THE STONEKEEPERS

Sally Chambers

"Go through, go through the gates!
Prepare the way for the people;
Build up, build up the highway!
Take out the stones,
Lift up a banner for the peoples!"
(Isaiah 62:10 NKJV)

"Behold, I lay in Zion a stone for a foundation,
A tried stone, a precious cornerstone, a sure foundation . . ."
(Isaiah 28:16 NKJV)

Elk Lake Publishing

The Stonekeepers

Copyright © 2015 by Sally Chambers

Requests for information should be addressed to:

Elk Lake Publishing, Atlanta, GA 30024

Create Space ISBN-13 NUMBER: 978-0991372782

Cover and graphics design: Anna O'Brien

Editing: Kathi Macias

Unless otherwise indicated, Scripture quotations in this publication are taken from the New King James Version, Holy Bible. Copyright 1979, 1980, 1982 by Thomas Nelson, Inc., Publishers. Used by permission.

This is a work of fiction. Names, characters, businesses, organizations, places, events, and incidents are either the product of the author's imagination or are used fictitiously. Any resemblance to actual persons, living or dead, events, or locales is entirely coincidental.

Published in association with Diana Flegal, agent, Hartline Literary Agency

To my heavenly Father,
and to my parents,
Helen and Clint Kessell,
now with the Lord.
From the depths of my heart,
thank you.

Acknowledgements

None could have been more loving, patient, and supportive than my husband, Jerry, my children, Jim and Deborah and their spouses, my extended family, and my close friends. I'm thankful for your prayers, for listening, and for always believing in me.

I want to thank my agent, Diana Flegal with Hartline Literary Agency, for her ready help and encouragement. Thanks to my editor, Kathi Macias, for her faith in and love for this story and for helping me through the edits. And thank you to my publishers, Fred and Nora St. Laurent of Elk Lake Publishing.

My heartfelt thanks to those who read my earliest chapters, Donita Paul, Carrie Turansky; Marilyn Yocum, Marty Boshart, Rosemary Cocker, Heather Reeder, Brenda Kessell, Cheryl Poindexter, Carole Harris, the Tabernacle critique group, Julia Lee Dulfer's Workshop, from whom I learned and drew encouragement to continue.

Thanks to Marguerite Cox and Kathy Ide for their helpful comments, and to my brother, Jim Kessell, who created drawings of the stone gate.

A special thanks to my wonderful, patient, persistent, critique partners, Naomi Rawlings and Zillah Williams, I'd never have finished this without you. And to many dear friends, all of whom gave me valuable input and encouragement and have prayed for me, thank you.

About the Author

Sally Chambers lives in warmth and sunshine among palm fronds, revels in sea breezes, loves the feel of sand between her toes, and braces for hurricanes annually. She, her husband, and two married children call Florida home. Sally writes for young adults, new adults, women of all ages who enjoy inspirational stories that are a blend of easy drama, suspense, and light romance.

Chapter One

Nantucket, Massachusetts

There has to be an explanation.

Outside Lexi Christensen's bedroom window, the world shook. The fast-moving storm hurled shards of silver lightning, and thunder bruised the heavens above rain-swept Nantucket Island. She leaned over her empty cedar chest, and again smoothed her hand across the base. Surely she'd only imagined the solid base had moved as she'd dusted the bottom.

There. A small indentation shifted beneath her fingers. She pressed the end of the wide slice of polished wood and drew in a quick breath. As if hinged, the slender board rose straight up, revealing a compartment.

Someone had carved out a section just big enough for a business-sized—

The overhead light flickered. Another explosion of thunder rocked the house as lightning illuminated an envelope tinged yellow with age. She bent closer. Emblazoned in sweeping black script, her name, Alexia

E. Christensen, traced across the face of the envelope.

Why would an envelope bearing her name be in her cedar chest? How long had it been there? She'd never completely emptied the box, but with her first year of college looming, she'd decided to clean it out. Remnants of her life had been layered like tree rings in the chest. Plaster-of-Paris handprints from kindergarten, old books and diaries, rumpled report cards, loose photos, awards, and more lay around her in short, not-so-neat stacks.

Then she'd lifted the old paper liner from the bottom of the chest. And found this.

The handwriting on the envelope wasn't familiar, and the possibilities that twisted through her mind didn't offer a single credible explanation.

The storm quieted, moving eastward over the island. Twin fires of curiosity and anticipation burned through her fingers as she picked up the envelope. The thin wood cover fell into place with a soft *swish*.

A clatter of pans sounded from the kitchen. Mom, fixing lunch. Good. For a while at least, Mom wouldn't barge in with more orders or an interrogation. Right now, Lexi wanted privacy.

She stretched to ease the tension in her neck, then sat back with her knees drawn up under her chin. Her hands trembled with excitement—or was it apprehension—and for a second, she hesitated.

Do it, for heaven's sake. It's just an old envelope.

The glue easily gave way as she slid her finger beneath the flap. She pulled out a fragile sheet of thin, crackly paper, and unfolded it. Several lines of text were written in the same handwriting as her name outside the envelope. Most of it was faded, barely legible, ink almost obliterated by brown stains. But the words of the first line stopped her, made her suck in a breath.

Northbrick House.

THE STONEKEEPERS

Northbrick. A vivid image of the aging mansion filled her mind. Massive, elegant with tall pillars and mottled cinnamon brick—and abandoned. Every time she passed the place, she felt drawn to it like a metal filing to a magnet. She had no idea why.

Three weeks ago, her half-eaten breakfast had been forgotten when she'd listened to the one-minute TV news blurb highlighting that "Northbrick House was scheduled for demolition."

If the place hadn't wormed its way into her heart, she'd have walked away from the whole thing. But as one of the oldest estates in Nantucket, Northbrick deserved to live, and she made up her mind to make certain it did. She located contacts, but was frustrated with replies that sent her chasing up a chain of responsibility with no answers on how to help halt or even delay Northbrick's destruction. The historical association, always right on top of saving the old houses of Nantucket, seemed to be trying their best, but nothing had changed.

With the demolition date less than a month away, she had enough time to help save the mansion from the town's wrecking ball. She'd planned to go inside Northbrick House, take photos, make notes on points of why save the place, and compile it along with her research. Presenting it all to the Nantucket Historical Association's open meeting on Friday of next week was on her calendar.

And her plan to go inside Northbrick was already in motion—for tomorrow.

She shook her head and stared at the cedar chest then at the opaque sheet of paper she held. "How could I be finding this now?" She whispered the words into the ether, her throat raspy and dry as beach sand. Only her best friends, Jenni and Ridge, knew she wanted to help save Northbrick.

Was it a coincidence? A warning? Did she even believe in

coincidence?

As far as she knew, no connection existed between her and the mansion. Was there something inside the old house that might link her to the estate?

Goose bumps rippled down her arms. She looked at the paper. If she read the remaining lines, would it make sense or get weirder?

The paper quivered in her hand, her eyes skipping down past several single, widely-spaced, hard-to-read lines, pulled to the bottom as a wave of unreality engulfed her. Two sketches of a familiar shape—a six-pointed star—like the one she'd worn beside her cross every day for as long as she could remember. She closed her eyes against the barrage of thoughts, questions, in awe at what she held.

Her hand moved to the slender gold chain against her throat. She pressed her fingers against the tiny metal replica of the Star of David, held it out, and turned it over. The two entwined triangles were engraved on the bottom of the left and right angles with two letter A's. Just like in the sketches . . .

And for a fleeting moment, she was a little girl again, sitting on a whitewashed bench in a garden, cradling a small box in one hand, and in her other, something golden shining in the sunlight. "A is for Alexia, and A is for apple," Mom had chanted, smiling and pointing at little Lexi. "You are the apple of God's eye."

Dear God, hold me together. Help me to make sense of this.

One step at a time. Long, slow breaths.

The stairs outside Lexi's open bedroom door creaked and footsteps tapped down the hall. Muted thunder rumbled in the distance. She refolded the paper, stuck it back in the envelope, returned it to its hiding place, and covered the base with the old liner. Drawing in a deep breath, she forced a smile and looked up.

Her mother halted in the doorway and stiffened. Her face paled, and her expression alternated between concern and fear, eyes darting from the empty cedar chest to the piles of contents strewn around it.

Flashes of remembered teasing pricked at Lexi as she looked at the slender woman in her late fifties with silvery hair, and skin still porcelain-smooth. "Having fun with your grandma, Lex?" "Hey, Lexi, where's your grandpa?" It hadn't been easy having older parents or being an only child.

"Is everything okay, Mom?"

Her mother's eyes pinned hers. Panic lined the edge of her voice. Her lips pursed. "You . . . you've emptied the chest." Did she know about the envelope?

She stepped closer. "It looks like you've gotten things pretty well organized. But why don't I help you with this part?"

Lexi plastered on a relaxed expression, closed the chest, and sat on it, rubbing her hands on her jeans. "No need. I'm almost finished."

Her mother took a step backward and sighed. "All right, then. Well, I'll call you when lunch is ready." Just as abruptly as she'd come, Mom left.

Lexi sagged, elbows on her knees, chin in her hands, waiting until the stairs were quiet. One thing she could count on lately: interruptions. Mom's hovering had intensified and Dad's interference had become ridiculous. She didn't mind what used to be a normal question or two about where she was going and when she'd be home. Now they pressed hard into what she did, who she'd see, where she went, how long she'd be gone, if she had her phone. Heaven knew she always had her phone! Their questions went deep, as if they didn't trust her . . . .

Why? They had no reason not to trust her. It was more as if they were worried or fearful about something concerning her. She stood in

the middle of her room and chewed the inside of her lip. Her attempts to talk about it were met with a quick change of subject. They'd been thrilled with her choice of MIT over Georgia Tech since it was close to home. But instead of loosening up and letting go a little as her days at home came to an end, their usual protectiveness had increased to the point of those constant probing questions. For the past few months she might as well have worn an electronic ankle bracelet.

She pushed the bedroom door almost closed, opened the chest, and retrieved the envelope. Unfolding the sheet, she held it close to read the blurry second line.

Through the door, beneath the floor.

What door? What floor? Was this some kind of a joke? Had to be. But *Through the door* was logical, and unless someone had hidden something, the only thing *beneath the floor* of that old place might be a crawlspace or cellar. Or did it mean the space between the ceiling and floor of the second story?

Eerie to find the envelope today. The idea of entering Northbrick house without permission grated hard against everything she knew to be right. Breaking and entering? Illegal. Talking her two best friends into going with her? Aiding and abetting. Now, those disjointed phrases from inside the envelope seemed to grant her free rein to walk *through the door*.

On the third line was a date. She let out a slow breath. May 22nd, the month and day of her birth, but three years later. Had she been three years old when someone wrote this? Had the envelope been in her cedar chest since then? She couldn't remember not having the chest in her room and had never questioned its being there. A landslide of questions and prayer tumbled through her mind. This whole thing was otherworldly.

Finish it.

14

She returned her attention to the calligraphy-like cursive on the paper. The words below the date were almost illegible. Sunshine dimmed as she lifted the sheet to the light and narrowed her eyes.

Preserve these stones—you are c . . .

After the *c*, the sentence vanished into a hazy field of brown.

I'm what? Challenged? Called? Committed?

Confused, clueless, or curious would fit better.

What kind of stones would someone want preserved and why? And what did this have to do with her? Wasn't her life complicated enough with her parents' hovering and her getting ready to leave for college?

A leftover crescendo of thunder growled. Lexi opened her window and breathed in the cool air, squashing the urge to fold the sheet into a paper airplane and send it sailing into the breeze.

Did Mom and Dad know about this? The paper trembled in Lexi's hand, and she laid it and the envelope on her desk. She still hadn't asked about the stack of old photos she'd found in back of a desk drawer, and with Mom's reaction to the empty cedar chest moments ago, unless there was a right time, she'd stay away from asking her anything for a while.

Lexi touched the symbols on her necklace, tucked the chain into the neckline of her shirt, and paced the edge of the area rug. Where did she go from here? Maybe things would become clearer tomorrow after she took photos and made notes on the condition of Northbrick House—and looked for an opening in the mansion's floors.

Her iPhone vibrated in her jeans pocket. Ridge's tanned, handsome face grinned at her from the frame beside the line of text, and her heart flipped.

Hey, beautiful, r we still on for N'brick 2morrow?

Beautiful? Well, that didn't help with her struggle to keep him

carefully inside friendship and outside her stubborn romantic heart.

She swallowed hard and shot him a quick reply. *No changes. c you there.*

OK!

Ooh, his reply had been too quick, too sharp. Why hadn't she at least stuck a smiley face at the end of her text to soften her abrupt reply? Even if he'd never be more than a best friend, she cared.

He belonged to Jenni. Shoving the phone back into her pocket was easy; pushing Ridge out of her mind was not.

Before she could head for the stairs, her cell vibrated again. Jenni was inviting her into a Facetime live video call. Lexi touched *Accept* and laughed out loud at the image of Jenni with dark brown smudges on her forehead and one cheek. "Hey, what's up?"

"Had to show you my new look, bff. Mom has me pulling weeds."

"Seriously? Jen the flower-slayer? She trusts you?" Lexi laughed out loud. "I see she's got you on your knees in her petunia bed! What did you *do* to deserve the hard labor?"

Jen scowled. "Don't ask. My knees hurt. Do we still have to show up at the mansion tomorrow afternoon?"

We. Lexi bit her bottom lip. "Yep. One o'clock, sharp." Why couldn't she stop cringing when Jenni's "we" meant Ridge and Jen?

Jenni scrunched her dirt-dusted face into a pained expression, her blonde ponytail swinging as she shook her head. "Guess I'll let you go then. I've gotta get my hair cut."

"Mine's so bad, I ought to go with you."

"Ha! They could throw you into a wind tunnel and you'd come out the other side looking like an *Elle* cover girl."

Lexi grabbed a handful of her hair and rolled her eyes. "I don't think so!"

"See y'all tomorrow."

Lexi grinned and shook her head at Jenni's fun, on again, off again, southern drawl. "Right. Happy haircut, girlfriend." She ended the call and stuffed her phone in her pocket.

The urge to tell Jenni about what she'd found had nearly reached her tongue before she'd glanced at the bedroom door and stopped herself. Not enough privacy or time to go into it now. They'd learn everything tomorrow.

She glanced at the delicate sheet she'd laid on the desk, much too fragile to be carried around. A copy was good enough to show her friends. She placed the sheet into the copier, pressed *Start*, then made a copy of the face of the envelope on the reverse side. The copy sat in the tray as she put the original back into the envelope, returned it to the chest, and replaced the liner.

With Mom's weird reaction to seeing the emptied chest, and no way to tell if she knew about the envelope or not, it was better to return the original to the compartment.

She pulled her Bible out of the "things to take" stack on her bed and opened it to one of her favorite verses, Proverbs 3:5. *Trust in the Lord with all your heart.* The copy would be safe in the drawer of her nightstand tucked there, between the well-worn Bible's pages.

Lexi lowered the lid of the cedar chest, dropped the long cushion on the chest's carved top, and sat on it, idly finger-combing her hair. None of this added up. If she could find out the history of her cedar chest, a lot of questions might be answered. Right now she needed to put it out of her mind, finish cleaning her room, and get some fresh air.

The sun cracked the clouds and flooded her room with light, as a salty ocean breeze pushed air through the dormer window. Mom's call to lunch wafted up the stairs.

"Be down in a minute."

She scanned her room. Two plastic bags full of old clothes sat in the corner, ready for the Salvation Army. The bed remained covered with clothes, and the floor strewn with the contents from her cedar chest. Another couple of hours and she'd be finished packaging up her childhood.

Lexi slid into the breakfast nook. "Looks good, Mom."

Across the table, her mother nodded as they bowed their heads and gave thanks. Lexi bit into her sandwich, silence hanging between them like a thick veil until the family picture on the kitchen counter caught her eye. She drew in a sharp breath. The photos. This might be a good time to find out what Mom knew about them.

Her mother peered at Lexi from over the rim of her glass. "So. We'll box up the things from your cedar chest and store them in the attic. The chest will work well to store the extra bedding and any summer things you want to keep."

Lexi bit her tongue. A month ago they would have talked about what she'd want to do with her chest, not been issued an ultimatum. She swallowed and ignored the bossy overtones in her mother's voice.

"Mom . . . I found some old photos I've never seen before in the back of a drawer in Dad's desk. Do you—?"

"Your father has lots of photos. When did you find them?" Brows arched, Mom leaned back from the table, put her glass down, and wrapped her arms around her middle.

"A few weeks ago . . . I was just . . ."

"And what were you doing, going through your father's desk?"

"Looking for paper clips. But when I found a bunch of photos in a rubber band, I pulled them out and flipped through them.

"Photos of what?"

"Some were of you and Dad, standing on either side of an old man with white hair and a beard. He was dressed in a dark suit and wore a small black cap. He was holding a baby. When I turned one of the photos over, I saw my first name printed on the back."

Mom reached for her tea, fingers whitening with her grip on the glass. "And the other photos?"

"In some of them, I recognized myself at about two or three. The old man was in almost every one. Who is he?"

"Just an old friend of the family, dear." Her mother's eyes pinned Lexi's. "And I strongly suggest that you stay out of your father's desk." She rose from the table, picked up their empty plates, and went to the sink.

Had Mom's voice quavered? Lexi's insides froze along with her desire to know more. Something was very wrong. As if the photos and the past they held were none of her business, as if she were an intruder in her own home. This whatever-it-was between them went a lot deeper than old photos.

Frustrated, angry, feeling shut out, she escaped to her room to concentrate on separating clothes—and to take deep, calming breaths. What to take, what to leave, what to pitch. She grabbed a heavy white sweater and thrust it into the "Take" box. As she did, a small tray holding earrings, bracelets, rings, and a smooth white stone fell from the bed. The stone smacked against her sandaled foot. "Ow! Okay, the stone goes too." As if it wouldn't! She picked it up and put it into the drawer with her Bible.

She couldn't take everything, but her Bible, her necklace, and that stone went everywhere she did. She'd been around four years old when

she'd seen it on the beach in a tidal pool—perfect, round, snowy-white against the tan sand—all by itself in the clear water. She'd nearly fallen into the pool trying to grasp it.

"There are prettier rocks over here," Dad had said, pointing to another pool.

"No, Daddy, I want the Chief!"

Lexi shook her head, smiling at the silly little memory. Her Sunday school teacher, Mrs. Adler, had told her class that Jesus was the Chief Cornerstone, and Lexi had found her reminder of Jesus, her "Chief Cornerstone." Dad had plucked it out of the water, put it in the palm of her hand, and wrapped her small fingers around it.

Dad . . . Mom . . . How could anyone go through leaving those they love, even if they were at each other's throats sometimes? And even if they were only few hours away.

As she shoved the first box into the hall, the click of old Gilly's nails sounded against the hall floor. Lexi's beloved golden retriever wandered into her room, tail wagging, ready for some loving. Mom must have sprung McGillicuddy from his banishment to the basement for being underfoot.

"Two minutes is all you get, boy. I'm getting out of here for some fresh air." She stooped to stroke his silky fur, her throat tight, her eyes filling with tears. Dogs should have a place in dorms. "I'm going to miss you so much, old guy." Her tears turned to laughter as his rough tongue swiped at her salty, wet cheeks.

She stood and sighed. All this cleaning, packing, and decision-making required before she left for college was a pain. The plan was to get it done early to have time to have some fun with her friends before she left, assuming she and her parents didn't kill each other first. In two short months, she'd be settled in her dorm room in the efficient, sturdy structure called McCormick Hall. Having Jenni as her roommate should be interesting; Jen collected clothes like a squirrel hoarded nuts for winter!

A steely clamp of anxiety banded around Lexi's chest as she shoved the closet door shut. She dragged the last black plastic trash bag into the hall and took a lingering look at her bedroom. Thoughts, questions, and confusion looped through her mind. She needed fresh air. Maybe a drive would clear her head.

She washed her hands, splashed water on her face, and ran a brush through her hair. Grabbing her purse and sunglasses, she encouraged old Gilly down the stairs, nearly colliding with her mother at the bottom of the staircase. "Oops! Sorry."

"Goodness! Another inch and you'd be refolding this laundry." Mom's smile was as tight as her hold on the plastic laundry basket. "Where are you going in such a hurry?"

Lexi dug her fingernails into the palms of her hands. "Just to Jenni's. I'll be back in a little while."

Mom grabbed Gilly's collar. "Well, don't be too late. Do you have your phone?"

Lexi rolled her eyes. Did she ever *not* have her social lifeline with her? And she really didn't mean to let the front door bang shut behind her like that.

Lexi's Mini Cooper sat in the driveway behind Mom's white minivan. An unsettling flurry of excitement and anticipation flew through her. She'd soon be driving her car onto the ferry for the trip to the mainland, a moment she'd dreamed of since she'd made her decision to attend MIT.

Convertible top down, sunglasses perched on her nose, Lexi got behind the wheel of the Mini, reveling in the sun and solitude, island

breezes playing through her hair—and worries playing through her mind. College prep, edgy parents, Ridge, a crazy letter connecting her to the house she wanted to save . . . She doubted a drive through the rain-dampened back streets of Nantucket would ease the mountain of stress she seemed to be climbing.

As Lexi pulled into her best friend's driveway, Jenni's brother sent her a high-five from the front porch. She waved at him over the top of the windshield. "Is she home?"

"Nope. She just called and said she's still at the mall. Something about a monster sale on jeans. Probably won't be back for another hour."

Lexi grinned. "So she snuck off to shop without me, huh?"

"Yeah, and she might strangle me for telling you."

"Don't worry. My lips are locked."

She shook her head and chuckled. If Jen bought more clothes, even two dorm closets might not be enough. She'd have to invoke "stand your ground" law or the place could end up becoming a war zone.

Lexi backed out of the driveway. Maybe she'd talk with Jenni tonight. She should make the trip to Northbrick alone first anyway. Just being there, scoping it out before the real thing tomorrow, felt right. Jenni's brain practically left the planet whenever Lexi talked about saving the old place, but Ridge seemed more than interested.

Two blocks south of the estate, she turned right, maneuvering her chili-red Mini onto a narrow dirt side road heavy with trees, weeds, and brush, and parked. Better than leaving the conspicuous little convertible sitting in front of the estate attracting attention. She locked the car and backtracked to Northbrick Avenue. She kept up a brisk pace, anxious to reach the gate.

A few feet ahead of her, as if it had no beginning or end, the tall iron fence emerged from a dense tangle of brambles and trees. It continued on the slight grassy rise that edged the sidewalk along Northbrick Avenue for close to the length of two football fields before disappearing into the woods on the north side of the estate. Set in the middle of the sturdy iron fence, two tall gray granite sentinels held the entrance gate.

Soft currents of late June air held the sweet-sour scent of pine, wild honeysuckle, jasmine, and weeds as she neared the mansion. The low hum of bees blended with the soft music of birdsong. Every sensation nudged her with whispers—and twinges of familiarity.

Lexi reached the fence and followed it to the twin pillars. How many times had she stopped and walked her bike past these imposing seven-foot giants? Countless.

Northbrick House faced west, and unlike most of the stately old mansions on the island, sat back nearly a hundred feet from the street. She stepped from the sidewalk and climbed the four stone-and-mortar steps to stare at the gate. Heavy, rusted, no lock, and open just inches, it sagged onto the stones beneath it. She pushed hard against it, and might as well have tried to push an elephant. The gate didn't budge. It didn't matter. Ridge would open it tomorrow.

Beyond the gate lay unkempt grounds, a chaos of trees, tall weeds, wild trailing vines, and thick brambles. Strange how dirt and dead weeds appeared scattered along what she could see of a wide, flat stone walk, as if someone had recently tried to clear the path. With no other way in except through this gate, she'd soon follow those stones to go into the house.

She set her cellphone to video, holding it between the bars, panning it across the house and grounds, then took still shots of the rusted black gate. Enough for now. There'd be more time and sunlight for photos tomorrow afternoon.

Lexi stuffed the phone in her jeans pocket and paused for a last look.

A tingly shiver scattered down her arms as her fingers curled around the cold metal bars, still damp from the earlier rain.

Through the door. The first words of the letter. Dare she follow the instruction?

The second line, *beneath the floor.* A cellar maybe. There'd be a lot to do when they went inside.

The sun rode low on the horizon, lengthening late-afternoon shadows. Wind moved dark strands of hair around her face. She shoved them away as a round, dark-gray, rat-sized lump skittered across the stone path behind the fence and disappeared into the weeds. *Just stay away from me, varmint.*

She needed to go home and tie up loose ends in her room. She hadn't exactly gone "just to Jenni's," but she'd be home in minutes. Time to leave.

She gazed at the abandoned mansion's ominous façade, the front door calling to her. Why did this place have such a strong pull on her? The paper involved her. How? Useless questions! There was only one way to find out. Should she? Lexi glanced around. No one in sight.

The iron bars iced in her hands. She tightened her grip and pushed. No movement. Instead, the ground beneath her feet thundered for long terrifying seconds . . .

Chapter Two

Boston, Massachusetts

Rick Vander wrestled with rumpled bed sheets and mopped beads of sweat from his forehead with the back of his hand. In spite of the overhead fan and open windows, trying to sleep was pointless, especially after the day he'd had.

Adding to the emptiness and futility of slow summer sales in the furniture business he'd inherited from his parents, he'd received an annoying phone call from his college buddy, Greyson Quinn, last night.

Rick, I'm in deep. I need your help, buddy.

GQ always needed something, and it always seemed to involve money. He'd ignored the message and gone to bed early. Dumb idea.

Vander rolled over to check the clock. Three-thirty in the morning with no hope for sleep, but it'd be 10:30 a.m. in Riyadh. His Saudi Arabian friend should be up by now. Forget about sleep; use the time.

He kicked the tangled sheets away, sat up, and grabbed his jeans from where he'd tossed them last night. Stepping into them, he hopped out of his bedroom, yanked them up, and took the stairs three at a time.

Entering a humming den of hard drives and blank-faced computer monitors, he typed in his ID and password to enter the online chat room. He smiled as Alpha-Z's name popped up.

Salim al-`Attar, aka Alpha-Z, had amazing talent when it came to everything related to computers. But he didn't fit the typical image of a tech geek. According to what Vander had learned through the online communications they'd had over the past several months, Salim was tall, handsome, and well spoken. He'd mastered six languages, was a brilliant mathematician, was headed for a prestigious American college, and had taught himself to play the guitar. Pretty impressive for a nineteen-year-old kid.

Computers made the world smaller—and the money-making possibilities larger. Figuring the Saudi teenager might come in handy sooner than later, Vander had told GQ about the "computer guru" he'd met online. Ever the manipulator, Quinn had immediately starting probing Vander on how they might use Salim's skill sets.

Now he wondered if telling GQ about Salim had been a less than brilliant idea.

Riyadh, Saudi Arabia

Salim al-`Attar sat in the midst of the electronic center of his spacious bedroom, his lanky frame sprawled over the black chair in front his computer screen. Heavy drapes covering large windows let very little of the bright Arabian sunshine into the dim room. Soft electronic whirs emanated from several computers networked across a line of desks. Screensavers covered wide, thin-line monitors, and keyboards sat wirelessly paired with fat, sculpted mice.

He tried to focus on his latest project. But memories of the twenty-seventh day of the last observance of Ramadan twisted his stomach into a knot as, once again, he relived them.

Strong in his Muslim faith, Salim had been fasting as he always did during the holy season. His father had left on yet another business trip, and the servants were busy with duties elsewhere in the house. Isolated, he lay on his bed, waves of sadness and wrenching loneliness threatening to overwhelm him. *Unfair. I am faithful to Allah. I should not feel this way.*

He'd soon fallen into the midst of a vision—or had it been a dream—into a peace he'd never before experienced. And the Man who stood between two others had reached out to him.

Then Salim had slept. He had awakened restless, with a relentless need to know about the Man who offered such peace.

He rose and paced, long deliberate strides, his forehead damp with tension from the memory. The vision had stayed with him throughout the months since then, leaving him only questions and wonder. He never dared to speak with anyone about his vision, and it never faded in its brilliance and crackling electric reality.

Amal rapped on his bedroom door then entered with fresh *shaay*. Salim smiled at the contrast of his muscled bodyguard wielding a porcelain pot of tea on a tray. Wordless, the big man nodded and stood aside as Salim poured his own shaay, sweetening it as he liked.

"Good timing, Amal. I needed a pleasant break. I will see you at noon."

The door shut with a thud. Salim downed the small glassful of steaming liquid then returned to his desk.

Tired of his current project, Salim consigned it to the computer's background and checked Facebook. He often found his friend Rick

in their favorite chat room during what was Vander's nighttime in the USA. But no new messages appeared on the screen.

At nineteen, Salim had already gained a reputation in the computer underground rivaling those of some of the most ingenious hackers in the world. He'd mastered many talents, but friendship wasn't one of them. He had no interest in cultivating relationships with people.

Rick Vander was one of the few exceptions to Salim's no-friends rule.

He'd met Rick in a secure online hacker's chat room several months ago. With much in common, they'd kept in touch almost daily since then. The American was a computer master and also an only child. Those similarities had led Salim to lower the bulwark of years against close relationships, and he'd formed a comfortable "big brother" bond with the American.

Some of their conversations had Salim suspecting Vander was even better than he was in his technological skill levels. Once he trusted Vander enough to brag about some of his capabilities, even the illegal ones, Salim soon followed a few of Vander's suggestions of how to slip through the new super-firewalls. All risky, dangerous, and illegal, Salim began to feel uneasy.

He ran his fingers over the keyboard, his heartbeat ramped with adrenalin at the thought of how close he'd come to getting caught with his techno-tentacles deep into an Israeli "file cabinet."

The only child of widower businessman Abdullah al-`Attar, Salim had plenty of free time to spend on his favorite hobby. His father's corporate offices were headquartered in Riyadh, but Abdullah traveled the world in the business of foreign oil sales. He indulged Salim with limitless funds that kept him in the latest electronic equipment.

Salim's father believed he used the equipment merely for playing games. And that was true, when he was younger. But out of boredom, Salim created a giant collection of privacy-destroying machines and spent every opportunity delving into other people's business. There were few computer systems in existence he hadn't hacked and probed.

Leaving the chat room screen on, Salim went back to an investigation he'd plunged into yesterday. *Ha. And the man thinks his computer is impenetrable.* A smile pulled at the edges of Salim's lips as he plumbed the depths of the Russian news agency TASS, and dug into a news contributor's spy source.

Moments later, he glanced at the twin clocks to his left. One glowed with Riyadh time: 10:32 a.m. Beside it, the second clock indicated Boston time as 3:32 a.m. A good time to check the chat room.

In the semi-darkness, Salim's thumb and forefinger smoothed his thin black mustache. On his computer screen, he traced the cursor down the list of clever names, handles of geeks like himself. Finally. With a click of the mouse, he grinned back at Rick Vander's smiling image.

The phrase *As-Salāmu `Alaykum* rambled across the chat-room screen. Salim warmed at the sight of the words he'd taught Rick Vander, "Peace be upon you."

Hey, hey, hey, little brother! Are you well? What mischief are you into today?

Wa `alaykumu s-salāmu wa rahmatu l-lāhi wa barakātuh. Salim typed the traditional reply, "May Allah's blessings be upon you." *Good to see you here today, my friend! I am well and, as you say, putting to use my many talents. You are well also?* He inserted a smiling yellow icon and sent the message. They exchanged more lines of small talk then switched to live video.

Salim felt frustration, anger, and boredom ease from his limbs like honey into warm bread as they shared their latest life-struggles. But

would things be better with the "why" of his vision continuing to prick at his soul?

Chapter Three

Lexi gripped the steering wheel in a chokehold as she drove toward Northbrick Estate. The morning had flown by. Last night when she'd finally called Jenni, she'd listened while Jenni went on and on about college and their dorm's closet space. A good thing since all Lexi could think about was the envelope with its strange letter. And then Jenni had interrupted her own monologue with "Oops, gotta go. Somebody's calling in. Ridge and I will meet you at the old house at one-thirty. See y'all there."

Lexi sighed and signaled for a turn. She'd been glad for the interruption. It provided an easy out from her temptation to tell Jen everything. This afternoon, she'd get some clear photos of the inside of the mansion, take good notes to go with the research she'd begun, and find something—anything—solid and believable, to tie her to the estate after finding the letter. At least that was the win-win scenario she prayed for.

She drove to the wooded area north of the mansion, where she'd told Ridge to park. The secluded lover's lane was quiet. Late, as usual,

he and Jen weren't here yet. She pulled in and glanced at the dashboard clock. One thirty-five. She'd deliberately been five minutes late, and had no plans to wait. She'd see them at the mansion. They'd show up. After all, they'd been in on wanting to help her with this plan from the beginning. She shook her head. Today their schedules matched—one of the few chances they'd have.

Late last week, Lexi and Jenni had been sitting on the top step of her front porch. After working their shift at White Oak Ranch, they'd been laughing and talking about college plans, when Ridge pulled into the driveway. He'd climbed out of his 1969 midnight-blue Chevy El Camino, his pet project since he'd saved enough from his after-school and summer jobs to buy it. His signature grin flashed from his suntanned face as he sauntered up the walk, clad in scruffy jeans and a Cincinnati Reds tee shirt, his dark, curly hair escaping from beneath a baseball cap.

Without touching the two bottom steps, he leapt up to their perch, the scent of motor oil and the dark smudge on his cheek evidence he'd just finished giving the El Camino some TLC.

Jenni moved her blonde, brown-eyed, skinny little self over for Ridge to sit between them. He grabbed the half-full can of Coke Jenni offered, took a few gulps, then handed it back to her. "Did you guys know the gate to the old Northbrick place is unlocked?"

Lexi nearly choked on her lemonade. "What?" That gate had never been without the chain and oversized padlock!

"I was on my way over to meet Mike at his house this morning. As I drove past the mansion, I noticed the gate didn't look all the way shut. I'd never seen it like that, so I stopped and checked it out. The lock and chain that are always there? Gone. Vanished. I figured they might have rusted and fallen off, so I looked around. Couldn't find them anywhere. Somebody had to have cut them off so they could bust into the house."

"That means I could get inside too," Lexi blurted out, her heart racing at the thought. "I know we've joked about going in before, but I plan on trying to rescue that old place."

Jenni's eyes widened. "No way. I know you feel all drawn to that spooky place. But you can't seriously be thinking about going in there."

Was Jen right? Maybe she really shouldn't be doing this. The legendary old house had been closed up as long as she could remember. No one she knew of had ever gone inside. All kinds of rumors about the mansion had circulated through town for years. The most infamous was about an old man's ghost roaming the house at night. Lexi never believed the tales, but they probably saved the house from vandalism.

Her research had uncovered one vague but possible item. The last owner of the estate had no heirs. That might explain why the house had remained unkempt and abandoned. But someone had to be paying taxes on it, and so far she'd found nothing about who paid them. One more unanswered question as the mansion sat here on Northbrick Avenue, dark, empty, as if waiting for something. Or someone.

Jenni tossed out a few of her ever-cautious "what ifs," her fingers vying with the island breezes to keep her blonde hair out of her eyes and her arm brushing against Ridge's.

"Well, you're not going in alone." Ridge's gorgeous hazel eyes focused on Lexi. "And I'm game to help."

A swarm of unidentifiable winged things invaded Lexi's stomach. She held his gaze, hoping he'd never look away.

When Jen chimed in with her agreement to help too, Ridge broke their moment of eye contact and patted her shoulder. "If we're going to do this, it has to be soon. There's no telling how long that gate will stay open."

Ridge was right. If they didn't do it soon, they might never get

another chance to go inside together. She left those thoughts unspoken. How could they admit aloud that this was *it*, the last carefree summer before they left for college and their lives changed?

Within seconds, they'd made plans to meet here this afternoon. Since Jen and Ridge lived next door to each other, they agreed to ride together.

Lexi checked her watch. So much for punctuality. What excuse would they come up with for being late this time?

Despite the muggy June air, exhilaration quickened Lexi's steps as she thought of what she might find inside the mansion.

Few cars lined the streets, and Northbrick Avenue was deserted as usual. *En garde* and stately in the bright daylight, the fence was more like a rampart. Thick granite posts interrupted the tall black iron pickets every six feet. Topped with arrow-like finials, the fence threatened to impale, daring anyone bold enough to scale it.

She stopped to pull burs from her jeans then neared the front entrance. The rumbling beneath her feet yesterday afternoon lasted for only a few seconds. Someone nearby must have been using a jackhammer—maybe. But what else could it have been?

The tall gate still hung ajar. She climbed the steps and pushed her sunglasses up on her nose for a closer look. Other than some deep scratches on the latch, there was no evidence it had ever been locked.

She gazed between the metal bars at what she could see of the estate's weed-tangled grounds and the faded face of the two-story edifice, tracing every detail.

Northbrick House. It must have been beautiful—about a hundred years ago. A white-railed widow's walk and four stately chimneys graced the roof. Chalky marks from aged paint smudged the red brick beneath the windowsills like frosty tears. Dull black shutters framed nine windows, five on the second floor, four on the first, and made dark holes in the façade that stared at her with unbridled curiosity and discomforting familiarity. On both sides of the house, a solid stone wall at least six and a half feet tall extended a hundred yards out in both directions. Boxing in the house as it made the front corners, the wall increased in height and disappeared into the unknown depths of the rear.

She ached to go inside. Another surge of doubt. She took in a deep breath and checked the phone for any missed calls or texts. She should just go ahead and call Jen. But they weren't that late. Irritation made her chew the inside of her cheek. One of them should have called *her* if they'd chickened out and changed their minds!

An argument between good judgment and temptation played tennis in her head. Temptation won. She'd do it alone. Turning off her cell, she thrust it back into her pocket, just mad enough to not want to be interrupted if they did call.

Another check of the street. Still quiet, deserted. With no one in sight, she pushed against the gate. It didn't budge. *Wish you were here, Ridge!* A second, harder shove. It still didn't move.

Lexi stared at the narrow opening. With a good-sized inhale, maybe she could squeeze through. She pressed her back against the smooth gray stanchion. The coldness of the stone penetrated her thin shirt as she inched herself along. Halfway through, the gate lurched and gave a hideous screech of protest against the stone walk.

Now you decide to move!

She froze, waiting, hoping no one heard the noise. The last thing she wanted was to explain what she was doing and why. An eternity passed before she tried again. This time she made it through and put some distance between herself and the gate.

A light thread of wind rustled through the long grass, breaking the silence. She walked halfway up the meandering stone path toward the

mansion's entrance, and paused.

Her eyes darted to a grimy windowpane on the second floor. Had there been movement—a flicker of light? Was someone inside? Battling a wave of panic and the urge to turn and run, she stood in place, watching.

No one's in there. It's nothing. Only a reflection. She pulled in a calming breath and kept walking.

Through the door. Beneath the floor. She didn't see any other way to enter except through the front door. The wide boards covering it might fight her for an easy entry, but she wasn't about to scale a stone wall to find another way in.

The wind pushed a cloud bank across the face of the sun, leaving her in shadow. Seconds later, Lexi stood on the porch, drawn to one of the two massive porch pillars. Had she been here before?

The base of the ornate column had suffered at the hands of a graffiti artist. She stooped to look closer and smiled. The markings looked more like the artistry of a child wielding something metal with happy abandon.

A sudden memory made her head swim. She could see herself as a child, etching letters as deeply as she could with the end of her little toy shovel . . . .

Lexi leaned against the massive column to steady herself. Was it possible? Could she have been here when she was a little girl?

She didn't have time to think about it—didn't want to think about it. She turned and approached the boarded doorway.

Attached to the brickwork to the right of the door, a rectangle of polished gray granite bore the number 1832. Lexi traced the figure eight with her finger. A date? The street address? She studied the weathered boards barring her way through. Whoever took the lock and chain from the gate hadn't tried to break in—yet.

The width of the old fashioned fan-shaped transom above the boards indicated a heavy, wide door below. The rusty nails that held the barricade together didn't look like much of a challenge.

Lexi grasped one of the looser-looking boards and yanked. It peeled away from the door so easily she nearly fell backward. She propped it upright against the wall, keeping her fingers away from the protruding nails.

With that single board gone, if she could get the door to open enough, she could do another slide-through.

The sun illuminated a large doorknob, painted black. Probably cast iron—and locked. She grabbed the knob and twisted. It spun in her hand then caught. She forced it farther, and the latch gave with a loud click. Lexi put her shoulder against the door and shoved. The heavy wood objected with creaks and groans, but it opened just wide enough for her to enter.

Through the door.

Dank, musty air swirled around her as she stepped inside. She coughed and rubbed at her nose. How long had it been since anyone had been in here?

She waited for her eyes to adjust then pushed the door almost shut—a little light, a little fresh air, and a quicker exit, if needed. Faint light filtered in from the dirt-encrusted transom and the slender panes of gold-colored stained glass on either side of the door. Wind moaned, whining its way through the slice of space between the door and its frame and sending a shiver down Lexi's spine.

She appeared to be in a cavernous foyer. Dust-covered floor, peeling, once-elegant wallpaper, the high ceiling, chandeliers dimmed with grime, doorways leading to rooms in every direction. She paused, staring at the grandeur of a wide circular staircase. The house looked

huge from the outside, but in here it was larger than she'd imagined.

When she took a step, the wood complained beneath her feet. Spider webs slid across her face and arms. She shuddered and waved them away, moving deeper into the foyer.

Without warning, the floor beneath her right foot gave way with the sharp crack of splintering wood, her shoe immediately becoming wedged between the boards. Lexi winced and bit her lip hard enough to taste blood as wrenching pain seared her ankle. She sat down fast and hard.

Please, Lord, not a broken ankle.

"Ow, ow, ow!" Struggling to keep her voice below a yell, she gingerly pulled her foot out of her shoe and moved it around. It was tender and would most likely swell up some, but she didn't think there'd been any serious damage.

She took a breath and peered through the gloom at the break in the flooring. Damaged floor or not, she had to get her shoe out of there. Not a good idea to go hopping around a strange dark house with one bare foot.

Huffing, she worked to free the shoe.

If she had any sense, she wouldn't have come inside in the first place. Dad always told her she had more spunk than sense. She'd been five or six when he first said it. The dare she'd taken from three older boys backfired when she'd jumped from the top of the monkey bars to a seesaw below. One of the boys had perched on the seesaw's end, but she didn't fly as promised because the boy decided not to stay put. She'd ended up with a big lump on her head. And her father had to flip her upside down under a water faucet to wash blood and dirt from her hair.

She smiled at the bittersweet memory. The relationship between Dad and her was so different lately.

Her smile faded. Jenni and Ridge—she'd nearly forgotten them. "Okay, you're forgiven. Come on, guys! Where are you? I could use some help here." She tugged at the shoe, aiming her grumbles at the no-shows.

Gritting her teeth, Lexi gave the stubbornly wedged running shoe a final jerk. It came loose with loud snap. An irregularly shaped short board flipped up and clacked to the floor. She'd pulled up a whole section of pine flooring in the process of getting her shoe out.

Great! The gap in front of her was a broken leg waiting to happen. She slid her shoe on and picked up the displaced board. It came out. It should go back. Odd how short and different it was from the rest of the floor. And the flooring in the center of the room had a much lighter finish than the wood near the wall. A carpet must once have covered the darker section, shielding it from the sun.

After several shoves and wiggles completely failed to refit the board back into the floor, she reached into the opening and ran her fingers beneath the edges. A nail or splintered wood could be blocking it. Musty air drifted up from below, making her cough. A thrill of excitement spiraled down her arms when she felt an angular wooden structure.

"What's this?" She leaned as close as she could. The soft, multi-colored sunshine filtering in through the transom gave her enough light to see the small shelf. Made of much thinner wood than the pine flooring, the shelf hung a little less than an arm's length away. It looked to be about four inches wide, almost like a hollowed out four-by-four.

Beneath the floor.

The words from the letter hit with the force of a slap. Could this be what the note was talking about? She shoved unruly strands of hair behind her ears.

Why not? Whoever made the hiding place in her cedar chest would

be creative enough to design this hidden shelf. Beneath the floor, a perfect hiding place. She leaned over to look again as the sunlight faded.

Please, Lord, no clouds, not now. It's dark enough in this place.

The shadows split into a rainbow of dim colors. She stuck her hand deep into the dark void. Something rolled and rounded was under there, tucked back, almost out of reach. Her hands shook with tension. She stopped and made herself take a few breaths. If she dropped it . . .

Just be careful and pull it out of there!

In seconds a small roll of paper lay in her hand. Rough-edged, delicate. Whatever had held the paper in its original rolled shape must have rotted away long ago.

Her heart raced, her hands still trembling as she placed the yellowed coil of paper beside the opening and felt around inside to see if there was anything else there.

The mansion remained cocooned in unearthly silence as she stretched to explore the recess. Barely breathing, she touched something firm and rectangular. She closed her fingers firmly around a small wooden box.

Moving slowly so as not to drop it, she inched the box toward her, then lifted it out.

"Well, you've been here a while." Her whisper tossed hollow repetitions back at her from the barren walls.

Breathless with excitement, she held the box up in the light from the transom. A band of tarnished, brass-colored metal encircled the middle, and a keyhole pierced its side. Lexi sat back on her heels and wiped dust and webs from a spot on the box with her shirt tail, revealing the sheen of a dark, fine-grained wood.

"Beautiful." But who had placed the paper and box *beneath the floor*? And why?

She tried opening the lid. Locked tight. A thorough search of the shelf didn't reveal a key. She set the box beside the paper cylinder, mentally kicking herself for not having brought a flashlight. *Ridge was supposed to bring one.*

She rubbed perspiration from her upper lip, looked at her watch. Where were those two? They'd had plenty of time to get here. Five more minutes then she'd call them. Lexi was looking forward to giving them an earful about keeping promises and being on time.

She moved the box and paper farther from the opening and worked to fit the rough-edged board into the floor. Was the thing ever going to fit? She shoved down hard on a corner. When she eased up, the board stayed in place. She got up and stood on top of it to make sure it remained flat.

An ear-piercing screech ripped through the quiet foyer. The unmistakable sound of the rusted gate.

Finally.

She jogged to the door, ready to yank it open wider and deliver her lecture. But a single glimpse outside snaked a rope of dread through her. She saw a tall solitary figure striding up the stone walk.

Chapter Four

Trapped! Lexi pushed the door shut just enough to tap against the frame, the wedge of light thinning to a sliver. She stepped away and inched back to where the box and paper lay.

Who was he? A house inspector? Realtor? Why was he here and why now? She hadn't seen much. Only that he was strident, imposing, and unfamiliar. She knew she had no business being in here, but did he?

Lexi's heart pounded. She'd done this to herself, made this choice. She'd have to face him head-on—or she'd have to hide. Maybe when he saw the boards over the entrance, he'd decide not to open the door . . . maybe. Either way, the man would be on the porch in seconds.

All her impatience had gotten her into was trouble. What she wouldn't give to be back in her car, where at least she'd be safe. Instead, she was alone, caught inside a dark, deserted house no one had set foot in for years.

Move!

Her muscles bunched, refused to obey as she stood beside the board she'd just replaced in the floor. Mind-numbing scenes streaked across her mind. Rooming with Jenni at college, Mom and Dad at graduation,

the wedding she might never have. Was she about to say good-bye to all her dreams? She closed her eyes, praying for the man to leave.

Heavy footsteps on the porch came to an abrupt halt near the door. A fresh wave of dread iced through her as scuffling sounds sifted in.

Whoever he was, he wasn't leaving. With the squeal of nails being wrenched from wood and the *thwack* of boards hitting the porch floor, her hope of being undiscovered evaporated.

If she didn't move . . .

The door creaked and groaned. Lightheaded, she flushed cold as she felt the blood leave her face. A slice of sunlight flooded across the floor and spread near her. Her legs lost what little strength they had and she dropped down, curling into a low stoop as the door opened wider and the man's long, dark shadow loomed over the spot where she cowered, watching.

Such a wimp she was! She should stand up and face him. But what if he had followed her? She could be in danger. What little resolve she had mustered to confront him melted.

Musty air laden with the scent of men's aftershave lotion swirled around her.

Oh, dear God, if she sneezed it was over. She held her breath.

His head lowered, the shadow-maker paused on the threshold as if adjusting to the gloom of the hall, then stepped forward and stood in place. The floor creaked loudly beneath the man's weight. He looked down, noisily tapping the floor with the toe of his shoe as if to test it.

You have got *to move. Now!*

A split-second opportunity. The staircase! It extended out into the entrance hall as if suspended, and the wide wood steps of the landing lay in darkness. Thank God, she was nearer the stairs than the door. Strength surged into her arms, hands, and body. She scooped up the box and coil of paper.

The man continued to test the floor with a series of taps and steps. Lexi matched his rhythm and soundlessly moved closer to the haven beneath the staircase.

She slid into the covering blackness and stood, quaking, beneath the steps, peering into the darkness. She could see and not be seen. And, if she was careful, she might not be discovered.

Her hands shook. She couldn't take a chance on dropping the box and paper. A narrow ledge to her left would work, a safe place to put them for now.

The tapping stopped. The dark-clothed figure pushed at the door and stepped farther into the entrance hall. The door groaned and almost closed. Lexi glimpsed the sharp-featured face of a tall man in a business suit and, within a shaft of muted light, the gleam of gold around his neck.

His eyes darted, left and right. Good. He hadn't seen her and couldn't see her now. Her fear abated. His agitated movements and sharp nose reminded her of a hawk on the hunt.

His tapping resumed. The man appeared to listen to the echoes, then suddenly cocked his head and knelt where she'd been crouched just a moment before.

Lexi's breath left her as he pressed down hard on the loose board, pulled it up, and looked beneath the opening—with a flashlight! She heard the distinctive click, and a glow of light focused on the gap in front of him.

How did he know about the spot in the floor?

Suddenly his head bobbed and snapped in her direction. The beam of his flashlight grazed the staircase.

She ducked her head and shrunk backward as far as possible. Her

heart banged against her ribs. More fervent prayer. She'd lost her mind coming into this house alone.

Lexi pulled in long, slow breaths and waited. She had to calm down. If she petitioned God one more time, she was sure He was going to stop listening.

There had been no noise for an eternity. Had the man seen her? Was he looking for her? Had he left the house? But the door hadn't moved or made a sound.

He hadn't gone upstairs; she'd have heard him. Was he somewhere else in the house?

If she shifted her position, she might have a better view. She moved forward, slowly, deliberately. The old floor creaked under her feet. Lexi sucked in a gulp of air and held it. Moving—not such a good idea. The door grated on its hinges as a gust of wind moaned through the opening.

"Who's there!"

He hadn't left the foyer. He stood in the darkness across the room and stared toward the staircase. His head swiveled from the stairway to the door and back.

Terrified, barely breathing, she pressed both hands tightly against her mouth.

He grumbled a few unintelligible words and began to move toward her like a predator after prey. A cone of light from his flashlight hunted for her, skipping over the barren walls and floor. Lexi crossed her arms tightly across her stomach. Would she be grabbed and questioned—or worse?

Without more warning than a distinctive growly *meow*, a huge white cat leapt from the staircase above her and raced through the foyer. It shot past the man and tore through the front door.

The man turned toward the door, bellowing threats of the loss of all nine of the cat's lives.

He hadn't seen her. Fear drained from Lexi's limbs and she leaned against the wall, grateful for the noisy, attention-diverting feline as the man returned to his search of the reopened floor.

He had to be looking for the box and paper. She had stumbled across the hidden cache by accident, but he went directly to the spot. Her desire to save the house, then finding the envelope, had led her here. But what brought him to the mansion? How had he known . . . ?

She shrugged. Whatever the answers, he didn't have the box, but she did. It must hold something important. There had to be more to all this.

He slammed his fist against the floor, swearing under his breath.

It's not there. So leave!

As if in response to her silent command and with no effort to close the gap in the floor, he got up and stomped to the door, turning once, his gaze piercing the dark corners.

Lexi held her breath until he yanked the door open and left.

His shoes rapped against the porch, down the steps, across the stone walk, and faded as he strode away. She waited, listening until she heard the squall of the front gate.

So tempting to just slide down the wall and collapse into the quivering heap she felt like. Instead, she stood, propped against the wall, and rubbed her face on the sleeve of her shirt.

Did she dare move from here? The door had stayed partially open, giving her enough light to find someplace else to hide. She picked up the box, and in the process, swept the paper from the shelf. It sailed downward along with something else that clattered as it hit the floor.

She retrieved the paper and searched for what had made the noise.

In seconds, she held the small tarnished silver object between her fingers. "A key . . . to the box?" Hands shaking, the key poised in front

of the lock, she stopped herself.

Not now. She slid the key into her pocket and sent a wary glance toward the front door. Staying in the foyer wasn't smart. It hadn't been safe to begin with, and the hole in the floor would have to wait until she was certain he was gone.

With no flashlight, forget about looking for another way out, she reasoned. But neither did she want to risk going outside yet. She stepped from beneath the staircase. To her right, closed double doors might open into a parlor or drawing room.

As she walked to the doors, the same familiar scent she'd encountered outside the house surrounded her, almost affirming she was doing the right thing. But the comforting floral fragrance disappeared as quickly as it came.

With her free hand, she pressed the handle of one door. Opening both doors as far as they would go, she left them wide and went inside.

A band of light escaped from between heavy draperies. If he came in again, dark corners and tapestry drapes made good places to hide, and they helped keep some of the heat out. She walked to a corner and set the box and roll of paper on the floor, then stood, trying to finger-comb the cobwebs from her hair as she looked over the large room.

Two old side chairs sat against one of the walls. An elongated shape, the size of a formal sofa, was covered by a white sheet. The ornate, dark wood legs of end tables showed from under more white sheets. Strange how familiar the room—

But she didn't have time to think about that. And the box could wait a moment more. She pulled out her cellphone, turned it on, and shot a few photos of the room from several angles.

Photo number five. Lexi aimed the phone's camera toward the dusty floor until the screen filled with the box and paper. She took two more shots then picked up the box. No more waiting.

Her heart pelted her chest with nervous thuds as the key slid easily into the keyhole on the side of the box. One twist, a metallic click, and the box yielded, unlocked.

"Okay, little box, what secrets do you have to show me?" She wagged her head and looked up at the ceiling. *Terrific, I'm talking to a box.*

The key back in her pocket, she pried at the wooden rectangle with her fingers until it opened. Her breathing quickened. In the folds of royal blue velvet lining, a shiny second key. Pristine. Perfect, it almost glowed. Small, similar to a skeleton key, she'd never seen anything quite like it. She took it from the box. A few tiny scratches but no tarnish. Possibly gold?

She moved into a ray of light and compared it to the yellow gold of her emerald birthstone ring. Old? Probably.

Lexi probed the soft lining with her fingers. Nestled deeper, she discovered an intricate ivory carving, a tiny double for the cat that had saved her neck. She picked the figure up from its plush bed and turned it over in her hand. It reminded her of old scrimshaw engravings whalers used to carve on whale's teeth. A word and numbers etched into the back read "Angel 1832"—the number engraved on the granite marker by the front door. Had the cat-image been carved the same year?

Angel was a good name for her rescue-cat; maybe it had an ancestor. Lexi smiled and shook her head. The real white feline had come from upstairs. What was up there beyond the beautiful circular staircase? She placed the tiny sculpture back in the box.

The shiny gold key teased her with its potential. It wouldn't open a safe deposit box or anything else modern, but would it unlock something in the house or on the grounds? The estate was huge. With no idea where

to begin to look, her hope slid down to join her toes. The answers to her questions were somewhere on this old estate, held tightly within the grip of earth, wood and stones, bricks and mortar.

The squall of metal scraping stone spun through the front door like sour bow-strikes to violin strings. Lexi stiffened, spiked through with fear.

Not again!

Chapter Five

Ridge turned off Northbrick Avenue onto a side street and maneuvered the El Camino down the worn track, cringing as brush scraped along the truck's front fender.

Oh, man, were they late! Toe-tappin' Lexi would be warped out of shape. He and Dad had finished the project in half the time he thought it would take, but his buddy Terry had called. They'd gotten back into an ongoing wrangle over whether Ridge should keep and store his El Camino while he was at college or sell it to Terry.

Beside him, Jenni huffed and squirmed in her seat. He couldn't blame her for being ticked at him. He'd forgotten the time, and they'd lost ten-plus minutes because of it.

Lexi's little red Mini Cooper sat in the sparse shade of a clump of scrubby trees. He pulled up close to the empty convertible and silenced the Chevy's rumbling engine, shaking his head with more regret.

"Let's see how long she's been here." He shed his seatbelt and went to the front of Lexi's car, Jenni right behind him. He laid his hand on the car's hood. "This thing is barely warm. She's been here awhile." Jenni

just looked at him with a sassy, smirky "Really?" expression going on behind her sunglasses.

He took her arm and aimed her toward the street to backtrack in a fast walk toward Northbrick Avenue. If Lexi was at the house, she wouldn't wait for them very long. He gritted his teeth and frowned at the idea that she might not wait at all. Adorable, with zip patience, stubborn as a trail horse . . . That was Lexi, and he'd never figure her out.

He should have gone ahead and parked the doggone El Camino right smack in front of the Northbrick gate. Then they wouldn't have so far to walk. But, no, Lexi had instructed him to leave his car parked with hers, south of the estate. Too obvious and too noisy, she'd said with that cute tilt of her head that flat took his breath.

"We should have parked closer." Jenni glanced over at him, her lips set in an anxious line. He nodded in agreement.

As soon as they reached Northbrick Avenue, Ridge stopped, certain he'd heard the faint grating sound of metal against stone.

"Wait a sec." Probably still mad at him, Jenni would probably keep right on walking. He put his hand up in caution.

"What's up?" Jenni paused and looked up at him, pushing damp curls of blonde hair away from her eyes.

"You didn't hear that?" Ridge cocked his head and listened.

"Nope. Not a thing. Except for the birds, this is the dead-quietest street in town."

Ridge reset his ball cap. He *had* heard something. "It sounded to me like the front gate moved. I'll try calling her."

Jenni rolled her eyes at him. "You've already tried twice. She's got her phone turned off. It'll just go to voice mail . . . again."

"Maybe she's turned it back on."

"Okay. We'll be there by the time you get her voice mail anyway."

Jenni moved nearer and grinned up at him, her wide brown eyes grabbing his as though he were the only person on the planet. He shook his head, held the phone up, and gave the voice command, "Call Lexi."

Jenni's face clouded. Uh oh.

Maybe he shouldn't have called.

Jenni's shaky grin faded. "Still no answer?"

Ridge pulled the phone away from his ear, ending the call without leaving a message. "Nope, still voice mail."

Jenni sent him an I-told-you-so look and paced a few feet ahead of him.

Lexi could at least have kept her phone on. Tension ratcheted up the muscles of his arms. He should have called her long ago. "I sure wish she'd let us know where she is."

It was too hot to jog, but they didn't slow down until they reached the black iron fence. He stopped in the shade of one of the large English oaks that lined the road and swiped at his forehead. "She said to meet her by the gate. We're close. We should be able to see her from here."

"Well, I *don't* see her. She's probably already gone into the house."

Ridge gave her a knowing nod, looking at the gate as they approached. Its position had changed since he last saw it. Maybe it had been the gate he'd heard. The thing was big, rusty, and sagging. Had Lexi moved it? Could she? He concentrated on the view beyond the slim metal fence posts. Except for a few trees, it was clear all the way across the unkempt grounds to the house. He glanced at Jenni. "See anything?"

"No. Nothing." Jenni stuck out her lower lip and blew a breath toward her forehead. "And that gate's open wide enough—"

"I saw that too." Ridge squinted against the bright sun. "I guess Lex could have wormed her way through there. She could be up there behind one of the pillars, out of our line of sight. We'll go in, but let's make sure

there's no one else snooping around here besides—"

Ridge's words hung in mid-air as the low summer buzz of squirrels, birds, cicadas, and bees abruptly ceased. An eerie chill coursed the length of his body. Had he heard a voice, or was he hearing things now? With a quick intake of breath, he grabbed Jenni's arm and pulled her back several feet from the stone steps and behind the wide trunk of an oak tree.

"For heaven's sakes, Ridge, what's wrong?" Jenni flattened herself against the tree.

He ignored her and peered through the waterfall of oak leaves as a white cat raced out from between the pillar and the gate. It cleared the four steps as if they didn't exist, bounded down the sidewalk away from where they stood, and vanished from sight.

"A cat!" Ridge breathed again, but Jenni had her eyes closed, leaning against the tree. "You okay, Jen?"

"That was not fun!" She fanned her face as pink settled back into her cheeks. "And we're not going another inch till my heart restarts!" She moved forward, peeking around him. "You scared me to death because of a cat?"

"It wasn't just the cat. I thought I heard a voice. And something's still not right." No cat had moved that gate.

A noise like boards scraping across the porch. The hair on the back of Ridge's neck rose, and beside him, Jenni tensed. He reared back, molded himself against the tree trunk, and stared. Someone descended the front porch steps, head down, and strode from the weed-choked walkway toward them. Ridge watched as the hunched figure of a man in a dark business suit furiously clenched and unclenched his fists with every step.

Somebody else was interested in this old place? Should he confront the guy? Nope. Nothing to confront him with.

"Who is he—a realtor?" Jen's voice was a shaky whisper.

"His suit is a little over-the-top for a realtor." The guy seemed more interested in the sidewalk than in his surroundings, never raising his head as he passed between pillar and gate. In a fast walk, he went the same direction as the cat, muttering just loud enough for Ridge to make out a few words.

Jenni nudged him. "What did he say?"

"Sounded like he was cussing out a floor. Pretty weird." Ridge kept himself glued to the tree, his hand clasped around Jenni's arm. She snuggled closer as the man blended into the shadowy forest of trees on the far side of the mansion's grounds and disappeared from view.

Within seconds, a car engine roared to life. If Ridge knew his engines, that would be a small sports car, and with the angry squeal of abused tires, there was no need to guess who was behind the wheel.

The smell of burning rubber drifted around them and he let go of Jenni's arm.

"I'm sure glad he didn't head in our direction." Jenni rubbed at her arm. "Do you think he saw us?"

"I doubt it. Probably would have stopped if he had. The guy was steamed."

Surely the man had some perfectly legit explanation of why he was there. He and Jenni had no good reason for being here, and Lexi—

Lexi! Ridge fisted his hands as Jenni's startled brown eyes locked onto his. She gasped as if she'd read his mind, and his heart squeezed seeing stark fear darken her face..

Thoughts of Lexi being alone in that house slammed at Ridge like a sledgehammer. If she was in there, she might be in real trouble.

His throat tightened and he swallowed hard. If anything happened to

her, he'd never forgive himself. "We need to get in there—now!"

He took off toward the gate, praying with every stride, Jenni in pursuit. Scenes of police storming the house and an ambulance being loaded with a lifeless form barreled through his mind.

Halfway to the porch, Ridge paused and stared. The open front door gaped at him from between decaying boards, a mouth full of blackness and gloom beyond its lips. He shook his head against imagining what they might find. *God, help us.*

He fisted both hands, his stomach churning with a mixture of anger and guilt. If that jerk had done anything to Lexi, he'd find him and give him a lateral transfer into the next universe! He should have stepped out from behind that tree and faced the guy.

Racing up the walk and onto the wide porch, Ridge's body tensed, steeled against what he might find as he headed toward the door. He kicked aside the boards scattered across the porch like discarded table leaves. He didn't know whether to feel amused or amazed at the job Lexi had done prying them away from the door. Or had the man done that job instead? Jenni hung back near a mildewed pillar.

"Let's go." Ridge hesitated on the threshold, motioned to her, then stepped into the huge foyer. "Leave the door open; we need all the light we can get."

"I'm not about to shut it." Jenni's voice quavered, but she followed him in, clutching at his arm again as they stood for a few seconds, their eyes adjusting to the darkness.

Ridge pointed to a gap in the floor. "Watch out for the hole. I hope she didn't step into that." Jenni released his arm, unwilling to follow as he moved farther into the entrance hall.

He stopped and turned to her. "Do you want to stay in here while I look for Lex?"

"No! I'm so scared, Ridge; I can't quit shaking."

He went back and took Jenni's hand, steering her into the area beyond the door and around the hole. "If it helps any, I'm scared too." Scared and mad.

"Lexi!" Ridge's deep voice reverberated throughout the empty hall. No answer. "Where are you?" *Lord, let her be all right.*

"Lexi, are you in here? Are you okay?" Jenni's voice echoed Ridge's, bouncing from wall to wall, sounding thin and hollow.

"I'm okay. I'm in here!" The words trailed out from a doorway to their right.

Jenni gave an audible sigh. "Thank God!"

Ridge prayed an inward *Yes!* But, until he saw her . . . "I'm not believing that until I look at you." They followed the sound of Lexi's voice and went to the open double doors of a large, nearly empty room. Fading light from the lowering sun shone from between heavy drapes. Silhouetted against them, Lexi looked so small.

"Are you *sure* you're all right? You should have waited for us!" Jenni pushed past Ridge and ran across the open space toward Lexi, firing a volley of questions all the way.

Ridge's legs felt as though he sloughed through quicksand as he went toward Lexi. He was ready with his own fusillade of questions, but as she turned toward them, he couldn't say a word. He stopped and stared. Face shining with perspiration, hair a mix of mahogany and charcoal clinging in damp waves around her face, falling all over her shoulders, deep blue eyes emanating fun and mischief, she was beautiful—and okay.

Thanks, God.

His stomach burned, a dugout full of fire ants that stung him with emotions he didn't want to deal with right now.

Chapter Six

Lexi couldn't keep her mouth shut, couldn't stay mad. Thank God they were here! Hands on her hips, watching Jenni and Ridge from across the room, she wrestled against a huge grin as Jenni flew through the doorway.

Ridge walked in behind Jen. He stopped short, staring at Lexi, his face etched with such a strange, worried expression that it took her breath away. She rubbed the back of her neck and squelched the urge to grab her phone, aim its camera, and capture those hazel eyes of his. Then his brow relaxed, his smile melting her heart, and for an instant his head bowed, lips moving.

A simple, thankful prayer for a friend. Another reason he was a best friend. She could never ask for more. She gave herself an internal shaking. Just be at peace with reality, and focus. She'd come here for photos and notes—which she had yet to make—and to find a connection. Which maybe she'd just found.

"Calm down, guys. I'm not hurt. I'm okay. Really, I'm all right." She tapped her watch and tilted her head at them. "And exactly where

have you two been?"

Ridge evaded her question and shot her a quirky grin. "The dust and cobwebs decorating your hair are a cool addition. Are you trying to start something new?"

Jenni parked herself in front of Lexi and gave her a quick hug. Leaving her hands on Lexi's shoulders, she pushed back, studying her. "You are totaled, girl! *What* have you been doing?"

Lexi had to smile. "Ignoring my questions is an art form with you guys. Thanks a lot. I'm fine—webs, dust, and all. It's simple. You were late, I decided to break—ah, no—come in here without you. You missed the whole thing. You should have seen me worm my way in here."

Ridge's baseball cap came off. He ambled over to her, a sly grin crossing his tanned face. "Okay, first we see a cat run out of here like the devil himself was after it. Then that guy shoots out of the house like a bullet and turns the air blue—something about a floor. And what's with the hole in the foyer floor, anyway?" He cocked his head and hung a thumb in his jeans pocket. "Let's hear the rest of your story."

Lexi paced along the windowed edge of the spacious room, her thoughts lasered on the human bullet Ridge described. "So, both of you saw him? He reminded me of a hawk—really beaky nose. Did he see you?"

"No, and with his head down, we couldn't see much of him either. How long had he been here?"

"I'm not sure, but he came in ten, maybe fifteen, minutes or so after I did. I thought it was you two when I went to the door ready to blister the air about you being late. I backed off the second I saw him; thankfully, he didn't see me. He started ripping boards away from the door. No way did I want a face-to-face. I grabbed the stuff I found and ran to the stairwell to hide."

Jenni moved closer to Ridge and fanned herself with her hand. "Did you recognize him? Had you ever seen him before?"

"No, neither, but he's someone I'll never forget."

Ridge's ball cap found its home again. "You said you 'grabbed the stuff you found'? What stuff?"

Lexi stopped pacing and locked her gaze on Ridge. "You asked me about the hole in the floor. What I found in that hole was what that guy was after, which is why he was, well . . . so . . . ticked."

She told them everything, replaying all that happened before they arrived. ". . . and it was the white cat that got the guy's attention, kept him from seeing me." She put her hands to her cheeks, her heart beating double-time as she recalled the scene.

Lexi couldn't look at Ridge or she might lose what little composure she hung onto. Jenni's eyes glistened as she pressed her fingers over her mouth. It could have turned out so much differently; all of them knew it. A wave of weakness vibrated through her limbs.

Show them.

Ignoring twinges of pain that still pulsed through her ankle, she stooped to pick up the box and roll of paper from the floor behind her. "These are why he was so mad. He didn't find what he'd come for, because I'd already found it all. Take a look inside the box." She opened the box, handed it to Jenni, and moved into a ray of light.

Jenni ignored the gold key and plucked the ivory cat from the blue folds. "Wow, this is beautiful."

Lexi nodded. "Kind of reminds me of a scrimshaw engraving."

"Wait a sec." Ridge's attention locked on to the cylinder of paper she held. "There's something written on there."

"I didn't see anyth—" Lexi frowned. She'd been so enthralled with the key and the carving that she hadn't noticed.

Ridge pressed down on the edge of the roll. "Right there. Black script . . . and there's another piece of paper inside that one."

Lexi gently tugged on an edge and held her breath as she unrolled a second sheet. Strong and translucent, the paper looked ancient. Parchment? Calfskin? It could be hundreds of years old, and she'd been treating it like . . .

"It looks old enough to be parchment." Jenni's blonde ponytail bobbed with her nod.

Lexi stared at the faded block lettering. A shiver coursed through her. She'd seen these same shapes countless times on a stained-glass window on the east side of her church's sanctuary. Two tablets, side-by-side, covered with lines in a language like . . .

Cryptic words inside envelopes, and now this. Too much. "Here." She thrust the duet of papers toward Ridge. Maybe he could comprehend what was inscribed on them. He took them from her outstretched hand.

Lexi's knees threatened to fold. If she didn't sit, she might get a nose full of floor, fast. Her eyes blurred as she slid down the wall and sat, cross-legged, fists beneath her chin.

Ridge sat beside her, and Lexi's heart flipped when it shouldn't have. Intent as he looked at the yellowed scroll, his large hands smoothed the ragged edges between his fingers as he settled himself against the wall and compared the two papers.

A sudden intake of breath, and a low, breathy whistle. "Listen to this." He held the paper that had protected the parchment closer, his words halting but deliberate as he read:

From God Himself came this decree:
"Two onyx stones you will engrave for Me.
In the order of their birth, deep into the lustrous faces,
Carve the twelve great names to mark their places.

And on the breastplate, you have been told,
Add twelve sealed stones, set forth in gold.
A time shall come when they are hidden,
And touching them will be forbidden.
Good sons of Aaron, I have entrusted you—
Preserve these stones—you are commanded to.
Be vigilant and wise as you prepare the way,
The stones' return to the Temple to forever stay.
When the time has come to pass, it will be true and clear.
I will choose My messenger, the day, the time, the year."

Ridge stopped reading, and Lexi's ears rang with the deafening silence of the estate house. Stones. Onyx stones? That was easy. Mom sometimes wore an onyx ring as black as the lacquered oriental desk in Dad's study. But stones? Twelve of them? Sealed? What did that involve? Nothing more lay under the floors other than bugs and dust.

But maybe she shouldn't be so sure. Stones were everywhere in this place. How would she know which stones were the right ones?

Ridge squinted against the lessening light. "There's more . . . different handwriting . . . like an afterthought." And he read again. *"O God, may Your chosen messenger be a worthy vessel to fulfill these words."*

He finished reading and looked from one to the other of the two unfurled scrolls. Lexi shifted her gaze to the faded lettering that made the old script so difficult to decipher. "The outside paper is a translation of the parchment. The parchment is ancient." Lexi drew in a breath and straightened. She'd spoken the statements with such authority . . . .

Jenni peered over Lexi's shoulder. "How can you be so sure? I can't read a single word, much less, letter, of what's on that parchment."

Why was it so clear to her? Lexi shrugged.

Jenni's hand trembled as she put the box down beside Lexi and

joined them on the floor.

Ridge let both sheets roll into their original shapes, then set them between himself and Jenni. "The last line sounds like a prayer to me," Jenni said, then looked at Lexi. "It doesn't match up with the lines on the older paper. Any ideas about that?"

Lexi's mouth went dry. Words she thought to say turned to ash, as if they weren't hers to speak.

Ridge's eyes sparked, drilled into hers, his deep voice gentle, clear. "I think it's a prayer, too. Maybe whoever wrote it wants the messenger to be one who believes and understands the message—and wants the messenger to follow the instructions on the parchment."

He'd said what she couldn't, and she wanted to hug him. Instead, she drew her knees up under her chin. Should she add to all this chaos and tell them about the cedar-chest-envelope or not? Pushing strands of hair away from her face, she looked from Jen to Ridge and cleared her throat.

"Before yesterday, I'd almost decided we should forget about doing this. I had practically coerced you both into coming with me today, and it really wasn't right. But then I found something that changed everything."

She hesitated. "I was stressing out over what to take to college, what to pitch. My room was a wreck, and if I didn't get it cleaned up . . . " She paused. "Anyway, you both know what a dumpster my old cedar chest is. I had to tackle that too." She suppressed an inward groan. So much for being linear and logical!

Jenni grinned and nodded, but said nothing.

"Mom's been threatening to clean it out for me if I didn't. So, no contest." She paused again then plunged ahead.

"That's where I found it—the compartment—hidden in the bottom of the chest. And inside, there was an envelope and a sheet of paper with words that made it okay for me to be here."

She left nothing out as she told them. The quizzical landscapes etched on their faces as she finished were photo-worthy, and her hand rested on the cellphone at her waist.

Ridge's baseball cap hit the floor, and he raked his fingers through his hair. "Did you bring the paper?"

"I couldn't. It's pretty fragile, but I made a copy." She pulled the folded sheet from her back pocket and gave it to Ridge.

Jenni mopped her forehead with a sleeve and leaned in over his shoulder to read. "Looks like some gibberish about a door, floor, and something about preserving stones that's totally unreadable. But the sketches of your Star of David give me goose bumps."

"Those drawings and the name of this house spelled out on there and my name on the envelope? How in the world am *I* connected to this place?"

Ridge stayed quiet as Jenni's eyes searched hers. "That envelope for one thing. And what you've just found in the foyer—two links right there. And we'll look for more."

Jenni shifted nearer Ridge, and Lexi studied the floor. *If she leans any closer, she's going to knock him over. Lord, I need help here.* Normal, natural, but did she have to see it?

How close Jen was didn't seem to matter to Ridge. He chuckled and agreed with Jenni, but his attention fixed on Lexi. "You know, if you think about it, you came through the *door* of Northbrick, you found the box *beneath the floor* in Northbrick, and the only thing left to figure out is about preserving some stones. I see the sketches as a way to help you get over any doubt that you *are* linked to this place."

Jenni nodded. "So that's what made it okay to come in here. I think

it's even more important than saving this house."

"It could even be the very thing that saves this house." Ridge muttered the words under his breath.

Lexi sighed and looked down at the small scrolls. Her mind cleared, confusion faded. Saving the house, finding how she was connected— equally important.

"What if the two are related? If we find those 'sealed stones,' maybe it will answer both questions." She folded her hands in her lap and looked up at them. "But how do we know where to look? Do they really exist? Are they hidden or locked away somewhere?"

Jenni pointed to the box. "Nothing else in there, right?"

Lexi picked up the box, turning it over and over in her hands. "No, I checked; there's nothing more."

Jenni reached to touch the base. "What about that?"

Lexi lifted the small case to look. Another star? Her backbone straightened in a rigid, icy lineup, she stared at the six-pointed star engraved on the bottom of the brass band.

Ridge bent near her and touched the gold star on her necklace. Lexi forced a slow breath as his fingers brushed her throat. Yes, Ridge, it matches the one on the box—and he smelled of leather, saddle soap, and sun. And oh, he was way too close!

Jenni gave a loud sniff. Ridge pulled away, his eyes on the engraving.

Lexi ignored both of them, laid the box in her lap, and pressed back against the wall. Why couldn't she remember if the Star of David had always been there alongside her cross? "All this feels so weird, like someone wants me to connect the dots."

The two symbols on her necklace cool against her skin, Lexi closed her eyes, engulfed in a vivid memory. She sat between her mother and father on a sofa in a large room awash with soft lamplight. Two men stood nearby, talking about something that seemed deeply important.

The only one not paying attention, Lexi gazed into a large, gilt-framed mirror that hung between brocade and velvet-draped windows on the wall opposite her. The mirror imaged a little girl with pale skin in a bright yellow dress, a yellow bow atop long black curls, and swinging feet encased in shiny, black patent-leather shoes. The little girl leaned forward to peer into the reflection—into her own deep-set, dark blue eyes—then examined the rest of the reflected room.

The mirror painted a picture of Georgian elegance. Heavy, ornate furniture. Cream and gold damask curves of the sofa where she sat. Her gaze drifted to the men. The taller of the two had a head full of silvery-gray hair, heavy dark brows over deep-set eyes, and glasses on the bridge of his sharp nose. He wore a dark blue suit, and with the paunch of his middle, one deep breath threatened to launch the two buttons of his over-stretched jacket in Lexi's direction.

She studied the profile of the old man in the black suit. Slender, shorter, with a small black cap that left a circlet of balding scalp edged with a spiky fringe of white hair. Except for the smile-creases around his eyes, the smoothness of his skin belied his age as much as his mustache and ragged white beard attested to it.

The old one looked at Lexi in the mirror. His beard wiggled and his mustache rose. The corners of his lips lifted in a smile that melted her heart. Then he winked at her. She watched herself put both hands to her mouth, suppressing the giggle that threatened to spill out. She had to grasp the edge of the sofa to keep from running to him to wrap her arms around his legs and hug him as hard as she could.

Movement in the mirror. A mound of snow beside her, a white cat sat demurely on the carpet next to her dangling feet. And she held something small, bright, and shiny that dangled from her necklace. She

saw herself trace its sharp angles with her fingers. Just as she did right here. Right now.

Lexi's arms tingled with a wave of awe. She'd been here before. Here in this room. Both men left an indelible imprint of familiarity, but the old man in black . . . Could he be the one in the photographs she'd found?

I loved him. But who is he?

Lexi opened her eyes and took a second look around the drawing room, and the words burst from her mouth before she could check them. "There used to be a big mirror right here above us."

She clapped a hand to her forehead, as much as to displace the disturbing memory as in disbelief she'd just blurted out nonsense.

Jenni shook her head. "Lexi, how could you possibly know there used to be a mirror there?"

"I don't know how, Jen. I just know. It's all so . . . so strange, like I remembered it."

Am I losing it, Lord? Help! Distracted, hands clammy, Lexi picked up the box, took out the gold key, and for long seconds, held it as if it were a life preserver.

Jenni rubbed Lexi's arm. "It has to be some kind of a coincidence, not a memory. Don't let it get to you."

Two strong warm hands closed around hers. With a soft squeeze, Ridge took the now less-than-shiny key from Lexi's limp fingers, letting one hand linger over hers. "Coincidence or memory, we have to find out what this key fits. And why you're going goofy on us."

Tenderness. Another reason she— Lexi forced her mind elsewhere, anywhere, to shake off the sensation of his fingers against hers. "What about the cat?" She scooped up the ivory carving and turned it over to look at the date. "Is this just something stuck in the box as an afterthought, or is it significant?"

"It could be a double for the one we saw run out of the house." Jenni tucked a wisp of blonde hair behind her ear and pursed her pink-lipsticked mouth. "The front was completely boarded up when you got here, right? You ripped a board off the door and opened it. So how did the cat get in? Where did it come from?"

She sent her blonde best friend a grin. "I didn't see it, but it could have followed me in, I guess. Thank God for that cat. If it hadn't been here . . . I don't want to think about what might have happened."

Lexi looked at the shadows lengthening in front of them. "It's getting late." She stood, brushing away the silky webs criss-crossing her jeans.

"You're right," Jenni said. "We can talk about this somewhere else."

Ridge put the carving and the gold key in the case, snapped the box shut, and handed it to Lexi. "Take good care of those, Lex. You got the other key?"

"Right here." She patted her jeans pocket. "And don't worry. I have a place to stash them."

"Okay." He grabbed his ball cap and pushed up from the floor.

Jenni gingerly rolled the parchment inside its covering. She gave the roll to Lexi and went with Ridge through the double doors into the entrance hall.

Lexi didn't follow.

There. She walked to the sheet-covered sofa, and turned. A splash of wonder cascaded through her, and she plucked the cellphone from its case. Pointing its camera toward the void oval shape on the far wall between the faded gold draperies, she took four shots in quick succession. The barren wall held shadowy muted evidence of the beautiful mirror she had once gazed into.

"Lexi . . . y'all coming?"

Jen's chirpy drawl had Lexi smiling. "I'll be right there. Just grabbing a few more photos."

She took several more shots of the room then joined them in the foyer. "So, do you two honestly want to help save this old place—*and* find out what makes me feel like I'm some clueless heroine of a second-rate mystery?"

Ridge shot her a crooked grin. "No way would I miss out on doing either."

"Are you kidding?" Jenni put a hand on Ridge's muscled forearm. "Don't even think of shutting us out of this."

Lexi couldn't help noticing Jen's emphasis on *us*—and that Ridge didn't make a single move to escape Jen's grasp.

"Okay. I wouldn't let you sneak out anyway. You're in this as deep as I am." She looked at Jenni. "With our early shift in the morning, we should still be home fairly close to nine. Would it work if we met at the library at ten to do some research? I'll email you both some info on what I want to look for. "

Lexi barely heard their agreement. She glanced at the flashlight hanging from Ridge's belt and then into the depths of the corridor leading toward the rear of the house.

"Uh oh. You're not finished with your plunder yet, are you?" Ridge put his hand on her shoulder.

A shiver raced from her shoulder to her toes. Did he have to do that? "There has to be a way to go in and out from the back of the house, right?"

Ridge turned toward the hall. "Yep."

Jenni pulled a cobweb from her t-shirt. "Maybe the cat got in that way."

"Okay, let's go see what's there." Ridge unclipped the light and turned it on, aiming it down the hall.

"Ahh . . . no. I'm not going." Jenni planted her feet, unmoving, staring down the beam of Ridge's light.

In the ray of light, Lexi saw the maze of shimmering cobwebs and grinned up at Ridge. "Go ahead and check it out. We'll stay here."

Ridge shook his head at them and strode into the dark hall, flashlight in one hand, the other flapping at webs. He returned in minutes.

"No one's getting in or out through the rear of this house without a crowbar. Good news is that there's a door, and the bad news is that the door and every single window of every room I checked is boarded up tight. And I mean tight. Everything's been nailed shut from the inside. I couldn't budge those boards, and there wasn't a pixel of light shining through any of them."

"Guess we'll have to scale the stone wall to check out the rear grounds." Lexi turned toward the center of the entrance hall. "One more thing."

Ridge's chuckle echoed in the quiet. "Let's see—you want to check under the floor again?"

She stuck out her hand, palm up, and wiggled her fingers, waiting for him to hand her the flashlight. "Got to make sure; here, hold these for me a sec." She gave him the box and paper and tilted her head at him. "And, if it's empty, just know I intend to search every inch of this estate to find those 'stones.'"

She went to the middle of the hall and knelt, laughing when Jen and Ridge dropped down beside her to look for themselves.

Nothing. The board replaced, she was ready to leave.

Jenni followed Ridge outside. Lexi paused on the threshold for a last look at the foyer before she pulled the noisy, protesting front door shut behind her. One of the last hands to have touched that knob belonged to a man she hoped never to face again. What kind of tangled web was she getting them all into?

71

Chapter Seven

Lexi parked her car and walked toward the impressive Greek Revival architecture of the two-story Nantucket Atheneum library. If Ridge and his El Camino were anywhere nearby, they were out of Lexi's view. She jogged up the steps, passed between two massive fluted columns, and entered through the double doors.

The solid, reassuring scent of old books and furniture polish permeated the atmosphere of the familiar, quiet library and filled her with a sense of well-being. The clock above the checkout desk read exactly ten as she scanned the area. No Jenni, no Ridge. The urge to tell them what she'd overheard before she'd left the house burned like an unscratchable itch.

She drew in a deep breath, little twitches of impatience curling her fingers around the straps of her canvas bag as she looked for a place to sit. Her friends had always teased her about her punctuality quirk. Maybe she was quirky, but was it such a big thing to be on time?

She spotted a cozy corner with a reading table and shelves filled with periodicals, and pulled out one of the wooden chairs to sit. Nothing between her and the entrance—except her tapping toe. She pressed her

sandal to the floor; at least from here she could keep an eye out for them.

Bookshelves beckoned, and all the resources of the library pulled at her to start researching. Pacing would have been more effective. Instead, in between people-watching, she grabbed a pad and pencil and began to sketch the face of the clock.

Across the room, a lone librarian with a perpetual smile and a tiny pair of reading glasses perched on her petite nose staffed the desk. Her long blonde ponytail swung like a pendulum as she checked books, answered questions, and directed patrons.

Lexi almost laughed out loud. The librarian's swishing hairdo brought memories of a straw-colored palomino, the first horse Lexi had ever saddled—and of the day she and Jenni met.

They'd both been fourteen when Jenni and her family moved to the island from Alabama. Lexi was two months into her first part-time job at White Oak Ranch. Jenni saw the stables and came to ride for an hour. While Lexi saddled a horse for Jenni, they talked non-stop. A week later, Lexi talked Ray, the stable manager, into giving Jenni a part-time job. The girls soaped saddles, pitched hay, mucked stalls, curried horses— and rode together every opportunity they had.

South met north in the two of them. Jenni was fair-skinned and blonde, compared to Lexi's dark hair and perpetual tan. They shared May birthdays and loved pepperoni-pineapple pizza, but their love of horses had drawn them together.

And after four fun years, they still held their part-time jobs—and would until they left for college. Lexi pushed away from the heavy mahogany library table, her throat aching with thoughts of no more crazy days of roping, saddling, and riding—and aching for a pillow between her back and the spindles of the chair. The wall clock taunted her, chewing up time, relentlessly swallowing the minutes in sixty-second gulps.

The clock she'd doodled had eyes and a face that probably mimicked her own—a frowning, grumpy mask. Her cellphone vibrated with a text message from Jenni.

I'm almost there. Ridge will be there asap—he says.

Right! So Ridge wasn't bringing Jen, and he'd be even later. Lexi punched in her reply, *ok c u soon*. She shook her head and stuffed the silly sketch into her canvas bag as Jenni walked into the library. Tall and slender in her faded blue jeans and hot-pink tee-shirt, Jenni pulled out a chair and plopped down across from Lexi with a huff.

"I thought I'd never get out of the house. Mom had this whole list of things I *need* to be buying for the dorm and that I *need* to pack. It's going to feel so good to get out from under being told what I *need* to do." Jenni's grin was apologetic. "Hope you haven't been here long."

Lexi swallowed a few words of frustration and plastered a smile above her chin. "No, only a few minutes. At least you're here. Guess we ought to wait for Ridge. You know he's going to drag himself in here half asleep."

Jenni laughed and scooted her chair closer to the table. "We should've told him nine so he'd get here by ten."

"Mmm, especially since *he* didn't have to work the early shift at the stable before coming here this morning. And speaking of the boy . . ." Ridge ambled through the door and joined them. "Glad you could make it," Lexi whispered in response to his disarming grin.

"C'mon, I'm on time—sort of! Steve needed a jump for the T-bird. That battery was deader than yesterday's headlines." Ridge matched her whisper, his gold-flecked hazel eyes flashing more mischief than apologies. "Are you still ready to do all this?" He gave her another lopsided grin as he sat, arranging his muscled six-foot frame across the

chair on the other side of Jenni.

That was fine with Lexi. He made spectacular eye candy. "I can't wait. I'm going nuts wondering what this is about."

"Yeah, we need to look for the name of the last owner—the hermit-slash-ghost." Jenni chuckled.

Last owner? Lexi straightened and bit down on the pencil. Ha! Jen had just given her the perfect intro to tell them about this morning. The pencil dropped to the table. *Here goes nothing!*

She gazed into the space between Jenni and Ridge, glad she'd chosen this out-of-the-way corner, and kept her voice low. "I can give you the answer to that question right now. He may have been a hermit, but he's no ghost." She paused and grinned at them. "Right before I was ready to leave to come here, Mom and Dad were in the kitchen talking. I was headed for the kitchen when I heard Dad say 'Northbrick House.' They hadn't heard me, and I was grafted to that wall, listening for what they'd say."

She'd heard her parents mention Northbrick and Cohen before, but though it made her feel strange when she heard the names, they meant nothing to her . . . until now.

She drew in a breath. "With three houses on the street and only two lived in, they had to be talking about Northbrick Estate. Then Dad said something like '. . . review the Aaron Cohen Trust.' I'm thinking it makes sense that a man named Aaron Cohen could have been the last owner of the mansion." The elderly man in the photos wedged into her thoughts, and she hesitated.

"I wish I could have made out every word, but Mom did say something about taxes. That was it. I didn't hear anything more, and you probably have as many questions as I do." Lexi tilted her head toward Ridge. Maybe he'd have some input on what it all meant.

She was sweating, on the edge of her seat over how her parents had anything at all to do with Northbrick.

Jenni cleared her throat and looked at her. "How do you figure your parents are involved with the Northbrick Estate and its taxes?"

Lexi hesitated, and Ridge interrupted, his expression thoughtful. "It could be for some reason they actually pay the taxes on the place."

She wanted to hug him again. Warmth she'd rather not have felt rose in her face. For Ridge to jump in to help her like that was beyond sweet. "I suppose so. And along with the envelope, that would be one more solid connection I have to Northbrick."

"But why would they be paying the tax? And what in the world would the trust thing have to do with it?" Jenni's eyebrows arched, her questions coming in an unusual flood of curiosity.

Lexi shrugged. "I guess you might be able to pay taxes *from* a trust, but I have no clue about how that would work, or why they'd do it."

Ridge picked up his cap. "I'll go online later and see what I can find out about the whole trust, tax angle."

Silence dominated the table for a few seconds before Jenni spoke. "Well, that brings up a heap more questions."

"It sure did for me, but I had to leave before I felt any guiltier for eavesdropping—or worse, got caught."

Ridge looked at Lexi. "What about Cohen's name? Does it mean anything to you?"

Lexi's stomach slid into knots, thinking of the photos again. But until she could show them, she wasn't ready to tell them about the photos yet, and the name probably didn't have a thing to do with the pictures anyway.

"No, but it means something to them. I hear them say Cohen or Northbrick; they hear me in the vicinity, they go silent, as if they're

either hiding something or trying to shield me from something." She looked from Jenni to Ridge and back with a shrug. "It happens a lot more often lately, and it's strange how I feel when I overhear them, almost like he's some long-lost relative."

She leaned back in her chair. "I know you're wondering why I don't just go ahead and ask them about all this." Jenni nodded, but neither she nor Ridge said a word.

The library wasn't the place to tell them how she really felt, that her parents had seemed to put up a wall—that she'd built one too—and that it was too deep, too hurtful to talk about. Heat burned her cheeks with a wave of resentment, then regret. What were the words in the Psalms about asking the Lord for guidance?

She pushed her fingers through her hair and held her head in her hands. "If I'd told them I was going into the house, they'd point out every risk in the book and forbid it. They'd end up being more hovering and protective. And even if I'd shown them the envelope and paper, the paper doesn't really say much of anything. So I decided not to show or ask—just do it."

More silence. Lexi dug her heels into the setting cement of pure determination. She had no doubt about why she was so driven. Finding the envelope Thursday, and the box and parchment yesterday. They *had* to understand. It was becoming screamingly evident that Northbrick and everything about the place involved her. But how and why?

Jenni turned and said something to Ridge. Lexi crossed her arms on the table and closed her eyes. She could see him again, the old man in the reflection. She saw herself as a little girl, looking up into his kind eyes. His gentle hand folded around hers as they walked together in a garden overflowing with flowers, and his strong arms lifted her to a bench. He sat beside her, placed his polished wooden cane between them, and put a small box in her hands. The sweet scent of roses and gardenias filled the air, and she looked up at rough wood rafters. A roof—a gazebo.

"You may open your present now, little Lexi."

Startled at the nearly audible words, her back muscles went rigid and she sat straight up in her chair.

Ridge leaned across the table, hands extended toward her. "You just lost a couple of shades of tan. What's up?" His fingers were micro-inches from hers and it didn't help a bit.

Jenni chuckled. "What planet have you been exploring, girl?"

"Planet? How about another dimension? It was one of those memories I keep having." Lexi's pencil fell to the floor and rolled under the table.

Ridge shot her a grin and bent to retrieve it. "Well something sure made an impression. What?"

His tone encouraged her as he handed her the pencil. Lexi rubbed the small of her back as she told them of the old man, the garden, the gazebo, the box. "And that box wasn't anything like the one I found yesterday. It was smaller and square, like a ring box."

"Okay, that was weird." Jenni gave a slow quizzical nod at Lexi. "You think it was the box your star came in?"

"No way I can know for sure." Lexi shook her head, but even she thought it was small enough to have been the box that held her gold Star of David.

Ridge's eyes caught Lexi's and held on. "Maybe you can figure out some way to ask your mom and dad a few questions about this Aaron Cohen person they were talking about."

Lexi pursed her lips. "I don't know how I can do that without making them wonder why I'm asking, but I'll try."

"Hey, I thought you said you couldn't wait to do some research."

Jenni grinned at Lexi, clicking a fingernail against the face of her watch. "We'll never find out anything if we don't get started."

Lexi glanced toward the stairs. "This place is a hive this morning. We should get up there and see if any of the computers are free."

Ridge straightened and put his elbows on the table. "Okay, what do you want to do first?"

"I want to know what the gold key unlocks, but nothing in here's going to tell us that." Lexi pushed the pad and a pen toward Ridge.

Jenni fussed with her tortoise-shell hair clips. "We should find out who built the mansion and when."

"Blueprints will help." Ridge twirled his baseball hat on his finger. "If we could locate plans of the place, we'd know the year of construction, who the original owner was, and maybe spot a couple of hidden passageways." He cocked his head and sent Lexi a mischievous smile. "You know—where they used to hide whatever thing the key unlocks. Who knows what they might have built into a place that big?"

"Mmm, as if they'd include that info on any blueprint." Lexi watched him write "mansion: address and year built; house plans, blueprints" on the pad. "I think we've pretty much figured out it was built in 1832, with those numbers being engraved on the plaque near the front door and on the back of the cat carving."

"True," Ridge said. "Could just be a street number, though. And it may not be all that important, but we should look for any other buildings on the estate. We don't know what's behind the rear walls."

Jenni scooted nearer Ridge. "I wonder if anyone else has lived there over the years. And if so, how can we find out who they were?"

Lexi nodded. "I'd like to find out why it isn't lived in now, and why it isn't for sale. As far as I know, there never has been anyone living there or any *For Sale* signs. But that should be easy to find out." She paused. "Who do you think—?"

"I think we should try to find out who that guy was that walked in on you yesterday." Jenni put her hand on Ridge's forearm and looked at Lexi.

Images of the darkened foyer and the man with hawk-like features flooded Lexi's thoughts. "Maybe we can come up with some way to ID him, but that's sure not going to happen in a library. Plus, I don't know how we can track down someone we've only seen once, and even then, none of us got a very good look at him."

Jenni fixed a questioning gaze on Lexi. "You told us he went straight to where you found everything. Didn't you wonder how he knew where to look?"

Ridge stared at the pen he twirled between his fingers. "Not gonna find that out in a library either, but I figure if the guy's familiar enough with the area to know about the house, he probably lives and works on the island. And if he knew exactly where to look, whatever he was after must really be worth finding."

Jenni's nod matched Lexi's. "Otherwise, why would he have stormed out, blistering the air with nasty-grams when he didn't find anything?"

"You're right about him being mad, but that still leaves the question of *how* he knew where to look for it. And three more people just went up those steps to the computers, guys." Lexi stuck her pencil between her teeth and reached for her bag.

Chapter Eight

Jenni hooked her thumb toward the wall clock. "We've got enough of a list to start, but we need to do it before noon. I'm meeting Mom for lunch."

Lexi glanced toward the stairs. "Hopefully one of the computers up there is free. I'll try to locate old newspaper articles about Cohen and find his obituary. Where do you two want to begin?"

"We'll go up with you. Jen and I can see if we can scare up one of the volumes covering the island's history or any books or records with some background on the estate. If you concentrate on Mr. C., that should cover it."

It was obviously okay with Jenni, who moved closer to Ridge as he stuffed his notes in his jeans pocket. He sent her one of his mind-bending smiles and edged away from Jenni. Lexi gave him an inward high-five, then mentally booted herself for being so happy about a one-inch space between them.

Upstairs in the Atheneum's great hall, Lexi headed to the reference desk as Jenni and Ridge went to the card catalog. "Happy hunting, guys.

Come and get me if you find anything interesting."

She checked out two promising CDs, but the third and most interesting CD was already in use. Computers brought this old library into the twenty-first century, but if she didn't find what she needed, she'd try online from home later.

She looked across the room at the four computer-laden tables. The only vacant chair was beside a man in a stern-looking business suit.

Lexi walked toward the table—and froze. Inches away from the empty chair, her eyes fixed on the young, dark-haired man she'd be sitting beside. As he hunched over his monitor, lightning flashes of the man in the mansion fired through Lexi's mind, even as a familiar scent assailed her nose. The same scent that fused with the musty air in the foyer as the intruder had entered. Had she walked straight into yesterday's nightmare?

He broke his concentration to glance up at her. His face! A chill clamped the nape of Lexi's neck and raced down her torso. Her bag slipped to the floor. Expressionless, he went back to his research, barely acknowledging her presence.

He has to be made of stone. Dark, craggy features. His nose and cheekbones protruded from his face like chiseled granite, and heavy eyebrows hung like cliff tops above deep-set brown eyes. Trimmed to within an inch of his open-shirt collar, not a strand of his dark, freshly styled hair strayed. His black mustache looked groomed to droop on either side of his thin lips and reached for the base of his chin. Even his suit looked menacing.

Everything matched with her memory of the near-encounter in the mansion. Adrenalin surged. She wanted to turn and run.

But she'd found him. Maybe finding out about him would happen in the library after all.

THE STONEKEEPERS

Her hands shook at the sight of his sharp-angled brow and beaky nose. It was too much. She needed to sit but her knees locked. She hung on to her composure and studied him from the corner of her eye as she struggled to get the first CD out of its case.

Lord, how do I handle this?

She pulled in a deep breath. Trust. Calm. She could be calm. Just take another deep breath and everything will right itself. Even if it was him, he couldn't possibly know who she was . . . could he?

For heaven's sake, sit! Her hands were wedges of ice, her fingers icicles as she set the freed CD and case on the table and pulled the chair out. Her eyes fastened on his monitor, then widened. Centered on his screen, a newspaper article showed a photograph of an elegant old house. She gripped the back of her chair, knuckles whitening. *He* had the other CD she'd wanted. He'd looked up the mansion.

Turmoil morphed her thoughts into a desire to know everything he knew, but danger spiked out from him like the quills of a porcupine.

She couldn't move her eyes from his monitor. A mistake. She'd paused too long. The man glared at her before turning to make notes on his cellphone. She forced herself to sit. She had to stay now. What choice did she have? Too obvious to simply get up and leave. Her hands trembled, and she prayed he wouldn't notice.

I can't do this. Lord, don't let me start falling to pieces now.

Her thoughts aligned. She gathered up her shattered nerves and smiled at him. "This is a different computer than I'm used to. CD goes in here?" She spoke with all the warmth she could muster and tried to keep her hand steady as she put the CD into the drive. The gold chain wrapped around his thick neck glittered, and she fought the temptation to look at it.

He snapped his phone into a case on his belt then faced her. His

sharp eyes blackened and latched onto hers for seconds that dragged by like a walk through eternity, his words, acid. "If you need some help, I suggest you see the librarian." And in a single swift motion, he removed the CD from its drive, stuck it in its case, and switched off his monitor.

A gentle answer turns away wrath. The scripture surfaced then sank in her thoughts. Gentle? How would that work with a guy who'd threatened to kill a cat for getting in his way? She'd like to smack him silly for scaring her into mindless oblivion yesterday. She swallowed instead.

"Thanks. I think I can figure it out." Her words seemed to catch him off-guard, and he slowed his moves to leave.

"Do I know you?" His gruff voice matched his looks, and his eyes continued their piercing gaze.

Had that been a glimmer of recognition? He knows me? Lexi hesitated. Maybe not. "I don't think so." The time she took to engage him now might be an opportunity to learn something about why he came to the mansion yesterday. It wouldn't hurt to try.

"Are you an attorney?"

It had been a good, but easy, guess. She detected brief surprise flitting over his otherwise composed face, but it disappeared as quickly as it had come. His answer followed, cool and brusque.

"As a matter of fact, I am." Beneath his mustache, a slight smile crossed his lips then faded. He did an abrupt turnaround, picked up the CD and a file from the table, and stood to his full height, towering over her. Smoothing the front of his storm-gray suit, he gave her a curt nod and walked away. Lexi almost expected him to click his heels together as he turned.

THE STONEKEEPERS

Minutes ago Ridge had spotted two vacant chairs side-by-side at a monitor/keyboard-laden computer table two tables away from where Lexi sat. Good, but she was hidden from his view. He brought up a site listing books of island history and tried to concentrate. Sitting next to him, Jenni was engrossed in picking through online databases and jotting notes.

Ridge blew out a breath and nudged Jenni, pointing to a listing on his screen. "This might hold some answers for us on the house. It covers the history of the island all the way back to 1602." He highlighted the title, opened the site, and scanned the contents. "This is going to take some time."

Jenni leaned in to look. "Yes, and that's one volume they're not going to let us take out of here." She scooted her chair closer. "Lots of great old photos."

Ridged wrote down the URL. "I'll pull it up at home later to see if there's anything we can use." He sniffed and rubbed his nose. Some kind of flowery perfume, and it wasn't Jen's. His comfort level dropped a degree. Shifting in his chair, the hair on the back of his neck started to prickle.

Something wasn't right. Something was going on in the library besides research, and he leaned back in his seat, straining to check on Lexi. Stunned, he tried hard not to stare.

He touched Jenni's arm and kept his whisper low. "Scoot your chair back a little and turn around. Take a look, but make it slow, and *don't* panic." She followed his instructions and his gaze to where a man in a business suit rose from his seat beside Lexi.

Ridge's determination not to stare fell apart. He gaped. Jenni grabbed his arm and held on. In seconds they both made a swift about-face as the man strode past them toward the reference office, trailing the thick sweet scent of aftershave. He dropped a CD into a return box, and went toward the stairway.

Jen's manicured nails dug into Ridge's arm. He looked down at the pink-polished pincers, then at her. Too pale. "You okay?"

She sucked in an audible breath, then released his arm and rubbed her nose. "Yes, but I'm going to hurl if I ever smell that aftershave again. Isn't he . . . ?"

"Yeah, and he wore Fort Knox around his neck. The way he walked—same guy we saw yesterday at Northbrick. I think that was Lexi's Hawk."

Jenni nodded. "I thought that the second I saw him."

Ridge continued to watch the dark-haired man until he was out of sight.

Shocked, Lexi sat, hard-wired to her computer, unmoving. The man hadn't asked her name, but after the look of recognition he'd let slip, her name probably held no mystery for him. She fumbled to remove the CD and shut down the computer. Where were Jenni and Ridge?

Back on the main floor of the library, Lexi sat, elbows on the table, chin in her hands, opposite Jenni and Ridge. "So you saw him." She pressed forward. "He's the one who scared the stuffing out of me yesterday."

Ridge nodded and grinned at her. "It'll never happen in a library, right?" His grin turned into a chuckle. "Never say never. But, you're right. He was either that man or a body-double for the guy we saw yesterday."

Jenni wrinkled her nose. "His passion for aftershave is no secret."

Lexi nodded. "That's what clinched it for me too. But more important, he said he's an attorney."

Jenni's eyebrows rose. "He volunteered that? Or did you ask him? How do you know for sure?"

Lexi grinned at her. "No, yes, and I'm not positive, but we can check online when we get outside. A lot of law offices put photos of their attorneys in their ads. Maybe we can match the face with a name."

Ridge pulled his baseball cap from his back pocket. "Good. Let's check out these books and get out of here."

"I'm more than ready to do that." Lexi sighed, tired of whispering and anxious to breathe some fresh air.

Five minutes later they sat on a bench outside the library and pored over Lexi's iPad, searching through Nantucket's law firms for photos.

Lexi had to bite her tongue to keep from saying I told you so. She jabbed her finger toward the younger of two men in the color photo ad, but paused, stunned, staring at the older man. Dad's business attorney? There must be some mistake. "This is the guy, but something's not adding up. He's—"

The tap of a cane against the wide red-brick sidewalk caught their attention, and a wide shadow fell across Lexi's iPad. The sound ceased, and the shadow hovered.

Chapter Nine

Unbelievable. Attorney Greyson P. Quinn, Jr., tugged at the gold chain circling his neck and left Nantucket Atheneum public library. Nerves on edge, his stomach soured, as upset from running into the girl as he was irritated with the elderly library clients who hogged the steps. No one took him by surprise, but recognizing Lexi Christensen, he'd been thoroughly jolted.

At the base of the steps, he squinted in the brilliant sunshine, then fast-walked through the library grounds, past the white perimeter fencing to the sidewalk. Pulling his sunglasses from his suit pocket, he slid them onto the bridge of his nose. Heat radiated from the worn cobblestone street, and instant sweat trickled down his neck. Another shirt for the laundry. Forget the library; he should have gone straight to the office this morning.

A laughing couple bumped his arm. "Hey, watch where you're going." They passed by, ignoring his growl. Quinn's skin crawled at the sight of smiley-faced islanders filling the sidewalks and doing their Saturday-morning shopping. They added one more brick to the load of

his frustration.

His chance encounter with the girl saturated his thoughts. When she first saw him in the library, she'd flashed a brief look of fear. Why? Only if she knew something—something about him. She'd seen the mansion on his screen, but she couldn't possibly connect him with the old Cohen place; it was too soon.

Three days ago an article, featuring White Oak Ranch, its riding stable, and a photo of her, holding the reins of two horses, appeared in the *Nantucket Inquirer and Mirror*. The name "Christensen" had jumped from the page, and he'd immediately connected her with the documents he'd recently handled involving the Cohen Estate.

He shook his head. Maybe he was reading more into this than he should. But he'd lay money on his conviction that she had recognized him. Her expression hung in his mind, smoldering like embers from a dying campfire.

What if . . . ? Quinn slowed his pace and rubbed his temples. What if she'd seen him go in or leave the mansion yesterday? He stopped and studied his reflection in the display window of a shop. Not likely. He'd been too careful. But there was another possibility. He pinched at his dark mustache as the overwhelming conviction that someone had been in that house when he was hit him as if he'd been body-slammed. Had she been inside the mansion before he'd gone in? Maybe the noise he heard had been more than a cat. The sounds could have been the girl trying to hide in the shadows. His breath left his lungs with a huff, and the mirrored image shot back a reddening face full of irritation and anger.

If it had been the girl, maybe she knew about the box. And if she knew about it, maybe she knew where to look for it. He glowered at his reflection.

THE STONEKEEPERS

She probably had it—took it right before he'd gotten there, and replaced the board. It made sense. The only others who possibly knew of the box were his father and Rodney. He pursed his lips. No. Not them. Both were ridiculously beyond honest.

Fact was, the box was gone. His hands curled and tightened into fists. And what other answer was there? None. The girl had the box. Simple as that. And now that she had it, what did she plan to do with it, and how soon?

His stomach burned. She wasn't supposed to learn about any of this for another two years. The young woman completely infuriated him. It could have been so easy. Now he'd have to resort to some other way to get that box.

Timing was crucial. Aggravation crept down the muscles and tendons of his arms as he strode toward his Porsche. Whatever he did, he had to do it fast. He knew only that whatever the box held was "of considerable value." She may not have any idea of the value of what she'd found, but if she'd gotten this far, it wouldn't be long before she did.

His thoughts muddled with anger, he opened the door of his red roadster, but had to jerk the car door back as several bike riders whizzed by. "Blasted bicycles!" Why the islanders had such a loving relationship with their bikes, he'd never understand. They did nothing but get in his way. Quinn folded himself into the seat behind the leather-covered steering wheel and turned the key in the ignition. Except for the purr of its engine, the sleek sports car left the curb without a sound.

Cool off, Greyson. He couldn't trust his temper when he drove in town. Too many run-ins with the local *gendarme* lately, and he didn't need another. He thrust an antacid into his mouth and chewed hard to quench the fire in his belly. He was tapped out. Money problems weighed heavy. As heavy as the recent painful punch he'd taken because of them.

Just drive and think. He shoved away his rage and frustration and drove like a little old lady down Federal Street, the seed of an idea taking shape.

Shopping done, errand done. Opposite the library, Jacob Carver left his accountant's office to return to his truck, but instantly halted, surprised. Young Quinn, Jr.? Jacob leaned against the wall of the small business office to rest his aging, achy legs . . . and watch.

Mmm hmm. No doubt about it. The son of a prominent local attorney strode down the library steps, almost knocking over an elderly woman on his way to the street.

Lord, help him! Boy always was rude.

Jacob watched Quinn pause in front of the display window of a shop and curl his hands into tight fists, smacking them against his thighs.

Well, what ails you? Humph. What doesn't? Jacob shook his head, ready to move toward his truck. But again, he stopped as three young people emerged from the library. He immediately recognized one of the two girls. Both Lexi Christensen and Quinn coming from the library within minutes of each other? Right bothersome. His breathing grew shallow. This was too much of a coincidence after what he'd seen and heard from his driveway near the mansion yesterday.

Frowning, Jacob scratched at his snowy beard. He needed to talk to Lexi, and it might be easier with her friends present. She probably wouldn't recognize him, but if he explained a little, maybe she'd be open to a visit with him and his wife. He'd invite her friends too.

Good. They'd stopped and sat on a wood bench beside the library. He grasped his cane, sheer urgency pressing him forward. He crossed the street, praying his legs would hold out a little longer. Breathing a bit labored, his cane tapped rhythmically against the sun-warmed cobblestones. He reached the sidewalk and made his way to the bench where the trio studied an electronic gadget.

Tap. Step. Tap. Step. Lexi held her finger poised over her iPad, about to tell Ridge and Jenni who the older man in the photo-advertisement was. As a shadow crossed the face of the tablet, she glanced up then flipped the cover shut.

A man with a head full of tight white curls leaned on his cane and stepped toward her.

"Excuse me."

The man shifted the shopping bag on his arm and seemed to be trying to catch his breath.

"I'm sorry . . . to interrupt . . . but I wonder if I might be of some help to you."

The old man appeared harmless, but why did he look directly at her? And why did his lilting Caribbean accent sound vaguely familiar? She returned his stare, strange *déjà vu* skipping down her backbone. Ridge stood and moved in front of her and Jenni, blocking Lexi's view. Well, that was mighty protective. But, no, she didn't need any protection.

She waited and watched Ridge's muscles tense as he spoke to the elderly man. "No. We're doing fine, thanks. I don't think we need any help."

Lexi looked at Jenni then dropped the tablet into her book bag, stood, and stepped around Ridge. Surely they didn't look as if they needed help. Maybe he did? She studied the source of the friendly voice. No,

he was okay. He'd make a great Santa Claus, but his round belly was far from little. The blue denim overalls were clean and all but covered his old plaid work shirt. So what was it about him? Not quite as tall as Ridge, the man's dark brown eyes again fastened on hers. If it hadn't been for his broad smile, she would have been more uneasy than she already was.

"Lexi Christensen, isn't it? That was a nice article in the paper last week."

"Thank you." Lexi couldn't stifle the amazement in her voice.

Quinn yanked the steering wheel into a sharp turn, dodging yet another duet of bikes at the Easy Street intersection. He slowed the Porsche and made a right turn, uncomfortable in the gray leather bucket seat. Too big and too tall, he wasn't a good physical fit for the sporty car, but he liked the looks he got.

He shoved his sunglasses up on his nose, crammed another Tums into his mouth, and grimaced with thoughts involving his father and recent events.

"Grey." He spat his father's nickname toward the windshield, coloring the single syllable with his anger and frustration. The name suited the man, matched his hair.

A week ago, he'd seen Grey take an old filing box from the file storage area and remove an unusually thick folder. No big thing . . . until later, when he went into his father's office to locate a law book he needed to reference. He'd turned to close the office door and glimpsed his father bending, a little too quickly, to lock that same thick manila folder in a file drawer in his desk. Not fast enough for Quinn to fail to see the bold black letters on the tab. *Cohen, A.*

He'd heard or seen the name before. But when and where? *Something you don't want me to see, Dad?* Curiosity twisted through Quinn's mind like kudzu through a forest. Why did that particular file deserve special attention?

Then, within hours, the Cohen name brought him to a standstill outside Grey's office, listening, pulse banging in his temples as Grey spoke to Steinman, a new man, a potential partner in the law firm.

"In May of next year, we'll begin preparation to comply with the wishes of our deceased client, Aaron Cohen. I want you to become familiar with this file, one of our more unusual cases, Rodney."

Heat flooded Quinn's face. *Rodney Steinman. Super-hero.* Three times so far this year, he'd been given cases Quinn should have handled. What had Steinman ever done to earn Grey's favor? Nothing. Not one thing.

Papers shuffled, and Grey had continued in his maddeningly genteel voice. "As outlined in Cohen's instructions, by May twelfth of the following year, the trust is to become fully active."

Grey had paused, and Quinn assumed Steinman had nodded his understanding. His father cleared his throat and added, "You should also know there's a sealed envelope in this file that's to be opened only under certain precisely drawn circumstances involving the Christensens' daughter. They are fully aware of the envelope and the details and will inform us if those circumstances occur."

Quinn slammed his foot against the accelerator, listening to the Boxter's responsive engine. That eavesdropping session had set him on a determined course to see the contents of the Cohen folder. He'd break into the drawer and look for himself.

And two days later, it had been so easy to get what he wanted. Alone

in the office, he'd easily picked the locked drawer and pulled out the fat folder. Inside, he found an envelope that listed "conditions" to be met before opening.

This envelope is to remain sealed until one of the following conditions occur.

Alexia Evengeline Christensen attains the age of twenty or she enters Northbrick Estate house prior to age twenty, but having attained age sixteen.

In the event the latter should occur, Alexia, her parents, Jason and Molly Christensen, and Attorney Greyson P. Quinn, Sr., or his legal representative, shall meet at the earliest possible date following knowledge of her entry.

At either designated time, these documents are to be reviewed and Alexia Christensen is to be made fully aware of the entire trust and its provisions.

Below Cohen's instruction, along with a notary's signature and stamp, all parties had signed the statement—except Lexi Christensen, who, according to the date, had been about four at the time.

"Conditions" wouldn't be stopping him from opening the envelope! He steamed the seal then sat in his father's desk chair and slid the contents out of the envelope. Several sheets of paper revealed the location of a "box, keys, and instructions," all the answers to Grey's mysterious directions to Steinman.

Well, he had first-hand knowledge, and there'd been an entry all right. Just a little too soon. Quinn banged his fist against the car's polished wood-grain dashboard. The Christensen woman had his box.

Quinn's black mood mushroomed. It was a sure bet there had to be more to this. Had Cohen laid out further instructions elsewhere? Whatever rested in the all-important box had to be something of considerable value, or else the wealthy, eccentric old man wouldn't have gone to all this trouble.

He had flipped through the balance of the folder. Not a thing that related to the "box." Nothing but legal documents pertaining to the sale of Cohen's business firm in Boston . . .

He jerked up straight, the leather executive chair complaining beneath him. Jewelry business! Cohen had been in the jewelry business. Thoughts of diamond-studded tiaras, pearl necklaces, gold bracelets, and emerald-encrusted rings. Sweet little items that would have translated into money—and still would if his plan worked.

The Boxter shot forward around a poky SUV toward the next intersection. *Slow down.* It looked as if someone else hadn't. Flashing lights ahead.

Stomach churning, he ground his teeth, wishing he could pass the line of stopped cars, like his father had passed him over. If it happened again, Quinn's hot breath would blister the old man's face. Cases translated into money. He needed money and more time. He'd gotten himself mired, deep in debt, in desperate need of cash. *Not* good that the girl had the box. He'd have to work fast to get it back.

The law office was close, an easy drive from the library. Squirming, agitated, still thinking, he pulled into his parking space near the front of his office building. At least the name on the door hadn't changed. Yet. Frustration fused with temper, and he banged an open hand on the steering wheel. Wincing, he aimed the air-conditioner vent toward his face. By now, it was possible her parents knew. And if they did—well, that was a problem he'd have to deal with.

He smoothed his mustache, and looked at his watch. There was still time this afternoon to call Dan Sangster in Boston. If he could get the less-than-honest private detective to fly into Nantucket as early as tonight, he

had plenty of work for Sangster to do. Bugging the Christensen house and phones was a priority.

He snatched his sunglasses from his nose and studied himself in the rearview mirror. Lips curved into a smirk, and eyes flared like charcoal embers. The smirk widened.

Charging Sangster's fee to the firm's account was easy enough; he had legitimate excuses with the cases he currently worked on. He'd call Rick Vander, too. Vander's connections could grease the plan he had.

A thrill shot through Quinn. He was all-in on this one, and the odds were in his favor.

Chapter Ten

Home from the library a few minutes before noon, Lexi stepped into the kitchen, mind still reeling from meeting Jacob Carver and from finding out the identity of the Northbrick intruder. Ridge was right. If for no other reason than her own peace of mind and heart, except for asking anything about Attorney Quinn, Jr., she would ask Mom and Dad some questions. But could she ask without a monster confrontation? Her hands tightened around the books she held. *Let the timing be right, Lord.*

The kitchen glowed with sunshine reflected from the maple table tucked into a windowed alcove. Gilly ambled over, and Lexi stooped to stroke his soft fur. "Hey, Gilly-boy, where's Mom?" She couldn't be far. The air was fragrant with the scent of freshly baked cookies.

Gilly pawed at Lexi's sandal and gave her bare ankle a sloppy kiss. He stayed beside her, his feathery tail slapping against the cabinets as she went to the fridge. She'd been blowing out three candles on her birthday cake when this grown-up version of the once lively puppy with chestnut eyes and golden fur had been delivered in a big wicker basket—

by whom? Another flash-memory that sent chills down her arms. Warm gray eyes smiling at her.

Gilly on her heels, Lexi went upstairs, trying to shake the odd sensation the recollection left behind. Her purse and books found a home on her unmade bed. If she didn't get better with her housekeeping, Jen would be threatening to throw her out their dorm window. But the bed stayed a jumbled mess, and Lexi sat on the rug to give a winded Gilly some ear scratches.

Footsteps in the hall. Mom. Lexi sighed, an audible groan beneath her breath. Derelict daughter that she was, she'd be in for a lecture for sure.

Lexi stood and tugged at the bed sheets as her mother walked in. "Hey, Mom, you've been busy. I smell cookies. Hope you plan on missing one."

"Well, they're not for us. I'm taking them to church on Sunday for the café. Did you find what you were looking for at the library?" She motioned toward the rumpled bed, her eyes lingering on the books. "Those sheets look more than ready for the wash. Is there any reason you left your room in such a mess this morning?"

Lexi closed her eyes and resisted the temptation to chew on her tongue. *Yes, Mother, my alarm didn't go off and I was almost late for work, and I didn't want to be late getting to the library!* But if she wanted answers from Mom, she'd better watch what she said.

"I should've put them in the laundry before I left."

Her mother's brows met in the middle.

Okay. Not what she said but how she said it. She'd be wiping the sarcastic drips from the floor if she didn't control her voice. Try again.

"Uh, where's Dad?" Better, but not by much.

"He had a meeting this afternoon and won't be back till about four.

We'll leave for the restaurant as soon as he gets home."

Good, they'd be eating early. She'd nearly forgotten they were going out to dinner tonight. The sun didn't set until well after eight, so she'd have hours of time for what she wanted to do. But would Mom be open to answering any questions? They were barely talking, and heaven help her if Mom saw the messy countertop and dirty towels behind her closed bathroom door.

Lexi sat on the rug beside Gilly again. "I'm meeting Jen and Ridge later. We've got a bike ride planned and we may go to the beach for a while." She swallowed hard with no intention of adding that they had one other stop scheduled.

Her mother seemed to stay on the edge of angry as she sat on the blue-and-white braided rug beside Lexi. "We should be home early enough for that." Mom stopped and shook her head. "But don't be out too late. You've been gone all morning long. Be home no later than nine. You know how we feel about you biking after dark."

Lexi stiffened. More of Mom's recent micro-management.

"You're such a glutton for back rubs, Gilly." Her mother reached to stroke the dog's golden coat.

"You spoil him, Mom." Lexi wrinkled her nose at her mother as she tried to unknot the frustration in her stomach. Oh, this small talk was mind-numbing. Would there ever be a right time to get some answers? *When, Lord?*

Now.

Now? Really?

They did have time. The rest of the afternoon remained wide open to the possibility. Her nerves caught fire at the idea of facing her past. She'd gotten the shove she needed.

"Mom, I've got some things to ask you."

With a tenuous smile and a nod that said, "Yes, I'm listening," her mother continued to pet Gilly, but turned to Lexi.

No hedging. Ask and see what happens. Lexi willed her insides to cool down. She tucked her knees beneath her chin and wrapped her arms around her legs—tight.

"Whenever I pass the mansion on Northbrick Avenue lately, I remember bits and pieces of things about an old man . . . ." Lexi turned and took in her mom's impassive expression and cobalt blue eyes for a split-second before she continued. "And every time I walk by or into a room when you and Dad are talking about someone named Aaron or Cohen, you instantly change the subject. Why?"

Lexi let go of her legs and raked her fingers through her hair, tension pulling at her insides. "It's really bothering me."

Her mother drew in a sharp breath. Her piercing gaze rolled waves of discomfort and unease through Lexi. Was Mom still ticked about her unmade bed? The mess in her room? Things were so fractured between them, had she made a mistake by bringing this up?

But as if she'd made a difficult decision, Mom's blue eyes softened and her delicate features relaxed as she sat taller.

"Well, maybe you are ready for a story. It's a long and interesting one." Mom stood and held out her hand. "I made a pitcher of iced tea, and our sandwiches are in the refrigerator. Might be nice to sit outside for a while."

Lexi took a deep breath. So there really was a story she needed to hear. She grasped her mother's hand and stood, hoping her shakiness wasn't noticeable.

Mom's eyes fixed on the pair of dirty jeans and two wrinkled tops that decorated the desk chair. A chase of ice water slid through Lexi.

Uh oh. Stay on track here. No diversions. She motioned toward the chair. "Okay, I'll take care of ⸺⸺⸺. Promise."

The sun rode lower in the west, throwing white-hot rays earthward, warming the sultry air. Pale gray clouds crowded the horizon, threatening rain. The thick canopy of oak leaves offered shade as they sat in cushioned redwood chairs, their trays on a square table between them.

Gilly settled in a puddle of sunshine. Not about to speak first, Lexi's chest tightened and she pressed back in her chair. Mom gave her tea a long stir before she looked up.

"There's good reason for you to have strong feelings when you go by the house on Northbrick—and why you have questions about Aaron Cohen, the man you've heard us talk about."

There it was. *Aaron Cohen.* Lexi's head bobbed and she gripped her glass. This morning's overheard conversation, the obituary, the articles she'd found, all raced through her mind. Where would this go? Her heart missed a beat, but Mom didn't.

"Dad and I had just gotten married. He was twenty-three, and I was nineteen when we met Aaron Cohen, the owner of Northbrick Estate.

"Back then, your dad interned at the Maria Mitchell Observatory and worked part-time repairing electronics at McVickers'. I worked at night as a nurse's aide at the hospital.

"Mr. Cohen's wife, Anna, was forty-two when she and their newborn son died during childbirth. Their baby boy, their only child, was given the name Aaron III, for his father and great-great-grandfather." Mom rubbed at her arms and seemed lost in thought.

Names, ages, so many details. How did her mother remember it all? "That's so sad and frightening. Weren't you close to forty when you had me?"

"Yes, I was." Mom sighed. "I suppose that's why I remember her age.

"I assisted in the delivery room that night. A team of doctors and nurses did everything they could to save Mrs. Cohen and her baby. Nothing worked. When it was over, Dr. Havstrom took off his mask and gloves, and left to talk with Aar—Mr. Cohen.

"One of the nurses asked me to go with the doctor." Mom's shoulders dipped and she reached for her glass. "Mr. Cohen . . . Aaron . . . stood in the waiting room in front of the window. It was a clear night. I remember the moon was nearly full, and he was silhouetted in the lights of town." Mom stopped and twisted the frost-covered tumbler in her hand then placed it on the table.

Heavenly Father, help Mom share these things. Lexi held her breath, with images of the gentle man in the photos darting through her thoughts. The fingers of her mother's hands wrapped around the ends of the chair's arms, whitening as she gripped harder.

"Aaron's face . . ." She shook her head and stared into the depths of the quiet yard as if he stood before her. "I waited by the door and watched Aaron's face change from expectant joy to a mask of shock as the doctor spoke to him, nodded, and moved to leave. Aaron turned toward the window, and I heard the sound of ripping cloth. In Jewish tradition, he'd torn the cloth of his suit jacket, his grief unbearable."

Lexi's throat closed, and she held back tears as Mom's voice wavered and she paused, eyes misting.

A sense of selfishness and overwhelming compassion seared through Lexi as she touched the star on her necklace. Her voice broke as she struggled with her whispered words. "You were so young, Mom. It must have been awful for you to be there and see that." She leaned closer, wanting to touch Mom, comfort her. But she held back as their eyes met, and a tiny smile crossed her mother's lips.

Mom shifted her gaze and stared at the darkening horizon. "I couldn't let this man be alone, so I stayed. I wouldn't have left Aaron for anything in the world.

"I stood there a minute, tears rolling down my face, not knowing what to say. Maybe I should have been stronger, but how I felt didn't matter.

"I went to Aaron and put my hand on his shoulder and prayed for the Lord to bless and comfort him, to hold this grieving man in His loving arms. And for a while, we were just quiet together.

"He didn't pull away from my touch. It was as if he knew how terribly sad I was for his loss—his wife and little son." Mom flicked an oak leaf from the arm of her chair, then smoothed the dampness from her cheeks before she spoke again. "When I asked if there was anyone I could call, I could almost feel strength fill him, and I'll never forget the look in his gray eyes. He thanked me, but said there was no one to call."

Mom picked up her glass from the table and looked across the yard again. "He asked me if I'd been there, with his Anna. When I said I was, he thanked me for being there, for caring. He held my hand for a minute. He still had tears in his eyes, but there was something else." She touched the cross on her necklace. "It felt like peace."

Lexi's fingers touched the symbols on her own necklace. The passion in Mom's voice made Lexi's throat hurt, and she blinked away tears, her eyes fixed on her mother.

"Aaron wore a tiny pin, the Jewish Star of David, and I saw him look at my cross."

Lexi pressed her fingertips against the star's points, wondering if his at all resembled hers.

"We sat together and talked until your dad picked me up at the end

of my shift. That night began a special friendship between Aaron, your dad, and me, in spite of our different faiths. Aaron asked us if we'd attend the funeral, and the next afternoon we went to the simple, private service.

"Not even a week passed before he came to visit us. He couldn't seem to thank us enough for the things we helped him with, but we were just glad to be able to help.

"Aaron was a wonderful friend."

Mom turned fully toward her, her eyes seeming to search Lexi's face. "You should know this. He prayed for Dad and me every day during years of us waiting, wanting to have a child. When we were so distressed, he understood, and when we told him you were to be born, he was as thrilled and happy as we were."

The man with the gentle gray eyes had prayed? He'd been thrilled and happy when . . . "

Suddenly studying her fingers, Mom's words slowed and softened and stopped. Lexi's insides clenched as her mother's lips set into a thin line and she looked up, her eyes gazing into Lexi's.

Was that all? Was it over? Startled, Lexi searched the frustrating veiled depths of her mother's expression.

No! There was something more . . . .

Chapter Eleven

Gilly whined in his sleep and changed positions. *Mom, what's wrong?* Lexi uncurled her legs and pressed her sandaled feet into the thick summer grass. Tiny muscles near the gentle line of her mother's jaw moved as if she waged an internal war. There *was* more.

Tell me, Mom! But the words that formed in Lexi's mind didn't make it out of her mouth before the tight line of her mother's lips softened and unsealed.

"Aaron was ecstatic the day we asked him to be your godfather."

Godfather?

The word shrieked its way down Lexi's spine and carried no less power than if she'd touched a live wire. She sat upright in the chair, the glass of sloshing tea in a chokehold. "Godfather! Aaron Cohen was my . . . my godfather?"

Her mother nodded. "Yes, sweetheart, he was."

Numb, Lexi waited for the statement to penetrate the chicken soup her brain had become. She put her glass on the table and grasped the arms of her chair, fingernails digging into the undersides of the unyielding

redwood.

Why did you keep him such a secret? She wanted to scream the words, wanted to hear more, wanted anything that would help sort out the shards of her fragmented memories . . .

Be still and know . . . .

The words, whispered to her heart, calmed her spirit. *You know me so well, Lord.* She needed to listen. She dipped her head and took a deep breath as her mother continued.

"It was new to him, the idea of being a godfather, but he accepted. And how he loved you! He showered you with gifts, toys, teddy bears, and attention." Mom paused and looked up before she spoke again. "He held you in his arms and prayed for you at your baptism."

Ohh. Tears burned Lexi's eyes, and her heart squeezed with a love she could barely contain. The photographs she'd found in Dad's desk had portrayed it all. A gentle man with silver hair and beard in a black suit. Tenderness and love, etched on his face. In his arms, a baby— her. The image burned a square in her mind, the unbelievable facts reverberating through every fiber of her being. A godfather who loved her. And she was remembering.

A turbulent vision of the envelope, box, and parchment, and the vague memory of soft gray eyes, swam through Lexi's thoughts. Why had Mom waited until now to tell her this? What did it mean? Why . . . ?

A time. A time for every purpose under heaven.

The muscles of her arms trembled, tears dried on her cheeks. Sea birds soared overhead. No question, she needed patience. A breeze sighed through the trees. Deep, even breaths. *Listen.* She coaxed her fingers to relax as her mother spread a watercolor of the past onto the canvas landscape of the present.

"Aaron died when you were four. You came to us early one morning, sobbing, asking where your Uncle Aaron was. A few minutes later the call came from Aaron's gardener, Jacob Carver."

Lexi drew in a sharp breath. The man she'd met this morning. She'd learned a little about him, but not this detail.

"When we got to Northbrick, you stayed inside with Malea, Jacob's wife. She cooked for Aaron and kept his big house spotless and in perfect order."

Yes. Mr. Carver had mentioned Malea this morning.

Mom's gaze settled on Gilly, her silence moving into overtime. Lexi fought to stay quiet. She had to know more. This was far from ended.

No more quiet. "What happened? Was there a funeral? Why didn't the house—"

Her mother abruptly rose from her chair.

Uh oh. She'd asked too much too soon.

"I don't have the time, Lexi. Your laundry won't do itself. That's all you need to know right now."

No! Hot anger raged red, and Lexi turned her back on the inner warnings that she should let this go. She needed to hear everything. Now. It wasn't fair for her to be left out again. This man who had loved her surely would have wanted her to know about him. She jumped from her chair and stood blocking her mother's way.

"Mom, I have a right to know." Her voice was low and deadly, as if it came from someone else. But she was helpless to stop the anger-launched words. "You can't just tell me that much and then get up and leave. You should have told me this a long time ago."

The shock in her mother's eyes forced Lexi backward. Lexi turned, dropped into her chair, drew her knees up, and buried her face. The storm of rage dissipated, every nerve tingled, but the deep injustice remained. Her parents didn't care enough to tell her. They just didn't

care. She should get in her car and drive, get away from here for a while.

Her mother's voice was strained, and Lexi heard the rustle of her sitting down in the chair beside her. "It never occurred to me you'd feel so strongly about this. You were so young."

Mom sighed. A deep shuddering sound, then stillness. Lexi tensed with a ray of hope. Would she say more? The last vestige of anger drained from her limbs, and the urge to leave no longer held any power.

". . . we had to protect you . . . young . . . it was vitally important . . ."

Empty words. Limp, with her forehead still against her knees, Lexi drifted, half-listened as Mom spoke.

"While Aaron was alive and Jacob still cared for them, the gardens were a masterpiece, like a fairytale fortress to me every time we visited him. They were huge, private, and hidden from the rest of the world."

Lexi raised her head. Gardens? Masterpiece? Fairytale fortress? The descriptive words didn't begin to relate to the overgrown, weed-infested Northbrick Estate she'd seen.

Mom glanced at her, expressionless, and continued. "You have to go through the inside of the house to get to the rear gardens, you know. They're completely surrounded with that solid seven-foot stone wall. It's a wall without a single break, except for some kind of a gate Jacob used to talk about, one I've never seen. There's no other way in.

"Jacob led your dad and me through the house, out into the rear gardens—the hidden gardens; that's what Jacob called them."

Were Mom's memories hers too? Or was it her imagination creating colored segments of the scenes Mom described as her eyes hazed with tears.

"I barely listened as Jacob reminisced about how Aaron walked in his botanical wonderland every day. But that's what he'd been doing on the November morning when he died. We went past the maze to the center of the garden and found him, sitting peacefully in the gazebo, with his long black overcoat wrapped around him. His cane by his side, he looked as if he were asleep. It was the way he would have wanted it to happen.

"We didn't have much time. Aaron's doctor was on his way, so Jacob went back to the house. We stood there, Dad and me, holding each other, remembering how you'd sit on Aaron's lap, put your little hands on either side of his face, and sing him the songs you learned in Sunday school: 'Jesus Loves Me' and 'Jesus Loves the Little Children.'"

Mom stopped, smiling through her tears, and touched her cheeks with her napkin. "But Aaron loved it best when you sang his favorite, 'Father Abraham.'

"He always respected our beliefs, but he was devoted to his Jewish faith. We were amazed at how patient he was, listening to you tell him about your beloved Jesus."

Lexi tasted salty moisture at the corners of her mouth and held back a bubble of laughter. How could that dear man have endured her pushy younger self?

Her sandwich sat, untouched, drying out in the sunshine as Mom's words swept luminous brushstrokes across the fabric of Lexi's mind.

"We always wondered if the things you said made a difference to him. All we could do is trust that God knew." Mom shook her head and smiled. "And, you know, sweetheart, as young as you were, you understood why you couldn't see your godfather anymore. You soaked up every word your daddy said as he talked to you. Often you'd tell us Aaron was 'in Heaven with Jesus and all the angels.' We believed you were right."

Mom looked toward a corner of the yard, tumbling with pink roses. "And for a while, we'd find you, tears covering your little cheeks, sitting

on the bench over there in the rose garden." Her mother looked at her and sent her a soft smile. "You'd always say, 'I'm okay, Mommy. I was just remembering Uncle Aaron for a minute.' Then you'd go right back to playing."

Her mother's voice lowered to a near-whisper. "Aaron helped us plant that rose garden. I wish you could remember how you tried to help too."

Her face pale, Mom leaned back and closed her eyes, looking exhausted, even a little relieved. Lexi swallowed hard, her thoughts splintering in a dozen directions. Was that all she'd hear? So much more to learn about the house, about the taxes, why the house stayed empty. Did Mom and Dad know the place was in danger of being torn down? And did they know the story behind her cedar chest? Had they known of the envelope? And what about what was under the floor? Lexi's stomach churned, sick. Dizzy.

Mom opened her eyes. "I know you have questions, Lex. There are other things I need to tell you, but Dad will want to be here."

Other things? What was so important or different that Mom wanted Dad to be here when she was told? As busy as Dad was, when would he have time? Mom's statement sounded as flat and final as a death knell. It looked as if she wouldn't be getting any more answers today.

Resignation rushed in like high tide and engulfed the clamoring beach of need-to-know. Okay. She wouldn't press for more, not now.

Their glasses held only dregs of tea-flavored ice water, and she offered to refill them. Mom nodded, seeming grateful for the break.

Lexi filled the tray and went into the kitchen. What a bunch of confusing details. She was being way too pushy and impatient, and any shred of self-discipline she had was busy climbing out the window of her mind. She couldn't shut it off. *Just try to stop and think.*

She had a godfather, and his former gardener, Jacob Carver, was the man she'd see tonight. There were gardens, and what else had Mom said about the wall?

In the midst of pouring tea the phone rang, and the ID announcement grounded her: *Call from Jenni.* Lexi caught it before the second ring and called out the back door before her mother could pick up the outdoor extension.

"I've got it in here, Mom. It's Jenni. I'll be out in a minute."

"Hey, Jen, I've been talking to Mom. The man Mom and Dad spoke of—Aaron Cohen? Mom just told me he was . . ." She stopped herself. Now wasn't the time.

"What?"

There's *so* much I have to tell you, but . . ." Lexi pulled in a breath.

"But what?"

"It'll have to wait. I want to get back outside with Mom. We'll talk tonight. As long as the weather holds, I'll be at your house at seven-thirty. Later!"

"Okay, okay! See you then."

She'd said enough. Jen didn't need to know she wanted Ridge to hear all this too, wanted him in on every word. She'd wait and tell them both. The right time would come.

Why did she and Mom always have to butt heads? Thoughts of Mom's disapproving stares at her room, her remarks about an unmade bed and a stupid heap of unwashed clothes, her hovercraft act over a simple bike ride, taunted her. And where was the truth? *They love me. What reason could they possibly have for not telling me I had a godfather?* Something had to have happened for them to keep that fact from her. But what?

Whatever their reasons were, she'd find out soon enough.

Lexi shook her head. She finished filling the glasses and went to the screen door. Gulls wheeled and soared overhead. Lexi loved watching them from the sandy-beige-colored beaches that ringed the island, and right now, she yearned for a long, lazy walk on that beach.

A few drops of rain splattered around her, then stopped as the clouds cast an arch of heaven-to-earth rainbow and the sun glowed lower in the west. The side trip to Jacob Carvers' home didn't look as if it would be postponed. Anticipation edged through her thoughts. What would it be like tonight?

Gilly had his golden head in Mom's lap when Lexi put the tea-laden tray on the table, and he didn't move as his brown eyes searched hers. He gave a little whine and plopped down beside Mom's chair as if he wanted Lexi to come closer. Mom's head still rested against the pillow-back of the chair, eyes closed and cheeks damp with tears. Lexi didn't hesitate. Love overflowed her heart, and she wrapped her arms around her mother and whispered, because she couldn't talk out loud. "I'm so sorry for losing my temper, Mom. Thanks for telling me as much as you could today. I love you."

Chapter Twelve

Jacob Carver shook his head and plowed his hand through short, tight curls from forehead to crown. He sat in the glider on the porch of his small home, his forearms resting on his knees. Overdone it, he had, with all that bending and kneeling at Northbrick this afternoon. He studied his brown fingers, calloused and toughened from years of tending the earth. Every bone in his eighty-one-year-old body thrummed a painful tune through him as he rocked.

Beside him, Malea stirred. Her warmth against his arm sailed a gust of comfort through him, just as it did each time they'd touched for the last forty-nine years. She looked mighty pretty. She wore that bright yellow-flowered housedress he liked so much. He liked how nice it skimmed over her ample figure too. Of course, she wasn't terribly happy about where the ample parts of her were. He smiled at her, loving every snow-white curl that went all random and tendrilly around her face.

Malea sent him a smile that blended into the few wrinkles of her smooth brown skin and made her face soft. It was good to come outside onto the comfortable porch this warm June evening. A snug little habit

they'd gotten into, sitting together on this worn white glider to rock, talk, and think a while. But this time they waited for guests, and Jacob stayed quiet with his thoughts.

A buzzing fly made a landing strip of his forearm, and he batted it away with a sigh.

Malea squeezed his arm. "Having the children come is dredging up a heap of memories for me too, Jacob." She brushed at the wrinkles in the lap of her dress. "Best years of our lives."

"Mmm hmm." She was right. Those many years they'd worked for Aaron Cohen and lived on his estate, they'd grown to love and respect him. To this day, Jacob missed the man. He'd become a friend and had entrusted Jacob, nine years his junior, with information about his goddaughter's future. And if Jacob's suspicions held, Lexi would be learning about her relationship with Mr. Aaron sooner than he thought she might. He hoped so. The only reason he knew of for Molly and Jason Christensen to keep that secret was to let her have a happy, carefree childhood—until it was time.

Jacob swallowed hard and frowned at the weathered wood floor of the porch. It wasn't his business, no matter how he disapproved of their not telling her. In their way, they were protecting her, and it was from more than simply knowing Mr. Aaron was her godfather.

His achy muscles twitched with uneasiness over seeing the younger Quinn this morning. *Humph.* Truth-be-told, Jacob was just as protective as Lexi's parents. Good Book was right. He'd no right to judge. He straightened against the ladder back of the glider and pushed. It responded with muted squeaks and a smooth rocking motion.

Rumbles of distant thunder drew Jacob's eyes to the skyline. Along with the easterly sea breeze, a brief rain had cooled the air earlier. Gray clouds still pushed along the horizon, brightened only by occasional rays of sunshine that sparked gold around their edges. "Hope they don't get wet. Doesn't look like we'll be having more rain, but you never know."

Malea rubbed her thumb against his forearm and gazed at him. "Those children won't melt."

"No, I suppose not." Jacob smiled at her calling them "children." If she thought of these three college-bound young adults as children, she was in for a surprise.

Malea studied his face and frowned. "Are you feeling okay? Don't worry yourself about them, Jacob."

"Not worrying, Sugar. I feel good." A twang of guilt for fibbing about his aching bones rustled through his chest.

"Now, Jacob, you're not telling the truth." Malea slid her small hand down his arm to rest on Jacob's large, rough hand. "You've got worry lines from your head all the way down to your toes." He turned his hand beneath hers, gave a gentle squeeze, and ignored her.

Her fingers laced through his. "Jacob, out with it. What's bothering you?"

"It's just no good." The glider stilled. He stretched his legs out and muttered the words toward his dusty old work shoes. "No good at all, seeing Grey's boy twice in two days. I never see him. It's downright odd. Don't have a single comfortable feeling about it."

Malea looked at him and shook her head. "Boy? Greyson Junior? Oh, my, Jacob, he must be in his late-twenties by now."

Jacob's insides twisted. "That boy never has been one you could trust. He's up to something for sure. I feel it in these old bones." He blinked and wagged his head. "He always did have way too much time on his hands. Always into something, up to something, or wrecking something."

Malea pushed to keep the glider moving. "Mmm hmm, I suppose that's true. But trouble's been brewing long before now. You know that. His father's always spoiled that boy—bailed young Quinn out of every problem he ever had."

Jacob did know that. He sat back. "How many cars did he go through? Three? Four?"

"Too many," Malea said. "Good Lord's had mercy, though. At least he's never hurt anybody, or himself."

Jacob pinched at his nose. "Lord's got to do more than mercy-showin' to get that boy's attention. Here he is, finished with his fancy college, walked right into a ready-made career in his daddy's law practice, and he's *still* got his nose where it doesn't belong.

"Bad feeling I had, seeing that sports car parked near the mansion yesterday." Jacob narrowed his eyes. "I know it was his. No other car like it on the island. If that boy was pokin' around the house, I'd like to find out why."

"Well, it's none of our business, Jacob."

Jacob ground his teeth and pushed hard against the wood planking of the porch. The old glider creaked and protested. "Nope. But it could become our business if he messes with that house. He about tore the road up when he left, awful mad about something." Jacob stopped and shook his head, feeling defensive. "It was him. Know it in my bones. Just bothers me that he was near the place."

"Lord knows, I can't think of any good reason he'd be there," Malea said, her voice troubled. She traced the outline of a flower on her dress and joined Jacob in giving the glider another push.

"And then seeing him in town this morning at the library. Guess it's a perfectly normal place for a lawyer to be, but Greyson? On a Saturday?" Jacob leaned forward and scratched his beard. "And then those young people being there, too."

"But something good came out of it; you saw Lexi again. Good Lord's hand is in this, just like it's always been."

Jacob turned and smiled at her. "His hand's been at work in our lives for the whole trip." He put his arm around her and pulled her into a hug. They rocked in time to the glider's squeaks for a long while before Malea spoke again.

"I could stay out here all night, but the cookies are cool by now—and the children should be here soon."

But she stayed beside him, and Jacob couldn't resist chiding her. "Lexi's not a child anymore, Sugar. You'll see."

Dirty earth-smudges covered his knees. He'd spent hours this afternoon setting out the large bed of summer flowers inside the northern edge of the mansion's hidden garden. It had taken him most of the spring to finish pruning the privet hedge. He couldn't let that get out of hand. The hedge made up the walls of the intricate emerald green maze filling the center of the garden. He and Mr. Aaron designed that labyrinth, and they'd ended it right at the walkway where the summer flowerbeds began. Now, one more June planting without Mr. Aaron had gone by.

He shook his head and shrugged, looking at his denim overalls. "Probably should have changed clothes."

"There's no time now, and you came by those dusty patches rightly, down on those old knees, praying and planting." Malea laid her head against Jacob's broad shoulder.

Jacob smiled. "Remember how Lexi used to watch me plant?"

"I remember Mr. Aaron carried her through that puzzle of green hedges before she could even walk. She took her very first steps in that garden."

Jacob turned to plant a kiss on the top of Malea's head. "Only two more years till the old house and its hidden gardens will belong to her." He leaned back in the swing with a chuckle that spread into a contented belly laugh.

Malea slipped out of his embrace and stood. "I best get some ice and sodas put out before they get here."

She began humming before the screen door shut behind her, and Jacob was left to his thoughts.

What would this meeting be like? How much should he tell Lexi tonight? How much did she already know? He glanced down the driveway. It wouldn't be long now before he'd be asking her some questions. Then he'd have to make decisions on what to say. A flash of silver from between the thick boughs of the pine trees along the drive caught his eye. He reached for his gnarled wood cane and rose from the glider.

Chapter Thirteen

Did dueling pistols come three to a case? *Really, Mom, Dad, you're following me all the way to the door?* If she didn't leave, she'd be late getting to Jenni's and they'd be late getting to the Carvers' house. Dad's meeting ran longer than expected, dinner had been rushed, this afternoon's conversation with Mom hadn't come up, and the last two minutes were a cross between an interrogation and barked orders. Lexi gritted her teeth and gave those minutes a quick burial. Her jaw ached with the challenge to keep silent.

Don't slam the door!

At least she'd made a civil exit. The insistent chirp of her cellphone began as she reached the end of the driveway. Juggling her bike and phone, Lexi checked the ID, and her heart knotted with frustration. Again?

"Hey, Jen, what's up?" She chewed on her lower lip as Jenni spouted apologetic words, explaining she was running way late, that she should go to the Carters without her.

Lexi sighed. Things were running true to form. "Okay . . . got to go

. . . incoming from Ridge. See you there later."

She clicked Jenni off and Ridge on. "Not you too, Ridge."

Ridge cleared his throat. "Yeah, Jen just texted me. Sorry, but Dad needs me to help him finish up a project in the garage before I can head out. We're almost done. I won't be long, and I'll meet you there. I shouldn't be more than ten or fifteen minutes late."

He sounded a little defensive. She should forget about the bike ride, take the car, and go —should but wouldn't. She battled to keep the mixed flurry of disappointment, impatience, and annoyance from creeping into her voice. "Okay, see you there later."

"No problem then?"

Lexi laughed and tried to back off a bit. Was there any way she could possibly stay mad at him? "Of course not. I'll see you guys whenever." She figured Ridge heard a little of the irritation in her voice because he didn't argue that she should wait for them. Good thing because she wasn't about to be late.

She jammed her sandals against the bike pedals. She could learn a lot in the time she'd have alone with Jacob and Mrs. Carver. The rush of the bike's tires rolling against the asphalt sent a shiver through her. So Jacob Carver knew all about her being Aaron Cohen's goddaughter when he talked with them this morning, and he hadn't said a word. Would he say anything tonight? Traffic was light, and her mounting frustration with Jenni and Ridge lessened with the passing minutes.

A surge of nostalgia brought a mist of tears as she rode down the familiar streets. Nothing would ever be the same once she left this beautiful island. She'd never walk the halls of a high school with friends again or cheer Ridge on at a Friday night game. No more working at the stable, horseback rides, and moonlight walks on the beach, and in spite of all their head-butting, she'd miss Mom and Dad. Everything was about to change.

The sea breeze caressed her bare arms and pushed her along, giving her a burst of energy. She coasted, hair flying, and lifted her face toward the deepening blue of the Nantucket sky.

Thanks, God, for all I have. Please get me through all the changes. And through what I'm about to do right now.

She rounded the corner onto Northbrick Avenue and passed the first house on the street. Near the mansion, she slowed and walked her bike past the estate. Her godfather's house—Uncle Aaron's house, not just an historic old house she was trying to save. Not anymore. There was an envelope, box, keys, and more that piled up and pointed at her.

Fear stabbed at her belly and split her between the urge to curl up and cocoon, or to let go and trust she'd find out why. She got on her bike and made her way toward the last of the three residences on the street.

The Carvers' driveway lay a few feet ahead. She'd passed here as many times as she'd passed Northbrick Estate. Never had the simple driveway held her attention as it did now. A rare and literal forest of pine trees and shrubs hid the house from the road. Only Jacob Carver's mailbox announced its existence.

She turned the bike into the drive, savoring the beauty of summer. Rainbow patches of heavy blue hydrangeas, pink and white gladiolas, lilacs, and wild roses still held glistening drops of leftover rainwater. She drew in a breath of fragrant air, loving the scent of flowers mingled with the ocean-salted air. Reaching a curve in the long drive, anticipation filled her stomach with butterflies.

She passed a dark green pickup parked near the house and rode up to the white picket fence surrounding a homey cottage. The line of fencing looked freshly painted. It angled around the yard in a neat square with a gate beneath a wide arbor in the center.

Hundreds of yellow roses clung to the arches of the white arbor above her as she walked her bike through the open gate. Her thoughts rambled like the roses. What would she learn tonight? How much could, or would, this friendly, interesting man tell her?

"Hello there!" Jacob Carver's warm, raspy voice hailed her. "We'll be sitting out here on the porch. Just leave your bike propped against that tree if you like."

"Hi, Mr. Carver. I'll be right there."

As she reached the top step of the porch, Jacob extended his hand in a gracious welcome. Beneath twin mini-avalanches of snowy eyebrows, his brown eyes twinkled and his broad smile deepened. The sense of recognition tugged at her, just as it had this morning. But now she knew where and when she'd seen this man before, her godfather's former gardener. Should she tell him what else she'd learned from her mother this afternoon? Maybe, but she'd wait. Surely this visit would answer some of her questions.

"We're so glad you could come—and please, call me Jacob."

"Thanks for inviting us, Jacob."

"And where are your friends?" Jacob looked behind her and down the drive.

"It's only me for now, but Jenni and Ridge will be here soon."

"Good. We'll just visit some till they come along." Jacob led her across the wide verandah and motioned for her to sit. "Mrs. Carver is in the house getting us something cold to drink. She'll be out in a minute."

Lexi chose one of the comfortable green chairs he indicated. Several were arranged in a semi-circle in a corner near a small wood table. A dog-eared, legal-size file folder lay at the table's center, and what appeared to be torn, ragged edges of newspaper clippings poked out from the top. Her curiosity piqued. The folder was there for a reason, and she guessed she'd see the contents sometime during their visit.

Nerves edgy, Lexi settled into the chair and tried to enjoy the comfort of the Carvers' front porch. The mixed scent of roses, jasmine, and citronella from the single candle on the porch rail permeated the evening air, and some of the tension eased from her limbs. The cool easterly breeze nudged the clouds into motion. It would be getting dark early.

The screen door opened, and a sweet, grandmotherly face sent a smile toward Lexi . . . .

I knew her too.

Jacob stood to hold the door as the woman came out, carrying a tray laden with sodas, glasses of ice, and cookies that smelled of chocolate, peanut butter, and oatmeal. He put his hand on his wife's arm. "This is Mrs. Carver—Malea. She's been mighty busy this afternoon. Downright heavenly smells coming from that kitchen today."

"It's nice to meet you, Malea, and I think I'm about to be very glad you were busy baking."

Malea put the tray on the table. "I have a few more things to take care of in the kitchen. You two go ahead and chat and I'll be out a little later." Lexi couldn't help smiling as Malea put a huge chocolate-chip cookie on a napkin and set it in front of Lexi before she went back inside. Did Malea know how much she loved those?

Jacob sat opposite Lexi and offered her a Coke as the screen door shut behind Malea. "I think you must have a lot of questions. And they probably begin with, 'Who in the world are you? How do you know me?' and 'What do you know about Aaron Cohen?'" He paused. "Am I right?"

Lexi looked up into brown eyes that shone with gentle kindness, and nodded. "Yes, those and quite a few others. This afternoon I learned

Aaron Cohen was my godfather and that Northbrick Estate belonged to him. And my mother told me a little about you and Malea, so at least I know why you looked familiar to me this morning."

Jacob's luminous eyes sparked with genuine enjoyment. "Good. Then you know Malea and I worked for Mr. Aaron for many years." He hesitated then bit into his cookie, chewing as if he had eternity to finish it.

Hands in her lap, palms moist, she laced her fingers, twisting them. Why hadn't she made a list? What questions should she ask? She didn't even know how she should frame her questions to get the answers she wanted. Her mind lapsed into a vacant white-room.

Listen, for I will speak of excellent things, and from the opening of my lips will come right things.

The words from Proverbs spoke to her heart, and her hands relaxed. But she'd say no more about what Mom told her today. She would hear as much as possible from this man.

Jacob ran his fingers through his hair, reminding her of Ridge's endearing habit. She took a deep breath but kept silent.

"Well, now, where to start answering some of your questions." He paused and looked at the unopened folder.

His face—round, light brown, framed with a silvery wreath of hair—was gentle as he spoke. He seemed to choose each word with care.

"I suppose the fact that I am Mr. Aaron's gardener is as good a place as any to begin."

Lexi held tight against the jolt that shot through her. Had he just said, "I *am* Mr. Aaron's gardener?" Would the pieces of the puzzle ever fall into place? She couldn't think of a single thing around the old mansion that could qualify as a garden. And how could he be working for a man who wasn't around to pay him?

"As long as I live, I'll never forget the reading of Mr. Aaron's last wishes. We sat there in that attorney's office, Malea and me . . ." He looked at Lexi and smiled. ". . . along with your mother and father, and you."

My parents were there? And me? Why? Beneath the table, Lexi squeezed her trembling hands together.

Jacob paused and pulled in a breath. "Then Mr. Aaron's attorney, Greyson Quinn, Sr., handed me a packet of papers that made this house and land belong to Malea and me, free and clear." Jacob sat back and rubbed at his stubbly beard as if he were unsure of how much he should say.

Thankful that Jacob gazed out over the grassy yard, Lexi's surprise registered all the way to her toes. The generosity of how Aaron Cohen had provided for Jacob and Malea was stunning, but so was the fact that Quinn, Sr. represented both Dad and Uncle Aaron. An image of the scene in the law office constructed itself in Lexi's mind. She'd recognized the name this morning, but not the man. The older man was Dad's business attorney. The younger was his son, the man she'd seen at Northbrick and in the library. She took a deep, quiet breath. She had to listen. Jacob had more to say.

"Right along with the house, Mr. Aaron left us a generous amount of money and a stipend that comes to us every single month for as long as the good Lord allows us to live. Mr. Aaron thought of everything."

So that's how he's paid. Lexi straightened, absorbed by the sight and sound and presence of this man who worked—works?—for her godfather. But the monthly income didn't explain the phantom garden he was supposed to be taking care of.

Jacob had stopped speaking and glanced at her.

That look again. As if he knows more and can't, or won't, tell me.

Please, Lord, lead me in what to say, and when.

Jacob swiped his hand across a dusty knee, cocked his head at her with a grin, and continued. "I catch a glimpse of you 'round town once in a while. And to this day, Malea and I still talk about how Mr. Aaron loved you. Yes, indeed, Mr. Aaron would've been very proud of his goddaughter." He reached to pick up the folder.

Malea appeared at the screen door, wiping her hands on an apron. "And you've grown into quite a beautiful young lady, too." Her musical Jamaican accent and her broad smile made the compliment easier for Lexi to accept, but her cheeks still flooded with heat. Before Lexi could thank her, Malea spoke again. "And you have the brains to match."

Malea sat beside Jacob as he opened the folder and pulled out several newspaper articles. "Here." His warm smile curved the tips of his mustache upward. "We've got several copies of these. Maybe you'd like to have them. Do you keep a scrapbook?" He handed Lexi two articles that had recently been in the *Nantucket Inquirer* and *Mirror*. One included her name on the dean's list from last year, and the other the photo-feature article covering White Oak Ranch.

"Thank you." Lexi floundered, a little at a loss for words. "I do have a scrapbook, and I'd love to have copies." It was almost the truth. She didn't really need the clippings, but it was humbling and endearing that they'd saved these things about her. She smiled and thanked him again, putting the news articles on the table beside her. Jacob reached down and massaged his knees as if they hurt him.

Lexi turned at the sound of two familiar voices. Jenni and Ridge rode up the driveway to the gate and left their bikes beside hers. She stood, relieved to have them finally arrive. There was already much to tell them on the ride home tonight.

Jacob reached for his cane and rose, walking to the edge of the steps.

"Hello. Welcome. Nice evening to sit out here. Come on up."

Ridge and Jenni joined them on the porch. "It's nice to meet you, Mrs. Carver," Ridge said, as Malea's small hand disappeared within his warm handshake.

Lexi couldn't take her eyes off Ridge, absorbing his unforgettable grin, his sincerity.

Beside Ridge, Jen's blonde hair curled in tendrils around her face in the damp air, and her handshake was as sincere as Ridge's. "It's a pleasure to meet you, Mrs. Carver,"

Lexi squeezed her eyes shut against the burning behind her eyelids, thankful for her friends. They were here for her when she needed them.

"We're glad you could come." Jacob motioned for them to sit, and they took Jacob up on his offer of cookies and a soft drink. Jenni eyed the folded clippings on the table as Malea smoothed her dress and sat next to Jacob.

Good. Malea would stay and talk. Maybe she'd have more to add to the story.

Jacob's eyes brightened. He fixed his gaze on Lexi and launched into a question. "You've read or heard about that developer wanting the city to tear down Northbrick House, right?"

Lexi stiffened and nodded, but Jacob didn't seem to notice, and continued.

"It looks as if the house has gotten a stay of execution as the city reviews some documents Attorney Quinn's given them. They'll have to deny the developer's request after they read those."

She stifled a gasp and caught the look of surprise on Ridge's face as Jen squirmed in her chair. No more photos and notes, no more worries on how to help save it?

But Jacob didn't wait for her reply. "Have you talked with your

parents about the house yet, Lexi? You know, Mr. Aaron wanted them involved if you ever went into the old house on your own." The man with the kind smile leaned forward as if to make an important point. "You *did* go in, didn't you?"

Lexi's stomach lurched. A dark cascade of hair fell forward, veiling her face as she studied the ten peach-polished toenails sticking out from her brown sandals. *What did he mean by that? Does he know? Maybe he saw me?* The soft glow of the porch light became a spotlight. With or without the permission the paper in the envelope seemed to grant her, guilt of breaking and entering pinched as if handcuffs had been slapped on her wrists. Her cheeks burned as both Ridge and Jenni stayed silent.

"I . . . uh . . ."

No chance to respond with Jacob's chuckled interruption. He pushed back in his chair. "Uh huh. You sure enough did! Mr. Aaron was right about a lot of things, and he certainly was right about you more than likely going into Northbrick House long before you turned twenty."

Lexi's head bobbed up. *Oh! What does he mean, long before I turn twenty?* She ran her fingers through her hair and twisted it into a rope, pulling it forward over her shoulder. Jacob's gaze remained on her, but an easy laugh rippled up from deep inside and rolled out in such genuine good humor that Lexi immediately felt better, even if she was totally confused.

"I don't understand . . ."

Jacob held up a hand in self-defense. "Hold on, hold on. Like I said this morning, I'll tell you all I can." His expression turned serious. "But before I do, you need to know that you might be facing a problem. Did you find anything when you were in the house?"

THE STONEKEEPERS

Jacob held Malea's arm with one hand and his cane in the other. Together they walked almost to the end of the meandering driveway as their three guests steered their bikes to the gate to leave. They stood and watched until the trio disappeared around the corner of the deserted street—or was it deserted? Jacob tensed as a swirl of headlights flashed through the trees at the other end of the street. The car pulled a u-turn and headed the direction in which the three young people had gone. Malea's knowing eyes met his.

He held her arm a little tighter. "Greyson? I wouldn't put it past him. Boy's nothin' but trouble." An uneasy shiver sifted through his weary bones as they turned toward the house.

"Probably just a coincidence, Jacob. Let's get back. I know those knees are giving you pain."

He swallowed. Bless her. She was always trying to reassure him. She knew his knees well, and he gave her no argument as he leaned heavily on his cane. Fireflies decorated the yard and the forest behind it with their tiny flickering lanterns.

"Those young people had a lot of questions, all right." Jacob slid his hand down Malea's arm and twined their fingers.

"And you answered every one the best you could without betraying the confidence Mr. Aaron trusted you with."

"Mmm hmm, as much as I could." The porch swing lured him with every step. "That glider looks mighty good to me. Let's stop there a minute."

Jacob stepped onto the verandah and sat in the swing, Malea beside him. "I wonder if Lexi will get herself into that garden."

Jacob took the last sip of soda in his glass, hanging onto it as a furry

white form leapt in a graceful arc from a chair to settle on his lap. Jacob grinned and raked his fingers through the cat's soft coat. "Oh, she will. I know she will. I just wish I could be there to watch her face when she does."

"Well, I'm glad you didn't go and tell her."

"Nope. Couldn't do that. She didn't directly ask anyway, and it's not our place to rush things. She'll find her own way." He paused and rattled the last of the ice in his glass. "But I am getting anxious to bring the front gardens back to life again—and to go back inside the house."

"After all these years, I can't imagine what it looks like in there. I dread seeing it after such neglect." Malea looked up at him. "But you've been so faithful with the care of the gardens."

Jacob patted his wife's arm. "And I know how hard it was for you to let go of keeping up that house. But you've honored Mr. Aaron's wishes, and he'd be pleased."

Moments later Jacob held the screen door for Malea to go into the brightly lit cottage. "Come along, Angel, time to go in." The fluffy shadow of a cat rubbed against Jacob's aching legs as if to nudge him through the door. But Jacob paused at the threshold and looked over his shoulder.

"Just how long will it be, little-girl-Lexi, before you find your way?" Jacob sent the words toward the reflective eyes of a white-tailed deer on the other side of the fence. With a flick of her pale flag of a tail, the doe bounded out of view.

He shook his head and chuckled. "Not long. Not long at all."

Chapter Fourteen

Home from the Carvers a few minutes after nine, Lexi's mind churned with the need to think, to sort out the events that had flipped her life upside down. The sound of Dad's voice wafted through the partially open study door. Two other voices came from the kitchen, along with the *clink* of spoons and cups. One hand on the banister, Lexi paused beside the stairs.

"Thanks for letting me borrow these, Molly. I'll bring them back Monday." Marie Delaward from next door sounded as though she was about to leave. Good. If Mom was busy with the neighbor, Lexi might avoid any heavy discussions tonight, but there wasn't much time. As late as it was, Mom would be checking up on her as soon as the door shut behind Mrs. D. Lexi put the newspaper clippings on the bottom stair and went into the kitchen.

"Hi, Mrs. D. Hey, Mom."

Her mother turned, and Lexi didn't allow a split-second of delay. "Sorry for interrupting. I just wanted to tell you goodnight. I'm going to check my email and go to bed early."

She gave her mother a light kiss on the cheek. "Love you. See you in

the morning. 'Night, Mrs. D." Lexi left the kitchen with Gilly padding along beside her and her mother's "Sleep well, honey" floating after her.

If she included Friday, this had already been one very long weekend, and it wasn't over yet. The warm pelting from her shower soothed some of the tension from her muscles, but her thoughts stayed hyper with information she wanted to dump into the computer. She couldn't forget or leave out anything that Jacob and Malea had told her. The blank monitor on her desk beckoned as she pulled a fresh tee-shirt and a pair of soft drawstring pants from a drawer.

Maybe she was a little paranoid, but first things first. She went to the window seat. Gilly followed, flopping down beside her, his limpid brown eyes fixed on her. Built permanently into the windowed alcove, the storage space beneath the seat held extra quilts and blankets. She removed the cushion and raised the lid.

Reaching in to push some blankets aside, she had to smile. As a little girl, she'd often watched, fascinated, when Dad repaired things around the house. An access panel for her bathroom plumbing was in the wall right above the end of this seat. And below it, inside the window seat, when the old tub had been replaced . . .

Never too old to have a stashing place. She chuckled out loud as her fingers touched the area in back of the large hole she'd cut into the wall so many years ago. Good. Nothing had been disturbed. Her hiding place had held most everything she'd ever treasured, and as of yesterday, it held the cedar-chest-envelope, box, keys, parchment, and the ivory cat. Before she slept tonight, Jacob's folder of clippings and her notes would be there too.

She ruffled her fingers through her hair, letting it air dry, and went to the computer to open a Word document. What Jacob Carver had told her couldn't be trusted to her memory. She wanted to capture every mental note on paper. If Ridge and Jenni did the same, the three of them could start piecing some of this puzzle together.

Jacob said I might be facing a problem . . . . Lexi stopped in the midst of typing the line, fingers poised above the keys. After she'd made her red-faced confession that, yes, she'd been in the house, Jacob's expression had switched from lively to dead serious. She'd only nodded in reply to his question about finding anything, and he hadn't pressed her. But then he'd warned her to be careful and aware of anything out of the ordinary. He'd said no more. Dropped it like a hot rock. Why? She should have questioned him more. Probed. Heaven only knew why she'd let it go so easily.

Her desk chair creaked as she leaned back. But what was Ridge's comment later? That Jacob hadn't needed to say anything more.

And he hadn't. Jacob's body language and tone of voice as he spoke of seeing the attorney leave the library said it all. The hair on Lexi's arms rose with the chill that pulsed through her. Fear? He'd called it a "problem" she might be facing. In retrospect, it felt more like she might be in mortal danger.

Jacob had been vague when he answered some of her questions. Had he deliberately skipped over things that, of course, weren't her business? She'd probed as best she could about why the big place hadn't been sold, or even put on the market for sale. And he'd slammed shut like a door when she and Ridge had asked about payment of property taxes. He'd been slow and thoughtful as he spoke of Northbrick and seemed to try to keep their focus on how Aar— No, she couldn't call him by his given name or Godfather. Uncle Aaron, maybe? As if the words were right, warmth fell around her shoulders like a gentle hug. Lexi smiled and finished the note. . . . how Uncle Aaron had doted on her and had been so close to Mom and Dad.

The single slip he made was when he said something about her parents and Quinn, Sr., being in the midst of "fighting city hall" over the demolition of Northbrick. He'd covered it quickly, changed the subject, and firmly cut her off when she attempted to ask more about why they were involved. Apparently Northbrick was safe, but he'd been downright skillful in dodging the questions that would really give her answers. But that slip alone ripped open the wound of frustration with Mom and Dad. One more thing they'd kept from her.

Jacob knew. He knew much more than he'd told her. He'd almost acted protective. Was that it? Was he protecting something? Walking some skinny line of what he could and couldn't say? But why was it all such a big secret?

She pushed back from the desk and threw up her arms. She hadn't learned much of anything of any importance. Nice visit. But that was all.

Fifteen minutes later, she pressed *Print* and tried to relax. But the chill hadn't left her.

One last quick check of Facebook, email, and an online group she'd helped to start last year. An email from Jenni reminded her of their early-morning report time for work at the stable Monday.

Thanks, Jen. A sigh slipped from between her pursed lips. She'd almost forgotten she'd told Ray she'd finish detailing the show saddles, a ritual before White Oak Ranch's autumn mini-rodeo. She'd miss everything about that job.

The printer purred and spewed out two single-spaced pages covered with recalled conversation and things to do. Lexi pulled the sheets from the printer and stuck them in the folder with the newspaper clippings. All of it went into hiding inside the window seat.

She had to get some sleep. Her imagination was in overdrive, her mind whirling with facts and fictional filler. Sleep had been hard to come by the last few nights, and Sunday morning would be here before she could blink. She threw on a robe and headed for the stairs. "Come on, Gilly. You need to go outside for a minute, and I still need to tell Dad goodnight."

Wandering behind a grass-sniffing Gilly through the darkened front yard, Lexi could still hear Ridge's voice, resonating in her mind. Then Lexi's thoughts took a U-turn and she stifled a chuckle, remembering.

Soon after they'd met, she and Jenni had wheedled his whole name out of him. "So how did you get the name Ridge?" Lexi had asked him.

Jenni turned on her southern charm with a sugar-sweet accent, and pulled his name into two syllables "Yes, Re-edge, tell us how!"

Jen was so outrageous with all her flirty eye-batting and head-tilting, bless her drawly little heart. And she held nothing back when she shared with Lexi how she felt about him. But all Jenni's efforts seemed to sift through Ridge's man-brain without notice, or maybe he just chose to ignore her. Either way, he changed the subject about his name at least five times before they wore him down.

He'd slapped his baseball cap on backward, a tuft of his curly hair poking out, making it look like the rear end of a longhaired puppy. "Pesky women! All right, all right. Mom and Dad named me after my great-granddaddy on my mom's side."

And there it was. He'd good-naturedly huffed out "Ridgeford Judson Louis Scott." Then he added he'd never been happy about being saddled with a name like Ridgeford.

And in that moment, he captured Lexi's heart . . . .

But he belonged to Jenni.

Derek Jentzen looked more like a fullback for the Miami Dolphins than a Sunday school teacher. Lexi stared up at the muscled man, from her seat in the young-adult classroom. Maybe half her dad's age, he dwarfed the teacher's desk he sat beside. Half an hour ago the ten chairs around two tables in front of him had filled with her friends. For the last fifteen minutes, they'd been in a hot discussion sparked by a single question: who wrote the Book of Exodus? *Moses, of course.* But Lexi kept her mouth shut and listened.

Lexi looked at her watch. That was skillful. In less than a minute, Mr. Jentzen had maneuvered them out of a fiery impasse and into the midst of Exodus.

"So if you want to follow along . . ." The big man got up and stood in front of his desk. " . . . I'm reading from the second book of the Bible, Exodus, chapter twenty-eight, beginning with the first verse."

Pages rustling around her, Lexi opened her Bible. She put her finger on the first verse and stifled a yawn as Jentzen read. Ho hum. Nothing but instruction from God to Moses about his brother, Aaron.

Now take Aaron your brother, and his sons with him, from among the children of Israel, that he may minister to Me as priest . . . . They shall make the ephod . . . . You shall take two onyx stones . . . .

Lexi's attention spiked, her heartbeat racing. Surely she'd read this before, but the words seemed new, fresh. The more her teacher read, the stronger her interest grew. The words took off in a direction she hadn't anticipated. She did some speed-reading ahead of him. Her finger moved south from verse nine, slowed as she skimmed down the page, and came to an abrupt stop on the twenty-first verse.

And the stones shall have the names of the sons of Israel, twelve according to their names, like the engravings of a signet, each one with its own name; they shall be according to the twelve tribes.

A tiny gasp rolled through her, her fingertip burning as she pulled it down the page of her Bible.

Words of scripture curled upward in twists like smoke from the page and seared their way across Lexi's mind.

Aaron. Two onyx stones. Engrave. Twelve names. Breastplate. Twelve stones. Gold settings.

The inscription on the parchment suddenly came alive. She sat straight up in the chair, her jaw clenched to keep her mouth from dropping open. Mr. Jentzen gave her a brief glance but continued to read.

She looked over at Jenni and Ridge. The shock of seeing, reading, hearing the words passed like a seismic wave between the three of them. Rigid, Lexi planted her eyes on the Bible verses and tried to read, to listen. But the page was a blur, and she didn't comprehend anything else Derek Jentzen said . . . or was he still reading?

Why was it quiet? She stole a look at Mr. Jentzen from beneath her eyelashes, then held her breath as he focused on Ridge, Jenni, and then her, with open concern.

Uh oh! Had she been that obvious, given away the fact that something he read had affected her, something she had no intention of discussing? Her insides shook along with her composure.

"Lexi, are you all right?"

Before she could respond, he laid his Bible on the desk and walked toward her.

Her cheeks were on fire, probably flaming red. "I'm fine, Mr.

Jentzen." Lexi prayed for words to explain. "Mmm . . . it's just that what you read struck me as interesting—fascinating, actually. The . . . uh . . . names sort of . . . and the stones . . . they . . ." Oh. She was rambling, not making any sense!

Mr. Jentzen didn't appear to notice whether she made sense or not.

"Very interesting, I'd say." He smiled; the intense worry lines eased from his face and were replaced with a half-smile. "Which part impressed you so much?"

Lexi looked at Jenni, and was met by a blank expression and a tiny shrug.

Mr. Jentzen pressed his point. "Was it about what the high priest wore? Something about the ephod?"

The overhead fan rotated in lazy circles, clicked in rhythm, and pushed cool air around in the ensuing silence. Someone snickered and . . . everyone looked at her.

Lexi swallowed hard. If she could turn this around, just maybe she could slip out of this embarrassing clog in her morning and learn something. She straightened and tugged at her sleeve. "The breastplate. It was covered with jewels. Do they still exist? Does anyone know what happened to them?"

Jentzen rubbed at his chin. "I don't believe anyone knows. And if you jump ahead a little, Scripture tells of the Jewish Temple being plundered, everything taken, and the Temple destroyed—not just once, but twice before Christ was born."

The heat left Lexi's face, and tension seeped from her body as the rest of the group moved in their seats, seeming to lose interest.

Jentzen returned to his desk, picked up his Bible, and turned a page. "After the Book of Exodus, except for a brief line in Leviticus, I don't think the jeweled breastplate Aaron wore is mentioned again in

Scripture. All of the gold, silver, bronze, and precious stones were taken by the enemies of Israel and disappeared literally thousands of years ago."

He paused and looked across at Lexi. "Lots of interesting history here. Does that help answer your question?"

"Um, I think so. Thanks." Sort of, but not really. She crossed her fingers under the desk, nodded, and attempted to appear satisfied. Hopefully that would end anymore talk of the jewels. But this quarter's study of Exodus and the gifted artisans, Bezalel and Aholiab, had accomplished its purpose as Derek Jentzen challenged them to consider what their talents were.

Please, Lord, just help me get through the rest of this lesson.

With class dismissed, Jenni met her at the door. Ridge hung back, talking with Terry and Nate. Neither she nor Jenni said a word as they walked into the sunlit garden near the sanctuary. They stayed quiet until they reached the trio of stone benches and sat. Lexi stared at the Bible she held in her lap and shook her head. Seconds later, Ridge sat beside her and broke the silence.

"Well, *that* turned out to be a pretty awesome lesson." He gave Lexi's shoulder a light squeeze. "I couldn't believe what DJ was reading, stuff nearly the same as what we read from the parchment Friday."

Lexi didn't move. The warm gentle pressure of Ridge's hand sculpted her in place. "I've read it before, but it never sank in. So much detail is in the Bible."

She didn't wait for a response. "I'd sure like to see if there's anything more that matches up with what's on the parchment. I will *never* be able to concentrate in church today." She looked at Jenni, curious not only about her take on what happened, but to see if she'd noticed Ridge's hand still on her shoulder.

Jen's eyes were glued to Ridge's hand. "I don't think any of us will,

but I'm wondering, too. There could be more."

She really should wiggle out from under his hand. "We need to compare notes from our talk with the Carvers. We still have a bunch of stuff from the library to look at, and now this. Anybody object to getting together this afternoon to sort this out?"

"Fine with me. The beach or a backyard? I'm open." Ridge gave Lexi's shoulder an almost imperceptible pat then moved his hand to run his fingers through his breeze-tousled hair.

Jenni's shoulders relaxed and she turned to Lexi. "It's too hot and windy to manage books at the beach. How about my house at around two-thirty?"

Ridge nodded. "I'll be there. I've got a couple more thoughts about what we're getting into here."

"Two-thirty works for me," Lexi said.

Jenni got up. "We should look at more than one translation of the Bible. That might help."

Lexi agreed. "I'll bring my iPad. I've got three translations on there. Don't think we'll need anything more."

Ridge held out his Bible. "Armed and ready."

Lexi slung her purse over her arm and stood. "I'll bring the copy of the sheet I found and the one I made of the Northbrick parchment. Maybe we can decipher more of what they mean."

"It all sounds good, ladies, but if we don't get moving we're going to be late." Ridge rose and started toward the sanctuary.

By quarter after two that afternoon, Lexi had the dishwasher loaded and humming. The talk with Mom hadn't been brought up. Lexi was relieved it hadn't. The conversation during their early Sunday dinner had been light and focused on her college plans. Her questions would come later. Maybe tomorrow. Today, her mind didn't stray far from the weird relationship between the Bible verses in Exodus and the cryptic words on the parchment. She wasn't even close to being ready to deal with more.

Dad strode into the living room, coffee mug in hand, Mom right behind him as Lexi headed for the door. With her New King James Bible in one arm, along with some folders, her iPad, and her book–filled canvas bag in the other, she nearly escaped, but her dad took one look and halted in his tracks. She had to smile as he and Mom raised quizzical eyebrows, neither saying a word.

"We're doing some research in the Book of Exodus." At least she wouldn't have to argue about going to Jen's this afternoon.

"Well, there's a first time for everything, I suppose." Dad's hand was warm on her shoulder as she opened the door. She nosed Gilly out of the way with her foot, and Dad grabbed the dog's collar.

Lexi's heart melted a little at his smile and touch. Was it her imagination, or were things a little less strained between them?

"Thanks for dinner, Mom. It was great. See you later." Mom started to speak but instead took Gilly from Dad back into the living room.

"Nice out. Drive safe, honey." He waved at her and shut the screened door.

She'd left the top down on the Mini after church, and it was still a top-down kind of a day. Tossing everything into the passenger seat, she was about to get into the car when something lying on the front porch caught her eye. A blue folder she'd carried out must have slipped from her arms. She dashed back, bent to pick it up, and froze.

"Something more is going on, Jason. I can feel it."

Mom's voice floated through the screened door, and Lexi listened. A familiar creak came from an easy chair in the living room. There was no way they could see her where she stood.

This is unbelievable. I could give classes on easy, effective eavesdropping!

"True. That might well be after what the two of you talked about yesterday. Whatever it is, though, it seems to be much more important to her than any discussion about her godfather and his estate."

The *clunk* of a mug being set on a table.

"I keep thinking of everything Aaron said about us probably having to tell her about the trust before she turned twenty." Mom's voice sounded tight and unnatural. "I really dread dealing with all this."

"We'll get through it. It's been on my mind, too. We dealt with it back then, and we will again, but we need to ask her if she's been in the mansion, and we need to ask her soon."

I'm involved in a trust? What's that all about? Lexi sat down hard on the porch step. She certainly wasn't ready to answer the question they planned to ask about her being in the mansion.

How many more surprises would blindside her? Lexi drew in a deep breath, pushed up from the step, and silently walked away from the porch, blue folder in hand.

Chapter Fifteen

Next door to Jenni's house, the black Land Rover Ridge's dad used in business and his mom's sporty white four-door lined up in their driveway. Lexi chuckled, slowing as she drove past. Ridge's cherished El Camino had been relegated to the street in front of his house.

The Scotts had moved to Nantucket soon after Jenni had. Four months older than Lexi and Jenni, Ridge kept their friendship fun, but he'd melted Lexi's heart after his first football game. He'd made the winning touchdown, and at the victory party, he sidled up to her and stood way too close, a cute, sheepish grin on his face. Thrilled for his win, she bear-hugged him, and his hazel eyes had pinned her with a look that turned her heart inside out. But then Jenni bounced up and dragged him off, and Lexi buried her feelings. What he meant by that look she'd never been sure of, and he'd said nothing.

A batch of butterflies fluttered in Lexi's stomach as she maneuvered the Mini Cooper around Ridge's Chevy. In the midst of deciding on a college last month, Ridge and his dad left to tour MIT and Duke, and ended up with a fishing trip off the coast. For nearly two weeks, she

hadn't given a flip about eating, sleeping was fitful, and forget about concentrating on anything for more than two minutes. It was a bitter taste of what it would be like without him, and the turmoil of emotions still confused her. She wanted the best for him, but she'd be miserable if he chose Duke.

Lexi sighed and pulled into the driveway of the Sheldon's New England saltbox house with its silver-gray shake shingles and white clapboard siding. Jenni jogged down the porch steps, her hair a curly mass of gold in freefall around her shoulders. "Looks like you could use some help with that armload."

"Hey, Jen, thanks."

Jenni grinned at her. "I hope we learn something from all this stuff." She wove her free arm through Lexi's as they walked around the side of the house. "I've got us set up at the picnic table. It's much cooler out here. Dad's at church, helping to put the new playground equipment together, and Mom took the boys to the beach to meet their friends. She'll be home any minute. And would you believe my guy is already waiting for us in the backyard?"

My guy? Lexi sent Jenni a sidelong glance and all but crossed her fingers. "I'm totally impressed!" Jenni'd been open about her feelings for Ridge, but her "my guy" assumption was a stretch. Things had shifted into a vague uneasiness between the three of them since they'd begun making decisions about college. Unless Ridge made some radical changes, Jen was setting herself up for a huge hurt. So far, he was same-o non-committal Ridge. Jen just wasn't reading him right.

With an internal shake of her head, Lexi bit back the warning and handful of advice she'd been ready to give. With her own confusion over Ridge, she had no business handing out advice. She'd never said anything to Jenni; maybe she never would. Lexi's feelings weren't part of the picture.

Would they ever settle back into their easy relationship, or was this three-way friendship in for a crash-and-burn spiral? Her chest tightened and her throat closed. There was too much going on in her life. Don't think about it!

A threefold cord is not quickly broken.

God was in control of the details—if she'd let go. She had to trust. *Help, Lord.*

"Sodas, water, glasses, and ice—everything's over there." Jenni motioned to the redwood table close to several trees. "Help yourself. Mom said she'd pick up doughnuts on her way home."

"I'm drooling already, and you're late." Ridge's lopsided grin and teasing dissolved Lexi's reserve, and with her knees totally untrustworthy, she plopped down opposite him. Not too long ago she would have threatened to bop him with her Bible—or done it.

She blinked hard. Where had those times gone when they were younger and easy in their fun and friendship? Move over, Peter Pan. "Never grow up" wasn't going to happen, so just forget it.

Jenni sat beside Ridge and reached across his arm to open his Bible. The big blob didn't move or object! *Mmmmf. Closer than peanut butter and jelly.*

Great. Not much success with forgetting things. But Ridge watched her, not Jen, as she opened her canvas bag.

"I brought a copy of the parchment. The original is safe at home." She handed the copy to Jenni. "I still can't get over how the words on this sheet compare to what we read this morning."

Ridge raked his fingers through his thick hair and leafed through the pages of his Bible. "Sure took my head to another level."

"Mine, too." Jenni looked at Lexi. "Too many of the words match up

for it not to be connected."

Lexi nodded. "Anybody had time to study what we read this morning? I sure didn't."

Ridge slid a sheet of paper onto the table. "I had a few minutes and found this. Take a look. It was on a site that focused on what the priests wore in the Temple. There's a drawing of what the original ephod and the breastplate might have looked like based on the description in the Bible."

"Wow." Lexi let out a slow breath, gazing at the sketch. The vivid, full-color artist's conception of the high priest's jewel-encrusted breastplate showed brilliant gems that seemed to glitter in the afternoon sunshine. Her heart skipped a beat. This was significant. Weren't jewels also called stones?

Jenni shaded her eyes with her hand and leaned in to stick her finger on one of the two black shapes on each shoulder of what looked like a vest. "There are two other jewels on that thing they call the ephod. It's hard to see, but there's something written on both of them. Onyx. They were supposed to be onyx."

Ridge cocked his head. "Yep. Onyx is a black mineral."

Smart aleck! Lexi picked up the parchment copy. "This says 'Two onyx stones you will engrave for Me. In the order of their birth—'"

Ridge put a hand up. "Wait a minute."

She stopped and laid the copy on the table, watching as he ruffled through his Bible to an earmarked page and scanned down the verses.

"Here. Genesis 49:1. This is where Jacob calls his twelve sons to come to him just before he dies. One-by-one, by name . . ." Ridge put his finger on an identical phrase in the parchment copy. " . . . *in the order of their birth*, Jacob tells each son what's in store for him in the last days. The first son was Reuben; then there was Levi, Simeon, Judah,

Zebulun, Issachar, Dan, Gad, Asher, Naphtali, Joseph, and Benjamin, the twelve sons."

Lexi looked back at the drawing then pulled out her iPad, connected to an online Bible site, and pointed to verses in Exodus. "This is where Mr. J started to read this morning. Verse nine is where it really begins to line up with the parchment."

She leaned back and looked at them. "So the brothers' names were to be written on the black stones, six names on each stone. Reuben's first on one, and Dan named first on the other. *And* all twelve individually engraved on each of the breastplate stones."

Jenni flicked a pine needle off the table. "Jacob's sons, the twelve tribes of Israel. But after Jacob had the wrestling match with God and God changed Jacob's name to Israel, they're also called the sons of Israel."

Lexi barely heard Jenni. "So there were fourteen stones total. What if they weren't lost or stolen, but were kept safe—hidden?" No way. Her thoughts bubbled like the fizz in her soda. "It's been *thousands* of years. I guess it borders on crazy-insane to think he might have had them."

She couldn't sit still. Aaron Cohen *had been* a jeweler. She sucked in a deep breath and pushed off the bench to pace.

Jenni twisted her ponytail. "If Aaron Cohen had them, maybe we could find them."

"And we do that how? Aaron Cohen only left a single clue that says he had them." Lexi shook her head and moved to stand between the trees. "One gold key. To what? And where does one find that 'what'?"

Ridge's eyes fastened on hers. "Clues or not, everything that's happened so far points to the possibility he did have them. There are too many coincidences. Think about what you've found, what you've heard." He paused and shot her a grin. "And what you've *over*heard.

And how do you explain all those things Jacob Carver said? There's *something* going on here."

Yes. There was. Too many pieces fit together for the stones—for any of this—to be coincidence. She sat on the bench next to Jenni. Too much eye contact with Ridge.

Jenni leaned forward on her elbows, her chin cupped in her hands, her eyes on the parchment copy. "This says it's forbidden to touch those stones."

Lexi smiled at Jen's frown and dark tone. "True, but four lines down from there, it says they're supposed to be returned to the Temple. Somebody has to touch them to get them there."

"If we ever do find them." Jenni's southern accent pulled at her words. "Remember what happened to the guy who touched the Ark of the Covenant? He was only trying to help keep the Ark from falling, and y'all just look at him!"

Ridge twirled his cap on a finger. "That Ark was a whole other ballgame, Jen. But all the 'what if's' in this sure make me wonder."

Darth Vader's theme music in *Star Wars* marched through Lexi's mind as long seconds of quiet hovered over the three of them. She got up and wandered to the tree again. "I wonder what *preparing the way for the stones to return to the Temple* means. It sounds as if whoever finds them is supposed to get ready to take them to Israel, but to what temple? There isn't one. It hasn't been rebuilt yet." She brushed an ant from her jeans. But hadn't she heard that it was under construction?

"Well, at least it says when the time comes, it'll be clear." Jenni paused then added, "To whomever."

"And what about the 'messenger' person?" Ridge narrowed his eyes at Lexi. "From every angle . . . it looks to me like that might be you."

He could have nailed her to the tree with his hazel eyes seeming to look for a way into her thoughts. Nerves blazing, she paced again, scuffing her sandals across the short grass.

"I was thinking the same thing." Jenni's fingernails tapped the top of her Bible. "It makes sense. You really could be the messenger."

Heat crept into Lexi's face. "You two are totally nuts." She was far from ready to think about unraveling that section of the parchment. Everything rolled toward her like a rogue wave, threatened to engulf her. She stood beside the table. "You're jumping to conclusions. Let's stick to figuring out the rest of this thing." She stifled a gasp at the sharpness of her words. She really was on edge.

Ridge shook his head, his hands up in an I'm-backing-off gesture. "Okay, okay, it's cool. We'll tackle the messenger part later." He flipped through his Bible, looking at strategically-placed sticky notes. "Back to deciphering. I looked up a bunch of info on the temple."

They were deep in conversation when Jenni's mother called from the back door that there were doughnuts in the kitchen. Jenni tossed her pencil on the table and went to get them.

Lexi waved at Mrs. Sheldon, relieved at not being peppered with questions about what they were doing with a table full of open Bibles.

Jenni brought back a plate full of powdered sugar temptation, and settled into her "jelly" position next to "peanut butter."

"This is so unreal." Lexi sat across from them and bit into a doughnut and nearly dropped it when Ridge picked up a napkin and reached to brush off her chin. Her face flaming, her heart jumped at his touch. What was he doing? Jenni gulped in a short breath, and Lexi wasn't certain how to read the look on her face.

Ridge cocked his head and sent Lexi an innocent grin. "What's unreal—the doughnut-dust on your face or what we just read?"

"Neither." Lexi forced herself to breathe and shrugged, rubbing at her chin.

Please, Lord, that did *sound neutral. Didn't it?*

No.

Ridge looked stung, and her heart squeezed. His tender chin-wipe couldn't have meant anything more than cleaning up her powdered-sugar face—could it?

She raced to smooth out the rough place. "It's just that this whole thing is weird. The idea that . . . um . . . Aaron Cohen might have owned any ancient, missing jewels. And then, the thought that we might find them . . ."

Lexi drew in a quick breath. She'd come close to calling Aaron her uncle. She dipped her head and rubbed at her arms as a warm reassurance washed over her. She *did* fit somewhere into this puzzle. That fact didn't seem to change the awkward tension around the table, though.

She filled her glass with water instead of more caffeine-charged soda and bypassed another doughnut. Between Malea's cookies and Jen's doughnuts, she'd had enough sweet stuff to last her a month. It was also sweet when Jen moved closer to Ridge, and he didn't seem to object. Not so sweet was the tiny, heart-sinking let-down as things felt natural again.

Lexi took a library book from her bag. "Our guess about the construction date of the mansion being 1832 was right." She put her finger on an article. "This also describes the fire of 1837, when the whole town had to be rebuilt. Northbrick House was one of the few buildings that didn't burn to the ground."

"We talked about that fire in history class." Ridge pulled the book closer and looked at the page. "It was a bad one, really changed things around here. Lots of people left the island because of it."

Jenni nodded. "We might not have had any of this info if someone hadn't been able to save the old records. Did you find anything else?"

"Only a few archives that go way back, and those list births and deaths." Lexi glanced at her notes. "No evidence that anyone except generations of the Cohen family ever lived in Northbrick, and almost every one of them were born there and died there."

She closed the book and put her notes aside. "By the way, there's more besides what Jacob Carver told us last night and what I told you on our way home."

Lexi left the table and sat on the grass, pressing her back against a tree trunk. She'd grabbed their attention. "I haven't had a chance to tell you everything I learned about Aaron Cohen. Mom said there was more, but she wanted to wait until Dad had time to talk with us."

Lexi pulled up a long blade of grass and picked at it. "Aaron and my parents were friends for twenty-seven years. And except for Jacob and Malea, he lived alone on the estate."

Jenni and Ridge listened, shocked, surprised, and engrossed, for ten minutes before Lexi finally changed trajectory. "Just before I left the house this afternoon, I heard Mom and Dad talking again."

Ridge's eyebrows reached for the dark curls that dangled over his forehead, and Lexi grinned, unable to take her eyes from his cute, quizzical expression. "I know. My eavesdropping is getting to be a habit. But they *were* discussing the Northbrick Estate, and I wasn't about to miss that. They mentioned the trust again and said they needed to ask me if I'd been in Northbrick house."

"Why—?"

She held up a hand before Ridge could assail her with his questions. "Before you ask, I have no idea why they'd want to know if I'd been in there. Since Aaron is my godfather, I'm definitely in the middle of this, this . . . whatever-it-is, but I don't intend to ask them more right now.

What *does* have my interest is a gate."

She looked up and held back a grin, glancing from Ridge's silly expression to Jen's. "Really. A gate. Mom mentioned one when we talked. Some kind of door or gateway through the rear stone wall of the estate. And what makes it really strange is that Mom said she'd never seen the gate. I plan on finding it. Tomorrow. Are you two coming?"

Ridge had been staring at her since she'd said the word *gate*. "Unbelievable." He shook his head, got up, picked up a pinecone, and tossed it to her. After the riptide of emotions today, the pinecone landing in her lap brought back some fun. As if all the strained undercurrents between the three of them had smoothed out.

Ridge hooked his thumb in his belt and cocked his head. "The ball is officially in your court. I'm ready to help, but why don't you want to look around inside the house first?"

"You're reading my mind, Ridge," Jenni said. "Why *don't* you want to look inside first?" Her best friend's expressive brown eyes blinked at Lexi.

"I wish I knew. A hunch, maybe." Lexi thought about pitching the pinecone to Jenni but changed her mind. "The whole thing is strange. I just don't think what we're hunting for is in that house. " But why in the world would she start looking in a has-been garden full of weeds and dead flowers? Logic said she should search inside. But nothing about this was logical.

Ridge snaked his fingers through his hair. "The parchment is pretty cryptic, but as far as I can tell, it doesn't give any hints about where we'd find whatever-it-is."

"Well, that gold key sure won't open any safe deposit box."

"Oh, so you're thinking there's buried treasure?" Jenni wrinkled her freckle-sprinkled nose. "Okay, I'll go along with digging behind the wall first."

Ridge laughed. "We might as well start by finding your mysterious gate. There's no way aside from a demolition crew that we'd ever get into the gardens by going through the house." A glint of mischief sparked from his hazel eyes. "*Treasure Island.* Bring your picks and shovels."

"No. No picks, no shovels," Lexi shot back. But how would they go about storming an impenetrable seven-foot wall? "First, find the gate or scale the wall. After we're in, we'll go from there. When do you want to start looking?"

"Tomorrow," Jenni said. "We have the early shift, so why don't we meet at Northbrick mid-morning?"

Lexi twisted the watch around her wrist. "That'll work. We'll have at least till noon. Okay with you, Ridge?"

"Clear. Dad's out of town, so other than a few chores, I'm open."

"Then we'll meet there at ten." Lexi tossed the pinecone to Ridge and gathered up everything she'd brought with her.

Ridge drop-kicked the battered pinecone across the yard, and they walked around the house to the front yard. "By the way, I finally looked up trusts. They're used in a lot of ways for a lot of reasons, but only one sounded like it might fit. That kind of trust holds property of any type that somebody holds for somebody else, for their benefit." He shot a grin at Lexi. "And that 'somebody else' can either know about it—or not. A lawyer fixes it up all nice and legal-like."

Trusts? Lawyers? Thoughts scrambled through Lexi's head in directions she didn't want to think about.

Ridge propped himself against the corner of the house. "You know, that probably means the 'Aaron Cohen Trust' your parents talked about. It could hold the property that belonged to him—for someone."

"Mm." Lexi nodded. "That makes sense, and if we look up who

currently owns the house and it shows a trust, we'll have the answer. But it's logical to me, if there is an 'Aaron Cohen Trust,' that it's a property trust and the trust holds or owns Northbrick Estate, however that's handled. And common sense says any taxes due would be paid by the trust—and someone has to manage it. Right?"

Ridge smiled at her and nodded. "Yep. Simple as that."

Jenni bounced around in front of Ridge. "And that means the town had to have let the trust manager know they wanted to condemn the house. They had to notify someone." She redirected her gaze to Lexi. "Probably your parents. Do you think they know?"

That was a good question. With her insides in cyclonic turmoil, all she could do was stare at Jenni and shrug.

Ridge glanced toward his spit-polished El Camino. "Just a gut feeling, but I think they know about the whole thing."

Lexi's breath left her, as Ridge formed and spoke the words that described what she felt. She looked up at them. "It's the 'why' of so many things that's getting to me. Forget why they've never told me about Northbrick. What I want to know is why the place didn't get sold after Mr. C. died. Why let it sit there empty, wasting away for all those years? What's the logic and reasoning behind that?"

Ridge opened the car door for her then leaned in close with a shake of his head. "Mystery to me."

Lexi laughed. "Uh huh. The Northbrick mystery, one I'm ready to solve. See you at ten."

PB and J stood, arms touching. She gritted her teeth, waved, and backed out of the drive.

Jacob said the house was safe, at least for a while. The less-than-subtle change of gears in her head drove her thoughts forward. Next step, find that gate and get into the rear gardens. Reason and logic didn't enter into this, just a nudge that whatever the key opened was somewhere behind that "gate." And just a hunch that the words and phrases of the parchment would help her find it. Her godfather had written it. He had placed it where she would find it.

Why, why, why? She pounded her fist on the steering wheel. Craziness!

Chapter Sixteen

This insane weekend had stretched its tentacles into the dark, early morning hours of Monday. In a way, the fog pleased Greyson as he wheeled the Porsche toward his law office. Nantucket was living up to her nickname. The locals called her *The Little Grey Lady of the Sea* for the weathered gray shingles covering their homes and frequent fog that rolled in from the sea. Low, billowy clouds of the stuff hung damp and heavy in the air. He hoped it made him less likely to be noticed.

But the loan shark's goon had the same advantage. They'd tracked him here from Boston, stalked him before, except this time he was ready—even expecting—trouble. Could he help it if his payments had been too slow? And if the idiot hurt him and kept him from working, they wouldn't see any payment at all. A chill ran up his spine, and he checked the rearview mirror. Visibility was poor, but as far as he could tell, no one followed.

So what if he was paranoid? Anyone would be. Greyson rubbed his still-tender right side, remembering the kidney punch he'd received one night a week ago. He hadn't seen the face of the gorilla that landed it. Running late, he'd stupidly parked on the deserted side street and barely

gotten one foot into the car when the iron-hard fist struck, catching him completely unprepared. Doubled over in the driver's seat, he heard only the verbal threat, "Time's runnin' out, man, and there's more where that came from if we don't see the money. Boss's givin' ya fifteen days." And then the flash of rounded metal in the shape of a gun brandished as a warning. Even now a stab of terror left him in a cold sweat and quaking. He'd finally scrounged up enough for another payment, but his huge gambling debts had put him in a deadly position.

Money. He needed lots of it, fast. His best chance to obtain it was as close as the box and key he'd missed retrieving from Northbrick, and he was on his way to start solving that problem. The single file he'd slipped out of Grey's locked desk had to have come from somewhere. His search for the source paid off when he'd looked through the storage room of pending and dead files. He'd found the file box with its subtle labeling on a bottom corner shelf.

Minutes from now, he'd take it from the office. And he had hours until the office opened at eight-thirty to go through the file box for info. The possibility of learning how much cash the items might translate into kept him focused. Old Cohen had been maddeningly vague about what was in the box under the mansion floor. He glued his eyes to the road and tried to stop worrying over the risks he was taking.

Squirming in the tight space of the leather driver's seat, he smiled. He'd been wise to hire Dan Sangster, a private detective out of Boston. The man was talented and skillful. It should pay off.

A year ago, Greyson had ridden with Sangster while checking on a case he'd worked in Boston. Great at details, the man depended on his police scanner's streaming broadcast. He constantly monitored it for advance warning that he might have been spotted when he'd snooped around the houses he surveilled.

THE STONEKEEPERS

Greyson peered into the pea soup fog swirling in the low-beams of his headlights. The sooner he got the Christensen house "wired for sound" the better. He had wanted Sangster in Nantucket immediately, but he hadn't arrived until late last night. Now it would be a matter of waiting, and watching for an opportunity for Sangster to bug the Christensen's house, phones, and cars.

It would be later this morning before Greyson had time to firm up plans to try for the box again. If the girl's parents hadn't contacted the law office by then, it would be a strong indication she hadn't yet told them she'd been inside the mansion. That meant what she'd taken was probably hidden somewhere in her bedroom.

He hoped.

But let's get this little job over with first. Greyson drummed his manicured fingers over the smooth leather steering wheel and nudged the gas pedal. He needed to watch his timing. The fiasco inside Northbrick House Friday morning had sharpened his awareness. He needed to slow down and be more deliberate. Waiting tested his patience, but he had no choice.

Turning onto a main road, he drove directly into the older downtown area. Stands of gaslight lamps lining the cobblestone streets smeared hazy golden light over the damp sidewalks. Nearing the law firm, he turned off the car's fog lights and slowed, looking for anything unusual.

Nothing.

So far, so good.

Turning into the office parking area, he chose an out-of-the-way spot and watched for any lights to come on in nearby buildings. It remained dark, misty, and quiet.

He checked the digital clock on the Porsche's dashboard: 3:15 a.m. He'd timed his arrival to avoid the routine security checks of the office

complex. He'd get in there, grab what he needed, and be out within minutes—only this time, he'd have the *entire* Cohen history in his hands. A sandstorm of regret ground down his spine. He should have been smarter sooner, dug deeper, not stopped with that single envelope when he'd first found it.

Greyson gave his surroundings a final check. All clear. He had no intention of reviewing the material at the office. Too great a risk. He needed light, privacy, time unobserved. He'd take the documents home to study. He got out and sprinted toward the darkened building, every shadow a hovering threat.

Fifteen minutes later, Greyson reset the alarm system, in his hands the burgeoning Cohen file box. He shut the heavy glass exterior office door behind him. Done, and still plenty of time before the next security check. His reflection in the door glass mirrored the satisfied smile beneath his mustache as he turned the key in the lock.

The fog had thickened, a blanket of dirty whipped cream, great for covering his activities, but he'd have to watch his driving. He gave the parking lot a cursory glance and put the file-filled container in the passenger seat.

Settled behind the wheel, he smoothed his mustache. If he handled this right, he'd have the files back at the office well before daylight, long before the secretary arrived. He eased the car into the street for the short drive home . . . and stomped the brakes. He'd narrowly missed crashing into the sleek black Corvette with no lights that ripped past him and disappeared into the twisting fog.

Greyson sat, frozen, hands seized on the wheel, waiting, expecting the black silhouette to roar into view, its doors to fly open and—

Nothing.

They were taunting him. Terrorizing him.

THE STONEKEEPERS

Wending his way through the ghostly haze, it took him longer than usual to reach his beachside townhouse. Security lights came on as soon as he was in range, and the area looked normal. He punched the automatic garage-door opener and pulled in, breathing a relieved sigh as the garage door met the concrete with a *thud*. All was well.

Inside, he safed the alarm system and started a pot of coffee. The orange message light on the phone blinked a silent demand for him to listen. His insides churned, but he ignored the orange summons. Just more of the same irritating phone calls.

Nerves taut as guitar strings, Greyson walked through his house, checking doors and windows for signs of entry. He stopped at the fish tank to feed his neglected exotic fish. His lone Serra piranha bumped against the glass, staring at him. Its jutting jaw, full of an ugly mouthful of razor-sharp teeth, chewed at the water as if ravenous. Probably was. Greyson thumped the glass. Fascinating fish. Reminded him of how he felt leaving Northbrick House Friday—sans box and key—ticked and empty-handed.

The whir of the printer clearing its ink jets sounded from the corner of his study, but his desk didn't offer enough workspace. Annoyed, he abandoned it for the dining room and dropped the heavy cardboard file box on the wide dining table. The smell of fresh-perked coffee wafted in from the kitchen. He poured himself a mug full before he sorted through the papers and folders spread over the polished walnut wood table. A headache threatened and his stomach twisted like a corkscrew. He ignored both and rummaged through the first folder.

Shoving his chair away from the table, Greyson pushed his shirtsleeve

up to check his Swiss Breitling watch, a graduation gift from his father. An hour had passed since he'd begun sifting through the files. He shook his head, tossed a folder onto the growing mess of papers, and reached for an expansion file. It contained more material than the others, and a large manila envelope with a dark red wax seal caught his attention. He hesitated, but the seal could easily be duplicated. He broke it open, pulled out the contents of the envelope, and leaned forward to scan the papers. His breathing quickened and he sat upright, utterly fascinated, then pounded the table with his fist.

"Ha! Got it!"

The words exploded into the silence of the room. He'd been right. What the box contained *was* valuable, priceless to the point he had to squelch the sensation in his gut that told him he might have trouble fencing it. There were international and historic implications to this. He'd have to move with care and stealth. His hands shook as he held a single sheet of paper. No wonder Cohen had been a recluse surrounded by secrecy. He had something to hide, all right.

Greyson stood and gave a vicious kick to a carved table leg. He'd let Lexi Christensen take that treasure cache right out from under his nose. He took a swallow of lukewarm coffee and paced the silver-gray dining room carpet for long moments. Calmer, he picked up the manila envelope and several folders, and took them to his study.

He glanced at the screensaver full of waving palm trees, tossing ocean waves, and deserted beach covering the monitor, and dropped the paperwork on the desk. *Maybe the sunny island of Bali could use another beach bum.* If he did this right, no one would suspect his involvement. But before he bought a villa in an Indonesian paradise, his gambling debts had to go. He gave the desk a one-way high-five slap, and loaded the more than dozen documents into the scanner.

Half-an-hour, three cups of coffee, six Tums, and two aspirin later, he'd reread, scanned, and copied all the paperwork he needed and backed up everything on a flash drive. With the envelopes resealed and the files restored to the briefcase, he was finished. Greyson leaned back into his chair, yawned and stretched.

Not again. The raucous warbling of the desk phone jarred his frazzled nerves. The calls came at all hours now. He looked at his watch: 6 a.m. The "debt collector" left calls and threats daily; the last one had come at midnight, before he'd left for town, and a second while he was away. He hadn't thought he'd get another so soon. Whether he picked up the receiver or not, he knew the voice he'd hear.

The answering machine caught on the fourth ring. Greyson turned up the volume and listened, hands damp and trembling from agitation and caffeine.

"Your last payment bought ya till the end of July, then watch your back." The grating bass voice rumbled out a smoldering threat that hung in the air like thick, black smoke. Greyson stared at the phone, an image of the gun flashing through his mind.

"Don't bother to pick up. I don't want to hear your voice until I see the color of your money. You know where I am, and don't think of running. We're watching." A click, then nothing.

Greyson threw back a gulp of ice-cold coffee and waited for his hands to stop quivering before he erased all the messages. Running had crossed his mind, but that was before he knew what the girl had found. His stalkers watched him when they could, but they couldn't know his every move. It had been simpler when his old man just bailed him out of his jams. This time he was on his own. He was in too deep.

Two big problems stood out like the Boulder and Grand Coulee dams between Greyson and what he wanted. Getting that box, and turning

its contents into money. If he messed this up . . . Another twist of the corkscrew in his belly. Like the wicked, biting jaws of his piranha, time closed in and devoured chunks of his life.

He rubbed his temples, anxious to call Rick Vander. He trusted his old college friend, and had already given him a heads-up that he had a "project" in the works. Good thing Rick was used to his projects.

Rick knew people who could make things happen, but to get his help Greyson would have to give him details he wasn't ready to spill yet. Making connections was as far as Greyson wanted Rick involved. Nothing should go wrong, but if they did, Rick would help—for a piece of the action, of course. But Greyson didn't want to share any money he didn't have to. Hopefully, it wouldn't come to that. He picked up the desk phone and pressed Rick's name on speed dial. Yeah, he'd be ticked at what time it was, but this wouldn't wait, and Rick always answered.

His voice groggy, Vander turned the air purple with a few choice words, ending with "Quinn, you're berserk calling at this hour. Don't you ever sleep, man?"

Greyson sat at the desk, twirling a pen, ignoring his friend's annoying protests. When Rick finally shut up, he filled him in with as much as he wanted his friend to know.

It took five minutes. Greyson hung up, satisfied he'd sufficiently tweaked Rick's curiosity. Rick had his back.

Sleep hadn't been on Greyson's agenda tonight, but he'd accomplished everything with an hour to spare. He chewed on an antacid as he switched off the coffeepot, lights, and overhead fans.

Getting the file box back in place at the office would be a snap. Showered, shaved, and dressed, he checked his alarm system and headed back to the office. The fog was dissipating, lifting along with his spirits. Maybe he'd miscalculated his timing on getting into the Northbrick house, but it wouldn't happen again. Too bad Sangster couldn't have gotten here sooner, but with or without him, he'd get that box from the Christensen girl.

Chapter Seventeen

Lexi was ten minutes early getting to Northbrick Monday morning. Twice since last Thursday she'd left her car in this dense, wooded area and walked to Northbrick Estate. About to do it again, sparks of anticipation and apprehension zinged down her arms as she parked the Mini Cooper.

Have I lost my mind, Lord, trying to invade a long-dead garden to look for something I don't even know exists? And if no gate existed, how would she scale that seven-foot wall? Was she even looking in the right place for whatever the gold key unlocked? Would this be an empty, foolish search?

She hooked a bottle of water to her belt and checked her cellphone. With no sign of rain, she left the convertible top down and jogged toward the sidewalk. Jenni had texted that she and Ridge were on their way and that they'd catch up with her.

Except for a light wind through the tops of the trees, nothing moved on Northbrick Avenue. Deserted and quiet, exactly the way she wanted it. She hesitated, gazing up the road toward Jacob Carver's driveway. He'd said she'd find the way through the wall. How could he be so sure?

But weirder, why was she so sure he was right?

The low rumble of the El Camino's engine sounded, and in minutes Jenni and Ridge strode toward the steps where Lexi waited on the walk on the other side of the iron gate.

"Hey, guys." Lexi's heart bounced an extra beat as she watched Ridge take off his sunglasses, arm muscles rippling beneath his khaki-tan tee-shirt in the mid-morning sun. But Jenni's hand was on his other arm. Lexi blinked. Reality check. Think of something else!

Ridge grinned at her. "Good Monday morning, beautiful. It's hotter than Indian kindling out here. You ready for this?"

They stood, facing the house. She looked at him from over the top of her slipping sunglasses and winged an eyebrow, wishing he really meant his "beautiful" comment. "I'm ready. Did you bring a compass?"

"Did you think I'd forget?" Ridge laughed and pulled the compass out of his jeans pocket. "We were right. The place faces due west."

Lexi shaded her eyes and bent close, watching the needle swing. They'd already sketched out a tentative plan to split up and search for any breaks in the rear wall. She pointed to the left side of the house. "Okay. Unless you want to do this some other way, I'll start at the north wall and work toward the back." She swung her arm and pointed to the right side of the house. "Jen, you take the south wall. Ridge, you get to walk the farthest to check out the rear wall." She shot him a smile.

"That'll work," Ridge said. "All right with you, Jen?"

Jenni twisted a hunk of her blonde ponytail. "Whenever you finish, come get me." She took off her sunglasses and looked at him from beneath long eyelashes. "We'll find Lex wherever she is on the north wall."

Lexi came way too close to rolling her eyes. *That* would probably leave half the south wall unsearched. She pointed toward the north wall again. "Anyone who finds anything that even resembles a gate, mark it, and come and get me. No yelling and no whistling." Lexi looked straight at the potential whistler.

"Nope, not even a whistle." Ridge readjusted his grungy Cincinnati Reds baseball cap, his tanned face a handsome mask of "who, me?" innocence.

Lexi bit her tongue as Ridge went with Jenni to the right corner. Lexi jogged down the walk to the left, fighting her way through waist-high weeds. The massive stone wall was mortared in a tight connection to the front corner of the house. She followed the shorter wall, too tall for even Ridge to see over, giving it a cursory scan. Who'd put a gate they wanted to hide in a front-facing wall? She turned into the thick forested area along the side of the wall, tromping through scruffy bushes and scrub, looking for anything that could be construed as a gate.

Underbrush crackled beneath her shoes, and wild rose thorns and brambles tried their best to snag her jeans. Everything including the heat seemed intent on holding her back as she inspected every foot of the forbidding stone barricade.

The sun was merciless, as she breathed in listless, heated air. Before long, perspiration glued strands of her hair against her forehead, and her old blue Nantucket High School tee-shirt clung to her like a second layer of skin. She mopped at her face with her shirtsleeve.

There had to be a way in. But so far only solid, slate-colored stone and mortar had passed beneath her exploring fingertips. She'd looked at over a football-field length or more of the wall and not a single entry point—no gate, no evidence there'd ever been one.

Heavenly Father, am I on the right track?

Ask and trust.

Okay then. Where is it?

A strong scent dropped around her like a mist. She stood back from the wall. Gardenias? Couldn't be unless they grew wild *inside* the wall. There certainly weren't any out here. She shook her head and continued to look for fissures, cracks, cuts, anything that might signal a gate.

Nothing.

Her hands and fingers filthy, nearly numb, slid beneath a heavy cascade of ivy. Strange. Shouldn't ivy cling? This didn't, and unlike the ivy nearby, these green leaves were bruised and shredded as if they'd been storm-battered.

Wait a sec. What was that? Something different, something sharp, uneven in the mortar between the stones.

She held her breath. Muscles and nerves strung taut, she examined the stonework. A crack, barely noticeable but definite, lined a rounded stone edge and went straight toward the ground, disappearing into the weeds below.

"Yesss!" A hissed whisper as an icy wave of anticipation washed over her. She shivered despite the heat. Could this be the entry, the gate into whatever lay beyond this rock wall? She stared at the suspicious break in the mortar. How was it even possible? How wide would an opening need to be? Her fingers played along the wall, searching for more evidence than what might be a simple settling crack.

Two of her fingers slipped into a second fissure, minutely wider than the other, a break running from as high as she could reach, down to the ground—and close to three feet from the other break.

Proof!

She clamped her lips together to keep from yelling for Jenni and Ridge to come. She needed to go find them, to tell them to forget what they were doing and—

But something wasn't right. Her focus changed, drawn to the ground in front of the wall. Tall grass and brush lay matted flat in a rough two-foot-wide semi-circle, and a trail headed off into the woods. Animal trail? Someone or something had been here before, more than once, and not long ago.

She swiped sweaty, dirty hands down the front of her jeans and scanned the nearby brush and brambles. A flash of red. A ragged shred of cloth hung on a twig, and she untangled it. Someone's shirt had a hole in it. Jacob Carver's? Maybe. She hooked the cloth back over the bush. She'd show it to Jen and Ridge later.

The wall seemed to beckon, to challenge her. She should probably mark it and find Ridge, but she couldn't.

No more waiting. She moved her fingers over the wall, explored, tested every line, rough indentation, and chunk of rock, for a sensible way to move a ton of stone wall. Nothing. No levers, no hidden switches, and hinges were impossible.

On tiptoes, she ran her fingers as far toward the top of the seven-foot wall as she could reach, and pressed on each stone around the perimeter of the three-foot-wide segment that rimmed the giveaway break. Still, nothing moved.

A different angle, maybe. She stepped back and to the side. "Uh oh." A lump beneath her foot moved.

Noise and song from cicadas, insects, and birds muted, and eerie silence blanketed her. Lexi's heart raced. She held her breath and looked down at the same instant an almost imperceptible, deep, pulsating sound came from the wall. Her eyes moved from her feet, up the cold gray stones of the monstrous wedge of wall, as it began to slide away from her.

Deep thunderous rumbling shook the ground, a shaking like when she stood—

Run! She had to run!

But fear encased her body, trapped her within an icy cage of immobilized flesh. She could only watch as the entire section edged forward, quiet now, gliding on some unseen track, defying logic. Fear melted into fascination, and a dozen reasonable ways this could be happening flashed through her mind . . . every one discarded.

This was the way into the walled fortress, the gate. She stooped to take a closer look at the base. Whoever designed this was genius.

Three wide-slotted steel tracks were imbedded in a base of concrete. Large rollers that appeared to run on huge ball bearings lined the inside of the tracks, and disappeared up into the stone at the base of the gate. The mechanics reminded her of photos of the space shuttle roll-out transporter.

"Gate? Lord, this isn't like any gate I've ever seen." Her whisper was lost in vibrations that shook like the aftermath of an earthquake. What else could she call it but a gate? The bottom looked twice as wide as the top. Heavy black grease covered both the track and the rollers. It was obvious someone maintained it, but who? She rubbed at a gritty line of perspiration on her cheek with the back of her hand.

The wall-gate, or whatever it was, rolled to a solid halt against some kind of stop, the noise resounding with a heavy rasp of concrete against concrete.

Watch over me, Lord. I'm going in. She stepped around the wedge of mortared stone and pushed her way through the lush shrubbery inside the entrance. The gate had rolled to within inches of a large concrete birdbath. Twin evergreens on either side helped hide the steel tracks all the way from the birdbath to the opening in the wall. Would the thing roll back and seal her in this place? She paused, watching. It didn't move.

Maybe she should look for a way to close it, but open or shut, she took a risk. If it closed, she'd have to find a way to climb back over or the way to open it from inside. If it stayed open, she hoped Jenni and Ridge would be the only ones to follow her in.

Her attention shifted to the birdbath. The chubby snow-white bodies of three cherubs surrounded the bath and disguised what was used to stop the gate. Three sets of sculpted cherub wings stretched outward, effortlessly holding an oval basin high above their heads.

What is this? The birdbath's snowy whiteness blended into the healthy deep green of the plants—plants that weren't supposed to be healthy or green. Lexi sucked in a quick breath and covered her mouth with both hands. Where were the unkempt grounds, the weeds, dead flowers? She pivoted in a half-circle, expecting ugliness and overgrowth like the front of the house. Instead, she stood, stunned.

Treetops stirred with soft sighs, and the sweet mixed fragrance of roses and jasmine filled the atmosphere. And gardenias. The sight of the creamy white petals of dozens of gardenias had her smiling. She locked her fingers against the back of her neck and looked up, breathing deep droughts of the perfumed air. Behind her, rustling sounds of water rippled and bubbled in the birdbath. A breeze played with the damp wisps of unruly hair around her face and cooled her overheated skin.

Mom's masterpiece, her fairytale fortress. Alive and in full bloom.

"I am Mr. Aaron's gardener." So this was the work of Jacob Carver, her godfather's caretaker. Bless him. He'd never stopped caring for the hidden gardens.

She had to walk. To see it all. Take it in. And maybe remember her godfather, Uncle Aaron. A concrete patio covered most of the expanse around the birdbath. Low shrubs lined both sides of the white concrete walkway and flared out in front of her. Other walks of fieldstone began

at the edge of the patio and meandered into four directions before they disappeared into the landscape. Not a single weed invaded the lawns, and not a blade of grass had escaped trimming.

One of the stone walks circled a pond full of plump goldfish and wide lily pads. Another led to a fountain of water falling into a rock-strewn brook. The water gurgled its way to somewhere she couldn't see.

It was Eden imagined, and it reminded her of the oil painting hanging in her parents' bedroom. She shook her head. Maybe the artist had seen this place.

Staying on the concrete walkway, she wandered in awe until the oddly familiar sight of a white granite bench beneath a wide, rose-covered arbor came into view. And a few feet away, a gazebo nestled in a hammock of gnarled oaks and surrounded by flowerbeds. For a few seconds, barely breathing, she hesitated, absorbing it all. Hadn't Mom told her she'd been here before? Lexi's eyes misted with tears. This was where they'd found Uncle Aaron.

"I am *Mr. Aaron's gardener."* Again, Jacob Carver's words of Saturday evening broke in waves on the shore of her mind. The work of Jacob's hands nodded at her from the heart of every blossom, from the face of each serene pool. So alive, so loved and cared for.

She went to the bench and curled up on its smooth, cool surface. As if Uncle Aaron had expected her and prepared this place for her, she remembered. His kind face, gentle gray eyes looking into hers.

She turned to lie on her back and gaze at the scented pink and white tangle above her.

Must have been thunder. A moment ago, and lasting nearly a minute, a low growling rumble sounded close by as the ground beneath Ridge's feet seemed to roll. But he looked up at a clear cerulean blue sky. No noise or movement followed, and Ridge finished his fruitless search then stomped through thick brush, retracing his steps to the south wall to find Jenni.

"Get off me! Ouch!"

Jenni's voice wafted from somewhere in front of him. A few feet away, he stopped short. Grumbling with every breath, Jenni was bent over, pulling at something that seemed to be crawling up her jeans. She looked up at him from between splayed blue-jeaned legs. Her blonde ponytail swung in an arc, sunglasses dangled, eyebrows met in the middle, lips set in a grim, upside-down bow, and sweat dripped from the end of her nose.

"What!"

He couldn't help but laugh. "Oh, boy, what mangled you?"

"I was attacked by a roving band of wild rose monsters." She scowled and rubbed the scratches on her arm as he helped pull the thorn-covered vine from her pant leg.

"There are plenty of those around here. They got me too." Ridge chuckled as he pulled away more thorns and burs.

"Ouch! Be careful. There's skin under there."

"Okay, okay, I think you're thorn-free." He looked at the nearly full bottle of water hanging from her belt. "Better drink some of that."

He unscrewed the top on his own water bottle and downed almost half. "Did you find anything?"

"No, but I about got knocked off my feet with that thunder a few minutes ago. Sure doesn't look like rain. Did you feel it? And have you heard anything out of Lexi?"

"Yeah, I felt it. Don't know what the noise was, but I'm not so sure

it was thunder. Too much blue sky. And, nope, I haven't heard a word out of her. Let's backtrack to where she's supposed to be." He wiped away the sweat trickling down the back of his neck. The short break helped, and they pushed through the brambles along the rear wall to the northeast corner.

"I can't believe how big this wall is." Jenni swatted at a gnat and stayed close to Ridge. "And I don't mean just tall either. It must have taken *years* to finish it."

Ridge nodded. "Looks like they used native rock. There's a place at the end of the island where the bluffs have had a lot of rock taken out. That's probably where these boulders came from."

They made the turn at the corner and their shoulders touched. He lengthened his stride, the image of Lexi, alone, standing near the drapes in the mansion fogging his head. The woman was always getting herself into trouble. Why would today be different? They should have stayed together to do this.

Ridge studied the area. "All the brush is intact as far as I can see. Doesn't look like she got this far." His gut seized. No trace of her. No evidence she'd set foot here. He'd been so certain she would have made it this far by now. And she was nowhere in sight. His fists tightened into bulges of knuckled flesh as they continued trekking beside the north wall. Where was she?

Jenni spotted the break before he did and pointed ahead. "Ridge, look at the wall. Up there. There's an opening!"

Jenni stayed several paces behind as he plunged ahead, sweat blurring his vision. Half dreading Jenni was right and worried about what they'd find, he wielded his machete, chopping his way through the green and brown thicket.

Machete mid-swing, Ridge stopped, gawked at the gap in the wall, and gave a low whistle. "No way." Railroad tracks, giant rollers, and massive ball bearings? He allowed himself two seconds to stare at the mechanics beneath the stone wedge then motioned for Jenni to follow him. "She's already in there. Let's go!"

A wary expression covered Jenni s face and disbelief filled her eyes. Ridge stepped through the open space with her close behind him. He pushed through the evergreens and was dumbfounded by a panorama that rivaled a big city botanical garden.

"Wow! So much for this being a dead garden. It's about as alive as you can get." He glanced at Jenni and grinned. Jaw dropped, eyes wide, speechless, she looked as surprised as he was. But Lexi was nowhere in sight.

The pain in his gut didn't let up until they found her moments later. Dark hair spilling over the snowy-white granite bench, she lay beneath a wide, whitewashed arbor, knees pulled up, her eyes fixed on the roses entwined overhead. And he stood there like an imbecile as his hands unfisted and his heart quit fighting with his ribcage.

Jenni shook her head and pulled her cellphone from her jeans pocket, poking Ridge's arm with her finger. "You *did* bring your cellphone, right?"

"Just so happens . . ." Ridge set his iPhone camera to video and panned the sight on the bench as Jenni aimed and clicked her own. He chuckled and shook his head. "I had a feeling we might get a few memorable shots on this mission."

Too quiet. He stopped panning and lowered the cell. Well, was she going to smile or snarl at him?

Chapter Eighteen

In his office, Greyson nursed a cup of black coffee, exhausted from no sleep after his four-hour "Cohen research venture" early this morning. It was nearly ten o'clock before he felt reenergized.

He needed to free himself up, clear the way to continue making plans for the break-in without more pressure than he was already under. He pulled up his calendar and checked his schedule. No major adjustments. This week was light on appointments.

He called Janet in and instructed her to clear his calendar for the next three days. She tilted her head and shot him a disapproving look. But her expression quickly changed to downright contrite as he dictated the note to his father that he'd be flying into Boston tomorrow on a two-day business trip.

At noon, Greyson changed into jeans and a tee-shirt and left the office. He grabbed a quick bite of lunch from his favorite bistro and squeezed the arm of his waitress as he left, still chuckling at the way she'd squirmed beneath his grip. But she'd appreciate the generous tip he'd left before he headed out to rent a car.

In less than an hour, he drove away from the rental firm in the driver's seat of a new Lexus. On a reconnaissance trip to take photos of the front and sides of the Christensen place, he'd also check out fencing, trees, bushes, entrances. Anything that might become a snare to his plan to break into the Christensen house had to be noted.

His eyes darted from the road to the rearview mirror, his mind wandering, thinking of the past weekend. Good thing he had switched cars. After recognizing Lexi Christensen in the library, he'd taken a risk driving the Porsche by her two-story house late Saturday night. His red sports car stood out like a beacon among the islanders' cars.

Now in the rental Lexus with its heavily tinted windows, he was less conspicuous. He'd charged the rental fees to his law firm and paid the storage costs for the Porsche in cash. If he ever needed an excuse for having to lease, well, the Porsche was in the shop for repairs.

Late Sunday evening he did a final drive-by and couldn't believe his luck. Apparently some people weren't too worried about their privacy. It had been easy to pinpoint the girl's upstairs bedroom. No closed drapes, no shutters, no shades in the windows. As he passed her house, he'd clearly seen her pacing back and forth, phone in hand, oblivious to whoever or whatever was outside.

Greyson slowed the car and parked in a secluded spot a block away from the Christensen house. He put on a dark blue long-sleeved shirt that displayed a reasonable facsimile of the local electric company's logo.

He tucked the blue shirt into his jeans and tightened his belt. It was time to get this done. Greyson glanced into the rearview mirror . . . and stopped breathing. Not . . . quite . . . time. A patrol car pulled up and parked in the street several houses behind him. He shrunk down into the driver's seat and moved the rearview mirror to watch. Two uniformed officers exited their vehicle and walked up the driveway of a house, paused, probably knocking on the front door, and then disappeared from view.

Greyson relaxed. They were there for some other reason. He'd wait a few minutes to make sure, but it didn't look as if they were interested in him.

The biggest snag he'd run into so far was Sangster not arriving until late last night. Not having the house and cellphones bugged was a huge disadvantage. Sangster would be working on that today, along with a dozen other things, to prepare to place the eavesdropping devices and more. Sangster assured him he'd have everything set by tonight—set, but not working, as he had to fly back to Boston early tomorrow morning.

Greyson wouldn't be covered for his planned break-in, a risk he was willing to take. As soon as Sangster got the bugs installed and activated, the detective would be monitoring them from his Boston office and report in with the Christensen family's activities.

By doing his own drive-bys, he'd avoided involving Sangster—in this part of his plan anyway. Yeah, he took a lot of chances, but he was careful. Having Sangster leave as soon as possible was best.

Movement. Shadows reflected in the mirror. He let out a breath. Nothing to worry about as the two officers left the house and neighborhood by the way they'd come.

Get this done. Greyson pulled a hardhat and toolbox from the backseat and left the Lexus. Nantucket Electric Company had just gained a new lineman. A surge of power plowed through his muscles, and he couldn't help exaggerating his brazen saunter through the yards, scrutinizing the poles like a pro.

He donned the hardhat and made his way to an electric pole directly behind the Christensen residence. He made a pretense of checking the

pole and lines as he studied the grounds without interruption and used the voice-activated recorder in his shirt pocket for his notes. No one stopped him and not a soul questioned him.

Jenni's twitter of laughter wiggled its way into Lexi's reverie as she lay on the bench in the garden. She shaded her eyes and turned toward her friends—and grimaced. Photos! She'd been too overwhelmed to even think of pulling out her cellphone to photograph the gardens.

She twisted on the bench and sat up. "Sorry I didn't wait, but I figured you'd find me. Walking through that weird stone gate was like being sucked into a whirlpool. Yanked me in, and I couldn't leave. Can you believe this place?"

Before they could answer, she stood, looking beyond them, and punched the air with her forefinger. "Did you see the maze?"

"It really is amazing." Jenni eyed the flowered arbor and walkway.

"No, Jen, not that. This!" Lexi laughed, walked over, and stood between two privet bushes shaped into tall upright rectangles. "I think this is the maze Mom was talking about."

"Must be, because that's exactly what this is—a maze." Ridge came up behind her and put his hand on her shoulder.

Lexi slipped from beneath the disconcerting warmth of his hand and went through the entrance, out of sight behind the green shrubs. She rubbed at her shoulder and stuck her head out from behind the greenery. "I've seen pictures, but never thought I'd actually see one of these." She waggled her finger at them. "Well, are you two coming with me?"

Jenni shot a vivacious grin in Ridge's direction, her long ponytail swishing side-to-side. "Uh-uh. I've heard of people getting lost in those.

You two go on in if you want. I'll stay out here. Send up a flare if you get stuck. Surely *someone* will save you."

"Nope. If one of us goes, we all go. Come on." Lexi jogged back to the entrance and grabbed Jenni's arm. "Get behind her and shove, Ridge."

Ridge's lips quirked into a lopsided smile and he took another photo of the two of them pulling in opposite directions.

"Okay, I give, but we *are* leaving a trail." Jenni wedged herself between Ridge and Lexi.

You didn't have to do that, Jen. I'm staying out from between you two—or can't you tell?

Ridge picked up a twig. "You know, leaving a trail isn't such a bad idea. It is pretty monotonous in here."

Lexi studied the dense green shrubbery. "And at the risk of defacing a shrub or two . . ." She snapped a branch from the base of the hedge and handed it to Ridge. "Hansel and Gretel and pebbles and crumbs all over again."

"Not quite twenty-first century style." Ridge dropped the marker in the center of the path, pointing the broken end in the direction they headed. "But," he added, tapping his phone and grinning, "we've got the GPS in this thing to get us out of here anyway."

"Yeah, if you know how to use it. This better be worth it." Jenni wiped sweat from her forehead as they followed the twists and turns and dead-ends.

"It will be if we find what the gold key fits." Lexi pushed at her sunglasses and mopped her own face.

Ahead of Lexi, Ridge stopped in a clearing and stood with arms akimbo. "Looks like we've found the center of this puzzle."

"Or we've walked ourselves right into the middle of a new one."

Lexi stared at the protruding front of a small whitewashed structure set into the grass-covered rise behind it. Dark green holly bushes edged the base, and two cherubs, identical to those that held the birdbath, stood on either side of three concrete steps that led to a door. "What *is* that? A crypt, maybe?"

Jenni moved closer to Ridge. "Maybe, but wouldn't it be a lot bigger?"

Ridge closed the distance to the building. "I don't think it's a crypt, but you're right. If it was, it'd be bigger than this. This thing's built more like an old root cellar." His baseball cap came off, and he tunneled his fingers through his hair twice before he put it on again. "If it is, it's a pretty doggone fancy one." He glanced back at Lexi and beckoned.

Lexi went to the steps and took off her sunglasses. "A root cellar, huh? Okay, Einstein, how do you know about root cellars?"

"Hey, I'm serious." Ridge nudged her arm and flashed her a grin that weakened her knees. "My grandparents had one. Built it into a hill behind the house on their farm. I used to play in it when I was a kid—and mow the whole thing." He paced the front of the white structure as if sizing up the entrance. "The biggest difference here is the entry. This thing's got steps, a porch, an upright door, and it's downright ornate. Most root cellars are pretty ordinary and have slanted, near ground-level, double doors. You have to lift one of the doors, lay it back, and go down some steps to get in."

Jenni tucked wisps of hair behind her ears. "Why in the world would anybody put a root cellar way out here if they're using it for storing potatoes and stuff?"

Lexi looked in the direction of the house and nodded. "A body could starve to death by the time the fruits and roots were delivered to the kitchen." She smoothed her hand over the cold marble feathers of a cherub wing and shook her head. "It doesn't seem practical, but maybe there's a good reason for it."

Jenni plopped down on the lowest step near the railing. "I don't know about you two, but I'm hot and tired, and like it or not, I'm sitting for a while."

Lexi set her jaw. "Not me. This girl's not sitting this one out. I'm going in there."

Ridge jerked his head up. Cellphone camera in hand, he backed up, took two quick shots of the building, then aimed at Lexi. She stood beside the stone angel, her stomach flipping as he moved closer and put his arm around her shoulders, getting face-to-face with his silly grin.

"Okay, nutcase, we could try."

Chill! His arm around you doesn't mean a thing. Breathless, Lexi moved out from under his closeness, the warmth of him, before Jenni thought more of it than she should.

Ridge didn't seem to notice as he studied the door. "There's no lock. Probably nothing in there but fossilized fruits and vegetables, maybe a few rats and spiders."

Jenni leaned forward, staring at the pedestal beneath the statue to her right. "Wait a sec! This is weird . . . ."

Chapter Nineteen

Lexi sucked in a breath. Something was carved into the statue's base. A word? She knelt on the grass and traced the letters with trembling fingers, the ground, solid and reassuring beneath her shaky knees. "*Wisdom!* Jen, does the other one have anything written on it?"

"*Vigilance.* That's what's on this one."

But by the time Jen crouched to look, every word etched into the two statues—and on the rise of each step—had seared into Lexi's vision. Her head was in freefall, and she grabbed the railing. *Please, Lord, help. This is too much.*

"There's more than just 'wisdom' and 'vigilance' scratched into those pedestals." Ridge pointed at the top step and read the word engraved on each one. "*Prepare—The—Way*"

Ridge turned to look at her then Jenni turned her eyes to Lexi too. They stood, gawking at her. How could anyone feel strength and weakness at the same time? She gathered in the breath that had left in such a rush, got up from her knees, and went to stand beside the "Wisdom" angel. They knew; Lexi knew. Those words—every one of

them—reflected words from the parchment. She could have recited them from memory. Instead, she pulled the copy out of her pocket and unfolded it.

Jenni moved close and slipped her arm around Lexi's waist. Ridge looked over her shoulder. A cooling breeze followed a warm wave of gratitude, and she blinked hard, tears stinging her eyes as, heart pounding, she read.

"'A time shall come when they are hidden; be vigilant and wise as you prepare the way.' There couldn't be more obvious signs that we're close. We've got to go in. Something is there. I can feel it."

"All right, Sherlock, let's go." Ridge took her arm in his and pulled her to his side. She let herself revel in the firm comfort of his grip.

Behind them, Jenni chirped loud and clear, "You two go right ahead. I'll be out here keeping the angels company." She looked as if she was about to park herself on the top step again.

But what Jen said stopped Lexi in her tracks, Ridge with her. "Wait. We don't have any idea what we'll find inside this place. We've prayed about everything else, so . . ."

"It wouldn't be a bad idea to hang with the angels for a minute." Ridge took off his ball cap and dropped it over an up-stretched angel wing, then looked at her with an expression that held an invitation for her to pray.

Lexi bowed her head as the words came. "You've brought us this far, Lord. Thank you for being with us, leading us. Please show us what you want us to find and do." Lexi paused with a shiver of anticipation as Jenni spoke.

"Heavenly Father, all this seems to revolve around Lexi; please give her guidance."

Ridge cleared his throat then spoke, his voice warm, rich. "Thanks,

Lord. Keep us in your will, doing the right things. All in your name. Amen."

Lexi went up the steps to face the white door. Hand on the discolored brass handle, she pressed down and pushed. The door opened with an audible *click*, moving noiselessly inward.

"That was almost too easy." She let go of the handle and stepped back.

A wave of cool air and the pungent scent of earthy dampness washed over her, and she crossed the threshold into eerie, quiet darkness. Beside her, Ridge pulled out his flashlight. The yellow beam splayed across the walls, floor, and ceiling, illuminating cracks and creating ghosts of undulating shadows. Shelves lined parts of the cellar, and well-worn flat stones covered the floor, every edge perfectly matching the stone beside it.

Swarms of bright dust particles swirled in the beam of light as Ridge moved it along the walls. "This place is just as high-falutin' inside as it was outside. Looks to be about twenty-foot-square. The walls are different, and no root cellar I've ever seen had fieldstone floors."

Stones.

Preserve these stones; you are commanded to.

The words raced through Lexi's mind. *Fieldstones? No. Stones.* There must be a ton of stones in this place, but the parchment wasn't talking about the stones beneath her feet. Pure anticipation kicked her heartbeat up a notch. "The floor looks a lot older than the brick in the walls. Why?"

Ridge pointed the flashlight toward one of the thick wood support beams near the door. The light illuminated an old gas lantern hanging on a chunky rusted nail. Lexi lifted the lamp from its hanger and heard the slosh of fluid inside.

"Sounds like it still has some oil in it." Jenni still stood in the doorway, fidgeting.

Ridge played the light over the shelves and around the room. "Too bad we didn't bring matches, and I don't see any. Looks like we're stuck with the flashlight."

Lexi took a few steps and nearly fell over a round basket. Several stacks of them, woven with narrow strips of shaped wood held together with wire, sat piled in a corner. Her eyes followed the bobbing light. Shelves held rows of quart- and pint-sized glass jars containing some unknown edible, probably not so edible anymore. Maybe those jars held vegetables and fruit intended for Aaron's family.

"Well, they're not quite fossilized." Lexi tossed the comment toward Ridge then pointed at an ancient wood sea chest standing in a corner. "Let's take a look in there." She grinned at him. "Never know what you might find in chests."

"Nope." Ridge repositioned the flashlight. "Me or you?"

"I'll try it." Excitement rippled through her as he held the light high. She knelt and fought with the stubborn lid.

"Need some help?"

"No, I've got it."

"Watch out for fat little four-legged, long-tailed things." From the safety of the threshold, Jenni's cute accent stretched things into *thangs*.

"Easy for you to say, girl, standing over there ready to run for it." Lexi lifted the lid, halfway expecting an attack of squeaky mice as she propped the top against the wall. She gingerly rummaged through a stack of musty old drapes and blankets.

Ridge looked over her shoulder. "There's nothing, not anything alive anyway."

After the experience with her cedar chest, Lexi inspected the top and sides and tapped on the bottom. "No. Nothing here that the key would open, no papers, and not a hint of a hiding place." Disappointed, she dropped the lid and stood, wondering where to look next.

"I sort of think this is a bust." Ridge moved the light to follow her.

"So far." Lexi watched her animated shadow silhouette against the wall several feet away. What was that? She stopped moving. The wall looked odd, really strange, as her gaze roamed over the rough topography. Newer brickwork showed uneven ridges. Hesitating, she inhaled a slow, jagged breath. A familiar pattern emerged, formed with bricks similar yet different from the rest.

The back of her neck tingled, and her heart looked for a way out of her ribcage. The symbol. It seemed to lift away from the brickwork, float toward her.

The light wandered away from the wall.

"Stop! Wait, Ridge. There! Something's different about those bricks. Can you shine the light right there?" Lexi pointed, waving away cobwebs glowing gold in the ray of light. She went, irresistibly drawn toward the center of the wall as Ridge focused the light over the bricks.

Jenni hadn't budged from her spot. "Doesn't look like much of anything to me. For Pete's sake, be careful. You have no idea what kind of spiders are in there. Those webs are everywhere."

"Take it easy." Ridge held the light steady while batting away webs. "She's found something. Looks like there might be a couple of loose bricks." He stepped closer.

"It's more than that." Lexi moved to the side to give him a better view and glanced at him over her shoulder. "Can you see it yet? It's the star of David." She grabbed her cell and took three photographs of the wall.

Jenni had braved her way into the room. "Wow, I see it! Somebody made that with the bricks? Unbelievable."

"Very cool, the way it was done." Ridge drew out the words as he

slid the light back and forth over the brickwork.

"Wait!"

The beam of light halted, motionless in Ridge's hand. Lexi stood close to the wall, scanning the bricks, slowly sweeping those that were close to eye level. Her gaze reached the center of the star, and the shadows changed. There was an indentation between two of the bricks.

She picked up a stave from a broken fruit basket near her foot and scraped the webs away from the barely protruding edge of the brick. "Ridge, can you focus the light here?"

The brick was in the middle of the octagonal center of the star. Could those two equilateral triangles indicate an opening? A thrill scattered through her. Cautious, hands damp from perspiration, she pushed at the brick. It gave slightly with her nudge, sending a miniature dust storm of dry mortar to the ground.

Ridge took a step closer, shining the light over the area where Lexi worked. Using both hands, she put her fingernails into the narrow slots at each end of the loose brick, wiggling and prying, flinching at the way her nails scraped against it.

Yes! She gradually worked the brick out of the wall until she held it in her hands.

"That's one." She chewed on her upper lip, trying to rein in her anticipation, and laid the brick on the floor beside her. Nerves edgy, she worked to free the next brick, sliding it out with relative ease.

"Can you see what's in there?" Jenni had ventured closer and stood beside Ridge, both of them all but breathing down her neck.

Lexi laughed. "Now who's impatient? I can't see a thing yet, but it won't be long."

Ridge chuckled, and the two backed off as he steadied the light.

"That should do it." Lexi took the last two of the rectangular red blocks out of the way and added them to the stack on the floor. The opening gaped at her like a toothless grimace. She stood back, brushing dust from her hand, then took a series of photos.

A long, drawn-out "Wow!" came from behind the flashlight, and Lexi followed Ridge's stare. He had trained the light directly into the gap and caught the reflected glimmer of bright gold.

"Can I have the flashlight for a minute?" Lexi stuck her hand out behind her without looking. "Today, maybe?" She wiggled her fingers as he finally placed the light into her hand.

She aimed the beam into the wall. The bricks had been a façade. Behind the first wall, a second wall faced her, constructed of the same stone as the floor they stood on. But built into it, a deep, wide niche held a large wooden box with a gold-colored latch, and it sat atop something else.

They took more photos, using all three of their cellphones, before Lexi memorized the sight inside the opening then gave the flashlight back to Ridge. Plunging both hands into the void, she grasped the heavy box and, breathless, inched it carefully toward her through the opening.

"I think . . . we have found . . . what that key opens."

"That is one awesome box." Ridge fixed the flashlight's beam on the box, staring at it in rapt fascination.

Tears bit the back of Lexi's eyes, and she drew in a breath of pure appreciation. Even covered with dust, it was beautiful.

"So, smile!" Jenni lifted her cell and clicked. "Sans the gold top, it looks exactly like a miniature of your cedar chest." Lexi blinked hard at Jenni's matter-of-fact statement.

Hands trembling, Lexi gently blew what dust she could off the top and rubbed the rest away with the hem of her shirt. Jenni was right. Overlaid with a paper-thin layer of gold and decorated with cherubim,

palm trees, and open flowers, the top of this small replica looked exactly like the top of her cedar chest.

"It's in perfect condition." Grateful for the frequent whir of Jenni's cell-camera, Lexi lifted the box, turning it. The sides and base shone with the deep burnished luster of newly finished wood.

The key-shaped notch in the center of its side begged to be opened. Digging the gold key out of her jeans pocket, Lexi obliged. The key fit into the lock like butter melting into warm bread. Turning the key clockwise, the lock gave a satisfying *click*.

The warmth of Ridge's hand on her arm stopped her. "It's risky opening it in here. You could drop it. Don't you want to take it outside where you can see?"

She'd been so caught up in wanting to open the box, she hadn't considered the fact she could hardly see, and her hands were shaking. Lexi relocked the box and slid the key back into her pocket. He'd probably stopped a disaster. She could have dropped it, damaged it, or lost whatever it held.

Lexi couldn't let go of the box, but Ridge already had the light poised on the book that still lay in the niche. He looked at her with a smile that clearly asked if she'd like him to retrieve it. He could have jumped in and not waited; Lexi loved him for his patience with her. "Thanks."

Jenni held the flashlight as Ridge drove his hands into the opening and pulled out a large, dusty, leather-bound volume. He traded it to Jenni for the light.

"Nothing else behind that wall, was there?" Jenni asked as they walked out of the root cellar into the heat and sunshine.

They'd been so enthralled with the box and book, they hadn't checked further. Lexi glanced up at Ridge. "I didn't see anything else, but do you want to take another look?"

"Sure." He nodded and walked back inside, lifting the flashlight, ready to make a second inspection. Lexi sat on the top step and put the box on her lap, picking at the webs on her shirt.

Ridge sported a somber grin as he sauntered back through the doorway. "You don't want to know what else is in there."

"We missed something? What?" Lexi shaded her eyes to look at him.

"Only a nest of big fuzzy arachnids is all." His eyes sparked with the humor Lexi loved. "Nah, just kidding. Nothing else in there."

"Oaf!" She shot him a frown and brushed away more dust and webs.

Jenni wiped perspiration from her face. "There has to be some shade around here. It's like a sauna outside compared to how cool it was in there. Give me a tree and a breeze—either, anywhere!"

Ridge pointed to a spot opposite the way they'd come into the clearing. Amazing shade trees, as large as they could be on this windswept island, cast welcome shadows, enticing them to the grassy area like an oasis. "How about over there?"

Lexi stood. "Looks good to me." She headed toward the thick green lawn that embraced a large oval pool. A waterfall on the far bank gurgled over smooth stones, ripples and eddies swirling outward. Beneath the trees, several small concrete pads edged with blue, purple, and red summer flowers held white benches. A white-columned water fountain offered a promise to quench their thirst. Fragrant star-jasmine climbed over a granite boulder close to the waterfall, where several ducks protested the invasion of their privacy.

"It's okay, guys. Take it easy. We come in peace." Ridge took a

package of saltines from his shirt pocket.

"Boy Scout." Lexi tilted her head at him.

He held up his hands as if in self-defense. "What? So they're left over from lunch."

Walking closer to the uneasy birds, he scattered crumbs on the grass. The ducks pounced on the crackers as if they hadn't eaten in a week.

Lexi watched the line of snow-white ducks trail behind Ridge. "Looks like you've made a flock of new friends."

He turned and shook a warning finger at them. At his heels, the lead bird instantly dropped in her tracks, quacking wildly and flapping for balance. Jenni and Lexi doubled over with laughter.

"This book weighs a ton." Jenni held the dusty volume in both hands then placed it on one of the shaded benches. "Wonder what's in it. It looks old and pretty well used."

"It could be a log or a diary, but it's probably just household records." Lexi placed the box beside the book and eyed the fountain. "Anybody thirsty? We're going to die of a heat stroke instead of curiosity if we don't get some water soon." But that might be a fib. If she didn't open that box soon . . .

"I hope it works." Jenni dabbed at the sweat on her forehead as Ridge twisted the shiny chrome handle. The fountain responded with a sparkling curve of water.

The last to drink, Lexi rinsed the dirt from her hands, splashed cool water over her face, then attempted to dry off with the sleeve of her tee-shirt. Okay. Deep breath. Deal with the butterflies. But her stomach still whirled as she returned to the bench. She sat, rubbed her hands against her jeans, then picked up the chest and held it in her lap. Her thumbs smoothed over the satiny wood finish, and she couldn't stop the shiver that scattered through her.

Ridge lay flat on his back on the grass in front of the bench and took off his sunglasses. Jenni stripped off the black band holding her honey-blonde hair, redid her ponytail in two swift motions, then sat next to Lexi.

"Well?" Ridge flashed a grin up at her. "Exactly how long are you going to make us wait?"

Lexi squelched a bubble of laugher. "You two are about to bust with wanting to know what's in here." And if she didn't open the box soon, *she'd* explode. "Okay. Chill and pay attention." She dug the key from her pocket, and in seconds that dragged through endless time, she flipped the antique latch and lifted the lid.

Chapter Twenty

The sun poked ragged, leaf-shaped shadows through the trees onto the grass around where they sat beside the pond. Jenni looked over Lexi's shoulder, and Ridge propped up on his elbows to watch.

More connections. Lexi gripped the raised lid, heart fluttering as she held her breath and lifted an edge of the soft blue-velvet layering.

With a breathy whistle, Ridge leapt to his feet. "Looks like the same soft cloth as in the other little box."

Jenni shook her head at him as he rounded the bench. "Vel . . . vet, Ridgey; it's called velvet."

Ridge bent over Lexi's shoulder, the warmth of his face close to hers.

Was *this* what the parchment spoke of? She stared into the box, then dug deeper, exploring the contents, lifting, holding, opening, pulling breaths that seared her throat. Her hands burned with the heat of what she touched. From the warming sun? Her vivid imagination?

Jenni gripped Lexi's arm. "That actually looks *real*."

"Real or not, this . . . is . . . incredible." Lexi fought for every word against the paralyzing awe that seized her voice. Never had she seen

or dreamed she'd ever lay eyes on anything so unique. Dizzy, her head spun with the idea of what she held in her hands.

Ridge walked back around the bench and stood in front of Lexi. "There's nothing fake about the stuff in that chest." He flattened his palms against his forehead and laced his fingers into his thick hair, pure admiration in his tone.

"It's all very beautiful, but I don't think we can be so sure." Jenni threw out the challenge, but her voice indicated she thought Ridge could be right.

"Why would someone go to all this trouble if it wasn't the real thing?" The angled edges of the wood chest dug into Lexi's fingers as her hands remained clamped around it.

She lifted her eyes, looking from Jenni to Ridge, and had to laugh at their expressions. Her own probably wasn't much different. "Thanks, guys. A lot of help and support you are."

Laughing helped, leveled out her tidal swing of emotions. She restored everything back inside the box, then closed and locked it. Cramming the key into her pocket, she put the box on the bench beside her. "So, where do we go from here? I don't know of any way we can deal with this without some advice."

"I think your parents know a lot more about all this than we think they do." Ridge paced the length of the bench and back. "I don't see that you have any choice but to tell them, show them everything. You know they'll help—whether or not this is real." He stopped and his eyes, filled with sincerity, fixed on Lexi's.

Jenni stood and stretched and inched to Ridge's side. "Umm, your mom still wanted to talk again, tell you more when your dad was home, didn't she?"

Lexi nodded and tore her gaze away from Ridge's hazelnut eyes, her nails biting into her palms. She hadn't said anything to either of them about the monster rift between her and her parents. Should she? Living with it was hard enough. No. She couldn't talk about it, and now sure wasn't the time. "I want to hear all they have to say, and *I* sure don't know how to go about seeing if this is authentic. I need to show them." She looked at her watch then deliberately sent Jenni a grin. "We'll be pushing it to get home by lunchtime. Think we can find our way out of here?"

A little after noon, Lexi parked the Mini in the driveway behind Mom's van. Dad was home for lunch, his big black SUV parked beside the van. So it would be now that she'd tell her parents.

I trust you for what I need to say, Lord, how to explain.

With a musty blanket from the root cellar sea chest draped over the box and book, she walked around the house into the backyard, mind roiling. How was she going to explain what she carried? What would she say to them? She went up the steps onto the porch then hesitated, staring through the screen door before she went into the kitchen.

And where, exactly, was her trust, her faith? More prayer. Throat dry, she sucked in a breath and hugged the stinky mound to her chest.

Dad sat on a stool at the counter, Mom beside him, a glass of juice in her hand.

"Ah . . . hi, Mom, Dad. We need to talk."

Her dad stopped mid-chew and plopped his sandwich onto his plate.

Mom's smile took a decidedly southern turn as she looked at Lexi, and put her glass down hard. "I think so . . . ."

Both of them gaped at her. What was their problem? Lexi looked

down at herself.

Oh. No wonder. She looked like a mini-train wreck. An instant mental image flashed through her mind. Sweaty, filthy jeans, scratched-up arms, windblown hair with who-knew-what decorating it, and holding a smelly old blanket that covered a stack of something unknown.

Then their expressions struck her funny, and she laughed. Dad guffawed, but she couldn't read Mom's smile. "Guess I'm some kinda sight, huh?"

"Where have you *been*?" her father asked, still chuckling.

Mom's gaze traveled to Lexi's feet, her faint smile fading. "For heaven's sake, leave those shoes out on the porch and wash your hands. Then you can tell us what's going on."

At the mini-interrogation and barked instruction, Lexi suppressed a flare of angry impatience, her laughter instantly quenched.

"Can't wait." Dad sat back, shook his head, and crossed his arms. His gray eyes reflected more patience than his words, and quickly tempered her reaction.

"Long story." She dried her hands and watched her mother's expression change as she tried to mask her emotions. Lexi removed the blanket from around the book and box, laid them on the maple table, and bent to take off her shoes. The blanket slipped to the floor.

Gilly ambled over and nosed at her hair and face. "Hey, Gilly-boy." Grabbing the fallen blanket in his teeth like a prize, he dragged it to a corner and curled up on it. Lexi gave him a quick ear rub and turned in time to see her dad get up from his seat. Had he seen the gold on the box? He walked to the table, leaning close, studying it. She halted mid-step and waited.

With his finger, he traced the edge of one of the gilded palm trees adorning the top of the chest. "Molly." He paused. "Molly, come look at the top of this." He gazed at Lexi and eyed her with such a serious, thoughtful expression that her heart turned over.

But she locked down, staying right where she was as Mom went to the table. The view Lexi had of her mother's profile portrayed unconcealed amazement. Or was she appalled? Her mother grasped the table edge for a few seconds, and Dad put a steadying hand on her shoulder. "I don't believe what I'm seeing, Jason. This . . . this . . ."

Dad cleared his throat. "Well, honey, I think we're ready to listen to what you have to say." Mom, wordless, sat on the bench at the table.

Lexi nodded. "I have to get some things from my room first."

She retrieved the cedar-chest-envelope along with what she'd found in Northbrick House on Friday, and returned to the kitchen.

Sitting opposite them at the table, Lexi's silent prayers were fervent. *How to begin, how to get through this.* For a few seconds, nothing but the rhythmic tick of the clock on the wall above her head and her own erratic breathing filled her ears. The atmosphere in the room had changed, charged with tension that hung like a thick veil between past and present, as if this single moment would forever alter her life.

God, help me do this right.

Gently, she pushed the journal and chest aside. She laid out the paper from the envelope, the roll of paper containing the parchment, the silver key, and the small box that had held the gold key. She kept the ivory carving in her hand, smoothing it between her thumb and fingers, looking down at it as she considered what she'd say.

She shifted her eyes from the carving to her parents, but their faces held nothing to reassure her.

Begin at the beginning and tell them everything.

She told them. From start to finish. Her fascination with Northbrick House. Wanting to stop the town from condemning and destroying the

house and why. Finding the envelope, going into the mansion, what she'd found there, and her library research about Northbrick's history and ownership. How Jenni and Ridge were involved. She explained the meeting with Jacob and Malea Carver Saturday night, told them of the scriptures in Exodus, and about finding the gate Mom had spoken of. She filled in as many details as she could, including her feelings and why she hadn't told them before.

She'd shoved a verbal avalanche down on them. Not waiting for questions or comments, Lexi moved everything she brought from her room aside and centered the larger chest between them. She took the gold key from her jeans pocket, inserted it into the keyhole, and turned the box toward her mother.

"Will you open it, Mom?"

Color rose in her mother's cheeks as her fingers closed around the key, and she hesitated. Lexi watched her blink back tears and study the design that duplicated the top of the cedar chest upstairs.

His elbow on the table, Dad pinched his chin between his thumb and forefinger as he looked at her. "I know you probably don't remember, but it was Aaron Cohen who gave you your cedar chest. He had it specially made for you in Boston, and he brought it to you on your third birthday—along with Gilly."

Lexi sat back against the cushioned bench as more of the puzzle fell into place.

Mom hadn't taken her eyes from the box. With an almost somber expression, her mother twisted the key in the lock, lifted the hinged cover, and laid it back against the tabletop. Then in a slow, deliberate move, she turned the box back to face Lexi.

Lexi reached into the chest, pulled up the soft rectangle of velvet, and smoothed it flat on the table. A stunned silence weighed like lead in the sunny kitchen as her mother and dad studied what she began to lay on the velvet.

Lexi stole quick looks at them. What did they think and feel? Maybe her going into the old house didn't surprise them, but what she spread out in front of them should.

Numb. That summed up her feelings when she'd first opened the box, and it did again now. Shattering the glass-fragile silence, she fastened her eyes on her father. "It looked authentic to us. What do you think, Dad?"

The handsome architecture of her father's face softened and he shook his head. "Honey, at first glance it looks genuine, but I think you know it'll take a lot more than a glance to determine if it is."

Mom had set her face into a familiar noncommittal mask, and whatever gripped her, tightened and held on as she stared. She didn't look open to accept any of this.

Dad got up and moved to sit at the head of the table. Lexi searched his face for some clue of what he thought, but he wore an expressionless façade. He ran a hand through his steel-gray hair and looked from Lexi to her mother.

"We need to think and pray about all of this, Lexi." He delivered his words softly, but with even firmness. "What you've found could well be extremely valuable. On the surface it appears authentic enough to warrant being checked out by an expert. But it will take time." He sighed, paused for a few seconds, and then locked his eyes on Lexi's.

"There's more to this than you realize, many more things we need to explain as well as things we will have to do, even if what you found isn't what it seems. Meanwhile, I suggest we find a safe place for this . . ." He tapped the box. ". . . until we can arrange for an appraisal." He raised questioning eyebrows at her.

She swallowed hard. What "things" would they have to do, and why? Silent seconds ticked by. Dad didn't say more and seemed to be waiting for her response.

She nodded. "I'll take care of it." He gave her a knowing smile, and a flush of heat crept into her cheeks. So he knew all about the little hiding place in her room. Across from her, Mom relaxed a little.

The insistent ring of the kitchen phone interrupted them, and Dad answered it. He smiled in recognition of the voice and nodded at Mom. "Yes. How are you, Bill?"

Bill probably meant their neighbor, Bill Delaward. He'd recently taken on the job of Neighborhood Crime Watch Captain and had called to talk to Dad several times since then.

"No, I haven't noticed anyone or anything unusual." He paused. "Is that right?" Dad's smile waned. "Okay. Good to know. I'll think about calling them. Thanks. I'll keep you posted."

He hung up the phone. "Bill's taking his new job seriously. He said he saw someone take their time driving by here several times. He hadn't thought much of it, but changed his mind when the car stopped and he saw the driver open a window and aim a camera at our house. Bill couldn't get a plate number. Newer car, blue, possibly a Lexus. The windows were tinted, and the car left before Bill could pull out his binoculars. He did say he got enough of a glimpse of the man to see he had sharp features and a dark mustache, but that was all. The camera hid his face most of the time. Bill felt it was unusual enough to call us, and suggested we let law enforcement know."

Mom shrugged. "I don't really see any particular need for us to be concerned. It's most likely a real estate salesman who wants to try to get us to sell. It's happened before."

But Lexi's blood parted company with her complexion. Sharp features. Could that mean a beaky nose? And a dark mustache? That driver might have been the attorney. Who else with that description would be driving by her house and taking pictures? He'd stormed out of Northbrick spouting about wanting what he thought she had.

A cold chill of understanding shivered through her. Jacob Carver had been right. By going into Northbrick, she may have put her whole family in danger.

"Dad, maybe you should go ahead and call the police." Lexi's voice faltered then strengthened. "I haven't told you about what else happened. I didn't think about it until now."

She told them about her close encounter with the man inside the Northbrick mansion and her certainty that the same man had been in the library on Saturday morning. "We found out who he was when we checked the business yellow pages on my iPad and saw the picture of him in his law firm's business ad. It wasn't hard to put everything together; too much matched for it to be coincidence." She finished by telling them of Jacob Carver's warning.

"Greyson's son." Dad's words were a guttural whisper; his face went pale, jaw muscles set as her parents exchanged glances. Was he angry? What did he know? Her father reached in his pocket for his cellphone and called his secretary. He'd be taking the rest of the afternoon off. His second call put the Nantucket Police Department on notice that there'd been a threat of break-in. Details of what happened were recorded and contact information taken. They'd be in touch.

What a crazy Monday. It was getting late and every muscle and bone in Lexi's body ached, exhaustion pulling out what little energy she had left. Within an hour, a detective had called. NPD had assigned two men to watch the house that night and to check periodically for the balance

of the week.

Stress had drained the color from her parents' faces and left deepened worry lines. Had it been her imagination that the tension between the three of them changed? They'd involved her as Dad made several other calls and formed plans about how he'd handle the chest. Before Lexi finally went upstairs, the lessened stress ended in hugs, with Mom near tears.

That had been over an hour ago. It was a step closer to peace, but with her mind full of all that happened, she was probably in for a night of tossing, turning, and little, if any, sleep.

She hadn't waited until morning to make calls to Jenni and Ridge. She'd let them know how her talk had gone with her parents, as well as about the surveillance of her house. She'd also spent time searching the Internet for sites focusing on the Temple in Jerusalem. Now her mind was slush, not the time to do any more heavy thinking.

Ready for bed, she turned out the lights and knelt on the window seat to push the curtains aside. A cooling breeze sifted through the screen, ruffling her hair and caressing her face.

Thanks, Lord, for helping me get through today, and please keep us safe tonight. I love you.

As long as no lights were on behind her, no one could see her there. She was satisfied the gold-topped case was safe, and no one would care about the old journal she had stuck in the drawer of her nightstand.

The unmarked police car Dad described was parked across the street a few houses down from their white Cape Cod home. She'd noticed it earlier and breathed easier knowing someone else watched while they slept.

She left her bedroom door slightly ajar and climbed into bed before sending up more thankful prayers, along with a few petitions. At least

God could make sense out of all this. She certainly couldn't.

Somewhere between the grays of drowsiness and the Technicolor dreams of deep sleep, she remembered she hadn't given Dad his cellphone back. She'd used it while her own was charging earlier. His phone now lay on her nightstand, and for a tick of time, she thought she really should take it to him.

Chapter Twenty-One

Greyson Quinn's nerves were near the snapping point as he left home. He clamped a hand against his chest, heart drumming an odd rhythm beneath. The muscles of his jaw twitched with his frown. This was no time for another anxiety attack.

Relax! But the self-reprimand didn't settle his heartbeat or banish his twitch. *Slow, deep breaths, Greyson, and think about where you are on this.*

He glanced at his car's dashboard clock and forced himself to concentrate. Tuesday morning, five minutes past two, and he was as ready as he would ever be for an invasion of the Christensen house. The couple of pieces of meat laced with knock-out drugs he'd brought should take care of the Christensen's dog, the only dog he'd seen yesterday. The girl and her family would be sleeping, and he was right on schedule.

It had been late Monday afternoon when he'd turned in the rented Lexus and exchanged it for this black Ford Mustang. The sporty convertible was right for the job, even if he had to keep the top up. No lineman's shirt tonight—he'd blend with the darkness. He wore a long-sleeved black shirt, a pair of tight black jeans, a black baseball cap, slim

black-leather driving gloves, and black running shoes. A lightweight black ski mask was wedged into his pants pocket.

As soon as he gained entry to the house, he'd "quiet" the girl and search her bedroom for the box, looking further if necessary. Her parents didn't appear to be involved yet, so she'd have been careful about where she'd hidden it. He was prepared to do whatever he had to, but he *would* get what he wanted.

So far, so good. He gave himself a mental pat on the back. Slowing for a stop sign, he double-checked his watch against the car's clock. Two-fifteen. Greyson swatted a high-five against the steering wheel. Right where he wanted to be at precisely the right time. He smiled despite his aching head and dug an aspirin from his pocket. He downed it with a few sips of bottled water—and nearly missed his turn.

Turn left, idiot! He spun the wheel and rounded the corner. He'd almost bungled something as simple as entering the neighborhood! Streetlights cast an eerie glow onto the damp road. The yards were wide and deep, generously sized in this older area of town. Flowerbeds exploded from nearly every yard. He sniffed and rubbed his nose. The abundance of flowers could explain his headache. He adjusted the air-conditioner, moving the vents toward his face.

Lots of trust in these neighborhoods. Crime had never been much of a problem for Nantucket. People left windows open and not many bothered to lock their doors. The residents of the Christensen's SW Ocean Drive home would feel safe in the darkness of this early morning. Lucky for him. Greyson had lived here all his life, and as he'd plotted the break-in, he figured all that carelessness would work to his advantage.

His thoughts turned to the documents he'd found in Cohen's file. "None of this would be going on if the girl hadn't gotten there and torn up the floor before me!" The grumbled words reverberated inside the car.

THE STONEKEEPERS

The purring engine revved and the speedometer crept upward. Greyson rubbed at his achy temples and tried to eject disturbing images of what might happen if he got caught. Lifting his foot from the gas pedal, he allowed the car to slow as he maneuvered through the light mist. The final turn lay ahead.

Thin fog and clouds blotted out the white sliver that was left of the quarter moon. A splattering of rain threatened to wipe out his meticulous planning. Wet streets reflected two silvery swaths of light from the car's headlights. He slowed, turned onto Stanton Lane, and mentally clicked through the things on his list.

Only a five-inch hunting knife hung in its sheath on his belt. No firearm. With his black belt in the martial arts, he was sure of himself. The night-vision binoculars that already hung around his neck, would be useful. He used them on his frequent weekend hunting trips when scoping out game, the only time he carried a gun. A toolkit filled with miniature stainless steel tools. He probably wouldn't need them, but they'd make things easier if he ran into locked doors, which could happen considering what he was after.

He smoothed his hand over his shirt pocket, over the soft, folded cloth and a tiny vial of ether he'd use to insure no interruptions. The ether would be simple to administer, silent—first to the girl, then her parents if need be. It would give him time to look through the girl's room, closets, drawers, and if necessary, time to search the entire house.

Several parked cars lined the street, a couple too many, but he saw no sign of movement in or around any of them. Wouldn't hurt to do one more drive-by. Turning the headlights off, he approached the curve of SW Ocean Drive to pass the Christensen house—and changed his mind, gliding to a stop. Still too risky, too obvious. And he was too nervous. *Stick to the plan, Greyson.*

He backed into a driveway and turned around, switching the headlights on again. The road ahead was empty of anything living, except a stray cat. As black as his blueprint for burglary, the cat darted across the street in front of him.

Slamming his foot against the brake pedal, he instantly regretted the move. The combination of slick pavement and fast braking threw the Mustang into a noiseless sideway slide. He held his breath and kept constant pressure on the brake. The antilock braking system kicked in, pulsing beneath his foot as he desperately steered around a line of trashcans. The car hit the curb, missing a green hydrant by inches, then stopped beneath a streetlight. Shaking, he watched a black feline tail disappear into the bushes.

That cat had just used up one its nine lives, and Greyson's head pounded like Japanese drums. Hands locked on the steering wheel, he looked around. No lights came on, no heads popped out from behind closed doors, nothing amiss. Greyson gasped in a deep breath and pulled onto the road.

One street behind the Christensens', in front of a vacant home with a *For Sale* sign in the yard, he spotted a shadowed, convenient place to park. From there it was a straight shot to where he wanted to end up. He angled the Mustang in close to the curb and got out, not bothering to lock the car. Staying close to the edge of some scraggly hedges, he worked his way through the darkened backyard and headed toward the Christensens'.

Only a little farther. A spike of fear burned down his spine. The metallic taste in his mouth reminded him he could face steel bars if this went wrong, and dread hammered through his mind. But stronger, the echoed words from the threats on his life crashed against the sides of his head like the headache he battled: "We're watching . . . don't try to run

. . . don't even think about it."

He *had* to have the money he'd get from this. Wincing, he felt the punch to his side all over again. Pay off the debts, get the loan sharks off his back, and leave the country. Thoughts of the flashed gun surfaced. His few payments had been a pittance. What he owed had grown to well over $300,000, and if he didn't pay up . . . Dead man walking.

He shook himself. Get a grip. Concentrate. He stopped beside the shelter of a tree for a few seconds. *Breathe, Greyson! One step at a time. There's a lot of money at the end of this rainbow.* For days he'd wallowed in thoughts of it, allowed it to rule his senses. It waited for him. Nothing would stop him.

Greyson squinted into the darkness. He had bigger plans than this island could offer. His airline tickets and passport were in his briefcase, locked in the trunk of his Porsche. And when he pulled this off, he'd stop gambling; he'd have no more worries about getting ahead in the law firm, no more worries about anything.

After he finished here, all he'd have to do is convert the stuff to cash. Rick had already set that up. Greyson would pay off his gambling debt, and Rick. He'd stash the rest of the money into an off-shore bank account, spend some time in the South Pacific or Rio, then settle into an apartment in Los Angeles.

A compact hedge of ligustrum created the property line between the two backyards. As he got closer, a low growl sounded from the other side of the bushes. He wiped the sweat from his face with the sleeve of his shirt. The ball cap came off. He switched it for the ski mask in his jeans pocket and pulled the itchy knit thing over his face. He slid a slice of raw meat halfway out of its plastic wrapper and tossed it over the green barrier in the direction of the growls.

Greyson stood in the shadows, impatient for the inevitable quiet as

the golden retriever's throaty threat turned to a guttural grunt, then to a juicy, snapping, chewing sound. The dog would sleep peacefully for at least half an hour. He had plenty of time.

Four musical chords sounded from the nightstand beside Lexi's bed, and she fumbled in the darkness to stop the noise. Dad's cellphone. She'd forgotten about it being there.

"Hello?"

"Mrs. Christensen?" The male voice spoke, his words infiltrating her sleep-laden brain.

"Miss . . . yes . . ."

"This is Lt. Withrow with the Nantucket Police Department. I need to talk to your father. Now, please." The man's tone was both stern and intense. "And no lights."

Something hard slammed into her throat. "No lights. I'll get him."

She glanced at the red numerals on the digital clock. Two-thirty! Sleep left her instantly; phone-in-hand, she dashed down the hall. The three small fluorescent nightlights spaced down the hallway emitted enough light for her to see. Praying as she ran, her heart flying ahead of her, she couldn't stop the uneasiness that increased with every step she took.

"Dad." She knocked hard on the bedroom door. "There's a call for you. Don't turn on any lights. Lt. Withrow with the police department needs to talk to you." Her voice quavered. Something was going on, and from the sound of the lieutenant's voice, it couldn't be good.

Her parents emerged from the bedroom, and her father took the phone. Barefoot on the cool oak floor, Lexi stood beside him, listening.

"Yes, this is Jason Christensen."

He paused, and Lexi held her breath, staring at his strong profile as he gripped the phone, the knuckles of his hand whitening in the soft light. "I'll meet you at the front door. Thanks."

He ended the call and handed the phone to Mom, speaking to them in hushed tones. "Lt. Withrow and another officer will be here in a minute. They were watching the house from the unmarked car, and it seems we might be expecting a visitor."

He looked at Lexi. His jaw worked as if he were trying to ratchet down the import of his words for her sake. As if she were a first-grader again.

And suddenly she felt like one. The attorney. He was after the box. She knew it. Lexi's mind shut down and she stood unmoving, unable to say a word.

I will never leave you or forsake you.

The words penetrated the fog her thoughts had become. And Dad was saying something, taking her hand, pushing at her.

"Let's go! You need to put on a robe. Mom will meet us downstairs. Remember, don't turn on any lights."

Lexi swallowed hard against the automatic retort. No time for stressing out over the small stuff. "I won't forget about the lights, Dad. I'll be right down." She turned and sprinted down the hallway.

In less than a minute, robe wrapped tightly around her, she stood behind her dad as he opened the front door for the detectives. The streetlight in front of the Delaward house was the only illumination in the dark living room as Withrow introduced his lanky partner as Mike Mankowski. The two-man surveillance team had been assigned late that afternoon, following Dad's call to the NPD.

"Is there a back door through there? We need to move fast." The

lieutenant pointed down the hall toward the rear of the house.

"Yes. Through the kitchen," Dad said and led the way. Withrow explained what had spurred them into action while Lexi and her mother followed the three men into the kitchen.

"We received a report that one of your neighbors spotted something suspicious and phoned in a complaint. He said he'd started to slide the glass door open to take his dog out when he saw someone around six foot, male physique, dressed in black, going through the front yard of the vacant house next door to his, walking in this direction."

Lexi shot her dad a concerned glance, thinking of what she had hidden in her room. He gave her a knowing look and a nearly imperceptible shake of his head. She breathed a sigh.

"Maybe something, maybe nothing." The lieutenant looked at Dad. "But if he's on his way here, you need to be in an upstairs bedroom and away from any windows."

Lexi studied Withrow's movements in the dim light, her attention drawn more to what he was doing rather than what he was saying. Her body iced as she watched his practiced hand unsnap and lift the leather cover from his service revolver, his beefy fingers closing around the gun. He pulled it out, checked it, and returned it to its holster.

Her mouth went dry. What had she done, invading private property, taking photos of things that didn't concern her, ripping away boards meant to keep her out, going into that house, and taking something she had no business taking? All she'd accomplished was to put her family, friends, and herself in danger.

Withrow motioned to his partner, who immediately moved with odd, staccato-like steps to the wall beside the back door.

Unmoving, Withrow looked out the window over the sink across from him then reached toward the wall beneath the cabinets. He pulled the nightlight out of the wall socket, and the room was instantly plunged into complete darkness.

The leather around the lieutenant's generous waist creaked as he spoke. "It's been about five minutes since we got the call. You need to go." The urgency in his lowered voice brought action as her father put his arms around her and Mom and they hurried toward the stairs.

Halfway up, Lexi's heart skipped a beat. "Dad, I totally forgot about Gilly! If he barks, he could be in big trouble."

"I just thought of him too. Sorry, honey, there's nothing we can do. I'm sure he'll be fine." Dad hugged her, tried to reassure her, but his expression disagreed with his words.

Mom's arm slid around Lexi's waist. "Dad's right. Gilly can take care of himself."

Lexi's throat squeezed. Five years ago, Gilly might have been able to take a chunk out of the man's hide, but not anymore. And if this was the attorney, she'd seen that creep's temper.

Mom closed the door to the master bedroom. Heart racing, Lexi caught a glimpse of the night sky through the partially open window. How long had it been—eight, ten minutes? How much longer? The thin, sporadic rain had stopped, and the house remained silent.

Father, please get us all through this and keep Gilly safe. Dad's hand enveloped hers, and the three of them sat on the bed talking in whispers, waiting. But for what?

Chapter Twenty-Two

Greyson peered over the dense hedge line. "Come on, dog, I don't have all night!" The drug-laced meat wasn't working as fast as he'd hoped it would.

Finally. He chuckled as the old retriever let out a muted groan and dropped to the ground as his legs failed him.

No sign of movement as Greyson scanned the backyard and the windows. Inky blackness filled the Christensen house. Quiet enough for an entry. He followed the hedge for a few feet, located the gap he'd seen yesterday afternoon, and went through.

He'd taken his time and done it right. The dog was on the grass directly in front of him, deathly still. "Good." He nudged the dog's limp tail with the toe of his running shoe, satisfied.

The night-vision binoculars thumped against his chest as he slow-jogged deeper into the yard. He paused and brought them to his eyes to look for his next target. For a moment, the dark night took on an eerie green glow. Hands trembling, he cracked the knuckles of both gloved hands and moved toward the side of the house to the telephone line.

Planting a hand on the hilt of his hunting knife, he jerked it from its leather sheath, the razor-sharp blade reflective in the dull light. With a single swipe, he sliced through the telephone and Internet wires. Not much he could do about any cellphone calls. Sangster still hadn't hacked into them, and there'd been no opportunity for Sangster to get near the house, so there'd be no intercepting any calls until at least tomorrow night.

Greyson had switched his own phone off until this little gig was over. Everything about his plan slipped item-by-item into place. He'd have what he wanted and be out of there before anyone was aware he'd broken in.

The night-vision binoculars dangled from their strap as he slid the knife back into its sheath and went toward the back door of the house. Noiseless, he took the three steps up to the porch, stretched out his hand—and stopped short.

Shadowy movement in the kitchen. No! His hand recoiled as if he'd been bitten, and his headache rolled a frantic throb against his temples. Don't move another inch. He stood in silent disbelief, listening, watching, waiting.

"If this guy's going to make an entrance, he should be here any second, Lieutenant."

The words wafted through the open window. Greyson felt the blood drain from his face at the sound of the subdued male voice and the gaze from eyes that seemed to stare into his own. His shaky gloved hand fell to grab his knife. He slithered off the porch, coiling himself within the protection of a large flowering shrub. Studying the shapes through the open window, his heart pounded. He *couldn't* get caught.

Calm down. Breathe. They didn't see you. He'd been lucky; he'd seen them. Two uniformed men stood behind the door, holding guns. He held the binoculars to his eyes and peered at the unearthly green figures from where he hid. If they'd seen him, he most likely would have ended up being tomorrow's news.

He'd been so careful, so thorough. He replaced the knife and pushed at the sides of his head with the palms of his hands. No one but Rick knew of his plan. Someone had to have spotted him on his way in. And the Christensens had laid a snare he'd narrowly avoided.

Backing off, he retraced his steps through the wet grass. They hadn't gotten him, and they didn't know who he was. He should be in the clear. He passed the corner where the drugged dog lay, cleared the hedge, stayed low, and zigzagged through the yards. Ripping off his ski mask, he raced toward the Mustang.

A siren squalled in the distance. Fury engulfed him. He yanked the car door open and jumped into the driver's seat. Trembling with rage and frustration but moving safely away from disaster, he smacked his forehead with his fist. Somehow he'd made a near-fatal mistake. Worse, he'd lost his best chance to get his hands on what he had to have.

He breathed in rapid gulps. Hands choking the steering wheel, he drew in several deep breaths, trying to calm down. He'd think of something else. No one could possibly know his identity. He'd been too precise. And he'd left no trace, not a single scrap of evidence that he'd attempted a break-in.

With a full-blown anxiety attack stalking his mind, he had to stay alert, stick to the speed limits, and watch himself at the stop signs he'd rather just run through. Constantly checking the rearview mirror, he made several turns onto various rain-dampened streets then left the area.

No squad car loomed on his tail and no more threatening sirens sounded. No one followed. Relief raced through his veins as his anger abated and his stress level evened out. He was safe. Away from the

Christensen neighborhood. On his way home. And already alternative schemes took shape in his roiling brain. But whatever he did, it had to happen fast.

If not, there'd be someone besides Nantucket PD breathing down his neck, and he might have to beg for more time to pay what he owed—if they'd even consider giving it to him.

He revived his cellphone and tapped Rick Vander's name on the contact display.

The voice was sleepy, but the man answered on the first ring. "Did you get it?"

"No. Somehow they knew. I nearly got nabbed."

"So you woke me up at this hour just to whine?" Vander growled. "Not a class act, Quinn. You're out of your league, trying that. I didn't figure you'd get the stuff. We should have done things my way."

Rick's sharp words stung, and regret shot through Greyson for having made the call. Acid rose, burning his throat as he tried to ignore Rick's sarcasm. "We'll just have to work things from Plan B." Greyson snarled the words, and his vain attempt at laughter twisted into a tight, forced finish. "I'm headed home. I'll call you later this morning."

"Fine. Talk to you then."

The connection abruptly cut, Vander had hung up. Red-hot rage rose in Greyson's chest. He fisted a hand and sledged it into the leather passenger seat. The mist outside the Mustang grew heavier as the digits on the dashboard clock read 3:30. He gunned the engine, tires screaming around the corner in a turn toward the beach.

Rick Vander dumped the phone receiver into its cradle, disgusted with Quinn's failure and no longer able to sleep. He thumped the pillow and lay back on the bed, his mind a sea of thoughts he couldn't do anything about at this hour.

Long ago, he'd slotted Quinn as a loser. But loser or not, Rick still looked forward to hearing what Quinn would say in the promised phone call. Exasperated, he ran his hand through bed-ruffled hair.

They'd been friends since their university days. Rick kept in touch with several college buddies, Quinn in particular, and for good reason. Quinn had access to his father's hunting lodge and liked to hunt. So did Rick.

It had been awhile since they'd gotten together, though. Early in his last year of law school, within weeks of each other, Rick's parents passed away. There'd been no family to help and no money to continue school. He'd dropped out and returned home to take over running the family's small furniture store, the only thing his parents had left him besides the house.

He decided not to sell his boyhood home or the store. Located in a busy suburb of Boston, the business brought in enough money to fund his hobby and keep food on the table.

Love that hobby! He had hacked into computers all over the world and lately had focused on business computers in the Boston area. He relished the challenge of nosing around in his business competitors' records. He was good at it, and he never knew what he would find. He rarely bothered to consider that what he did was illegal or that he might get caught. When he did think of it, he tried to tell himself he didn't care. And every day he was getting better at not caring—and not getting caught.

Rick rolled over, battling with the bed pillows again. Even with all Quinn's bungling, maybe there would be a much bigger payoff.

Something was up. He could read GQ like a book. He was holding back, knew more than he was saying. Could be that doing this job held more than he had first thought.

He threw a pillow on the floor. The one huge downside was that now he'd have to get in touch with his contact and cancel the appointment they'd had to exchange the goods for cash—at least for the time being.

Chapter Twenty-Three

Lexi surfaced through a jumble of twisted bed sheets and raised herself on an elbow to look at the clock. Ten till five. What an exhausting night! She'd slept fitfully for all of twenty minutes, and it was a wonder she'd slept at all. With a huff, she dropped back against her pillow.

It had been close to 3:30 when the NPD team left and the Christensens made a wild trip to the emergency veterinary clinic. They'd found Gilly unconscious, lying in the grass; beside him lay bits of evidence he'd been given drug-laced meat. Thank God he now dozed peacefully beside her bed. The house had finally returned to some semblance of normal.

Anger filled Lexi's chest. Her hands curled into fists beneath the covers, picturing the gargoyle of a man who'd come so close to killing her dog.

Dr. McPherson's words still bumped painfully against the corners of her mind. The sixty-something Scotsman put his arm around her, rolling his r's as he spoke. "Lexi, lass, we're very fortunate Gilly's still with us. Five minutes more and all the stomach pumpin' in the world would nae ha' saved this elderly canine gentleman."

Lexi had swallowed hard against the stream of tears that ran down

her cheeks. They'd brought Gilly home instead of leaving him at the clinic overnight. "Less stress," Dr. McPherson said, and he'd sent her a look that indicated having Gilly home would help her frame of mind as well.

He'd been right. She eased her arm over the side of the bed and rested her hand on the warmth of the retriever's silky fur, feeling his heart's strong, regular beat. God had answered so many prayers.

She turned onto her side and pummeled the pillow. The whole episode hadn't exactly been a false alarm. The man who drugged Gilly and cut the phone lines had been lucky. He must have seen or heard something that scared him away, but why did he want to break in?

Another disturbing image of Greyson Quinn, Jr., floated through her mind, and a chill slipped down her spine. The man knew entirely too much about her and about what she had. No one would talk her out of believing he had been the one invading her yard tonight.

He'd been in the mansion, but hadn't seen her, and in the library where he appeared to recognize her. But how? The last time she'd been in his law office was with her parents and the Carvers when she was four, and she doubted he had been there. What more did the man know about her, about everything?

The answer washed over her like an incoming tidal wave, and she sat straight up in bed as logic kicked in, clarifying her thoughts. That man had access to every single file in the law firm, including Aaron Cohen's. He'd seen through her life as if she'd been x-rayed without her permission.

She shuddered with an instant sense of vulnerability. He would have information about the trust, know her name, know she was Aaron's goddaughter. For him to make the connection to her at the library was as simple as recognizing her from the newspaper photo!

THE STONEKEEPERS

She drew her knees up and wrapped her arms around them. *For You have been a shelter for me, A strong tower from the enemy.* With the words from the Psalms, a gentle surf of thankfulness swept over her. God had sheltered and protected her in the mansion Friday. Yes, the attorney knew what he wanted and where to look. But she'd gotten to it before him, and the only sensible reason he'd want to break into her house was to take it from her.

Everything fit, but nothing answered the question of why he would want a simple little box, a piece of paper, and a couple of keys. The paper in her cedar-chest-envelope had all but told her where to look. He must have had the same clues to have gone to the same spot she had. But unless there was a copy of the parchment in the law firm's files, he didn't know there even was a parchment or what it said. He might be at a dead-end, and that might be why he wanted to break into her home—to take what she'd found.

Or was there some other reason? Her mind churned with unanswered questions, and she rubbed her temples. Maybe he believed she'd—

Lexi slapped both hands down onto the bed, her fingers twisting into the sheet as her eyes widened with the possibilities. Could he think she'd taken something bigger, far more important, from beneath that floor—like what they'd found in the root cellar? Except for traces she'd probably left inside yesterday, there was no evidence anyone had been in there for years, so Greyson obviously hadn't discovered that part of the puzzle.

She drew in a sharp breath. That had to be it. He had no idea the root cellar existed. He believed she'd already found and taken "the big one" from under the floor. But how could he know for certain? He had to be making educated guesses. Or was she being followed? Had their phones been bugged? That was doubtful, as the only opportunity would have

been last Saturday when they went out for dinner.

She straightened. And tonight! No one had been at home when they'd taken Gilly to the vet. Had someone been in here while they were away? Ridiculous. Surely not. She was just overtired, stretching things.

The man had escaped, but if the sequence of events had been different tonight, he might have come right into her bedroom to look for the box. And when he didn't find it, would he have forced her to give it to him?

She dropped back down onto the bed, glad to be wrapped in darkness, feeling the internal thunder of her heartbeat. Would she ever feel safe again? Anything could happen, and she'd never know when or where it might be.

But the box remained secure in her room, and everyone was okay. She needed to contain her negative what-ifs before they began controlling her.

Worrying wouldn't help. Being careful was the only reasonable thing she could do. Let go, have faith, and let God take care of it. Thankfulness came in a billow of praise, but not sleep.

Lexi switched on the bedside lamp, pulled the leather-bound journal from the bottom drawer of her nightstand, and dragged extra pillows up behind her. No one had asked about the book. The entire focus of everyone's attention had been on the gilded cedar box with its contents. There had been no time to open the book, until now.

She smoothed her hand over the cover. Dried and cracked with age, the brown leather still had remnants of gold leaf on the bottom right corner. She could barely make out the initials, A.C.

Pressing the spring-latch, she opened it, lifted a few pages, and tensed. This was no book of household records. It looked to be a diary, a journal, and a book of prayers.

She settled back against the pillows, turning pages and reading. The old-fashioned lettering, spelling, and language challenged her, and she determined to make sense of it all. Time drifted as she immersed herself, engrossed in details.

Rich with stories of the Cohen family, the volume formed vivid pictures of lives once lived. Her godfather's ancestor, also named Aaron Cohen, had been a jeweler in London. It was he who had begun keeping this journal. Scrupulous in passing information down through the subsequent generations, he'd recorded the family's history from older writings and stories previously kept alive by word of mouth. With obvious pride, yet deep humility, he devoted pages, written with now-faded black ink, to his genealogy.

Lexi stopped reading, let the book drop forward into her lap, and stared into space. With meticulous care, this man had traced his heritage back to the original Jewish high priest, Aaron, brother of Moses. Her godfather's roots extended back to Moses? The "let my people go—burning bush—Ten Commandments" Moses?

She shook her head. It had been one thing to find something historic, but this was almost too much for her sleep-deprived brain to take in.

Just read. She gave herself the order, pulling the book closer. Scattered through the journal's beginnings, she noticed a continual repeat of the phrase "preserving the sacred," and countless referrals to the G-d of Israel.

He wrote that he'd been born in England in 1791. Early in the year 1831, he told of having had an intense dream, "perhaps even a vision." Then in December, trusting, following where he sensed God lead, Aaron, his wife, daughter, and son, boarded a sailing ship and left England to immigrate to America.

Lexi paused and drew in a deep breath, sensing the centuries turn. In 1832, he had designed and built Northbrick House on Nantucket Island.

She laid her head against the pillows. What must it have been like for Aaron's daughter, Rebekah, to leave London and her good friends behind and cross an ocean in December? Lexi closed her eyes, filled with admiration over Rebekah's courage. The diary hadn't said how old Rebekah was when they sailed, but it did say the son, Levi, had been born in England in 1821. He'd have been age nine.

Surely there was something about how old Rebekah was as well. Lexi scanned the page again . . . and her heart did a cartwheel. Couldn't be! She looked closer, studying the nearly illegible handwriting. Rebekah's birth date was listed as May 22, 1818. There was no mistake. Out of 365 days in a year, nearly 200 years apart, they shared a birthdate. That made Rebekah thirteen when she boarded the ship.

The original Aaron had died at age sixty-eight. The handwriting on the page changed, and then came the statistic that Rebekah's brother, Levi, had married and had a son, Judah Cohen. Lexi paused and smoothed the fragile page. That made Judah her godfather's great-grandfather.

The phrase leapt out at her again. *Preserving the sacred.* Consistent, it appeared each time the handwriting changed and seemed to propel the history forward. Northbrick had been home to the Cohens in the milder months of the year, and the family lived in a house in Boston during the winter. All the children went to boarding school in Boston, going on to England or Israel to finish their studies. She scanned forward.

The daughters usually met and married husbands there or elsewhere in the United States. But every one of the firstborn sons had married and then returned to care for Northbrick and oversee the family's jewelry business in Boston. But what had happened to the business and his home in Boston when Uncle Aaron died with no heirs?

She pulled the lamp nearer her bed. Time condensed as the diary spoke of her godfather, Aaron, born to Judah's son, Benjamin, and his wife, Ruth. So the original London-Aaron was Uncle Aaron's great-

great-grandfather.

She untangled her legs from the sheets as Gilly stirred on the rug. She reached to soothe him a moment before she continued reading, poring over the book until the sun rained gold rays from between the edges of the window curtains.

What did it all mean? Dreams, visions, sacred vows, a sworn duty. Like mini-lightning bolts, the endless facts sparked through her thoughts. Woven throughout the book were tantalizing hints of something precious and a covenant kept. From what the journal/diary indicated, the Cohen family had always stayed to themselves—and they had protected a treasure.

No one ever knew they had safeguarded anything, until now. "Until the day I found it," she murmured. "Why me, Lord, and why now?"

Her deep sigh blended with the breeze that lifted the curtains as it freshened the room with cool, early-morning air. She reluctantly closed the book, her hand still touching it, and glanced at the clock. Six-thirty. Her fingers remained curled around the edge of the volume. She'd take a few more minutes, read a few more pages, then hit the shower. She moved the book to her lap, let it fall open at random, and stared at one of the last entries in her godfather's handwriting:

In the city of Jerusalem, the messenger will find the one—a Levite,

chosen of God. This one will return the lost treasures to the tabernacle.

He will restore them as they were in the beginning, and replace them in the

rebuilt Temple.

Seek this one.

She blinked hard, staring again at words that appeared to hover above the page.

. . . replace them in the rebuilt Temple . . .

The Temple *was* being rebuilt. She hadn't paid much attention to the

news coverage about it, but now, the timing . . .

There was more, but Lexi's eyes blurred. The truth streaked toward her, a shooting star that grew larger with each passing second. Aaron Cohen intended that she find this. She had seen her name. Her godfather had printed it on the envelope she'd found. With no heirs to keep the Cohen covenant, he had chosen her, not to continue to hide and protect the lost treasure, but to return it. And with the words she'd read, the time to return it was now.

"I'm the messenger." She spoke the words toward the ceiling in a loud, strangled whisper. She was to return what Aaron Cohen and his family had kept safe for all those generations—to Jerusalem, to someone she didn't even know existed.

The journal lay open on her lap, and she grabbed a fistful of pale-blue bed sheet in each hand, swallowed up in wonder and assailed with an unfamiliar and terrible doubt.

She was to find the Levite, but how? It was too much. Too fast. Too overwhelming.

Oh, God, please, just let me go back to normal, back to making college plans, to being plain old impatient, toe-tapping Lexi.

Tears ran hot down her cheeks, into her hair, onto the pillows.

The dream woke her with illusive reflective forms, muted colors and shapes. Angels moved in a mist that shimmered like sunlight on a morning fog. A white cat wove its way through ice-blue clouds, settling on a street paved with cobblestones that shone like lumps of rounded gold. And formed in an oval pool of silvered water, letters of ebony, a word: *messenger*.

A wave of comfort and a sense of peace wrapped around her like strong supporting arms. The beat of her heart and the breath from her lips slowed in the calm quiet of her bedroom.

She was not alone. *Thanks. I love you, heavenly Father.*

The breeze continued to ruffle the curtains in the bright morning light. She burrowed a little deeper between the sheets. The attempted break-in had faded in importance after her vivid dream. Since then she'd lain there, making plans to search for "the one—the Levite chosen of God." She'd found a piece of the lost treasure of the tabernacle, and she intended to return it.

She glanced across the room at the unresponsive computer. Along with the phones, he'd taken out their Internet connection. Would those things get repaired this morning? There'd be no access to any resources or information she'd need until that got done.

Gilly rose from his cozy spot beside her bed, stretched, and put his cold nose against Lexi's cheek with his wake-up kiss.

"You're not about to let me think or go back to sleep, are you, boy?" She roughed up the soft fur around his ears and studied his brown eyes, looking for any sign of problems. They were bright and alert in spite of his yawn. He snuffled at her hand. "You sure are feeling better, you sweet old guy. Give me a few minutes and I'll take you out." He flopped back down beside the bed, his dark eyes following her.

Lexi's mind shifted into high gear as she headed for the bathroom and a shower. Tuesday. She wasn't on schedule to work at the stable until this afternoon. Good thing. It would give her a few hours. She needed to call Jen and Ridge to tell them what happened last night, but not yet—not at seven in the morning.

Chapter Twenty-Four

Crazy-weird night! Lexi wiped the steam from the bathroom mirror and stumbled through the routines of lipstick and blush in a race to start the day. Hair still damp, she pulled on a fresh pair of jeans and a tee-shirt and fastened the leash to Gilly's collar. Based on noises from the kitchen, Mom was up and busy cooking. Lexi's stomach growled with the scent of breakfast as she went downstairs. "Hunger pangs or not, you come first, Gil. Let's go."

Gilly ended up taking her for their morning walk. He slowed as she followed him back up the steps to the porch and into the kitchen, thankful he'd come through such a close call so well.

"Hey, Dad." She leaned over to kiss him on the cheek and slid into the alcove opposite him at the table. Gilly found a patch of sun and lay down near the screen door. Mom set a glass of orange juice in front of Lexi.

"Morning, Mom. Thanks." They exchanged an air kiss, and Lexi downed her multi-vitamin with some juice. They talked about the previous night, but thoughts of the journal and her dream froze her tongue and her hands went damp with apprehension. She couldn't speak

about either one. The coffeepot beeped, and Mom left the table. Lexi relaxed a little.

She stood and picked up her glass to leave. "I saw the phone repair guys outside, Dad. Do you know how long before the lines are fixed?" She couldn't wait to get her fingers on the computer keyboard, but it would be penciled notes until—

The phone rang once and stopped.

Mom set her coffee cup on the table. "That was probably telephone repair. They've been working for the last half-hour."

Dad nodded his agreement. "Shouldn't be much longer."

"I hope it's soon. No Internet until that gets fixed." Lexi took a sip of juice.

Mom sniffed and hovered, refilling Dad's coffee cup. "Well, you could certainly do without the computer for a while. And you need more than just juice to keep you going. There's oatmeal. Why don't you have some cereal and toast?"

Lexi swallowed the taste of frustration as well as the juice at her mother's tone and expression. "Okay. I'll make some toast."

The phone rang. Dad answered, spoke for a moment then hung up, grinning at Lexi. "Looks like you're in business. Phones are up and running."

"Great! I want to do some research. Care if I take the toast upstairs with me?"

"Mmph." Mom raised an eyebrow as Lexi stuck two slices of bread in the toaster. "Just be sure to eat all of it while you're up there nose-deep in research."

Edginess was alive and well between them, and Lexi's thoughts clouded. She throttled her glass. "Yeah, I will, Mom."

Her dad looked at her, cleared his throat, and adroitly changed the subject. "Looks to me like Mr. McG, all laid out in the sunshine over there, is doing well. Nice recovery, considering his age. It was a pretty exciting night for him."

Thanks for the save. Bless you, Dad. "I know. I couldn't believe him this morning. He has more energy than I do."

Her father sent her a conspiratorial grin. "Speaking of energy, did you get any sleep, honey?"

"Some, but not enough. Dreamed a lot, did a lot of thinking. Are you still planning to take the box to that jeweler in Boston today?"

"Mmm. Chuck Thurston." Dad nodded, finishing his mouthful. "I'll call him from the office around ten and have Jeff fly me over in the Gulfstream. I need to take care of some company business while I'm there anyway."

"Sounds good, thanks." She added honey and milk to a mug of hot coffee and put it on a tray with her toast. "How long do you think it'll take them to let us know whether it's for real or not?"

"I think Chuck will make the appraisal a priority, especially if he agrees that what's in that box is what we believe it to be." Dad stood and pointed to his oversized briefcase. "I think the box will fit right inside here. Why don't you bring it down, and we'll check it for fit right now?"

Lexi eyed the plate of fast-cooling toast on her tray and dashed upstairs. "Okay. I'll take this stuff up and be right back." Cold toast was nearly as good.

Well, maybe not so good. She chipped away at crusty, cold toast, and sipped lukewarm coffee as she Googled for information. Dad had been right. The box fit perfectly inside his briefcase. He'd left the house soon after they'd checked it out, and she'd gone back upstairs, Gilly at

her heels.

Beginning with the Temple, she dug into a dozen sites covering its history, original furnishings, the priesthood, the new construction. Not enough. She had to go deeper. Who headed up the reconstruction? A committee? One person? Where was this Levite she was supposed to find? How in the world was she going to know he was "the one" if she did?

The power dipped. Her battery backup chirped a warning, then restored. She'd spent most of an hour looking and making notes.

"Am I ever going to find something, Lord? Please help." She blew the words toward the screen. She should have prayed the second she sat down to start this search. One more site then she'd quit for a while. She straightened, stretched, and sighed as it loaded. There hadn't been a single site so far that held any promising answers. She leaned in and stared at the monitor. But this one just might . . .

Her breath caught as the screen lit up with a recent photo of the huge structure rising in Jerusalem. Beneath it, descriptions and explanations that pulled her in and held her like quicksand, page by page, every one more gripping and interesting than the last. She read until she found the roots of the site, information that mesmerized her. Could it be?

She pushed away from the screen, tried to shake her fierce concentration, to think. But her gaze didn't move from the face of the man in the photograph. The man with eyes that exuded joy, gentleness, yet firm authority, a salt-and-pepper beard that reminded her of Uncle . . .

The room silent, air compressed from her lungs as if her heart would stop. Could the creator of this site be *the one*?

An hour later, there was no longer any doubt about the website or its creator. She knew enough. Since Ridge had left for work, he'd have to wait to hear this, but Jenni wouldn't.

Jenni answered on the third ring. "Hey, girl, what's up?"

"I've found him, Jen. He's got a phenomenal website. Everything is right there—photos, pages of details about the rebuilding of the Temple, everything." Oh, she was burbling again!

"Wait, wait! Slow down." Jenni's smile came through in her voice. "Who did you find? Where?"

"Sorry. I'm so hyped over all this. After everything that happened last night, I couldn't sleep, so I—

"Okay, hold it! What happened last night?"

"Uh . . . should have told you that first, but the man I found—

"Lex! Tell me!"

Lexi dumped her night full of lawmen, a break-in that didn't happen, Gilly's trip to the vet, Dad taking the box and contents to Boston for appraisal into Jen's lap. But she cut Jenni's questions short.

"And that journal—it's no household record book. It's more like a diary. Everything in it keeps pointing to the fact the Cohen family had been protecting something valuable . . . for generations. I'll read you a little." She opened the journal to a page where she'd stuck a bookmark. "Here's what Aaron Cohen wrote on one of the last pages."

Lexi read her the paragraph of instructions her godfather had written. Even as she spoke them again, the words pierced her heart and opened her eyes to what she had to do. She told Jenni about her dream, then of the website. "Avi, Avraham Solomon, the man who created the site, is a rabbi who lives in Jerusalem and heads up the organization building and *restoring* the Temple, not just rebuilding it. They're putting it back exactly as it was, recreating every single original thing that was inside. I'll text you and Ridge the home page info. You've both *got* to see it!"

She paused and held her breath. The dead silence on the other end of the phone line was deafening before Jenni finally spoke. "This is

unbelievable. That rabbi might just be the one you need to contact."

"It looks that way to me, too. I'll tell you everything else this afternoon at work—how Mom and Dad reacted and more about what Dad's doing this morning, more than I want to tell you by phone after what happened last night."

She hung up, glanced at her cellphone lying beside the monitor, and rubbed her forehead. Stupid! Why hadn't she used her cell instead of the landline to call Jen? But maybe her cell could be bugged, too. Was there a way someone could do that? She'd been fairly careful about how much she said, but what if the phones really had been bugged? Maybe even the whole house? She shook her head. No one else seemed worried. She was being paranoid. But the thoughts still clung to the edge of her mind.

Bleary-eyed, Greyson Quinn, Jr., sat in his law office with the door shut against the noise of gabby clients in the reception area. Everything including the creaky leather of his executive chair bothered him. Pill bottles beckoned from his desk. Should he take an aspirin or an antacid or a couple of each? He pushed at his temples with the palms of both hands, trying to decide.

He popped a Tums and dug out an aspirin. He'd reviewed every possibility of what could go wrong, and still he'd managed to botch a simple break-in. Someone must have seen him. How else had the cops known?

Exhaustion crept over his limbs, chilling him like the morning fog he'd driven through. If he'd messed up, it was from lack of sleep and worry over the constant phone calls woven through with heavy-handed threats.

THE STONEKEEPERS

Greyson pulled at his mustache. Whether he liked it or not, he no longer had a choice. He had to have Vander fully on board, and for more reasons than simply exchanging the goods for money.

The tick of the miniature Big Ben timepiece on his desk amplified his headache, prodding him to get the call over with. He stirred extra sugar into his café latte and took a deep swallow. He straightened, picked up his cell, and pressed Vander's business number.

"Vander's Home Furnishings," Vander answered in his raspy baritone.

Greyson skipped his usual friendlier, hey, how's it going, and launched directly into Vander's day. "There's a lot more to this than I thought."

"Why? What's up? What else have you got?"

"Can you have your contact in Saudi do some checking for me?"

"Sure. Why?"

"I don't want to discuss it by phone. We need a face-to-face." He cleared his throat and continued. "But sometime before we meet, I want you to find, rent, beg, borrow, or steal a Bible, and read the Book of Exodus. It'll give you some background you'll need to know."

"Exodus! This better be good. I don't have time for books, much less that one. And you need some sleep. You sound like you just fell off the ferry."

A few ugly retorts flipped from Greyson's mind to his mouth. Vander's sarcasm and mood swings stretched their friendship thin lately, but he needed what Vander could provide. Greyson bit his tongue.

"Just read it, Rick. I'll be flying into Boston late Thursday afternoon. I've made reservations for dinner at Antonio's. Meet me there at seven. I've already lost two business days, and my schedule here is full. I'm backing off until I catch up. Check your email in the next few minutes.

I'm sending you a list of things to do before we get together. Everything else will have to wait till Thursday. Trust me, this *will* be worth it."

He paused, if for nothing more than effect, then added, "Oh, and before this is all over, you may be going to Israel."

The last thing Greyson heard was a strangled "What?" before he tapped *End Call*, and shut Vander out of his morning. He entered the time he'd scheduled for their dinner on his desktop PC's calendar. It would sync with the rest of the office computers and mesh with other appointments on the schedule.

He shoved his cellphone into his suit-coat pocket and sat back to loosen his tie, smug that he was the only one besides his father who knew of the Israel connection. The Christensens had yet to notify the law office of Lexi's entry into Northbrick, and the delay bought him more time. Raiding the files his father guarded so carefully had paid off. He'd get his hands on the box soon.

The incessant pounding of his headache eased. He logged into his email to compose a note to Vander, supplying Lexi's email address, her parents' names, and other personal information he'd gleaned from their files. Vander would need to do some hacking and electronic eavesdropping. Having copies of all the Christensens' email and data on Internet sites they visited would help shape plans to locate and retrieve the box.

Gulping down the last of his latte, he reviewed his email to Vander, encrypted it, and sent it seconds before his cellphone vibrated with an incoming call. He glanced at the ID. Sangster. Maybe he had news.

By the end of their five-minute conversation, Greyson had filled half a legal-size sheet of paper with notes. He kicked his feet up onto the desk and looked over both the good and the bad news. *Dan has all the bugs in place. Cellphone calls and text messages are being intercepted.* Then

Sangster's single piece of bad news. *Unless you're FBI with a reason, Jason Christensen's office location and business lines are impenetrable.* No telling what he'd miss there.

"It's done!" Sangster had crowed. "Wasn't too difficult—just used the police scanner from a few blocks away. Some jerk had poisoned the family dog, trying to get into the place, but the cops had been called and he's in the wind. When the Christensens raced out of there to take the dog to the vet, it only took a few well-timed moves. Between the time the cops left and the Christensens got back, I had it finished. Busy place, your target house. Know anything about it?"

Yeah, but you'll never know. He reshaped his lips into a sardonic smile—the same house this "jerk" had just failed to get into. A cat burglar he was not, but there were other ways.

But a cold flush had swept through Greyson before he'd told Sangster that he had no idea what that was all about and had congratulated him on his quick work. Too bad he couldn't have had Sangster locate the box.

He looked up annoyed as his bothersome blonde, blue-eyed secretary knocked, then opened his office door.

"Mr. Quinn, Charles Warner is here for his appointment. Shall I show him in?"

He frowned and nodded, exchanging the empty latte cup for the thin file in her outstretched hand. There would be time for more thinking later. The day couldn't go by fast enough.

Chapter Twenty-Five

Thursday night, Antonio's Italian Restaurant in Boston overflowed with the usual scents and sounds of the dinner crowd as Greyson Quinn, Jr., pushed through the doors. Perfect. The noise would be great cover for privacy. Rick Vander had already commandeered a corner booth. He glanced at Greyson, nodded, then picked up his menu.

Greyson smoothed the front of his suit jacket and strode by the hostess, comparing himself to Rick with every step. He studied his college buddy's shorter stature, his pride lifting a notch. Pushing thirty, the man's disheveled blond hair flopped over his forehead and into his eyes like a kid's. Even in his business suit, he looked like a boot camp runaway. But he was a skilled hunter, Greyson had to give him that. And he knew his way around computers like no one Greyson had ever known. A good thing right now. He needed to know what the girl's computer held.

The jaws of anxiety vised around Greyson's head as the two shook hands and he sat opposite Rick. In seconds, a balding, overworked waiter with beads of sweat above thick brows brought water and hovered

beside the table to take their drink and dinner orders.

Antsy, waiting to say what was on his mind, Greyson drummed his manicured fingertips on the tabletop until the harried server left. In no rush, Rick leisurely sat back and sipped his drink.

Maddening! But Greyson slammed the door on his impatience when Rick opened his briefcase and reached inside.

"I have an idea you're ready for this." Rick's face held a wry smile. He shoved a manila folder toward Greyson, then leaned against the cushioned leather seat and threaded his fingers behind his head, watching.

Greyson pounced on the file and instantly regretted the move. *Not cool. Stand down, man. It isn't as if the thing's going to jump off the table and run.* He forced deep, even breaths and shuffled through the folder. *Nice job, Rick.*

He lifted the last page and stared at the sheet, the hair on the back of his neck at full attention. The words "Jewish artifact" in Rick's notes about her email confirmed the girl was about to do some traveling, but not a scrap of info on what the "artifact" was. Nevertheless, there was one piece of luggage that was *not* going to make the trip. He pulled in a breath, straightened, and looked at Rick with a rush of fresh enthusiasm.

Rick nodded. A slow smile of understanding crossed his lips. "You were right on the money about Exodus, but that's all I got before they started using some pretty stiff encryption."

Rick's concession hung in the dinner-scented atmosphere, and Greyson swallowed a dollop of smug satisfaction with no comment. He'd put two and two together and come up with the logical conclusion that the girl would be taking what she'd found to Israel.

He took a small spiral notebook from his jacket pocket. Ripping off a sheet, he wrote the name of one of the largest, most respected jewelry firms in the United States, and slid it in front of Rick. "There's more you need to know."

Rick's eyes widened. "Even Jewelers International? E-*ven*'. I know them. Old-line Boston firm. Weird name, but impressive. Means stone in Hebrew. Didn't some Jewish family on your island used to own them?"

Greyson nodded. "Yep. It sold a dozen or more years ago. Grey handled the sale."

"So where does Even Jewelers fit into the picture?"

"Dan Sangster called yesterday afternoon." Greyson rubbed his hands on his napkin.

Vander leaned closer and grinned. "Oh, yeah. Your slightly shady private eye with his slightly questionable credentials. Sure you can trust that guy?"

Greyson ignored him. "Dan's good at the basics, plus he likes being paid. He'll only know what I want him to know. The girl's apparently being pretty careful about what she says on the phone, so I don't think he'll learn much, if anything, from her." He hoped. Because if Sangster learned exactly what Lexi Christensen had in her possession, who knew how the man would react?

"What did Sangster have for you?"

"Facts. Late Tuesday morning, that firm," he said, pointing to the piece of paper, "accepted delivery of a sizable package. And that package came in from Nantucket, hand-delivered by Jason Christensen." Greyson checked the notes in his iPhone and glanced up.

Rick's expression read like a question. "So?"

"Early this afternoon, Sangster intercepted a phone call. And by the time Christensen showed up in Boston, he was outside Even's Jewelry, in his car, in full surveillance mode. Christensen had returned to pick up a package of what looked to be the same dimensions as the one he

delivered on Tuesday."

Rick gave a low whistle and pushed his napkin around on the table. "So, Christensen had the stuff appraised?"

"Looks that way, and there's another thing. Instead of taking the ferry to Hyannis and driving into Boston, Christensen used his corporate jet—both days. I think that's significant."

"Mmm, safe, fast transport. Guess it pays to be the boss."

"It could also indicate he needed, or wanted, the appraisal stat," Greyson said.

Rick pinched his chin between his thumb and forefinger. "Yeah, but from where I sit, the fact they had it in and out of there that quickly might mean it was worthless, a fake."

"Not from what I've learned about it, but I need more info from you—ASAP."

Great. He'd said a few words too many, and they hadn't gotten by Rick. The man's piercing green eyes drilled into him.

"I have an idea of what you want, but shoot." Rick looked down and doodled on his mangled napkin. "I'll consider it and the risks."

Worry niggled at Greyson's insides. Maybe Rick wasn't going to go for this unless he could see a bigger score. "Right now, I want to know just how much this stuff is worth. You shouldn't have a problem digging that out of their computer." Greyson pointed again at the slip of paper. "Besides delivery receipts, there should be detailed electronic records of their transactions and an inventory."

Rick wrote on the reverse of Greyson's slip of paper and stuffed it into his pocket.

"Well? Can you get to what we need?" Greyson tapped out an impatient cadence on the shiny tabletop and waited, watching Rick contemplate his silverware.

"Well?" Greyson leaned forward, feeling sweat bead along his hairline. "Can you?"

Rick's eyebrows met as he narrowed his eyes and nodded. "I'm still thinking about it, but it sounds like a piece of cake. And if I can't get to it, there's not a firewall in any computer security system in the world that can keep Alpha-Z out."

"Alpha-Z? Oh, yeah, the genius kid you know in Saudi. Salem, right?"

"It's Salim, but yeah, he's the one."

"Good." Greyson sat back and ripped another note-covered sheet from his pad and stuck it in front of Rick's plate. "A few more things for you to do."

Rick shrugged and looked it over and then shoved it back in front of Greyson. "So far, so good."

"Just be thorough." Greyson swiped sweat from his forehead, details flying through his mind. At least he'd locked in Rick's interest, and they knew the girl would be taking the stuff directly to Israel herself, though when she'd leave was still undetermined. Would Greyson have one more chance to relieve her of it before she left? If his last-ditch effort on US soil failed, getting Rick to agree to be in Jerusalem before the girl arrived to try again was crucial. One of them had to succeed.

Greyson took a breath and continued. "Between what you find and what comes from the bugs in the girl's house and phones, I can firm up plans."

Rick sat back and folded his arms across his chest. "I think . . . you mean . . . *we*." Rick interjected the words with a frown.

There it was. Greyson's stomach burned. He'd have to deliver more of a percentage or he'd lose Rick's support in this. He put down his fork and smoothed his mustache, wanting a Tums in the worst way. Greyson

couldn't take the chance of trying to handle this alone. Time to give Rick his fair share in this. "There's more that will make it a 'we' deal. Of course, I meant both of us."

He closed the folder, moved it aside, and tossed out his bait, a money-heavy proposal. During the next ten minutes, he noted the varying expressions of interest on Rick's face as he unreeled details he was certain would set the hook. This had to work. He'd paid Rick generously for the original, smaller favor, and it rankled him to have to offer a bigger percentage now.

Rick listened until Greyson finished, then set up a firestorm of debate, questioning the amount. With a final heated exchange, Greyson locked in at the maximum he was willing to split, then sat back, silent, his face set into a granite-hard mask.

No more.

Rick twitched and fiddled, first with his knife and fork, then with his collar and tie.

Hooked? Surely Rick was smart enough not to turn down a chance to make this kind of money. If he accepted and things went according to plan, they'd soon know just how big that amount might be. But seconds passed, and Vander said nothing.

Greyson's left eyelid twitched and he pressed his finger against it. Would he have to raise the stakes? Was there any other choice? *No. Wait him out. You've set the hook; just reel him in nice and slow.* Greyson snatched his iPhone up from the table and checked his email, anything to keep busy lest he start talking out of sheer impatience.

"Okay. I'm in." Rick reached across the space between them to shake Greyson's hand.

Greyson nearly dropped his cellphone. He put it on the table, smiled, and nodded, but his arm and proffered hand were as wooden as the oak flooring beneath his feet. "Good decision."

The waiter arrived with fresh coffee and ice water. Greyson gritted his teeth until the man walked away.

"If you need anything else, call, but call my cell, not the office. I don't want a hint of this getting to Grey."

"No problem, man. Chill! It'll get handled." Rick's eyes fixed on Greyson's. "Question is, can *you* handle it as rattled as you are?" He paused and leaned on his forearms. "Oh, by the way, I get the connection with Israel, but unless you figure you'll bomb on your next *big plan*, what's the deal about me going there"

Rick's attitude screeched across his nerves like the brakes on a freight train. "Backup." Greyson glared at him. "I'll fill you in as soon as things start to move. Just get your bags packed, and you or your hacker-friend in Saudi get that info from the jewelry company fast. If you don't have a passport, maybe he could manufacture that too." Greyson stuffed his notepad and cellphone into his suit-coat pocket. "Get back to me as soon as you can."

Rick sent him a smug "yeah, sure" expression, and Greyson clenched his teeth.

Reaching across the table, Rick gave him a friendly punch in the arm. "Take it easy, man; we'll make it work. We'll get the stuff one way or the other." He glanced at the folder beside Greyson. "Keep that. I've got copies." He looked away to pocket his notes and close his briefcase.

Greyson stuffed the folder into his briefcase, stood, and deliberately left the unpaid bill on the table. He left the restaurant and hailed a taxi to return to his hotel. His early-morning commuter flight back to the island couldn't happen soon enough. He'd scheduled a meeting with Sangster. The detective should have a lot more to tell him.

Nothing like being asked to meet for dinner and getting stuck with the bill. Steaming mad at Quinn for leaving him the restaurant tab, Rick hopped in his car and raced toward home. Raced until one of Boston's finest officially reminded him about speeding through residential zones and fined him $150.

Rick huffed into his living room, tossed his suit jacket aside, kicked off his shoes, and settled into his La-Z-Boy chair in front of the TV. In a week or so, bills, fines, or anything related to money might not matter at all. The meeting cemented his decision to be involved, and things were moving forward.

The television's blank face gaped at him. He grabbed the remote and turned it on, keeping the sound low. His thoughts rolled back to Tuesday morning and the phone call from Greyson after his pitiful B & E attempt. Breaking and entering, ha! Greyson had sent him an email with the information he could use to track the Christensen girl. Rick had hacked her computer and followed her Web searches until they came to an abrupt halt.

The girl had settled on a site that originated in Jerusalem and belonged to a Jewish rabbi, an Israeli by the name of Avi Solomon. By yesterday afternoon, their email devolved into the gibberish of encryption. Rick didn't have the time or desire to translate, but with a single phone call, Salim was all over it.

And now that file, with *most* of the translated email and hard-copy pages of the rabbi's website, the evidence Salim and he had gathered resided in Greyson's briefcase. Remembering Greyson's reaction as he'd read through the information, Rick had to smile. That info had confirmed enough to change both their lives.

THE STONEKEEPERS

With the agreement between him and Greyson tonight, Salim would play a much larger part in what they planned.

Rick raked a hand through his hair, and the tension drained like an overfilled sponge from his limbs. He collapsed the lounge chair's footrest, stretched, and flipped through the channels. Pausing at CNN, he shook his head. Some kind of big discussion about a meeting in Jordan between Israel and Palestine on nearly every news channel. Ever since the earthquake leveled nearly everything in Old Jerusalem two years ago, that area of the world had gone crazy.

An attractive but somber red-haired news anchor pointed to a map of Old Jerusalem and expounded. ". . . and the changes that placed administration of the entire site of the Dome of the Rock under Israel's exclusive control have been under fire from . . ."

Rick got up and headed for the kitchen, listening to bits of what he could hear of the anchor's dialogue as he grabbed a bottle from the refrigerator. "Israel . . . massive and swift construction . . . restricted to the original design . . . completion . . . less than two years . . . Ark of . . ."

Bottle in hand, Rick returned in time to see "Red's" co-anchor's expression reflecting the gravity of Red's words. The man picked up the thread of her report and continued. "In other news from that area, an investigation is underway regarding reports from several agricultural centers near the Gaza Strip of an unusual desert bloom . . ."

Rick interrupted, didn't need to hear it. "Earthquakes? Flowering deserts? The world's gone berserk."

He jammed his thumb on the mute button and sat back, his thoughts on Salim and their last conversation. Salim had been more than willing to pick up the slack on boring details like decrypting, and Rick sensed Salim's building enthusiasm over being included. They were involved in what Rick hoped would be the "job" of a lifetime. It helped that Salim lived the life and traditions, knew the ropes in the Middle East. He spoke

several languages and owned the newest tech equipment.

Sure, Rick could have done the hack-jobs, everything, by himself, but his protégé was faster and would be invaluable, and there had to be a backup plan.

Rick took a deep pull from the bottle. The primary reason he wanted Salim onboard was to let him take the fall if the situation got out of hand in Israel. He had no intention of there being any way to trace things back to himself. He needed Salim.

But if he was to make sense when he talked to Salim, he had to get some sleep. Already computing the time difference between Boston and Riyadh, Rick yawned, switched off the television, and went into the bedroom to set his alarm.

A few hours later, Rick sat on the edge of his bed, iPad in hand and already on Skype to make the overseas call. Salim's image filled the screen.

"Hey, Salim. I need your help, buddy. Glad I caught you. Are you alone? Can you talk?" The friendly responses were all affirmative, and Rick continued.

"You've done a great job with sorting out the emails for me, and I've got a couple more projects for you, but there's one thing I need first and fast. You said you could do passports and take care of reservations?" Rick grinned at Salim.

"It can be done."

"Good. What do you need from me to make it happen?"

Salim explained, and Rick made the list of what to send him, nodding at the dark-eyed image on the screen.

"Okay, watch your email—and your front door. I'll FedEx everything. And as I said before, it'll be well worth your time." Salim didn't really care about nor want the money, but Rick offered it anyway.

With Salim firmly onboard, Rick encrypted and sent the "keys" to get Salim into the jewelry store's computer system and more info on the American girl. He would do it all. "Just get back to me as soon as you can. The timing on this is going to be important, man."

Rick hung up and called Greyson. It wouldn't be the first time in Rick's life he'd risked everything, including prison time, for an unknown possibility. Rick had gotten an earful of how Greyson had already done a lot of "risking." So if Greyson wanted to spread that risk, bring it on!

Chapter Twenty-Six

The living room sparked with tension. Lexi sat in a side chair as far away from the front door as possible. She looked at her nails and shook her head. She'd been chewing on them off and on since she got out of the shower this morning. In spite of her pitch for postponement, she and her parents were keeping the appointment with Greyson Quinn, Sr., Attorney at Law, at nine this morning.

Ready to leave but far from willing, how could she face walking into the younger Greyson Quinn's law office? He wasn't supposed to be there, but what if he was? What would his father be like? If he was at all similar to his son, she was not ready to find out. She needed more time to deal with the fear that laced its icy tentacles down her spine. It hit her every time she thought of that man throwing Gilly poisoned meat and trying to break into her house.

She bit down on the inside of her cheek and tried to stop her insides from churning. Surely a few days wouldn't make any difference. She wouldn't be dishonoring her godfather's wishes to delay this appointment.

"Mom, I *still* don't see any good reason why we can't wait until we get back from Israel to see Mr. Quinn."

Mom's lips pinched thin, wordless as she turned to reach for her purse. Dad's deep, even voice sounded behind Lexi. "We've been over this thoroughly, Lexi, and I don't want to hear any more argument. We need to leave now to be there on time. Go get in the car."

With an inward sigh, she did. She was a child again as her father's black SUV moved through Nantucket's Monday-morning traffic. The atmosphere in the car was thick with the silence of three stressed people. *Lord, why couldn't I have simply said nothing and gone without a fight?*

Twelve days since she'd found the envelope and eight since she'd found . . . *Stop.* Things had gotten better with Mom and Dad, and she needed to keep it that way, to breathe and pray and look beyond this unwanted appointment. Focus.

Dad peered at her in the rearview mirror. "Don't worry, honey. This shouldn't take too long. And as I said before, it's just a routine reading of Uncle Aaron's will and getting some advice to help us with decisions."

Well, at least one of them was trying to be conciliatory. Not trusting her voice, Lexi sent him the calmest smile she could muster. How could receiving a substantial inheritance from a man you barely remembered possibly be routine? And what did "substantial" mean? Would she ever adjust to the fact that her godfather had made this business all about her?

Lexi held the car door open for her mother and cringed at the furrow between Mom's brows. Warmth crept into Lexi's cheeks with the reminder that this week hadn't been easy on any of them, that this wasn't all about her. Love surged and hot tears welled in her eyes as she slid her arm around her mother's waist and laid her head on her shoulder. "Mom, I'm sorry for earlier." And with a hug, the frost between them melted a bit.

THE STONEKEEPERS

The law offices were impressive, but as they walked into a large reception area, Lexi's nerves rattled with worry over the idea of running into Quinn, Jr. How would she react if she saw him again? Her heart beat double-time as she passed a closed office door with the junior Quinn's name engraved on a gold plate. Only when she crossed the threshold to enter the elder attorney's private office did she breathe again. It helped that his plush suite included a library and conference room and reflected a comforting sense of security. Tension seeped from her body with the light scent of pine and leather.

The attorney motioned to a semi-circle of chairs in front his wide walnut desk. "Please, make yourselves comfortable. Liz has a tray of fresh coffee and doughnuts if you like." He lowered his girth into the dark green executive chair behind his desk while his secretary poured coffee into china cups.

Liz closed the door behind her and effectively shut out the busy sounds of a successful law practice. Lexi mechanically stirred cream into her coffee and let the muted conversation between the attorney and her parents roll around her. She sat, praying she could compose herself enough to listen and make sense if she spoke.

"So the day has finally come." Quinn pinched his nose beneath his rimless glasses, nodded at her parents then targeted Lexi with his sharp gaze. "I knew your godfather well, Lexi, and a finer man has rarely walked this earth. He left nothing to chance, and I've not worked before nor since with as brilliant a mind as his." Tears welled behind his glasses and the attorney paused, straightening in his chair. "I miss Aaron Cohen to this day." He cleared his throat, his smile erasing wrinkles as it reached the corners of his mouth.

Lexi swallowed hard as, beside her, Mom stifled a sob. After a few additional words of welcome from the attorney, Lexi sat on the edge of

her chair, listening, fascinated by what her godfather had done so many years ago. More than a single trust for her, Aaron had set up several trusts. They were for the purposes of providing lifetime incomes for the caretaker and her parents, for the upkeep and tax obligations of Northbrick, the physical estate, property, and . . .

Lexi's mind blurred as he continued. Legal verbiage rained down—trustee, grantee, settlor, testamentary, beneficiary, title to trust property, executor, power to control, right to exercise. The words pelted her until he exchanged them for a language she understood.

". . . the Northbrick Estate . . . contents and surrounding acreage . . . held in trust . . ."

Lexi went numb. She pushed back in her chair, wishing its massive arms would swallow her as the gray-haired man continued to review the life-changing sentences.

". . . Alexia Evengeline Christensen . . . its ownership in trust . . . State Street Bank and Trust holdings . . ."

Only weeks ago Northbrick Estate had been an abandoned, tumbledown house on a deserted street.

Not anymore.

She was its new owner. Tears burned the back of her eyelids. She blinked hard, grasped the arms of the chair, tried to pay attention. She was too weak, too inadequate, and too full of turmoil to receive Northbrick Estate. She couldn't think, and as if they knew, from either side of her, the hands that had held her since birth touched her arms.

Oh, how she yearned for her confused prayers to be heard as Attorney Quinn's words sank in.

The Lord will give you strength; The Lord will bless you with peace.

Like a gentle incoming wave, the verse formed a message to her heart. She relaxed, lifted her chin, and fixed her eyes on the attorney.

Thoughts of taxes and upkeep rose in her mind, and when he finished, she questioned the amount of money the trust fund held. The silver-haired lawyer looked at her over his glasses, raised thick eyebrows, and gave her a broad smile.

"Considerable, Lexi," he said, matter-of-factly. "Considerable, as it involves stocks, bonds, and several banking institutions. A complete accounting will be ready for you when you return from Israel."

Dad had a few more questions, and Lexi watched him, admiring the way he interacted with the older man. Dad seemed to trust the attorney implicitly, and with all that had happened, she hoped she would be able to as well. She could not imagine how this gentle man could have a son so ready to break the law—and probably his father's heart.

The brief appointment left her head spinning with questions and details. But both would have to wait. From the moment she'd found the envelope, time had raced past like dry beach sand through her fingers. Determined to carry out Aaron's wishes, almost everything except the impending trip had been put on hold. Her days were a maelstrom of researching, making calls, and trip-planning. Jenni kept her grounded with laughter and prayed with her when excitement soared in her chest like a hot-air balloon without tethers. Ridge stayed close and helped her keep track of things, too often putting his hand in hers or an arm around her shoulders. Sweet, thoughtful hugs, and she wasn't so sure now that they didn't mean more than that. But he hugged Jen, too. If he'd just stick to hugging one of them, it would help. The man was confusion personified!

"That went well." Dad squeezed her arm as they left the attorney's office.

Yes, it had, but in spite of Dad's cheerful words, a thick sense of foreboding rose in her. Why? She shut the heavy car door, the *thud* of its closure echoing the thud of her heart.

Chapter Twenty-Seven

Jerusalem, Israel

The following Tuesday morning at the Foundation for Temple Restoration in Jerusalem, Rabbi Avi Solomon gazed at the monitor atop his battered oak desk. He finished the encrypted email addressed to Alexia Evengeline Christensen, reread it then clicked *Send*. Satisfied, he stood and pulled the chain on the overhead fan. It would ease the stuffiness of his cramped office. For a moment, he watched the white blades swirl, then sat back in his soft leather chair and swiveled away from the computer.

Had a decade already passed since he'd felt the urgings in his spirit? Driven, listening, praying, he had created a website and a weekly newsletter that focused on reconstructing the Temple. Without a single appeal, generous donations had flowed in.

The site's success filled him with as much surprise and humility now as it had then. A wave of thankfulness flushed through him. The kind hand of Adonai had moved so many to give so much. Elbows on the arms of his chair, he tented his hands, his forehead bowed to touch

his fingertips in praise. The success had enabled him to complete plans for the future hope of rebuilding the Temple and filling it with flawless replicas of the original contents.

He'd searched and found highly skilled wood carvers and workers in brass, bronze, silver, and gold. He'd looked for those with hearts for Adonai and belief in His coming Kingdom. The site had lured each of them, brilliant artisans who came from within Israel and around the world to recreate the furnishings. He'd employed them, provided living quarters, and given them materials along with detailed patterns to recreate the original work of King Solomon.

Now with the Temple rising, he stood on the brink of reality. Schoolboy excitement had his old heart beating too fast for comfort, and he pressed his hand hard against his chest. "*Adon ha-olamim,* Sovereign of the universe, grant patience and peace," he whispered.

Solomon glanced at his desk calendar and shook his head, hands gripping the supple leather arms of his chair as he relived the vision he'd had two years ago today. For almost that long, he'd kept it to himself.

A powerful desire to walk alone that morning had impelled him to leave his home immediately. Approaching the ancient Wailing Wall to pray, he was far from alone when he arrived. An unusually large crowd bumped and pushed against him, leaving him breathless and confused.

He had no memory of how the vision began, nor did he sense the passage of time as he leaned his body heavily against the ancient rampart. Noise, so much noise. It grafted him to the cold stones, compressing the air that wafted around him into silence as the vision unrolled before his eyes.

Light, so great a light. And words! Oh, the words whispered into his spirit! Fragments that seared into his heart and never left his mind.

I will do a new thing in Israel. Humble yourself. Do not doubt.

THE STONEKEEPERS

Listen. Receive instruction. Trust. You will receive a messenger.

Not knowing how he got there, he found himself back at the door of his home, dazed, his eyesight dimmed from brilliant, blinding light.

For the following thirty-nine days, he spent countless hours alone in his office in intense prayer and meditation. And the morning of the fortieth day, the earth shook.

Solomon's mind swam with remembered events, headlines, and part of an article, indelible with the news:

The 6.2 magnitude earthquake, which destroyed much of the old city and leveled the Dome of the Rock, left only the stone base, the Wailing Wall on the west, and the Golden Gate on the east. The result has been shock and no one to blame for the massive destruction. . . .

He bowed his head in amazement at the power of *Hashem.* Days after the earthquake an occurrence during a meeting of Jerusalem's Supreme Muslim Council created shockwaves that rocked the city and beyond. The Grand Mufti had fallen to the floor of the chamber in an ecstatic state and had been unable to see. *Blinding silver-white light, a Man, a voice, a vision.* Words and phrases emerged and circulated, all spoken by men who had staggered, stunned, from the Council meeting room.

Within an hour, an order had been issued. By mid-afternoon, administrative control of Temple Mount had been rescinded, and the Israeli flag quietly appeared where King Solomon's original temple once stood. Immediate gatherings of the foundations, societies, and institutes involved with plans for Temple reconstruction took place. Out of those conclaves came Rabbi Avi Solomon's appointment to oversee the rebuilding.

The rabbi rose from his desk and went to a massive table covered with a full replica of the first Temple. He stood, pulling at ends of his

beard, then paced, deep in thought. Did he dare compare his mission to Noah's call to build an ark? He drew in a quick breath at the familiar warm shiver of approval around his shoulders.

Noah labored in faith, never having felt a drop of water fall from the sky, and waited for a flood without a shred of evidence one would ever happen. At Hashem's command, he had labored 120 years to construct an ark.

Avi Solomon had evidence before starting his mission, a single earth-shattering event. By the hand of *Adon ha-olamim* two years ago, it had been an earthquake that cleared the holy site.

And now, as he had received Hashem's command, in the midst of Old Jerusalem, the Temple was rising on the mount for a third time.

Miraculous! He shook his head so hard his black yarmulke nearly lost its moorings. *Adonai is great.*

Retrieving several sheets of paper from the printer, he leafed through them, perusing a master list of items, materials, projected dates of completion, coded locations, and a catalogue of artisans.

A secure, central receiving site had thinned from having been swollen with raw materials. Gold, silver, bronze, brass, cedar, cypress, iron nails, hand-hewn stones, and more had passed through the facility. Moving quickly, the finished items transitioned into secured storerooms until they could be placed in their permanent positions.

Rabbi Solomon turned his chair toward the desk and traded the thick stack of paper for a single sheet, reading until his eyes rested on the last line. *Alexia Evengeline Christensen.* He had to smile at the significance of her middle name. Did she realize her name carried the Hebrew word for stone? He shook his head. One day he'd ask her. The sheet's heading began then continued with a lengthy, detailed description of the antiquities, their authenticity, and inestimable value. He pushed back against his chair and drew in a deep breath. Leather creaking beneath his weight, his concentration blurred.

The young woman had recently initiated an interesting email session. When searching for information, she'd come across his plans to rebuild the Temple. At first she wrote to introduce herself and tell him of finding his site. Her avid fascination, not only with the Temple but with the holy items he was having reproduced, intrigued him. But when she asked some pointed questions regarding the wardrobe requirements of the high priest, he abandoned his usual practice of dictating responses to his associates. He replied personally.

By their third email, she'd let him know the reason for her interest, and that reason had Solomon on his feet, praying and pacing before he touched the keyboard to reply.

His computer security was good and had blocked several unauthorized access attempts. He'd set up their digital IDs to encrypt the balance of their email communications, but nothing was completely safe from determined hackers. Their correspondence then moved to using videophone with her father involved.

Solomon closed his eyes, allowing awe of the memory to race through his heart. Receipt of documents from a Boston jeweler had revealed the meaning of his vision. History predating even King Solomon still existed, preserved for centuries, saved from destruction by countless generations of a single Jewish family. Antiquities had been safeguarded with the intent of one day returning the gift to Israel. The young woman was inextricably woven into his life's work, and there had been no turning back.

Outside his office, the voices and rustling of business reminded him that he didn't bear the responsibility alone. Solomon had chosen two close friends, Rabbis Jacob Yachin and Benjamin Asher, to be his

liaisons and representatives. Levites, descendants of the first Aaron, men of integrity, he had assigned them special duties in the rebuilding process. And though he'd noted an unusual level of coolness from his friends since he'd told them of his intentions regarding the delivery of the ancient treasure, they had also seen the indisputable proof that the articles to be received were indeed genuine.

The old teacher drew in a breath filled with admiration for the man whom Lexi Christensen explained was responsible for the incredible return she was to make.

"Aaron Cohen, my brother." He spoke the words into his office as Jacob Yachin entered, Benjamin Asher in his shadow.

Yachin raised his heavy eyebrows as if less than amused by something, while Asher moved to stand beside him, stone-faced.

What was this? Their faces looked mutinous, and an evil darkness haunted their expressions. Solomon's throat dried as righteous fear gripped him.

Not by might nor by power, but by My Spirit, says the LORD of hosts.

Instant in prayer with words from the prophet, Zechariah, galvanizing him, anointing his heart with peace, he motioned toward the file cabinet. "Ah, Jacob, will you find the copy of Miss Christensen's last communication please?"

Yachin made no move to comply.

Solomon peered over his glasses. "It is difficult to believe we are soon to receive this lost treasure of Israel. Yes?" He cocked his head and smoothed his gray beard. "And from a young woman in America."

Yachin cleared his throat, rasping his words. "And *that*, I—we—respectfully submit, Rabbi, *cannot* happen."

Asher stiffened beside Yachin. "The Law is clear—"

Rabbi Solomon narrowed his eyes and raised his hand in a demand for silence. "And my command is from Hashem."

The great care he'd taken to explain his plans for receiving the holy artifacts had met with a black barricade. Then his explanation to his friends had not been enough? His palms grew damp against the arms of his chair. He had been mistaken. Their silent agreement had instead been a silent protest. He got up to close the door, and the three remained standing. He would not invite them to sit. Not yet.

"I have not made myself clear. The autonomy I have been given by the Council stands, and my decision is final. We will bring Miss Christensen, her family, and her friends to Israel. For Hashem, and to honor Aaron Cohen and his family, I will accept the treasure on behalf of this grateful nation into my hands . . . from hers."

Yachin clenched his fists, eyes hardened with open outrage and indignation. "Lawlessness! No woman's hands should bear the weight of a single holy item. And a Gentile? Blasphemy!" Beside him Asher's head bobbed and he stood, rocking in place.

Avi Solomon's breath left him with the leaden power of the words his friend uttered. He turned and sat heavily at his desk. These devout men endured the same internal struggle he had put aside: that a Gentile, a woman, had possession of sacred artifacts and would return them to the Holy City herself. If they were to help him, they had to believe as he did, that Adonai would fulfill His covenants, and the third Temple was no small part of the future of Israel.

Would they understand nothing was beyond the power of Hashem, that all things are in Hashem's hands? *Adonai, help me.*

"Son of man, describe the temple to the house of Israel . . . make known to them the design of the temple and its arrangement, its exits and its entrances, its entire design . . . Write it down in their sight, so they may keep its whole design and all its ordinances, and perform them."

The prophet Ezekiel's words filtered through Solomon's thoughts.

The vision. He'd held his vision too close to his heart, and he had told no man. A deep sigh shuddered its way through his chest. Perhaps hearing of his vision would open their eyes as it had his. But would deeply imbedded beliefs and habits allow his friends to accept things formerly forbidden and unclean?

"Sit. Please sit. I am urged to tell you more."

Asher ceased his agitated rocking as Yachin spoke. "I will warn you, nothing you say will justify your actions and make right this wrong, Rabbi." Yachin's expression eroded from anger to puzzlement as the two sat uneasily opposite Solomon.

Solomon pinned his gaze on them, praying for their minds and hearts to open. "It *will* take place." And he unfolded his experience to them. The indescribable white light, the whispered words, everything poured from his mouth into their hearing as he related details that drove a divine wedge between old and new.

As Solomon watched, doubt and skepticism turned to shock then incredulous belief, as humility and awe crossed their faces. Hashem would allow a foreign woman to return an ancient Hebrew treasure.

Silence bathed the room until Yachin rose, opened a file drawer, then handed a folder to Solomon.

Asher's hissed whisper to Yachin as they left the office didn't escape Solomon's hearing. "His face! Did you see the light in his face, Rabbi?"

Solomon laid the Christensen file down, picked up a small framed picture from the corner of his desk, and studied the vivid color photograph. He'd soon be face-to-face with this remarkable, attractive, dark-haired young woman. Adonai's hand surely covered her life. Were his friends truly convinced? Had Adonai seen fit to align them with His plans?

But wishing he could have assurance did not get his work done. He replaced the photograph and opened Lexi's folder.

He felt every year of his age as he stroked his beard, mulling over the decisions made about timing, transportation to Tel Aviv and Jerusalem, lodging, and meetings. He'd sent an email earlier that airline tickets for Lexi, her family and friends, as well as details of their travel itinerary, would be delivered to them tomorrow. Hashem willing, the group of seven would arrive in less than a week.

All had progressed well. Too well. He held a deep breath, praying. Something about the arrangements bothered him. He shook his head, exhaling slowly. What had he overlooked? Why this deep concern burning in his belly?

Chapter Twenty-Eight

At White Oak Ranch Thursday morning, Lexi finished conditioning the western saddle, heaved it onto the storage rack, and left the tack room. The stable doors stood open. A light breeze swept in from the corral and feathered the air with the scent of horses, sun-warmed wood, dust, and straw. She stood on the threshold, an incessant little cloud of foreboding falling like night around her. Nearly two weeks had vanished between the attempted robbery and now. Her sense of being stalked had lessened, but Dad had fended off at least two reporters' phone calls since then, and two detectives had returned to ask more probing questions about why her family might have been targeted for home invasion. Too many people knowing too many details asking too many questions.

She kicked up a plume of dust and grimaced at the way her thoughts dipped deep into negative territory. She'd been thrilled with the decision that Jen, Ridge, his dad, and Jacob would be traveling with Mom, Dad, and herself to Israel. Most of the arrangements were complete. Still, snakes of worry coiled around her heart and struck at her peace of mind.

Father, something isn't right. Please increase my faith; I'm really

slipping here.

A few stray clouds laced through the arch of the azure sky, and the sun speared vivid rays earthward. As if God's arm encircled her, Lexi basked in the reassuring warmth. She had plenty of reasons to be thankful. The problem of rescuing history in the form of an old mansion slated for destruction had resolved the second it slipped out of the trust and into her hands. Then, late last night, the Rabbi faxed the itinerary for their trip.

Two voices wafted from outside the corral, Jen's thicker-than-syrup drawl, and . . . Lexi turned to look. Nick Avery? Cute new guy on the island. He'd been out here to ride a lot lately. The corral gate opened. Lexi pulled back from the stable doors and rolled her eyes. Should she eavesdrop or barge in with a brazen interruption? She should keep her mouth shut and just walk out there. But her feet stayed put at Jenni's honey-dripped drawl.

"Y'all are a genius with that lasso, Nicky. I thought li'l Josh was gonna jump out of his boots waitin' for his turn to rope that post. Thanks so much for helpin' me with the kids this mornin'. They loved it."

Nick's reply was lost in noisy hoof beats as four horses loped into Lexi's view and toward the water trough.

Then Jen's voice chimed clear. "Okay, then, I'll talk to y'all later."

About what? Move! Lexi crossed the threshold as the corral gate shut, her only glimpse of Nick, his backside. If those two were going to talk later, would Jen tell her?

Her thumbs flying over her cellphone, Jenni stopped just short of running into Lexi.

"Hey, girl, what's up?"

Jenni poked her lower lip out and held up the cellphone. "We haven't had a minute to talk all morning, and this thing has gone all goofy on me. I'm not getting any texts. And where's Ridge?"

Lexi grinned at her. "Which is probably why you didn't answer the texts I sent you earlier. And Ridge should be out here soon." They climbed the wood corral rails and sat.

Lexi angled her old straw hat to shade her face. "Well, are you going to tell me what's up with you and Nick that you're going to talk later?"

Jenni straightened and almost toppled off the rail. "Uh, nothing's up with Nick. I . . . he just wanted to know how we like the vet we use for the cats, but we didn't have time to talk much this morning."

Oh, there was something up all right, but what was the quirky expression that covered Jenni's face? Lexi backed off. She could be wrong. "We got a fax from Rabbi Solomon late last night."

"Then you know when we're leaving. Tell me! When?"

Lexi nodded. "We fly out of Logan International next Tuesday morning, have one layover in New York, fly straight to Tel Aviv, and from there we drive to Jerusalem."

"God's hand is in this." Jen shivered and rubbed at her arms. "Ever since that first day at Northbrick House, it's like I've been watching some kinda miracle unfold. I keep seeing you in the center of what God is doing—in every detail."

Lexi studied her dusty boots and nodded. "I feel like I'm opening a gift . . . a little at a time until I see all of it . . . if I really ever will."

"Hey! Where's your faith, girl? You'll see it all. Look here at me."

Jenni's gaze was arrow-straight as Lexi lifted her head. Jenni's words were slower than usual, and thoughtful. "You have a job to do. You *are* going to Israel."

Lexi dipped her head again to stop another rush of doubt and let Jen's words meander through the recesses of her mind. She held her breath, made herself count the two-dozen horses milling around inside the enclosure. The truth was she was a "doubting Thomas." She needed to touch the hands of Jesus, to see everything. Oh! She just lacked faith; her moods, her thoughts, were as up and down as dawn and dusk.

Jenni said something about it being too hot and her great grandmother's sunbonnet. Lexi tried to listen and nod in the right places. A piece of straw clung to her jeans. She picked it up and chewed on an end. At least Mom seemed to have come to grips with Lexi hand-delivering the box to the rabbi, and even wanted to be there when she did. Their head-butting edginess had eased up, and Mom had been an anchor when Lexi needed her. Dad guided her through the maze of travel plans, discussing them with her as they talked to the rabbi. Even Gilly stayed close, a friendly reminder to keep her feet firmly planted in reality. Why didn't any of it stop the twinges of breath-holding dread?

A man's heart plans his way, but the Lord directs his steps

Words from Proverbs slipped in and changed her focus. Long ago, her godfather believed in her, left instructions for her, trusted her with his secrets enough to give her all of Northbrick. If she believed the Lord directed her godfather's steps and her own, surely God would give her the faith and the strength to do everything Uncle Aaron had wanted her to do. She couldn't get through any of this by herself. She wasn't even about to try. Hadn't Jesus said he'd be with us to the end? Hadn't she felt his presence?

Beside her, Jen sat, quiet, and Lexi figured she'd given up on the sunbonnet subject. A sea breeze twisted a small dust devil around in the corral, and she sent the mangled piece of straw sailing to the ground. "Timing's going to be close and tough with the three of us leaving for school so soon after we get back. I'm so glad you're going to Israel with me."

"No happier than Ridge 'n' me are." Jenni nudged Lexi's black boot with her brown one. "I'm excited. I know you are too, but something's on your mind. Spill!"

Spill? No way! Lexi's throat closed. She couldn't put into words what was going on in her heart and mind. She couldn't voice how shaky her faith was, that she felt exposed, vulnerable, and fearful the treasure still wasn't safe, that none of them really were. Saying the words would make it too real. But Jen was staring at her, waiting for an answer.

Lexi pushed wind-tangled hair away from her eyes. She was way too stressed out. Her hands balled into fists. She should just keep it all to herself.

No, she wouldn't, not some things. "I'm worried about what happens when we get home and it's over. It's like there's a whole lot I need to do right here on the island. Then I think of the heavy class load I've committed to this year, and my knees get weak."

She'd told the truth but not all of it. Deliberately unwinding her hands, she placed them flat and damp against her thighs.

"If it helps, Lex, I haven't stopped praying for you."

"I know you haven't. Thanks. I feel every one of those prayers and . . ." She looked up, distracted as Ridge walked over in the boots Jenni and she had helped him pick out last year. A tiny shiver shimmied down her back. Aside from a coating of barn dust, Ridge looked like he'd just stepped off the cover of American Cowboy magazine.

And she was staring. Good grief, she had to shake herself out of this! Lexi wrenched her eyes away from him and jumped from the rail, Jenni right behind her.

Ridge put his arms around each of them. "I'll walk you to your transport, women. Don't know about you, but I'm ready to head home for some grub and a hot shower. Not sure which'll come first."

Lexi smiled up at him. "Me, too. And by the way, horse scent suits you."

Ridge laughed and gave her waist a gentle squeeze. "Okay, so I

stink a little. But horse *sense* I've got, and we need to use some of it in making the rest of our plans. Which reminds me, have you firmed up our leave-date with the rabbi yet?"

Lexi could have done without the little squeeze. It meant nothing, and he was just too close. She completely lost her train of thought as he looked at her with those piercing gold-struck hazel eyes. He obviously expected an answer, but the tanned muscles of his arm touched hers. *Work, brain!* She chewed her lip, groping for a quick recovery of both her wits and her breath.

"Uh . . . Tuesday . . . We leave Tuesday morning. The rabbi faxed the details late last night; tickets'll come tomorrow." She paused, ducked out from under his arm, and bent to brush an imaginary something from her jeans. No way could she think curled into his arm.

She tilted her head at him. "And no, we won't be taking the Gulfstream. Too many of us for that long of a flight, so it's commercial all the way." She caught disappointment flash across his face and grinned. "We'll take it from here to Logan though."

Even white teeth showed in his broad smile. "Sounds good to me." Ridge opened the corral gate, double-checking the latch, and they walked toward the spot where they'd parked their cars.

Jenni took off her hat and fanned her face. "I'm still not believing your rabbi's foundation insists on paying for our whole trip."

Lexi leaned against the El Camino's fender, ignoring Ridge's frown of protest. She ran her tongue over her dry lips and hoped she sounded more coherent than her thoughts were. "Just might have something to do with our special delivery. I keep thinking about his work and what plans he'll have for us when we get there."

Ridge's arm slid around her waist again, pulling her away from the fender, and she lost her breath—until his other arm curved around Jen.

Her heart did an odd double beat in her chest, and she squeezed her eyes shut. Why did it matter?

It may have been corral dust, but something gritty coated her throat as she pushed out of his grip and headed to her car. "Hey, guys, we're still on at my house around three this afternoon, right? We have lots to talk about, and my to-do list is growing." Her words sounded forced and raspy, and a wave of uneasiness shuddered through her. Something had to change.

Chapter Twenty-Nine

Riyadh, Saudi Arabia

Ejecting Alexia Christensen from his thoughts? Not as easy as Salim al-`Attar had hoped as he paced the edge of the multicolor carpet at four o'clock Friday morning. Beyond the vaulted arches of his windows, the sky rolled out in a star-scattered, midnight-black tapestry. He paused near the bank of computers at one end of his spacious bedroom.

A thrill of enthusiasm spun through him, and Salim pulled in a long breath, his spirits lifting as he recalled the email exchanges he'd decrypted. It had been a week since Rick Vander "introduced" him to the American girl and the Jewish rabbi, and all of it seemed pure Hollywood movie-fiction come to life. Correspondence between the girl and the rabbi involved everything from an abandoned estate to her college plans. He was riveted with interest.

Hours too soon, he'd bathed and dressed, and was ready to leave for the mosque to attend Friday prayers. Maybe prayer would reshape his shaken beliefs and end his searching and confusion about the Man in his

vision. Between Lexi and that wretched vision, his mind was a sea of endless conflict. He swallowed hard and dug into the pocket of his robe to finger his prayer beads. Why all this kite-like twisting in the wind?

He glanced at the two clocks near the monitors. Nine o'clock at night, Eastern Standard Time on the island called Nantucket, and four o'clock here. Would she be there, in the chat room, posting?

Salim went to the computer desk and sat, staring at the alignment of wide, flat-screen monitors, end-to-end down its length, then focused on one of the two in front of him. Euphoria sparked along his arms, then faded as he scanned post after post in the Christian chat room, none with Lexi's tagline.

Why couldn't he get the woman out of his mind? Curiosity, compulsion to know everything about Lexi overwhelmed him. He wasn't really stalking her. But if Googling her, checking her out on Facebook, and digging into her personal email and documents qualified him as a stalker, he was. Inside an old house, she'd stumbled across something priceless. That would have been intriguing enough, but this woman was also smart and interesting. Nearly every night, calling herself "Dove," she entered the chat room that was obviously Christian. He'd followed her in, lurking and listening, but never posting. She had something that drew him like a magnet—knowledge of the Jewish prophet, Jesus. She talked openly of Him and, as if He were alive, how important He was in her life. But the man was dead. Right?

Activity increased on the first monitor. He straightened and studied the screen. Dove. She was in. He leaned closer, reading the post she wrote to someone who called himself Jackknife: "Do you believe in God the Father, God the Son, and God the Holy Spirit?"

Salim nodded at Jackknife's answer. "But how can one God be a Father, a Son, and a Spirit at the same time?"

THE STONEKEEPERS

Pure idiocy! Annoying discussion. But he couldn't stop reading. Praying as his fingers flew over the ninety-nine prayer beads, he ended at the leader-bead with a whispered "Allah. There is no deity but Allah."

The spoken tribute only added to his confusion as he tried to absorb Dove's return post. "God is three Persons in One—God Who is our Father, God Who is His Son, and God Who is Spirit. Think about an egg, J-knife; it's one, yet three: shell, white, and yolk. Or think about ice, water, and steam—all are the same, but different. There is nothing impossible to God."

Then Lexi asked Jackknife a question that had Salim pounding his fist on the desk so hard it shook the monitors.

"Do you know where you're going when you die?"

The screen blurred. His father's double-edged dagger could not have pierced Salim's heart more deeply. Of course, he knew! Didn't he?

He blinked hard, but the question still hung in the box in the center of the screen, a searchlight singling him out. Until that moment he'd been confident of his answer. Not anymore. With laser intensity, the vision of the Man who spoke to him sliced into his thoughts.

Salim stopped eavesdropping and posted for the first time.

Moments later, he shoved his chair backward, lowered his elbows to his knees, his hands cradling his forehead. He gazed down into the sheen of the polished wood flooring beneath his feet as if it would help him understand, then left the computers and walked to his bed. He flopped down onto the silk covering and stared at the ceiling, the recalled vision achingly real.

In it, he lay on his back on top of a mountain. In a sky far bluer than any of the brightest days in Arabia, two men in white stood, side-by-side, watching him. Their eyes and expressions beheld him with great gentleness. The two moved aside, and a third Man appeared between them, His robes gleaming white and His face . . .

A knowing seared into Salim's heart. The Man, the great prophet, Jesus, of the Holy Qur'an, nodded and held out His arms as if inviting Salim to come to Him, to follow Him.

His heart and breath suspended, Salim's eyes fixed on the eyes of Jesus as He spoke words that burned into his hearing.

Believe me, that I am in the Father and the Father in Me. I *am the way, the truth, and the life, my son.*

And for a few breath-holding bits of time, the words and vision resonated.

Why had the dream ceased at that instant? Salim rubbed his arms, reliving the warmth of love and compassion that emanated from the Man's face.

He'd studied the Qur'an. Since childhood, he'd been taught of the prophets. He knew and deeply respected the greatness of the prophet Jesus. Yet, how had he known the Man was Jesus? And who was he that this prophet had invaded his dreams. He was not uneducated that he didn't know the myths of Jesus' crucifixion and supposed death. Why did Jesus appear to *him*? Did He want Salim to believe He was more than a major prophet?

He shook his head. An infidel belief. His mind and reason battled against the empty ache in his chest and consumed him with a desperate need to know more.

As the months had passed, he'd heard of others having dreams and visions during Ramadan, and some had risked ridicule to tell of seeing the Man Jesus. Salim researched everything he could find in the Holy Qur'an about Jesus. He'd prowled his father's library for old holy books and documents. Hours were devoted to Internet searches, sifting through information, finding and printing articles, filling a file with copies, notes, and his thoughts. The more he searched, the more confused he became, and his hunger to know more deepened.

His chest hurt. He closed his hand around the prayer beads, clenching them until his fist ached, and vowed he would meet Lexi in Israel, with or without Rick or his father's permission. A thread of uneasiness persisted. Why this sense that her life might be at stake if he did not go? His thoughts drifted to an image of the appraisal of the artifacts, and with the finality of his decision, his hands relaxed.

Slamming against culture, against tradition, more than anything, he wanted to meet Lexi. What would she be like? Would she act and speak differently in person? Could she answer his thousand questions?

He rose and returned to the computers. Back to work. Maybe burying himself in a project would fill the time before he left for the mosque. Salim picked up the list of instructions from Rick and concentrated on them.

Amal's unique rap sounded on the bedroom door.

"Enter, Amal."

The burly man brought a breakfast tray of steaming shaay, hot breads, honey, cheese, eggs, and olives. "Peace be upon you. I heard you up quite early, sir."

"Upon you be peace, Amal." Salim smiled and cocked an eyebrow at his servant. "Then I was not the only one up early. Here. Clear a space and set the meal up here. I'm in the midst of a project."

Salim caught Amal's eyes straying to the screens, but made no move to clear the monitors while Amal spread the food on the table and prepared to leave. But Amal might have some wise words; more friend than servant, never had he been untrustworthy.

"Stay, Amal. You will take the morning meal with me. I need to inform you of my plans; you're part of them."

"Sir, I have—"

"Nothing is more important than this, Amal. It would please me if

you would sit."

Nodding, Amal went to a cabinet for an additional gold-handled tea glass for himself, served his charge, prepared a plate, then sat opposite.

As they ate, the second screen switched between a live feed from a high-jacked security camera to images of receipts from a Boston jewelry store with the girl's father's signature, and an appraisal that Salim still couldn't wrap his brain around.

"What you see on the screen, Amal, involves a trip to Jerusalem— very soon. I have spoken to you of my American friend, Rick. Two days ago he informed me he would be going to Israel."

No need for Amal to know details of the alias and documents he'd created to get Rick across borders. And he'd keep how he'd unraveled Rick's request involving records secured in an American jewelry company's computer to himself.

He'd easily lived up to his Alpha-Z reputation when he quickly laid the supposedly safeguarded papers and photographs wide open for Rick. But the information the papers and photos held surprised Salim.

Hacking was one thing, but actually stealing records was another. He'd told himself not to feel guilty, but guilt was what he felt now as he thought about the violated paperwork. Stealing wasn't his preference, but for Rick, he'd do it.

Amal moved uneasily in his seat, but his expression betrayed his fascination. Maybe even a twinge of excitement? "So you have facilitated your friend's journey?"

Salim combed his fingers through his hair. "Nothing I couldn't handle. Travel arrangements from Boston to Tel Aviv are complete, and he's booked into a hotel room in Jerusalem under the name of Gerald Jamison, from Austin, Texas." Salim paused for Amal's reaction. He didn't add that he'd called for a courier for pick-up tomorrow morning.

Rick would receive the itinerary, fictitious ID, complete with passport and credit cards soon.

"Ah. Then we will meet Rick Vander, alias Gerald Jamison? Let us pray there are no more earthquakes while we are there. Allah was with us in Jerusalem when we missed the last one by only two days."

"The arrangements I have made for us are also final, and you will need to pack for us and be ready to leave on short notice."

Amal smiled, rose, cleared the desk, and left the bedroom. Good. Tension eased from Salim's taut muscles. This was no business trip with Salim's father, but he'd have no argument from Amal, even if the man wasn't aware that something more earth-shaking than a quake might occur.

Salim straightened and stretched. He didn't need Rick's money, but craving the challenge, he rarely wasted time thinking about the future or considering the consequences. It simply hadn't mattered if he got caught—until recently when he'd considered getting caught just might matter to him one day. He reached to remove the DVD of information from the jewelry firm and backed out of the live feed.

Now his fingers raced over the keyboard as he pushed himself to do the work. He ignored the risks he took with his illegal activities, even as his thoughts stirred with something else--the odd desire to stop. But why? If he didn't care about what happened to the items the documents described, he shouldn't care who got hurt by what he did.

Who? Name her! What if throwing Lexi to that wolf Rick meant she'd get hurt? He couldn't let that happen. An ugly sense of guilt clawed its way into his mind, along with an impending sense of dread about Rick's intentions.

At dawn, he watched the sun deliver Friday morning through the sheer window hangings as it spread lemon-yellow smears across the

blue sky, then rose to leave. Doubt filled his heart that his offered prayers would even begin to sort out his agitation.

Boston, Massachusetts

The FedEx envelope with its return address of Arabia burned in Rick Vander's hand. His breathing shallow, he stood in his doorway and ripped the container open, leafing through the contents, reading.

He leaned against the doorjamb, the envelope trembling in his grip. So much for electronic records being carefully guarded. Salim had lifted a file full of records and communications, invaluable information, from the jewelry firm's computer. The evidence Rick held made it worth the wait. Greyson Quinn had come to him with the find of the millennium.

The fence was going to love this. Private collectors would pay top dollar. Even splitting it, they'd make a fortune. Except . . . . He scowled, remembering Quinn's pathetic description of the plan he had in mind. There was no way Quinn would succeed.

Rick's sardonic laugh echoed down the hallway as he banged the front door shut and mentally booted Quinn from his mind. He would plant himself in Jerusalem and put his own hands on this treasure.

Anticipation drove his eyes toward the alcove where his bags were packed and waiting near the door. He needed a little more help from Salim, but he was ready.

Chapter Thirty

Boston, Massachusetts

Above scurrying waves of humanity, Logan International Airport terminal's endless rows of blurry white orbs reflected onto the polished gray flooring like runway lights. Lexi planted one wedge-sandaled foot in front of the other, stiff with a wooden sense of unreality. Maybe she was too tired. At four this morning, Dad's Gulfstream had flown the seven travelers from Nantucket to Boston, and they'd arrived at the airport hours early. Now they walked together in two uneven columns down the concourse, her parents in front, she and Jen behind them, and bringing up the rear, Ridge and his dad, Steven Scott, flanking Jacob Carver. There was nothing unreal about the gentle bump of Jenni's arm against hers as Jenni wrangled their two carry-on bags. Lexi loosened the safety strap that anchored her to the briefcase. She rubbed her chafed wrist but left the strap on, much less snug than it had been. She'd won the brief yes/no argument with her parents about who would carry the custom-made black leather case, a gift from the rabbi. It weighed in her

favor that Solomon had her name engraved on a small gold plate near the handle.

Security was tight, but they'd gotten special clearance for the briefcase. It still had to pass through the scanner, the only moment it would be out of her sight and hands. That she could deal with, but thoughts of what the case held . . . She gulped in air to slow her racing heart. At least the majority of their luggage had already been checked through, and they'd be boarding soon.

ID and passport parked in the pocket of her white jeans. Check. Purse inside her carry-on. Check. Aaron's journal. Check. It lay wrapped, packed beneath her clothes in the bottom of her luggage. Along with it, she'd stowed the new journal that chronicled her life from the moment she first walked through the door of Northbrick. From Nantucket to Jerusalem, her life had become worth journaling.

Images of Uncle Aaron in the old black-and-white photos fanned an odd mixture of excitement and anxiety in her chest as words from the parchment filled her mind.

"Preserve these stones—you are commanded to.
Be vigilant and wise as you prepare the way,
The stones' return to the Temple . . ."

Had she been vigilant and wise enough? The preservation part sent a chill through her. So far they were safe. Could she keep them that way?

"When the time has come to pass, it will be true and clear.
I will choose My messenger, the day, the time, the year."

She swallowed hard against the lump in her throat. Messenger. Everything had happened so fast. Her godfather's generational vow, the Cohen covenant, would be fulfilled in hours. She couldn't fall apart now.

Help, Lord! This is so huge, and I need to get it done for you with a little dignity.

THE STONEKEEPERS

"I'm such a wimp." Her eyes blurred with a mist of tears, and she choked back anger at her hammering emotions.

"Huh?" Jenni slowed her steps, looked at Lexi, and laughed out loud. "You look like you just flunked a final exam. You *can* do this. Do I have to get Ridge over here to give you another pep talk?"

"That bad?" Lexi glanced over her shoulder at Ridge and took a deep breath. "No!" If he got near her, for heaven's sake, she *would* fly apart!

A silly grin tipped up the corners of Jenni's lips. "Ridge has been great."

Lexi nodded. A flush of warmth swept into her cheeks, and she hoped Jen didn't notice. Ridge's soft heart showed itself when he stayed constantly beside Jacob, helping the old man with subtle gentleness. Jacob's reluctance to use a wheelchair slowed their walk through the airport, and it had been Ridge who encouraged them to respect Jacob's wishes.

"There's our gate, Dad." But her parents had moved too far ahead to hear her. Lexi turned at the *rat-a-tat* click of high heels close behind her. A young woman dressed in a svelte cream-colored business suit barged through the gap between Ridge and Jacob and rushed up to her in a scented wash of perfume and . . . garlic? For breakfast?

"Miss Christensen! Excuse me, Miss Christensen. I understand you're transporting some kind of ancient Jewish artifact. Is that correct?"

Jen's hand circled Lexi's arm, and Lexi halted, her mouth and throat desert-dry. The woman, press card dangling around her neck, microphone in one hand and cellphone in the other, closed the few feet between them like a starved barracuda. A man wielding a camera trailed the reporter, and if the camera's red light meant anything, captured Lexi's every move.

The area erupted into a media frenzy. Jacob, Ridge, and his dad vanished behind bobbing video cameras with call letters of CNN, FOX, MSNBC, ABC, CBS emblazoned on their sides. How had they gotten . . . ? Blinking red lights aimed at her like robot probes. A sea of faceless monsters floated in from every angle, hurling questions at her like darts. Lightning-white flashes blinded her with silvery round ghosts when she blinked. Lexi clenched the case against her stomach and froze.

A second reporter with teased blonde hair elbowed her way through the cluster of cameras. "I've been told you've had an artifact authenticated, Miss Christensen. Can you tell us exactly what you've found and how old it is?"

How did they know her? How could they possibly know what she had? Did they know where she was going?

"I . . . I . . . it's . . ." The words hung unfinished as Lexi stood rooted to the floor.

A squatty man with long hair rubber-banded into a ponytail targeted her with a verbal volley. "Isn't Israel your destination, Miss Christensen? Ultimately Jerusalem?"

Then they *did* know. Had someone—? Her stomach churned in rebellion. She, all of them, had kept their itinerary quiet. No one had any reason to know who they were, why they were here, or their destination. At least that was the intent. Why would anyone know or care about their plans?

Ponytail's microphone joined the others, inches from Lexi's lips. Something seemed to vacuum the air from around her, as if she breathed through cotton batting. One more word from anyone, she'd lose it and scream.

Her father moved between Lexi and the noisy mob; his voice boomed, annoyed and commanding. "We have no comment." His hand shot forward, slapping the man's mic aside; he glared at the reporter who stepped back, startled.

The disorienting scene undulated as if underwater, and Lexi pulled in a shaky breath. In the shoving, bumping mass, Jenni's hand jerked from Lexi's arm and Steve Scott tried to move closer.

The camera's penetrating eye never wavered from Lexi. She had to get away. Heat rose in her face, and her fingernails dug into the damp palms of her hands. Where was airport security? Breathe, she had to breathe. Craving space, she edged into a clear spot to her right then jolted at the *crash* of something large hitting the floor.

Instinct whirled her into the direction of the noise. A cameraman had dropped his camera. She watched him bend . . . to pick it up . . .

But the camera lay broken, scattered . . . untouched.

Icy prickles covered her like a snow-heavy avalanche. Déjà vu flashed the mental echo of a man in black rising like a mountain of lava . . .

Her mouth rounded in a silent scream. Run! She had to run!

The cameraman leapt from his crouch with an unearthly growl. A wide-shouldered, black-clothed blur, he launched himself at her like a crazed animal.

Time and terror iced the passing seconds, and froze her in place.

God—please—help!

A battering ram, he flew into her, a body-blow that doubled her over and sent her to the floor, jetting her into a wild backward slide. Breath crushed from her lungs, her head brushing the unforgiving marble as she slid. The case slammed down beside her, her fingers locked around the handle. Her thoughts a cyclone of panic, she gasped for air.

He was after the case.

No! He wouldn't touch it without a fight. She scrambled, tried to get

up. A flash. Something in his hand. A knife? Box cutter? Would he kill her?

Upright, agile, and fit, the man crossed the few feet to where he'd sent her sprawling.

Fear wrapped her, choked her. Fight him!

No time. He leaned over, his breath hot, his hand a vise, squeezing, bruising her arm. She couldn't shut her eyes, watching, as with a single fierce slice, the strap separated, ripped from her wrist; he yanked the briefcase from her hand, stood, and took off.

Her hand, wrist, and arm stung, throbbed from his savage wrench. She glanced at her arm. No blood. He'd somehow missed slicing her wrist. Pain stabbed through her side, curved her into a ball on the cold marble floor. Blackness threatened to envelope her, to suck the life from her. She shut her eyes and fought for breath, to pull back from the edge of oblivion.

"Lexi!"

Daddy. Her heart pounded, her lungs burned with every desperate gulp of air she drew. She opened her eyes to her father's anxious gaze.

Get up. She had to get up. Through tears of frustration, her father's arms supporting her, Lexi struggled to her feet, wincing. "Oh, Dad, I'm so sorry! He got the case."

The stunned crowd suddenly came alive, moving toward her. She shunned her aches and glanced at her mother, who tried to prevent a furious-faced Jacob Carver from hobbling after the man. Jenni pushed toward Lexi, tears on her cheeks.

A few feet away, Ridge caught Lexi's eyes with his, hesitated, then visually examined her head to foot before she sent him a tiny nod. In a split second, all six feet of him erupted into a full run after the counterfeit cameraman.

She watched Ridge vault over a heap of baggage in his way. "God, please, help him."

The media took off with cameras rolling, and everyone turned toward the chase. Lexi stood, numb, her eyes locked on Ridge, his muscular body in a full-out sprint after the man. No way would he let her assailant get away with this. And she couldn't just stand here like a fence post!

She clutched her side, slipped from her father's protective arms, and raced after Ridge, her shoes barely touching the floor, silently cheering him on. With every movement, the curves and angles of his body focused on his target. Lexi's heart stirred, sparking of something much deeper than admiration as she followed.

The briefcase flailing in his hand, the man in black bumped and buffeted his way through throngs of people, shoving anyone who got in his way. Ridge's stride increased, lessened the space between them.

No slowing down. Lexi dismissed the pangs in her side and wove through the crowd.

A few feet behind Ridge, another man joined the chase, shadowing him. Friend or enemy, Lexi had no time to worry or think about either as the strange, silent race continued.

An emergency exit door stood directly ahead, and pain greater than physical seared through her. The case couldn't vanish into the street!

Ridge . . . What was he doing? She slowed and stared as Ridge's muscles rippled and seized. He leapt, arms out, airborne in a flying tackle, and heaved himself at the thief.

The man, sandwiched between Ridge and the floor, smacked down flat on his face with a resounding *crack*. Decked. Two bloodied white squares, undeniably front teeth, skittered across the floor. His hat and dark glasses flew from his head and scudded away, along with the case.

Lexi suddenly had an unrestricted side view of his face. Both hands fisted, she pulled in ragged gasps of air and gaped at the man's sharp

features. "You!"

Centered on Quinn's back as if riding a bull, Ridge looked at her. He followed her line of vision to the thief's face, then to the bling around his neck. Recognition flooded Ridge's tanned, even features, and he tipped his head back and laughed. "Looks like your Hawk, aka Greyson P. Quinn, Jr., just got his wings clipped."

Lexi would have been happy to clip Quinn's head off then and there, but Ridge's laughter brought a smile to her lips.

An out-of-shape, out-of breath airport security guard jogged up and reported in on his lapel mic, but made no attempt to get between Ridge and the downed attorney.

Ridge kept the bloodied, winded attorney pinned and turned his attention to the briefcase that had ended up a few feet away. The man who'd followed Ridge during the chase reached to pick it up.

Lexi's heartbeat quickened as she watched the casually dressed man approach Ridge. Was Ridge about to have another chase on his hands? Ridge got up, wary, muscles tensed. Without a word, the man took a black leather folder from his pocket, flipped it open, and handed it to Ridge. Relieved, Lexi glimpsed the unique blue six-pointed star it displayed.

Gasping for air, Quinn pushed to get up.

"You! Stay put!" Ridge put one foot in the center of Quinn's back, took the folder, and read out loud. "Israeli Intelligence and Special Operations, Agent Zeev Birman?" The surprise in Ridge's voice matched Lexi's as the man accepted the returned badge.

Mossad? He could be. She'd heard they performed special covert operations beyond the borders of Israel, but this was a little less than covert. Did he know what she carried?

Dark brows raised, Ridge looked at Birman.

"Just protecting our interests, Mr. Scott," Birman said. He glanced at the engraved nameplate then gave the case to Ridge. "I believe this is what you were trying to retrieve."

Lexi stared. How did the man know who Ridge was?

Despite the small pool of red forming on the floor beside his face, Quinn interrupted them with a loud, lisped tirade of protests that the case belonged to him. Birman glared at the attorney, his voice steel-cold. "No, Quinn, it does *not* belong to you, and I strongly suggest you remain silent."

Lexi bit back a smile as Quinn looked at the imposing figure towering above him and shut his mouth. Birman turned, nodded at her, and left, blending into the crowd.

"Nice takedown, man," the ponytailed reporter hailed through a ripple of applause from the gathered crowd.

Lexi watched Quinn, playbacks of the attorney at the mansion and library flashing through her mind.

Her father's voice sounded behind her. "You all right, honey?" Suddenly light-headed, Lexi's knees trembled and buckled. He grasped her arm, steadied her.

She leaned against him, pulled in a breath, and stretched the truth. "I'm fine, Dad. Just got a little dizzy for a sec." She was all right except for pain in her side, and her discovery that it was Quinn who'd attacked her.

Dad turned her and studied her face. "If you're certain you'll be okay, I'll go check on the others."

"I'll be fine here with Ridge."

"Right. Back in a minute." He grinned and moved through a landscape of cameras and reporters.

Ridge, briefcase in hand, stayed near Quinn, as a security officer squatted beside Quinn, sat him up, and did a perfunctory pat-down. Stuffing gauze into the oozing gap in Quinn's mouth, he read him his rights and handcuffed him while another gloved officer retrieved the attorney's two front teeth.

For a moment—a long, pointless moment—Lexi watched Ridge, wanting to shut out the world to everyone, everything, but him. She wanted him to pull her into his arms, hold her close, to hear his comforting words, feel his strength, let all who was Ridge belong to her— just for a moment. As if he'd heard her thoughts, he fastened his hazel eyes on her, cocked his head, and walked toward her.

Maybe it was the ache in her side, but if he took one step closer . . . and if she didn't breathe, she really was going to pass out, right here, in front of him. No one's shoulders should be that wide. No one should have dark hair that curled around their ears the way his did. No man should have a heart as tender . . . . She couldn't tear her eyes from him, the sinewy glide of his steps, the way his arms challenged the seams of his shirt for space.

She blinked hard. Simply because his expression sent her stomach in a tailspin and melted her heart didn't mean his concern showed anything but friendship. It just couldn't.

He put the case down and took her hand, lacing his strong fingers through hers.

She pulled in a quick breath. "Um, you sure sent him flying. That was a great tackle." Yeah, as if she knew what a great tackle was! She threw her arms around him in a quick hug then tried to push away, but he held her close. And she couldn't help herself. Right there in his arms, she relaxed against the strength of his chest and closed her eyes for long, sweet seconds.

His lips brushed her cheek, leaving a trail of warmth as he whispered into her hair, "Hey, God even answers prayers on the run."

His breath tickled the top of her ear, and she shivered as he leisurely pulled back and held her face between his warm hands. He welded his eyes to hers as if to search her thoughts.

"That guy charged you like a raging bull. Are you okay?"

Lexi touched her tender side. "I'll probably have a few colorful bruises for a while, nothing more." She didn't want to admit her side ached like crazy, didn't want him worrying over her.

He held her at arm's length and frowned. "Not so sure I believe that, but okay."

She picked up the case. "Thanks for saving this."

He ignored her thanks and squeezed her shoulder. Then, releasing his gentle grip, he pointed at Quinn. "I think that bird will be grounded for a while. His ten-gallon Stetson and the aviator sunglasses did a fair job of camouflage, but what clinched it for me was the gold glitter around his neck."

Jenni sidled in between them, threading her arm through Lexi's as security gave Quinn a thorough search. "Glad you're okay, girlfriend. And Ridge, that was amazing. You got him!" She glanced at Quinn. Eyes wide, her head bobbed. "Isn't that . . . ?"

"Yep, we netted the Hawk." Ridge looked up as his father grasped his son's shoulder.

"All that football practice paid off big-time. Good work, son. Are you all right?"

"Yeah, thanks, Dad. I'm good, but that guy's going to need a dentist."

"Quite a tackle, Ridge." Lexi's dad shook Ridge's hand, and Mom wrapped her arms around Ridge in a hug.

Jacob turned to Ridge's father and pointed at Quinn. "You know who he is, don't you? Grey Quinn's son. Grey made him an associate in his law firm in Nantucket not long ago. Boy's in deep trouble now."

Lexi's dad looked at her chokehold on the briefcase and held out his

hand. "You were right about him, sweetheart, and I don't think he'll be much of a threat to anyone for a while."

Lexi didn't hesitate to trade Dad's luggage for hers. Letting him take over was smarter. She hadn't done so well with the job.

A trio of men in FBI-emblazoned vests approached, the tallest introducing himself as Agent Mike Kelley. Mossad? FBI? More trouble? They had to get to their gate soon. The case was safe in Dad's hand, but Lexi brewed with the same storm surge of resolution that had propelled her into Northbrick.

Trust in Me with all your heart. Her tension eased, but her questions didn't.

Kelley took a phone call then turned to the gathered group. "Looks like you've rated some special attention. That call came from a high-level official at the Israeli Embassy in Washington, DC. Although they don't foresee any more incidents, they've arranged for additional security. At this point, we have arrested and charged Quinn on several counts, and we have a lot of eye-witnesses and news and security footage. You'll still have the option of pressing charges, but we'll hold off any interviews with you until you return."

Kelley turned to Lexi. "You might like to know that calls from an unidentified male tipped every major newspaper and network in Boston about a huge story breaking at Logan International." He rubbed at his squared chin. "Telling them there'd been a major historic discovery, he apparently gave them enough info to convince them it was legit."

Lexi squirmed beneath a stern gaze that alternated between her and the briefcase, and Kelley shook his head as if what followed was inevitable. "The man gave info that pinpointed you, and from there, the story went national."

Quinn. It had to have been him. He'd singled her out and probably counted on the mob of reporters to give him cover for the theft, and he'd almost pulled it off.

He was certainly covered now and probably would soon be parked in a detention cell. But what if someone bailed him out? Surely they wouldn't let him go right away. But the idea he might try something more, from the confines of a prison cell or not, worried her. Her attempts to focus began a slow meltdown.

Quinn mumbled something about a phone call as he was hauled to his feet. Ridge picked up Quinn's hat and gave it to one of the burly officers. The man jammed it on the attorney's head and aimed him toward the main terminal. "'Fraid that's not going to happen," the officer rasped. "You have an appointment to meet and greet a few more of Boston's finest in about two minutes."

Quinn turned and leveled deadly cold eyes at Lexi, not breaking his stare until he received a sharp shove from behind. A glacial chill raced down her spine. Everything in her shrieked that this wasn't over yet.

Chapter Thirty-One

Jerusalem, Israel

Good morning, Heavenly Father, I love you.

Lexi shoved the bed sheets aside and stretched, reveling in the comfort of the room where she and Jen would stay for the next few days. The digital clock on the bedside table flashed 5:08 a.m. Good. Plenty of time to get away and think. But waking up in this historic place and about to keep an appointment with a rabbi at the site of the rising temple was pretty unbelievable.

She rolled over, praising and praying for a few moments before her mind wandered to Ridge. The mental guardrails she'd erected around her heart crumbled with thoughts of how his eyes melded with hers as if to drink her in as they talked on the flight, and the way his hand smoothed her arm in a tender touch. All of it had her head swimming and mind diving into places it shouldn't. She shook her head. Of course there was also how he'd helped Jacob, and his gorgeous take-down tackle of Quinn at Logan.

She grabbed her pillow and hugged it hard against her chest. Over the

last week or so, Jen's flirty, clingy little ways with Ridge had lessened, and he'd been all business as they finished plans for the trip. And Lexi hadn't simply imagined how close he stayed to her, almost hovering. Or maybe she had. Time had raced by, and there hadn't been much time to wonder about the changes between the three of them. And why was getting anything out of Jenni about Nick rougher than prying open an oyster? She sighed. So hard to let go and trust, but every shred of her life was in God's hands.

Enough. Get up! Get ready and leave. She should be thinking about why she was here. Propped up on an elbow in the dim light, she listened. A few feet away, Jenni's quiet, even breathing sifted from beneath the mound of covers.

Nothing but darkness and glistening city lights outside the window. Lexi slid out of bed, thankful for the humming air-conditioner and the thick carpet that muffled her steps. She'd come back later to change clothes for her appointment, but for breakfast at 6 a.m., dress was casual. She grabbed her beige cashmere sweater and black jeans from the side chair, then picked up paper and a pen from the desk. Jen would panic over her vanishing act if she didn't leave a note. Skirting Jen's bed, she went into the bathroom.

Moments later, showered and dressed, Lexi rubbed the steam from the mirror. Her hands trembled, along with her bottom lip, as she traced a sheen of deep pink lipstick over her lips. Unless she pulled herself together, none of her practice, research, and rehearsal of what she'd say to the rabbi would come out right. The reflection in the glass scowled, and her flushed cheeks received a dusting of blush. Was she ready for this?

Deep breath. Heart knowledge that with God all things are possible was one thing, but handing over a national treasure to a rabbi she'd never met at the site she'd never seen in a country she'd never been to? She should be relaxed, at ease, confident, full of faith.

Lord, I really need You. Please help me trust You and be ready for anything today.

The deep-set eyes in the mirror looked serene, but tiny worry lines creased her forehead. She dipped her chin. "At least keep me upright, coherent, and— What's with the tears, Lord? Please. Not now."

I am holding you by your right hand.

Lexi blinked hard and stepped back. The figure with dark hair sweeping over her shoulders looked back at her with the same blue eyes that had returned her gaze from the gilt-framed mirror so long ago. If her godfather were reflected here, he would have winked at her, exactly as he had done before.

She smiled. A tiny tremor of excitement rippled down her arms, and she let the thrill of being in Israel and bringing pieces of history infuse her with fresh energy. A final swipe of the brush through her hair. Good enough. She was ready.

The bathroom door creaked as she opened it. *Don't wake up yet, Jen. I need some time alone.* She hesitated for several agonizing seconds. Not a stir from the sleeping form.

She left the note beside Jenni's charging cellphone.

The elevator drifted downward to a stop, and the doors opened. So far everything worked toward having a cup of tea in solitude, but it was strange not having the case in her hand. Her eyes were drawn to the check-in desk across the lobby. The black briefcase lay in the hotel safe, out of her control. But was it safe? Was she? The fortitude she'd mustered wavered, faded with the wisp of dread spiraling up her backbone. She was a strobe of flashing emotions. What was she doing? Today should be the most momentous day of her life—if she could get

past her apprehension.

It is what it is. Deal with it. Lexi set her jaw, lifted her chin, and fought the impulse to turn and run back to the elevator. Instead, she walked steadily toward the restaurant. A twinge of guilt for leaving Jen spun through her mind, but she needed time to gather her thoughts. Ridge would meet Jenni and her for breakfast half-an-hour before the rest of the group joined them. She looked at her watch. Selfish, maybe, but she'd have at least three-quarters of an hour for herself.

The hostess smiled and came toward her, menu in hand, and Lexi pointed at a table in a secluded corner. From there, she could see the entrance and still have some privacy. The hostess led the way and left her with the menu.

Perfect. Only four other diners. Lexi settled into the cozy nook beside a wall of glass and concentrated on a view that showcased nodding pink flowers, verdant lawns, hedge plants, and trees in the flattering light of early dawn. In the heart of Jerusalem, the luxurious King David Hotel sat back from busy King David Street, buffered by walled gardens and overlooking the Old City with its sea of cars and people. Aside from the relentless beige of the desert and the golden "Jerusalem stone" structures, the city wasn't much different from any large American city. But what would the temple site look like? A plump, motherly-looking woman made her way to the table, and Lexi had to smile. The woman's rolling gait reminded her of the well-fed ducks that followed Ridge in Northbrick's garden.

"Good morning. What would you like to order?" The woman's uniform blended with the color scheme of the hotel, and her nametag announced her as Esther.

Lexi pointed to Earl Grey tea. "With honey, please."

The woman's sleepy brown eyes came to life. "Yes, ma'am. My

husband is a beekeeper and brings honey to the kitchen, fresh and sweet every day."

"Then I'd like some hot tea with plenty of your husband's honey and some cream. Two more will join me in a little while, then four others a little later on, so just the tea for now."

Esther left and Lexi relaxed, absorbing the quiet atmosphere until it became too quiet. Muffled conversation from the four diners ceased, and with a sudden flash of unease, Lexi turned. Someone watched her. A man clad in typical all-white mid-eastern attire stood near the entrance, his interest focused on something or someone near her. She followed his gaze.

Two tables away, a fifth diner sat. When had *he* come in? No one had been there when she arrived. He didn't look any older than Ridge, and sat, almost regally, by himself. Twin jet-black cords held his white head-covering in place, and he wore a gold-trimmed, finely woven black robe over a white garment. His dark brown eyes locked onto hers, and the ends of his thin mustache rose as he smiled—as if he knew her.

She straightened, furrows of discomfort plowing up her spine. Arrogance? A tinge of condescension? His expression was too calm and too controlled to suit her. She tore her eyes away, picked up the menu, and studied it, embarrassed at their lengthy eye contact.

Esther returned with tea, but quickly left to serve another diner. Directly behind Esther, the young man in black stepped close to Lexi's table. She stiffened and glared at him, her hands drawn into fists at his approach. She'd warn him and call—

His piercing, cocoa-colored eyes pinned on hers and cut into her thoughts, but he did nothing to threaten her. He stood ramrod straight and spoke in accented English.

"My name is Salim al-`Attar. I cannot remain here long," he said, his

voice soft, urgent, "and I am sorry to interrupt you, Miss Christensen, but I must tell you something of importance."

Lexi pressed against the cushioned seatback, her heart in her throat. *He knows my name. Who is he, Lord? Please keep me safe.* How had he known she'd be here? Unless he'd hacked her computer and her research of this place and its hours, he couldn't. She grasped the edge of the table, vulnerable, open. *Breathe. Think.*

His dress and appearance were Arab, but here in Israel? No. She shouldn't be surprised. Arabs did business with Israelis. But he looked too young to be here on business.

She'd read of traditional mid-eastern and Israeli attire and protocol before their trip. It helped explain the soft black *bisht* worn over his formal white *thawb* that meant today was a special occasion for him. But all the research in the world wasn't helping her undo her tongue. Heat rose in her cheeks, and he rescued her with more explanation.

"You do not know me. I do know of you. I know what you have brought with you, and I know where you are taking it."

A knife of fear stabbed somewhere between her heart and her stomach. She ignored it. Her hands burned, circled the cup of hot tea. *Trust in the Lord with all your heart. Trust. The briefcase is safe.* She nodded, trying not to hold her breath, listening.

"I am from Riyadh, Saudi Arabia. I am in Jerusalem for a few days, touring the ruins of the Dome of the Rock—and for other reasons."

He seemed knowledgeable of western ways, but this man was *not* adhering to traditional Saudi behavior with women. How did he dare approach and speak to her? *Haram! Shame, forbidden!* But the words she should hurl at him refused to leave her lips.

She glanced at the doors and cringed. The man in white entered the restaurant and stood, rigid, his dark eyes on her, his face a mask of disapproval and stifled anger.

"Do not be concerned." He smiled, tilting his head in the man's direction. "He is my bodyguard." Salim-from-Arabia touched the chair opposite her. "May I sit?" His arched black eyebrows rose with his question.

Did she have a choice? At least she was in a public place. She nodded again, swallowing back an adrenalin-launched rush of alarm. The overhead fan creaked rhythmically, pushing breakfast-scented air around them. He pulled out the chair and sat.

His eyes didn't leave her face as he continued. "You escaped danger before you left America, but you face another danger here." He leaned forward, forearms and hands flat against the tabletop. "I do not know details of when or where, but I know of it because I helped to plan it."

Lexi regained her composure and the use of her tongue instantly. "You helped to put me in danger? And you planned it? Why are you telling me about it now?" She stopped, sighed, and backed away from the precipice of anger and indignation. He wouldn't tell her if he meant to harm her. "No . . . no. I'm thankful you're telling me now, but how are you involved?"

He raised his hand and smiled. "You are Dove?"

Dove! A shower of awe shot through her limbs and forced the air from her lungs. Calm. She had to stay calm. Her nails bit into the palms of her hands. She studied his eyes, his face—earnest, sincere, smoldering in his need-to-know—and kept her words slow, guarded. "I am Dove in a Christian chat room."

"I am Alpha." He allowed an inch less between them as he bent closer.

The recollection of a recent chat room session rushed into the instant gulf of silence between them. The chat room. *Fledgling Faith* had

become a diversion for Lexi, a ministry to others new to the faith. There had been an Alpha who joined the online forum.

She released the chokehold on her cup and put it down. "You . . . you are Alpha?" An entire script of incredible scenes screamed through her thoughts. Out of the blue Alpha had come, wedging into the midst of the chatting Christians. Never obnoxious enough to be ignored but probing with an almost desperate desire to learn, Alpha never revealed any personal details.

His "visits" started soon after she'd gone into Northbrick, and there was a moment when she became suspicious he already knew she was there before he entered the chat room. Alpha's questions always singled her out, sailing through cyberspace at her one by one, persistent with his need for answers. "Who is the Man Jesus? Why do I need to know Him? What has He to do with sin? How do you know He rose from being dead? Why do you say I need Him? I worship Allah; why do I need Jesus? Why does He call Himself the Way, the Truth, and the Life?"

Allah. One word revealed his Muslim faith, and she had taken him on, query by query, her own faith tested and strengthened. Then Alpha was gone.

Across the table, above his black mustache and tiny straight-line goatee, Salim's smooth dark face remained impassive, watching her. But his eyes held something she recognized. He had become a believer.

"I must go." His eyes darted, scanning the restaurant. "I will not see you again, perhaps not until we are in heaven. You should know that Jesus spoke to me last year during the fast of Ramadan. You have opened my heart to Him with your answers to my many questions. I can only say thank you—to Jesus and to you."

He held her eyes with his again. "You are in danger, but though I have caused it, you have my promise that I will finish it to protect you and what you are doing." He reached across the table toward her hand but did not touch her. "You will be watchful?"

"I will." Lexi nodded, sensing urgency in his words and actions. She didn't want to let him leave, but she couldn't ask him to stay. Flying in the face of all she knew about his strict culture, she closed the distance between their hands and placed her right hand on his.

"I don't deserve your thanks, Salim. Only God draws His children to Himself through Jesus, and you have caused a huge commotion in heaven. I'm sure at least half the angels are turning cartwheels up there." She tilted her head and grinned at the quizzical expression that crossed his face. "I mean, there are angels full of joy because you believe. I'll pray for you. And whatever danger I might be in, you can be sure God is protecting me as He always has. Even so, thank you for warning me. God bless you."

Oh, her "God bless you" sounded so stilted and awkward and final. She'd said enough, and withdrew her hand from his. He might be putting himself in jeopardy.

He smiled. "I did not say I would not talk with you again, Dove, only that I might not see you."

The grim man in white paced near the doors. Alpha—Salim al-`Attar—pushed away from the table, rose, and walked to the exit. Through the glass doors, Lexi watched a contrast in black and white as the two men swept through the lobby to the elevators.

Salim didn't look back, and she sat there, seeing him disappear from view, feeling as if she'd read the entire episode in a novel. How long she stared after him, she didn't know, but reality returned like the burst of a balloon with Ridge and Jenni's arrival.

Thanks for the peace I'm feeling, Lord. Please keep me walking in it.

"Pretty incredible place they've put us up in," Ridge said, as he and Jenni neared Lexi's table. "And it looks like you wanted it all to yourself." He stifled a cavernous yawn, glanced at the used teabag, and

her half-empty cup. "Tea? Where's the coffee?"

Jenni moved toward the cushioned bench-seat to sit beside Lexi, but Ridge gently steered Jen away and pulled out a chair for her opposite Lexi. Jen sat with a murmured "Thanks."

Ouch. That surely wasn't going to go over well. Lexi glanced at Jen, who'd already picked up a menu, her expression unreadable.

Ridge slid in close beside Lexi. The spot where his shoulder touched hers flamed, until Jenni looked up from the menu with a question that barely gave Lexi a second to gather her wits.

"Good thing you left a note, girl. I thought you'd been kidnapped. And turning your cell off? Nice touch. Have you been here long?"

Lexi's breath left her in a *whoosh* of relief that Jen wasn't going to . . . well, dispatch her with a table knife. She'd have to figure all this out later. "Long enough to have an interesting encounter with an Arab and to find out we might be in big trouble and to drink a cup of tea."

Her loaded answer misfired, shot past her friends without a single comment. They needed to get settled and wake up first, and Esther was headed toward their table. "Want to go ahead and order while we wait for the rest of the gang?"

Jen checked Lexi's cup. "I just need something to wake up with, and it's not going to be tea."

Ridge sent a charmer of a grin to Esther. "How about a couple of coffees, please?"

Lexi pushed her teacup toward Ridge. "Make that three, please, Esther, and several others will be here in a few minutes. We'll wait till they get here to order breakfast." Esther thanked them and left.

Ridge pulled out his cellphone and aimed its camera at Jenni, clicked, then handed the phone to her. "Take your best shot, Jen."

Every normal dynamic of their fun friendship boomeranged through

Lexi's thoughts. The pressure and warmth of Ridge's arm, the scent of him as he pulled her close, warred in her head.

Jen chuckled and held up the cellphone. "Okay, smile, you two."

How could she . . .? Nick Avery. It had to be. Nothing else fit, but why in the world was she keeping him such a big secret? Ridge pulled her out of her thoughts and closer to him.

Jenni took two photos and handed the phone to Ridge. "Okay, what's this about danger, and who's the Arab?"

Ridge nudged her. "Right. You still haven't told us about your Arabian knight yet. Let's hear it."

"So, you were paying attention." But she'd run out of time. It would have to wait. As if barriers were thrown up to stop her, Esther interrupted with a tray full of cups and coffee, and her parents, along with Jacob and Ridge's dad, walked toward them. She'd say nothing. Mom would only worry if she knew, and Dad . . . Surely with all the security nothing would happen.

Chapter Thirty-Two

Agitated, Rick Vander, aka Gerald Jamison of Austin, Texas, tripped over the threshold of the elevator into the elegant lobby of the King David Hotel. So far, not much had gone right. He'd overslept and gotten to the lobby later than intended. No phone call from Quinn, and for some reason, he couldn't reach Salim this morning. Quinn's silence meant he'd blown his final chance. No surprise. And according to plan, it was now up to him.

Security was routine and included the usual cameras. Nothing to be concerned about. He adjusted his floppy cloth hat and scrutinized the people coming and going. Sunglasses helped hide eyes bleary from his late-night meet with a discreet vendor. His cash reserves had been considerably lowered with the amount he'd paid for the item he now carried, but he might not be able do this job without it.

The girl wasn't in the lobby, but late as he was, he was still early enough not to have missed her. His nerves jangled on the edge of raw even with all the details under control, but he was ready.

"Ow." Stupid coffee was still too hot. Beads of sweat formed on his

forehead as he held a thick, folded newspaper in one hand and balanced the Styrofoam cup half-full of black coffee in the other. Acting the typical tourist was almost laughable. He set the coffee down, clamped the newspaper under his arm, and took a few minutes to leaf through a magazine, then searched for an armchair. He needed one that would give him the best view, like the one near the reception desk. Situated between the bank of elevators and the doors opening to the street, it offered unobstructed views of both. Perfect.

Sunglasses dangling from the cord around his neck, Vander retrieved his coffee and settled into the chair to scan the lobby again. The still-folded newspaper lay in his lap, heavy with its contents. One unsteady hand squeezed around his cup, and the other around the paper. He was ready to relocate if necessary. The young, clean-cut desk clerk eyed him, but an elderly woman approached the counter, and Vander relaxed as the woman diverted the clerk's unwelcome attention.

Vander glanced at his watch then surveyed the clusters of busy humanity that disgorged from the elevators. She should be here by now. He had her photo and a copy of the Christensen party's itinerary, but so far no one matched the photograph. Had he misjudged the timing? Or had Salim screwed up and given him wrong info? He sipped his coffee and gave an inward shake of his head. Either of them could have miscalculated. He needed to be patient.

In seconds, his breath quickened. Alexia. Lexi, Quinn had called her. A dead-on match to the photo in his pocket. He hadn't missed her. His grip on the newspaper tightened. Setting his cup on the table, he inched forward in his chair. A slender, very attractive young woman with dark hair, dressed in a loose-fitting white shirt and a black, ankle-length skirt, left the elevator and went to the front desk. A cute blonde and an older woman followed, also wearing the customary dress to visit holy sites in Israel. Three men joined them, and Vander recognized the tall, older man behind Lexi as her father, Jason Christensen.

Head lowered, he pulled in a breath and watched from beneath the brim of his hat. The desk clerk left for a moment then returned with an oversized black case and placed it on the counter. Vander stared at the briefcase. A flush of heat prickled the back of his neck and curled his fingers around the thick newspaper. The target. But who would carry it? As if in answer, Jason Christensen took the case and thanked the clerk.

Vander's shoulders slumped. His job might have been simpler if the girl had carried it. He got up and moved to the magazine rack, watching the group of seven as they crossed the lobby toward the revolving-glass door that led outside. They'd go directly to their car. He needed to keep up, but couldn't afford to broadcast his intent to anyone who might be watching. His movements leisurely, deliberate, he put on his sunglasses then waited a moment before he followed.

Fingers of uneasiness played down Lexi's spine. Hotel security—routine. Peering one-eyed cameras and uniformed personnel—everywhere. She'd told Salim she'd be wary, careful, and something wasn't right.

Heading up a long line of vehicles and parked much farther away than she'd expected, the white limousine waited, the driver beside it. If she could slip under Ridge's watchful radar without detection, she'd be the last one out as they filed through the door. A red-jacketed doorman stood beside the entrance as Lexi paused to let everyone else go by.

The brief pressure and warmth of Ridge's hand on her arm loosed a flurry of butterflies in her chest as Ridge, his dad, and Jacob left the lobby first. Mom and Jenni, then Dad, case in hand, followed. Lexi smiled at the doorman and exited, the last one to leave.

People of all shapes, sizes, and ethnicity were everywhere. Who could tell who was for real and who wasn't? Her heart thudded with images of the scene at Logan—and Quinn—careening through her thoughts. Her hand flew to her chest. Surely Quinn was still in custody.

Trust. Keep your mind fixed on Me.

She took a deep breath and reminded herself to keep praying.

She allowed some distance between herself and the others, then stopped to check the street in front of the hotel. To her left, a large white delivery vehicle stood stationary at the curb. What danger? The area looked completely safe. Had Salim been telling her the truth?

She turned toward the limo, but hesitated and glanced back over her shoulder at the white van. Had she seen a flash of black and gold behind the truck? Salim? No. Just her wild imagination again.

"Lexi, are you coming?" From several car-lengths away, Ridge's voice filtered through the cacophony of street sounds.

"Be right there." Nerves stretched, Lexi's attention remained on the van. Nothing out of order. She should stop this, turn herself around, and jog to catch up. Her family and friends would be okay. They were seconds away from the safety of the car.

Jagged reflective flashes from the opening hotel doors. Tiny hairs covering her arms rose, and liquid dread pooled in her stomach. Suddenly, she saw no safety, only a man who emerged from behind the doors, stopped short, and seemed to focus on—her!

The grim line of the man's chin, how he held his body, the way he moved. Lexi's senses blazed with a rush of adrenalin. Was this the danger Salim had warned her of?

She fisted her hands in frustration and strained to see his eyes. This wasn't happening. It couldn't be. Not again! Why couldn't she move?

With long, forceful strides, he came toward her, crossing the space between them at a speed that sliced dark fear through her. The man's face was shaded by a hat and dark glasses, and he carried a folded newspaper as if it were a—

Run! But her feet refused to leave the stones beneath them, and grit filled her throat. The man slowed as if he approached prey, a slight smile on his face as if teasing her.

Not this time! Hot anger flooded her limbs, and she braced herself. He would not get the case. Close enough to see his eyes dart between her and something beyond her, he jerked, sidestepping to his right.

Lexi's body shook, heart pounding as the man halted and yanked his hand from the midst of the folded newspaper. Her eyes riveted on the shiny black finish of a pistol. Imprinted along the barrel, the squared Glock trademark symbol, the number 19 and AUSTRIA; the gun was a near duplicate of her father's.

"Dad!" A scream ripped from her throat and slashed the air.

No! The silent protest became the fluid movement of her body, and she lodged herself between the gun and her father.

The man raged at her and punched the air with his weapon. His mouth twisted in fury. "Move!" The newspaper dropped to the stone walk. He took a step backward and brought the gun up in a two-fisted grip, aiming at her.

Breath squeezed from her, and she froze for seconds that tugged at time in horrible slowness. *Oh, God, please don't let anyone get hurt!*

Her mother screamed, Dad bellowed her name, and Ridge . . . But Lexi's gaze welded to the finger the man had locked onto the trigger of the wavering gun. She threw her arms around her body expecting, accepting burning pain.

A sharp *crack* and then another in split-second succession. Two instantaneous glowing yellow-orange flash plumes, the smell of

gunpowder. Two more bursts. The *ping* of projectiles ricocheting off glass reverberated in her ears, echoed through her mind. But her body hadn't moved with any impact; she had no pain.

She leapt backward as the man lunged at her, gun flailing. Two more shots and a roared demand, "Get out of my way, woman!" He made a move to go around her.

"No! Dad . . . !" Her scream withered, died in her throat. A rustling black wave of at least half a dozen men in dark clothing emerged from the hotel, street, and vehicles, and swept up behind the man. One grabbed the gunman and slammed him to the sidewalk in front of her. She stood near enough to hear the huff of his breath as he thudded hard against the stone walk.

The gun jetted from his grasp and skidded with a metallic scrape across the hard surface. Caught by their cord, his sunglasses crunched beneath his weight. His hat landed a few inches to the right of her toes— toes instantly set in motion, propelling her away from the man, who attempted to grab her ankles.

"Give it up, Vander!" One of the plainclothes lawmen rasped.

But Vander leapt to his feet, turned, and plowed his fist into the man's gut so viciously that Lexi winced with sympathy pain. Ignoring the blow to his mid-section, the man straightened, caught Vander's arm mid-air, and deftly twisted both it and Vander. Vander grunted in pain, and with his wrists behind his back, succumbed to handcuffs. One of the men retrieved the firearm as three others picked Vander up and deposited him in the black SUV that squalled to a stop alongside the delivery vehicle.

The relative silence of the scuffle was surreal, and there was no sound behind her. *Dad! Mom!* Lexi wheeled, fear surging through every nerve, looking from one to the other, her voice lost within a choked whisper. "Oh, Daddy, you're not hurt. Mom, you're okay? Thank God! All of you, okay?"

Her eyes hazed with tears, and she swallowed hard, breath coming in short, choppy gulps. In seconds, Ridge's voice and touch blurred her thoughts, and she grabbed and held onto him, her knees soft clay. Mom and Dad were at her side, hands on her, arms around her, and the air filled with panicked questions. The others closed in, shaken and concerned but unharmed.

The man who'd taken the gunman down spoke quietly on his cellphone then walked over. He looked from Lexi to her father, down at the briefcase, and back. "You had a close call. The man hunts game for sport. It looks as if he either was having a bad day or didn't really intend to harm you. Is everyone all right?"

That voice. Lexi stared. Agent Zeev Birman, Israeli Intelligence. She'd been so intent on the gun and its owner that she hadn't seen his face. Had Birman been on their flight?

"Agent Birman. Thanks." Her father scanned the gathered group, nodded, and shook the agent's hand. "A little unnerved, but it looks as if we're all okay. We're grateful for your help."

Birman divided his attention between Lexi and her father and hooked a thumb toward the SUV. "We've been doing some surveillance on this man, but if it weren't for a tip we got early this morning, we might not have been aware of his intentions today. His name's Rick Vander. He owns a furniture store in Boston, and apparently he's an associate of Greyson Quinn, the attorney who tried this at Logan International. Neither of them will be doing much of anything for a while."

At the mention of Quinn's name, Lexi heard a muffled gasp from her mother. Her worries that Quinn might somehow try again had been right. Lexi put her arm around her mother's slender frame and hugged

her. Her parents' protective hovering had been completely justified.

"Your statements have been waived at this point, and you should have no further interference." Birman's cellphone interrupted and he checked the caller ID then looked at Lexi. "Sorry, I have to take this call. I'll be available if you need anything. We'll keep our distance, but won't be far from wherever you are." Birman handed Dad his business card, nodded at Ridge, and sent Lexi a warm smile before he got into the SUV to leave.

She scanned the street and walkways as a dozen people exited the hotel, probably kept from leaving by the covert detail that intervened in the shooting.

Salim—Alpha. Had he seen this? Was he still nearby? Surely he'd been involved in stopping the thing he had said he'd helped plan, and when she saw or spoke to him again, she had every intention of asking him what had happened.

The driver closed the door of the limo, but the Lord would be opening another door for her moments from now.

For He shall give His angels charge over you, to keep you in all your ways. And they had been in charge—of a raging dark battle. But was it over?

Please let it stay over, Lord.

Chapter Thirty-Three

"At least this thing's built like a Sherman tank." Ridge turned from the side window toward Lexi, who sat opposite. The sleek limousine pulled away from the hotel and merged into traffic. "Looks like Birman was right. Vander couldn't hit the broad side of a barn, or maybe he didn't aim to. Glad they were prying bullets out of trees and buildings instead of us. Are you feeling any better?"

Thankful Mom and Dad sat far enough up front not to hear her, Lexi dipped her head and slid her fingers into her hair, drawing in a long breath before she looked up. "Honestly, I'm still shaking."

Jen's eyes met hers. "Me, too. I had no clue what it felt like to think you were about to die, but I do now."

Lexi put her hand on Jenni's arm. Ridge's hazel eyes softened and fastened on Lexi's as he settled into his seat. "You know, that was one crazy move. He could have killed you the way he was waving that gun around."

"All I could think of was Dad. It was my fault he had the briefcase. So, yes, it was insane, but you'd have done the same thing." She tugged

at her long skirt and smiled. Surely Salim had something to do with it. There hadn't been time to fill them in on all the details about her meeting with Salim before she'd left the restaurant to change clothes for her appointment, but there was time now. Lexi pinned her gaze on Ridge. "I'd sure like to know how this Vander guy knows Quinn and how they pulled this stunt off half a world away from each other. But earlier you said you wanted to know about my Arab? His name is Salim al-`Attar, and he's from Saudi Arabia. A little while before you walked into the restaurant, he came to my table. He said he needed to warn me I was still in danger . . . that he had helped to plan it."

Ridge's eyes darkened and he slid to the edge of his seat. Lexi matched his move. She had to derail his interruption or she wouldn't get through this. "He told me he knew me and that he knew what I had and where I was taking it—"

Ridge interrupted. "This man, this Arab, he talked to you this morning and gave you a warning? He was part of what just happened?"

Anger razored through Ridge's voice, and if he could have stood, she knew he would have. She ignored him. "Salim promised me that even though he'd been involved, he'd protect me and what I was doing, but said I had to be careful and watchful. Either he couldn't say anything more, or he didn't want to. A few minutes after that, he left with his bodyguard."

Jenni listened, but the line of Ridge's jaw and his fists were white and clenched as Lexi continued. "So there were three men involved: Quinn in Nantucket, Vander in Boston, and Salim in Saudi Arabia. It's pretty obvious that the danger Salim told me he'd been part of—that he warned me about this morning—was Vander and what he just did."

Tension seeped from Lexi's body as she finished telling of Salim, and she leaned against the leather seat, silent at last.

"So the guy said he'd protect you?" Ridge's tone grated low, edgy. "Some protection that was."

How was she going to diffuse this? She lifted her hand, palm up. "How else do you figure Birman and the Israeli police showed up so fast? Way too fast to have been a coincidence. Salim had to have tipped them off. And if he hadn't, we could have lost the briefcase, maybe even our lives. Salim admitted to me he was involved, but there's something else he said that had nothing to do with Vander."

She pulled in a breath, praying for the right words. "God has worked huge changes in Salim—"

The limo slowed and pulled into a parking area. Lexi glanced at the case on the floor beside her and sighed. "I'll tell you about it later. But I believe, with God's help, Salim kept his promise to protect us and what we're doing. I think he was even outside the hotel when we came out. I'm pretty sure I saw him behind that white van. Didn't either of you notice?"

"I saw something, but just thought someone was back there unloading stuff." The anger dissipated from Ridge's voice as he spoke.

"I didn't see him," Jenni said, "which is probably a good thing. If I'd seen anything lurking in the shadows, you'd have had to scrape me off the sidewalk. I've been so jumpy since Logan."

Ridge shook his head. "Jumpin' Jennifyr."

And Jen filled the rear of the limo with her bubbly, contagious laughter.

Four all-business Shin-Bet special operations officers escorted Lexi's group from the car. Beneath the sapphire-blue sky, a light breeze swirled eddies of dust and heated air that smelled of wood and

earth and cement as she walked. The Wailing Wall, the western wall of the Temple site, towered above her. She stopped and stared up at the massive blocks, awe-inspired chill bumps spilling down her body. Another stone structure, but the walls the Cohen family built couldn't begin to compare with this.

The officers waited a moment then motioned for them to follow up steps, through an entrance, and onto an uneven plateau of rocky earth and shattered stone that crunched underfoot.

Ridge slid his arm around Lexi's shoulders and pointed off to her right. In the distance huge piles of drab rubble from the earthquake awaited removal. In stark contrast, pieces of the dome that had fallen victim to the shaking earth sat in separate heaps of broken gold, blue, white, and turquoise shards.

But why had only some structures gone down while others were left standing? Why the selective destruction of the quake? Why now, of all times in history?

Close by, two men stood beneath a covered pavilion; in its shelter, the Americans were shown to comfortable chairs. A nearby table held fruit, herb teas, small sandwiches and cakes, and several buckets of rarely-served ice. An aged man, with a smile as wide as the brim of the pitcher he held, bent to pour a glass of tea for Lexi's mother.

Lexi sat and picked at a piece of lint on her black skirt, combating nervous energy with slow, deep breathing. Everyone else seemed relieved to finally sit and unwind, but with the briefcase in her hands, Lexi couldn't eat or drink or stay put. She moved to the edge of her chair.

Her mother's voice broke through Lexi's uneasiness. "Are you sure you don't want Dad to hold the case, dear?"

"Yes, I'm sure, Mom. I just need to stand for a while. I'll stay close until it's time." Lexi managed a smile for her parents. "Promise."

Ridge stopped mid-sentence in his conversation with Jacob, his eyes questioning her. She shook her head at him before he could follow her, then got up and moved a few feet away. A few minutes alone to take some nerve-healing time might help ease the building tension in her neck.

Closer to the edge of the construction site, a wave of unstoppable realization billowed through her. Holy ground. She ached with the desire to remove her shoes, for there to be nothing between her and this holy earthen spot. The place of kings. King David, King Solomon, and Jesus, King of Kings. James and John, the sons of thunder, fishermen made fishers of men, walked here. The other disciples, and Mary . . .

Overwhelmed, humbled with her sudden small placement in history, she paused. She'd take it all in, but a little at a time. Not much longer before she stood closer to the rising Temple.

A long, narrow strip of orange plastic hung draped between a walkway and a "danger" zone. Every few feet on the ribbon, black markings repeated the lettering one of the officers explained meant *Construction Site Do Not Enter*.

Security here was as tight as her left-handed grip on the briefcase. Strategically positioned throughout the area, a special force of Israeli military, dressed in crisp desert-camouflage uniforms, was on guard. Their uniforms differed from the olive camouflage she'd seen nearly everywhere else. Watchful, alert, and fully armed, they blended into the background.

Outside the wall, barricades had been moved aside for their limousine. Traffic was restricted in every direction. The only noise from the few cars and trucks was an electric whine, as no other engines were allowed. Signs indicated only foot traffic was permitted this close to the

Temple. Eerie, muffled activity filled the site; an odd sensation for there to be so little noise when something this large was under construction.

And the temple, when it was being built, was built with stone finished at the quarry, so that no hammer or chisel or any iron tool was heard in the temple while it was being built . . . .

The words of King Solomon's edict of silence during the building of the temple centuries ago ran through her mind. What she'd read about the pre-shaping of the stonework must be happening here also. It seemed as though the architects and builders had taken the holy words to an extreme.

Near the structure, two men stood at a waist-high table and studied what might be blueprints. All over the site, swarms of men in hard hats congregated like worker bees around a hive. Rabbi Solomon had written that the initial phase of the reconstruction was complete and the second well underway.

Lexi scanned the site. Huge stacks of native rock quarried from limestone pits around Jerusalem were in place and ready for use. The rabbi's website had reports of storage buildings filled to capacity with cedar boards and beams, fir planks, and olive wood—beautiful, exotic timber.

All of this would soon come together to house what she would return to Israel. A twinge of dread iced through her. What would it be like when she went home to Nantucket? How would things change when she was back in her own home?

. . . do not worry about tomorrow . . .

As if to shake out her doubts, along with the Lord's words, like the brush of angel wings, a playful breeze wafted around her and reminded her of the whitewashed statues of angels in Aaron's garden. Vigilance, wisdom, preparation. She'd lived those words, and they were in her future and gave her hope.

THE STONEKEEPERS

A short distance away, a well-worn path meandered and widened, then extended into a much larger expanse of rugged beige dirt and stone. Beyond it, in vivid contrast on either side, areas of grass had been planted. She'd read that the earthquake uncovered hidden water sources from deep underground, and like Uncle Aaron's garden, trees and luxuriant flowerbeds spread out in orderly designs.

In the center of the grassy field, a large tent, open on all sides, held two tables and several chairs. Two men with cameras sat in a far corner, animated in conversation. Her stomach clenched at movement near the edge of the grass. An enclosed black vehicle resembling a large golf cart pulled up and parked.

Almost time. Her heartbeat quickened and her fingers gripped the case handle as three men left the vehicle and walked across the lush sea of green toward the white canvas tent. Wearing hats and coats of jet-black, each carried a briefcase. They paused and stood in the shade, talking and pointing for a few moments. One of the men handed his case to another, then turned to face her as the others continued to the tent, and he covered half the distance toward her in seconds.

Rabbi Solomon. A replica of the photo he'd sent, he paused and fixed his deep-set brown eyes on her. A crinkly smile stretched his graying beard across his chin. She smiled and hoped the warmth in her eyes matched the welcoming warmth in his as he called to her.

"Lexi! Welcome. We are pleased to see you." His rich baritone voice carried easily across the distance as he continued toward her, stooped to cross the plastic barrier, and came near.

She straightened and pushed her hair back from her face, shivering at the mantle of serenity misting around her. Her fingertips tingled as she reached to touch the symbols on the chain around her neck. The cross was caught up in the Star of David. She left them entwined and moved to greet the rabbi.

The slender, bewhiskered man dressed in black approached, his eyes fixed on hers. Rabbi Solomon smiled and stepped out of the boundaries of his Jewish tradition with the offer of his hand. Her hand trembled, small, enfolded in his firm grasp.

"*Shalom Aleichem;* peace unto you, Lexi Christensen. Finally we meet. Hashem is good and gracious to send you to us. I am Avi Solomon."

Lexi let her hand linger in the warmth of his. God had brought them together. And the depth and sincerity of this man's commitment to love God, his family, friends, and home, was as deep as the well of delight and enthusiasm in his brown eyes.

"*Aleichem shalom*, Rabbi Solomon. Yes, God is so good, and I'm glad to meet you. Thank you for all you've done to bring us here. It's beautiful, so . . . overwhelming."

"Ah, yes, a fitting place to receive the treasure you have brought." Solomon's smile broadened, and he released her hand.

Lexi's heart skipped a beat with fresh appreciation for this man of God when he paused and turned to her family and friends. His smile encompassed them, his eyes embracing the entire group even as he stretched out his arms to them.

An image of Uncle Aaron's smile flashed across her mind. Peace like a warm sea flooded her as everyone gathered under the shelter of the pavilion. Solomon's smile seemed to light up the atmosphere as he shook her father's hand then turned to her mother.

"Jason and Molly Christensen, I am proud to welcome you to Israel and amazed at the circumstances that have brought you here. My brother, Aaron Cohen, did well when he heeded Adonai's will for your daughter to become his heir and protector of the treasure she carries to us."

Lexi's head dipped with the weight of his words. The gentle squeeze of her mother's hand on her shoulder, her father's soft-spoken encouragement, and Lexi's eyes hazed with tears. Sweet thankfulness welled in her chest, and she swallowed hard. Dad reached to hold her mother's hand. They watched, encouraged, prayed for her, and it meant everything.

Solomon spoke quietly with Jacob Carver, Steven Scott, Ridge, then Jenni. Jenni's eyes shone with moisture, and her chin quivered. Lexi blinked back her own tears and sent Jen and Ridge smiles she hoped they'd read as "I'm really glad you came."

Rabbi Solomon turned back to her, and she fought off the shakiness that threatened her composure. "Are you ready to join us, Lexi?"

She nodded, but couldn't move as he spoke a few more words to Dad then lifted the orange ribbon to leave.

Heat rose in her cheeks as Ridge's eyes met hers, and he crossed the few feet between them. His strong arms slipped around her, and he pulled her close with tenderness that took her breath. His warm whisper rustled through her hair. "I . . . we love you, Lex. You can do this."

He loved her? His arms tightened in a hug, but he gave her no time to react. He led her to the orange ribbon and lifted it. She ducked under and onto the path. Ripples of excitement, and an echo of "I love you" coursed through her.

The leather handle burned in Lexi's palm, and she gazed at the earth beneath her feet. Somewhere in the distance a siren wailed, and for an uneasy moment her mind spun with memories. The attempted break-in just weeks ago, yesterday's debacle at Logan International, and the explosions that flashed from the business end of a gun less than an hour ago. She closed her eyes. Would there be more? Could she do this?

God, help and protect us.

Chapter Thirty-Four

Rabbi Solomon had chosen the time of day with care. Full of construction turmoil moments ago, the sun-warmed atmosphere grew quiet as work crews took their midday break. A light breeze swept through the tent, and they moved into the shade where the two other rabbis waited, not as reserved as they were when they welcomed her to Israel yesterday.

Asher's grandfatherly face held a sincere smile, framed by a full, graying beard, and dark eyes squinted at her behind rimless glasses. "We are very happy you are here." Asher's black hat bobbed with the enthusiasm of his words.

Rabbi Yachin's long white beard reached for his tie clip. He raised black eyebrows and fixed his gaze on her. "Indeed, it is good that you have come."

"Rabbi Yachin, Rabbi Asher, it's nice to see you again." Lexi nodded, smiling at each of them, not missing the sincere interest in their eyes, or when Yachin cocked his head and sent her a tentative smile.

They followed as Solomon left her side and went to a long wood

table. Beside the table Asher stood, eyes closed, his lips moving in silent prayer as he rocked in a tiny back-and-forth motion. Cameramen were a discreet distance from the table, nearly immobile behind their equipment, the muted sounds of their zoom lenses and camera clicks continuous. Their distance didn't stop a ripple of leftover apprehension as she eyed the cameras. She straightened and turned away.

Quick, nearly robotic, Yachin opened his oversized briefcase and withdrew a piece of alabaster-colored linen, along with a large, polished wood case. His hands trembled slightly as he spread the cloth over the entire length of the table and smoothed it out flat. He placed the wood box in its center then turned to Lexi. "If you are ready . . ."

Tension beneath the canopy tightened in wide bands. Blood pulsed hard with every beat of her heart. The sound of it filled her ears and pounded like surf against the Nantucket shoreline. Palms damp, she closed her eyes and prayed.

Therefore, since we are surrounded by such a great cloud of witnesses, let us throw off everything that hinders . . . .

Peace fell around her even as leaden silence filled the atmosphere throughout the tent. Lexi set her black briefcase on a folding chair, opened it, and lifted out the gilded cedar box. The breeze quieted.

Breathe My name.

Lord Jesus . . . Lexi handed the box to Yachin. He placed it on the linen cloth while she put on a pair of thin, fitted white gloves. She stole a glance at Rabbi Solomon, taking in the time-drawn lines etched around his smile and the softness of his expression, committing the scene to memory. Her fingertips tingled as she touched the lid and opened the box. The scent of cedar drifted upward, pungent and comforting.

She removed a leather pouch, untied its thongs, and withdrew a second sack, cashmere-soft, and opened it. A vibrant, deep red jewel set in gold filigree slid onto the pale cloth.

Her voice was strong and clear. "The first jewel of Aaron's sacred breastplate."

A reflected ray of sunlight caught the edge of the large, emerald-cut ruby and spun shards of fiery glitter across the canvas roof. In vermilion splendor, its worn markings spelled out the name of the firstborn of the tribe of Israel.

Audible gasps escaped the lips of the rabbis as they leaned close. Solomon, one hand on his beard and the other over his heart, stared at the stone and whispered the name in Hebrew. *"Rə'uven."*

He'd read the word so easily. "Reuben." Lexi's whisper echoed Solomon's translation and she removed another leather bag. She pushed out the topaz and placed it beside the ruby.

"Simeon," the rabbi intoned.

Lexi pressed a gleaming emerald from the third sack, set it at the end of the first row, then paused to watch Rabbi Solomon's face. These men were Levites, and this single jewel represented their heritage. He smiled, but not at her.

"Levi." Solomon's single word reverberated with joy beneath the canvas, and his expression broke with his voice. Tears trickled down his cheeks and mingled with the laugh lines around his mouth, burrowing into his beard.

Eyes still suffused with tears, he drew in a breath and transferred his gaze from the deep green jewel to Lexi. She pushed the fourth jewel from its pouch and began a second row of gems.

"Ah, for Judah, a turquoise." Solomon's words feathered into the warm air. *Lion of Judah, Lamb of God, my Lord, and my God.* The words surged into Lexi's mind as she lifted the fifth and sixth bags. She swallowed hard but didn't pause, and pressed more gems from their soft containers.

Solomon's voice filled with joy-filled emotion. "For Dan, a sapphire as blue as the sea, and a magnificent diamond for Naphtali. Exquisite, amazing, the beauty Adonai created."

Lexi placed three more jewels in a third row.

"For our brother, Gad, the jacinth. An agate for Asher, and for Issachar, an amethyst."

She laid the first gem in the final row.

"For Zebulun, beryl, and for Joseph, rescuer from great famine, an onyx." The last stone settled into place as the rabbi spoke the final name. "For Israel's youngest son, Benjamin, the jasper."

The twelve jewels cast colored splinters of light beneath the tent like a broken rainbow. Reflected sunlight? Unable to tell where it came from, a thrill flamed through Lexi as the light glistened, cascading over the gemstones in waves.

Solomon stepped forward and smoothed his hand over the linen cloth, then stood aside as Lexi took the second container from the gold-covered box. From more bags of leather and soft cloth, she extracted two massive, black onyx stones, both surrounded with delicate gold filigree.

"The two onyx stones for the shoulders of the ephod." *In the order of their birth, deep into the lustrous faces, carve the twelve great names to mark their places.* Six names on each smooth black stone face, deeply etched and gold-filled—the names of the sons of Israel.

Solomon remained beside Lexi as she took off her gloves and returned them to her now-empty case. She watched, waiting as the three teachers immersed themselves in the display, talking and studying the gold-embraced jewels. Yachin cleared his throat and tugged at the tip of his graying beard, and more than once Rabbi Asher glanced at the agate, then removed his small oval-lensed glasses to wipe away tears.

Long moments passed before Solomon donned gloves and opened

his large wooden case. He placed the jewels into each of fourteen compartments, replaced the box into his briefcase, and set it beside the table. Every gemstone, shaped and set in fine gold thousands of years ago, and authenticated from the filigree and markings as being original, had been appraised as flawless.

Would the jewels be safe? They'd been far from safe while they were in her possession. Her hands rounded into fists at her sides. Rabbi Solomon cocked his head and looked at her.

"You might be concerned about what will happen to this treasure, how it will be stored, but you needn't be. Heavy protection will continue until the jewels are placed in a secure vault. They will remain secured until the Temple is finished. Then they will be added to the breastplate and ephod being prepared for the priest who is to wear them."

The tension eased from her hands. "All of this has been God's business from the beginning."

"Indeed, it has." The rabbi's expression was both pensive and serious. "Constantly, I'm taught to accept new things." He looked at her from the corner of his eye, a smile widening beneath his mustache. "Like accepting that part of Hashem's plan to restore the Temple would include a Christian, an American woman."

Lexi nodded, the palms of her hands crossed against her chest. "As when I realized how unworthy I felt to fulfill the vow my godfather expected me to. It wasn't until after I read his journal that I began to understand and accept what he'd entrusted me to do."

The elderly teacher pursed his lips and bobbed his head. "Generations of your godfather's family not only cared for the treasure, but the meaning and history behind it. Hashem is surely pleased with Aaron and his family, with their faithfulness.

"And I am certain Adonai is pleased with your faith and obedience. In spite of everything you faced, you have done well, Lexi." He stilled, catching her glance with his own. Tilting his head, he held up his forefinger, eyes sparking with sincerity. "It was with Hashem's guidance and wisdom that your godfather chose you."

The sound of a car door drew their attention. The driver of the black transport got out and opened the vehicle's side door. The tent suddenly rustled with energy as the rabbis retrieved their briefcases and the press gathered their equipment to leave.

Lexi and Rabbi Solomon spoke for a few moments longer then returned to the place they'd first met on the pathway. As Solomon left her, Lexi turned from the pathway and looked toward the pavilion, thankful her family and friends waited there for her. Jenni stood talking with Mom and Dad, but Ridge didn't shift his gaze from Lexi as she crossed the crunching pebbles and brown earth. In just weeks this summer, their lives had changed. Wanting to explore an old mansion had put them into danger more times than she cared to remember.

She slowed, absorbing the atmosphere of this holy place. The stones were beautiful and they represented God's loving care since time began. Why now?

Jerusalem is at peace. The Temple is under construction. An ancient treasure has come home. My people are returning to Israel from all over the world. You know of a desert in full bloom and of the birth of an unblemished red heifer. These are signs. You walk the edge of history.

The answer, like the unveiling of a bride, filled her with fresh peace. The sacred cache had come full circle. She had delivered the message. *Mission complete, Uncle Aaron.*

Lexi turned to look at the site, remembering the final entry in her godfather's journal:

The garden was especially beautiful today. Little Lexi and I walked for a while, then rested together in the gazebo. She looked into my eyes, put her tiny hands on my face, and told me about her Jesus again. She makes me believe as she sings about Him in her sweet voice. It is because of her, and God's own familiar urging, that my heart is open to this Man of my own faith. I am reading the Book she gave me on His birthday. . . .

Lexi's whisper feathered into the breeze. "Thanks, heavenly Father." She took in a breath as a deep, unexplainable knowing enveloped her. In a time to come, she would see her godfather again. He had allowed "the Man of his own faith" to walk into his heart.

Epilogue

Nantucket, Massachusetts

Lexi looked up through the thick bower of roses covering the arbor. She'd dropped everything mid-afternoon to do errands but ended up in Northbrick's rear gardens. Alone. To attempt sorting out her life. That she'd leave Nantucket for college in two days was surreal.

She had parked in the old lover's lane and walked to the house to help clear her mind. A light breeze wafted through the garden, moving petals and familiar scents around her. Solitude settled like a mist, and she shivered with a sense of well-being that took her back to the path she'd walked with Rabbi Solomon less than two weeks ago.

Age, culture, none of the differences between them had faded the glow as they'd moved toward the pavilion together. Solomon had motioned toward Yachin and Asher, excitement in his voice. "We look forward to seeing all of you tonight, Lexi. The car will be at your hotel at six. The three of us and our families will join you there. They have heard only a portion of your story. Everyone is eager to meet you, including all

members of the Council. We will convene with the Council tomorrow morning, and they are on pins and needles, as you say, to hear of your relationship with Aaron Cohen and how the jewels were found."

Lexi nodded. "I've brought photos and copies of the parchment to give them, and I'm looking forward to both meetings. I'll bring Uncle Aaron's journal with me to the Council meeting."

The elderly rabbi turned to her. "There is no reason you shouldn't keep the box and book that belonged to your godfather. It is enough to have the ancient jewels in Israel. Before you leave, the original box will be in your hands, but as you would expect, the journal will take more time, as it will be examined, studied, and photographed. We have chosen a gifted student, a major in Jewish history and language arts, to copy the journal, and commissioned an artisan to replicate the case."

He tugged at his beard, eyes twinkling. "I would very much like to see for myself the place where you found my brother Aaron's diary and the gemstones."

Lexi reveled in a backwash of joy. Solomon's graciousness and genuine interest in Uncle Aaron and the thought of showing Solomon Aaron's beautiful garden infused her with enthusiasm. "We would be honored to have you, Rabbi Solomon. You're invited to come anytime."

"Then it's settled," he'd said, his smile radiating warmth. "When the copy of the journal is complete and it is convenient for you, I will personally return it."

Lexi twisted on the bench and lay on her back with her knees drawn up, the sight of roses blending with her thoughts.

She'd looked toward an intriguing future even before she left for Israel. The history of Northbrick made it a natural landmark, and she envisioned dozens of ideas for its preservation. Years of college, spring breaks, and summers at home, relationships, and plans that had three families, the historical society, even the community, talking about turning the estate into a historic site for the island. But more than that, it would be a way to honor the Stonekeepers, as Lexi had come to think of them—her godfather and his family. A single family, who'd obediently fulfilled a lonely responsibility to preserve a giant piece of history for generations to come, was an inspiration and would be remembered.

She shut her eyes and smiled at how Nick Avery had entered the picture now that Jenni and he were a dating constant—and how things had changed with Ridge.

Lexi couldn't stay on the bench another second. There were things unfinished, unresolved. Her heart squeezed remembering how Ridge ducked under the ribbon and sprinted down the path to pick up her briefcase. He'd held her hand in his, and walked the rest of the way close beside her as they joined her family and friends under the pavilion that afternoon.

She stood and paced the smooth walkway, grappling with the stabbing ache in her throat that threatened to flood her face with tears of love and yearning. How could she feel so much emotion and not die of it?

Oh, God, help me deal with this . . . with Ridge.

Nothing. Only the overshadowing of dark clouds overhead.

She left the walk and went to one of the taller gnarled oaks, leaning against it, pressing hard on the cool roughness of the bark.

Ridge had said "I love you" . . . sort of. Did he love her? It had been impossible to tell; they all been so busy and preoccupied after their return.

The lump in her throat hurt and her eyes blurred with tears she could no longer hold back. How could she be strong in so many things but so weak when it came to him?

This had to stop. She shuddered and drew in a breath filled with the scent of gardenias, leather, and . . . Leather?

Everything that was Lexi filled Ridge's mind and pulled on every shred of his being lately. Well, truth be told, since the minute he'd seen her alive and well in Northbrick's dusty drawing room weeks ago.

He'd returned from Israel and launched himself back into life and the pressures of making immediate, final decisions about college. Too much of everything except finding the time to be alone with Lexi was driving him crazy.

He should have called and stopped by her house on his way here, at least checked on her. Instead, he'd come straight from his last day at work at the stable and parked on the street in front of Northbrick.

He knew she'd be happy he'd decided to attend MIT, but there was more on his mind. Man, was he rotten at this. He fisted his hands, determined to figure out what he wanted to say. Maybe a walk would settle him and his jumbled thoughts before he told her.

Glad they'd been leaving the stone gate open, he went through, numbness setting in as he walked. And wishing she were here didn't ease up the weird ache in his chest.

God help me. I need some direction. His boots clomped against the stones as he strode down the pathway, and the haze in his mind cleared. He neared the center of the garden, stepping into the grass to quiet his steps. The ground seemed holy here.

Distant thunder rumbled of the storm to come. Overhead, charcoal gray clouds churned, heavy with the threat of rain.

The gazebo was empty, a good spot to wait out the storm. But muffled sound drew his eyes toward the trees. Instantly, his breath left him. She was here! The woman was as unpredictable as morning fog. Head bowed, her face buried in her hands, dark hair falling around her shoulders . . .

She couldn't be near that tree with lightning so close! He ran, the racing storm impelling him to where she stood. He couldn't speak, his breath still chained in his chest. Huge drops of rain pelted into his hair, down his forehead, drenching his shirt as he grabbed her arm.

Her hands fell away from her face, soft full lips parted in surprise, cheeks damp with tears from eyes so intense and so deep-sea blue he was instantly lost in them. She didn't look hurt. Why was she crying? Dark lashes held glistening wetness as she stared up at him.

"Ridge, what are you . . . ?"

Thank God, she was okay. He yanked her close "No! What are *you* doing under this tree with a storm coming?" She stiffened at his growl, but didn't resist him, letting him pull her into the shelter of the gazebo.

Would she push him away again, slip out from under his arm? Damp and smooth beneath his hands, her arms were warm, and the flowery scent of her perfume . . . He didn't let her go. Couldn't let her go.

His eyes snapped shut, the brightness of the flash blinding him for seconds, the noise, an ear-splitting crack, the air suddenly pungent with smoke. Shaking, scared, and soft, Lexi stayed wrapped and safe in his arms.

"Th . . . the tree . . . It hit that . . ." She tensed, put her hands against his chest, and pressed away from him. "Thanks." She looked up. "I didn't expect that."

Didn't expect what? For him not to grab her away from a tree trunk in a storm full of lightning? Not to hold her when she was scared out of her wits? No. Things had changed. He had changed. Had she?

Rain thundered on the roof, banged like his heart against his ribs as she backed away, uncertainty in her face, her eyes. He stepped closer and slowly drew his friend, the love of his life, to him, her skin sweet and soft against the late-day shadow of his beard. He held her, trailed his lips across her cheek, whispering the words against her ear, through her hair. "Lexi, I love you."

She leaned into his arms, her heartbeat quickening against his chest, her breath coming in tiny gasps. "I . . . love . . . you, too."

His hand slid up her back into the silky thickness of her hair. Her chin lifted, lips moist with tears and rain, blue eyes misty, closing. His senses rocked, consumed with tenderness, his lips brushed hers, and her arms slipped up to circle his neck before he nestled her to himself, crushed her lips with his, and deepened their kiss.

www.ingramcontent.com/pod-product-compliance
Lightning Source LLC
Chambersburg PA
CBHW062012170626
46813CB00001B/124